# Heroes, Legends, and Villains

## Dana Fraedrich

Other titles by Dana Fraedrich:

## SKATEBOARDS, MAGIC, AND SHAMROCKS
*Skateboards, Magic, and Shamrocks ~ Summer 2012*
*Heroes, Legends, and Villains ~ Autumn 2015*

## BROKEN GEARS
*Out of the Shadows (Lenore's storyline 1) ~ Autumn 2016*
*Into the Fire (Lenore's storyline 2) ~ Autumn 2017*
*Raven's Cry (standalone prequel) ~ Spring 2018*
*Across the Ice (Lenore's storyline 3) ~ Autumn 2019*

Dana Fraedrich

*This book is dedicated to all the authors who have come before me and produced such rich characters, compelling storylines, and captivating lands. The work of these amazing writers has nourished and inspired countless other imaginations for tens and hundreds and thousands of years. I hope this book spurs readers to seek out and discover the writers that served as my muse while I wrote it. Many, many thanks to all of them for Terturelia.*

*Heroes, Legends, and Villains*

ISBN: 1518657842
ISBN-13: 978-1518657849

Dana Fraedrich

## Table of Contents

# Chapter 1

Taryn trotted down the stairs of Wells, her dorm building, and waited impatiently on the landing.

"Are you coming?" she called up. Her voice echoed slightly off the walls.

"Yes! Hold your horses!" came the response from one flight up.

She sighed and wondered why exactly she didn't just rush ahead. Smitty would catch up; he knew where she was going. He appeared a moment later, walking down the stairs at a much more leisurely pace. They headed out to the parking lot together, Taryn almost skipping. She forgot all about waiting for Smitty, however, when she saw Ozzie unloading his car and ran to him.

"Oz!" she cried happily.

"Hey! Ryn!" Ozzie called back with a huge grin.

He caught her as she ran to hug him and returned the embrace enthusiastically, squeezing her as hard as he could.

"I'm so excited to see you!" Taryn said.

"Me, too," Ozzie agreed. He released Taryn and then called, "Hey, Smitty!"

Smitty strolled up to the car and gave Ozzie what Taryn affectionately called a man-hug.

"Hey, man, how you been?" Smitty asked.

"Good, pretty good," Ozzie replied. "You got my spot on the floor all ready?"

"Nothing but the best economy carpeting for you," Smitty joked.

They began to walk back to Wells, Ozzie and Smitty catching up as Taryn smiled at having her best friend with her for the weekend.

Things had not panned out the way Ozzie and Taryn had expected them to, not at all. Taryn was in the beginning of her junior year at college, while Ozzie was living back home with his mother, Annie. They had spent freshman and sophomore year together at the university, but circumstances had forced Ozzie to take the semester off. When it rained it poured, as Ozzie's mother liked to say. Despite his stellar grades, Ozzie had not been granted all of the same scholarships he had received in previous years.

There are students in more need of financial assistance. The selection process is unpredictable. There were more applicants than usual this year. We just don't have as much funding as we've had in the past.

All of these and more were what Ozzie heard when he appealed the decisions. In the end, he had to forfeit what small amount he had received. Back home, he was working as a server in a restaurant—he actually made more in tips than he would in retail or even an office—to try and save up, but he knew he wouldn't be able to make enough to pay for the other two years anytime soon, not unless he received a lot more in scholarships again. On top of that, he was wary about taking on student loans, as he didn't know how he would pay them back after graduation and he didn't want to be saddled with a lot of debt right out of school.

The whole situation clearly caused Ozzie a lot of heartache, despite his optimistic demeanor and words. Whether this optimism was authentic or partially an attempt to remain so, Taryn wasn't sure. Most people would simply see it as the former, but Taryn knew Ozzie better than anyone. She could tell, almost like a sixth Ozzie-sense, that it was not effortless when he talked about how it was all going to be okay. She had brought this up with him more than once, and he told her the same thing every time.

"I'm just not going to let myself get defeated by it."

Taryn had pressed the issue a few times, expressing how concerned she was, but Ozzie always told her not to worry. She let it drop then. He wouldn't lie to her and, even if he did, she'd be able to tell. Still, she worried about his future. Getting a college degree had always been a dream of Ozzie's, and it was hard to know if, much less how, that was going to happen now. He could go to a cheaper school, but that didn't help the fact that he had yet to declare a major, and most colleges required you to declare by your junior year. That didn't give Ozzie much time to make a decision, which he was also anxious about doing. He wasn't particularly in love with any one subject. They all had their merits, so how was he supposed to pick just one to focus on for the rest of his life?

Thankfully, the separation did nothing to dilute his and Taryn's bond. They were best friends through and through, and, after surviving an almost deadly quest, a few hundred miles meant nothing…especially when they had the Internet.

That was how Ozzie had stayed close with Smitty, too. Smitty—whose given name was Loren Smith, which he hated—and Ozzie had roomed together their first two years and were good friends. Smitty wasn't quite as easy-going as Ozzie, but they balanced each other out in that. He was also taller and not quite as much of a beanpole. He had blond hair and blue eyes and was an English major like Taryn. Had Taryn not come as part of the Ozzie-package, she probably would have become friends with Smitty eventually through their shared classes. Despite her wishes, though, Ozzie was still going to stay in Smitty's room that weekend because the campus had rules about co-ed sleepovers, even platonic ones.

They headed up to Smitty's room on the third floor, and Ozzie set his backpack and sleeping bag down in a corner.

"Too bad you didn't get the corner room," Ozzie said, looking around wistfully. "How's Alex as a roommate?"

"He's great, but gets up early," Smitty replied. His new roomie was currently at the student center having dinner.

"PoliSci majors, such overachievers," Ozzie replied. "Hey, Ryn, don't you wish we had had sleeping bags like this when we went camping?"

Taryn's first instinct was to shoot Ozzie a look, but two years of training made it easy to rein in the urge.

It was actually a little more than two years since she and Ozzie had returned from Leleplar, and most of the time things felt almost one hundred percent normal. *Almost* only because there was always a knowledge between the two that no one else shared. They had nearly died together more than once in that other world and then saved it. The two had spoken with creatures from myth and legend and experienced things that had permanently changed them. On top of that, they had gained and lost a good friend, Tynx, in the midst of everything. It made everything around them suddenly seem surreal when they thought about him, still out there but *somewhere else*, living a life of his own without them.

Instead of shooting the look, she simply smiled and said, "It was fine."

This was how most of their exchanges went when their adventure in Leleplar was referenced. It was always vague and carefully crafted so that the other people around them wouldn't catch that there was some underlying meaning.

"You probably won't need it," Smitty informed Ozzie. "It gets hot up here."

Ozzie, Taryn, and Smitty then spent a little while just chatting and then debating about where to go for dinner and what to do after. Smitty wanted Mexican and to go play mini-golf, Taryn wanted Chinese take-out and to come back and watch movies, and Ozzie didn't really care as long as he didn't have to drive and it was cheap. Taryn won the dinner argument, but completely lost out on her movie choices. Unsurprisingly, Ozzie and Smitty's votes to watch action comedies outweighed Taryn's choice for the latest Disney film.

"Watch it with Emily and the girls," Smitty said.

"Or with Kyla next time you go home," Ozzie added.

Taryn only grumbled a little, knowing the boys were right. It wasn't long before they had all piled into Smitty's beat up little Toyota and were on their way. They headed down a set of little back roads to avoid the rush hour traffic, Ozzie and Smitty doing most of the talking since they were still catching up. Taryn and Ozzie talked on the phone every day, sometimes more than once, and texted, so they were pretty much always up to speed. Even though Taryn kept Smitty updated on Ozzie-related news, there were still numerous subjects that they needed to discuss that Taryn had less than no interest in. She zoned out when they started talking about sports...or cars...or some other thing. Her mind was drifting off now in ways it didn't used to when something caught her eye. Smitty wasn't watching the road and was instead looking into his rearview mirror at Ozzie when Taryn broke in.

"Smitty! Look out!" she cried, pointing to the road ahead of them.

Smitty looked back just in time to see several deer leaping out onto the road in front of them. He swerved to avoid them, and the car went headlong into the ditch.

# Chapter 2

Ozzie opened his eyes and was confused for what felt like a long time by what he saw. Above him were leaves, a thick canopy of leaves. They might have been elm or oak or something familiar to him, but he couldn't quite make it out. He was lying down too, which was odd, on something uneven but not totally uncomfortable. There was something in his hand. He gave it an experimental squeeze—it worked like it was supposed to, so that was good—and realized what he was holding. It was another hand. He looked down blearily and saw that the hand he held was slender and delicate. He knew that hand; it was Taryn's. Finally, fear began to break through his confusion. He remembered the deer and the car and the screams.

"Ryn?" he said before he could think of anything else.

He got up—too fast—but he needed to make sure she was okay.

"Ryn?" he said again, and shook her hand in his.

She was lying on her stomach near him in the grass. He had been lying on the ground too, nestled in the roots of a large tree. He was about to feel for her pulse when he saw her chest rise and fall. Good! She was alive!

"Smitty?" Ozzie called, looking around.

He immediately spotted him just beyond the tree. Ozzie could see that he too was breathing. They both looked uninjured. But where was the car? Ozzie looked all around them, but it was nowhere to be seen. Besides that, there was also no road. They were surrounded by forest on all sides, a lovely, serene forest filled with birdsong and dappled sunlight. As Ozzie looked around them, an insane thought came to him. As soon as his mind began to wander in that direction, however, he heard a noise. He looked back to see Taryn getting up.

"Smitty, next time I'm driving," Taryn said groggily. "Got me?"

"Whatever," came Smitty's weary reply. He rolled over and sat up slowly. "That wasn't my fault. It was the deer."

The banter immediately made Ozzie feel better, and he squeezed Taryn's hand again. She was determined to continue her argument, however.

"It *was* your fault," came Taryn's quick response. "You weren't paying attention!"

"Hey, Ozzie," Smitty said, ignoring Taryn, "you okay?"

"Yeah, I'm alright," Ozzie replied. "You two? Anything hurt?"

Taryn and Smitty did mental checks while they became familiar with their surroundings. It seemed to be taking a few minutes for everything to sink in for them as well.

"I think I'm okay. Uh, where...where's my car?" Smitty asked. "We were all wearing seatbelts, right?"

Neither Ozzie nor Taryn responded. Ozzie was looking at her, waiting for her eyes to meet his. When they did, he could see that they were still absorbing information.

"Are you okay?" Ozzie repeated carefully.

"I'm not hurt," Taryn replied uncertainly.

That was all her brain could manage, as it was grappling with something far more difficult. She swallowed hard, and Ozzie could see that she was having the same idea he was. The forest, the lack of car, the way they were all uninjured despite being sprawled out on the ground...it couldn't be, but what else could it be?

"Maybe we were thrown really far..." Taryn suggested weakly.

"How could we have been thrown this far and still be alive?" Smitty demanded.

He was very upset about the loss of his car.

"Maybe we blacked out and...and wandered away," she tried again.

"Okay, maybe," Smitty agreed. "Let's go find my car."

He stood up unsteadily, but kept his balance. A moment later, he began to walk away.

"Smitty, stop," Ozzie said firmly. "You're not going anywhere. We need to stay together."

"Relax, we have our phones," Smitty replied, patting his pocket.

"Check your signal," Ozzie said simply.

Smitty did so, and Ozzie's suspicions were further confirmed when Smitty's brows knotted in anger.

"No signal?"

"No. Not at all."

Ozzie pulled his own phone out and checked it. Like Smitty, he had no signal, not even for the extended network. Taryn did not follow suit. Instead, she was looking around her fearfully, as if the forest might suddenly come alive and eat her.

"Taryn, it's going to be alright," Ozzie told her, squeezing her hand.

"You don't suppose that this is like last time, do you, Oz?" Taryn whispered. "It can't happen again, can it? Again?!"

Her voice was so full of desperation and fear, Ozzie's heart almost broke for her. Their journey in Leleplar had been very different for him than it had been for her. True, they had both been terrified during those times that they were nearly killed by bandits or dragons or the evil Shifter, Vurnal, but Ozzie had enjoyed most of the rest of their time there. Taryn, on the other hand, had been frightened for most of it. The few bright spots for her had been some of the people they had met, Tynx especially. Now that he thought about the possibility, Ozzie felt some of the same eagerness welling up inside of him again. Granted, he was older and more experienced about alternate universes now, but that didn't mean that his love for fantasy adventure stories had dimmed. In fact, he enjoyed reading them more now that he had actually experienced one, and he was slowly getting excited about the idea that he could do it *a second time*! He knew Taryn needed him now, though, so he put his growing enthusiasm on the back burner and focused on her.

"I don't know, but, wherever we are, you don't need to freak out. Okay? We're all fine. We'll figure this out."

"Is she in shock?" Smitty asked, coming forward. "Aren't we supposed to cover her with a blanket or something?"

"I'm not in shock," Taryn replied tersely, annoyance quickly coming forward to take fear's place.

"Good. That's good," Smitty replied. "How about we go and look for my car then?"

Taryn and Ozzie exchanged a glance, but nodded and stood up. Taryn made sure to hang her purse, which had miraculously stayed with her, across her body so that it couldn't be snatched easily. A quick inventory of it showed her that it still contained everything it should—wallet, keys, cell phone, various hair accessories, lip balm—but nothing they could use at the moment. All three walked close together just in case and headed in the direction opposite to the way they had been laying. Smitty deduced that by going back in that direction, they should find the car in no time.

"Isn't it awfully sunny?" Taryn asked no one in particular as they walked.

"What?" Smitty asked.

"It was late afternoon when we left. You'd think it would be darker by now…"

Smitty said nothing to that, and Ozzie knew that Taryn was reluctantly putting the pieces in place. True, he didn't know for certain that they were back in Leleplar, but, considering everything, nothing else made as much sense to him. They did eventually come upon a road, but it was not the one they were expecting to find. The road was old, *really* old, composed mostly of packed dirt and heavily worn cobblestones. Taryn knelt down with her head between her knees and took a deep breath.

"Taryn, it's okay," Ozzie said optimistically. He was trying to keep her from falling too far into fear. He knew how ugly it would get if she got really terrified. "We found a road. Look! It's even sort of paved."

"Funny," Taryn said dryly, but Ozzie's attempt at humor seemed to be working a little.

"May the road rise to meet you," Ozzie put a hand on her shoulder and began to quote in a terrible attempt at an Irish accent. "May the wind be always at your—"

"Paris?" Smitty said flatly.

"Uh, no. I don't think that's right," Ozzie said in confusion.

"That's what the sign says," Smitty said. He seemed unable to get past this fact.

"Paris?" Taryn asked hopefully, lifting her head. "Paris I can handle!"

They looked and saw a little signpost, which looked almost as old as the road, sticking out of the ground. It indeed said PARIS—3 on it in big, block letters. The arrow end of the sign was pointing down the road. There was another arrow-ended sign above that, which pointed in the same direction and said AMERICA—71 and one below pointing in the opposite direction that said GREECE—14. Ozzie, Taryn, and Smitty were all silent for a long time as they simply stared at the sign.

"Where is my car?!" Smitty cried suddenly, breaking the silence. "Oh man, my parents are going to kill me!"

"Smitty," Ozzie said calmly but firmly, "you have to forget about your car for a minute, okay? You have to stay calm and listen to me."

"To us," Taryn corrected.

It seemed she had come to grips with everything rather quickly now that, wherever they were, it was still close enough to home to share the same names.

"Really, Ryn?" Ozzie teased. "You mean you're *not* going to freak out like you did last time? I'm so proud."

He was doing this on purpose, too. If he got her ire up, she would be harder to scare.

"Oh, shut up. You might be a little more timid of strange worlds if you had almost died from eating bad mushrooms."

"Or I might be a little more excited because cute half-elves like to wander the woods of strange worlds."

Taryn blushed at that and seemed unable to settle on any one emotion to feel about that idea.

"What are y'all talking about?!" Smitty demanded.

"Sorry," Ozzie said quickly. "It's just…you're going to think we're crazy."

Smitty just fixed him with a hard *I'm waiting* look.

"Let's walk and talk at the same time," Taryn suggested. "Paris isn't too far. We can try and get information there."

It was as logical a plan as any, and they began to walk. Ozzie and Taryn began to tell Smitty about their wild adventure in Leleplar, to which Smitty just listened silently, his face closed. When they were finally done, they waited for him to respond.

"Just how stupid do you think I am?" he said finally, though there was a note of something besides disbelief in his tone, and there was no anger whatsoever.

"We can't prove it," Ozzie said reasonably, "but Taryn does have a scar from Tynx's attack."

She waved her wrist at Smitty, which bore a long, thin scar.

"You got that from working in the kitchen," Smitty said.

Or so the story went. The scar was not inconspicuous, nor had the wound been. Ozzie and Taryn had to lie to their parents, telling them that Taryn had accidentally dropped a knife while helping Ozzie make dinner the day after they had gotten back from Leleplar. They explained that the knife had landed on her arm and sliced right through the skin. Ozzie and Taryn had concocted the story together, but waited until someone actually asked before giving it as an explanation. Taryn's mother, Shannon, had not seen it until about a week later because Taryn had kept it covered with a variety of accessories and makeup. Shannon had been furious that Taryn had not told her about it sooner. She actually took Taryn to the doctor to get stitches, but it was too late by that time. Annie, however, seemed dubious more than anything, but said nothing. She made a habit of asking Taryn how she was feeling—not doing—whenever she saw her for a long time after that, too.

"I promise you, I didn't," Taryn said.

It was not Taryn's words, but the hard, not-to-be-challenged look in her eyes that made Smitty back off.

"It's just…it's not real," Smitty said.

"I get that," Ozzie said, "but how do you explain Paris and America and Greece being so close to each other?"

"Busch Gardens? That place has different countries, right? Or, better yet, a Renaissance Festival," Smitty said.

Ozzie actually laughed at that and said, "If it's a Renn Faire, I will buy your dinner."

It was a long walk, but the weather was nice, and the scenery changed quickly, which helped. There was an awkward silence between the three as they went. Taryn and Ozzie desperately wanted to discuss the possibility that they were back in Leleplar or someplace like it and what they could do if they were. They didn't want to alienate or frighten Smitty any further, however, so they kept quiet. The forest eventually thinned out and became farmland

and homesteads. There were green fields with cows and sheep and small ponds where they occasionally saw someone fishing. It was really quite beautiful, and even Taryn had to admit that it wasn't so bad. After an hour or so of walking, the three entered the city proper of Paris. It was clear long before, however, that it was neither Busch Gardens nor a Renaissance Festival. All the houses were made of dark beams and mud or plaster with thatched roofs, and the road eventually evened out so that it was comprised entirely of cobblestones. They had begun to pass people not long after getting on the road, and Ozzie, Taryn, and Smitty quickly discovered that their dress was anything but period. The boys stuck out like sore thumbs in their jeans and tee shirts, but Taryn was downright scandalous. Everyone they passed stared.

"What if they arrest me for indecency or something?" she murmured to Ozzie.

Ozzie didn't know how to answer that, and suddenly saw a...guardsman?...some kind of law enforcer. He grabbed Taryn's hand automatically. He knew she was right. Any one of them could be arrested without even realizing they had done anything wrong, but Taryn seemed to be the most at risk in that moment. The guardsman sneered at them, but didn't stop his patrol, and Ozzie and Taryn breathed a sigh of relief.

"Where are we going?" Smitty suddenly asked.

Ozzie and Taryn looked to him and saw he had been watching the guardsman, too. He was apparently worried about the same thing they were, which was good. Ozzie was relieved that he seemed to be thinking practically instead of freaking out. He knew Smitty pretty well, but, well, you could never really guess how people were going to react when you threw them into an alternate universe. Ozzie motioned for Taryn and Smitty to follow him and he led them over to a little alley. Parked there, they could talk without being overheard by one of the many people passing by on the road.

"I'm not sure," Ozzie confessed quietly. "We need information." His stomach growled just then and he added, "And food, which means we need money."

"How are we supposed to get money?" Taryn asked.

Ozzie didn't answer, but looked at her neck thoughtfully. Smitty followed suit, and Taryn furrowed her brows in confusion.

"Um, what?" she asked, placing a nervous hand against her throat. Then a look of appalled realization appeared on her face and she hissed, "No! My parents gave this to me for graduation!"

*This* was a lovely gold necklace with several precious stones set into it. There were two larger stones, a garnet and an aquamarine, on the ends of the setting, two smaller rubies next to those, and a medium sized diamond in the middle. Shannon and Donovan Kelly had given it to their daughter as a high school graduation/leaving for college gift. Each stone was a family member's birthstone, including a small ruby for Taryn's younger brother, Kael, who had died years earlier in a boating accident that had also killed Ozzie's father and nearly drowned Ozzie. Taryn loved the piece and wore it often.

"Ryn, I know how you feel," Ozzie said soothingly, "but we are in dire straits here. I promise I'll replace it when we get back."

"No," she groaned. "You don't have to do that."

She knew Ozzie was right and hated it. She quickly did a mental check for anything else on her that they could sell. Sadly, her necklace was the only thing of real value. She looked at the boys too, but they really didn't have anything besides the clothes on their back. She certainly wasn't about to make Ozzie spend any of his hard-earned money on a replacement necklace for her. She told herself it was just jewelry, but she couldn't help but feel very upset about giving it up.

"She could sell her hair," Smitty suggested. "Isn't that a thing?"

Ozzie and Taryn just looked at him as if he had just grown an extra head.

"What?" he said. "I saw it in a movie or something once...I think."

"I really appreciate your outside-the-box thinking, but I think the necklace is a better bet," Ozzie said.

"Well, we better make sure to get a fair price," Taryn said bitterly. "Let's find the ritzy part of town and sell it there."

Ozzie and Smitty agreed, and the three were off again. Taryn removed her necklace and tucked it into a little interior pocket of her purse. She was suddenly very protective of it, as it was now their only means of getting money. The three walked further and further into the city. Ozzie guessed that that most well-to-do part area would be closer to the center since they hadn't seen it yet. He was not quite correct in this case, though he wasn't far off. Ozzie, Taryn, and Smitty had entered the city from the north and headed south until they hit a river that ran through it. They guessed this might be the River Seine, but couldn't be sure, as they were not in the same Paris from back home. They then followed the river west until they came to a part of the city that looked too rich to be allowed. Before they had found the river, however, they found something else very interesting.

Ozzie, Taryn, and Smitty were walking down yet another grand street looking for a jewelry store that met Taryn's standards. Ozzie thought they must already be in the area they needed to be, but Taryn insisted they could do better. As they walked by a gargantuan building, Taryn stopped short and stared at a sign for a moment before looking to the building. Wonder, puzzlement, and a small bit of understanding were all vying for a place in her expression.

"Taryn?" Smitty said, having been nearest to her and noticed her behavior first.

He, followed by Ozzie, looked at the sign but couldn't figure out why it had made Taryn react so. It was a simple, hand painted advertisement that had been erected in front of the building. Surprisingly, the ad was in English and stated that *Faust* was being performed and that a woman named Carlotta would be playing the starring role.

"I know this," Taryn said, her mind clearly elsewhere. She looked back at the building and added, "It's the Paris Opera House."

"That's great!" Ozzie said. "What does that mean?"

Taryn came back to herself and said, "It's *The Phantom of the Opera*."

"I still don't really know what you're saying," Ozzie said.

Smitty, however, offered, "You mean one of the movies?"

"I actually mean the book," Taryn said.

"Oh wow," Ozzie said excitedly, "that's awesome. I didn't think we had *just* gone back in time."

"So…we're in a book?" Smitty asked dubiously. "How do you know for sure? It could just be a coincidence."

"I don't know," Taryn replied, pointing at the sign. "I just know that this right here is a scene in *Phantom*. Not the ad, but the performance."

"How do you know the author didn't base his book on real events?" Smitty asked.

"I don't, okay?" Taryn snapped, annoyed with all the questions. "I'm just saying it would be some kind of an explanation."

"So what do we do?" Smitty asked.

Taryn didn't have anything to offer, so Ozzie suggested, "Let's get our money situation resolved first—"

Taryn's face fell again at that.

"—and then we can come back."

Taryn and Smitty agreed to the plan and they set off again. Taryn mumbled to herself what she could remember about *The Phantom of the Opera*, trying to figure out from what part of the story the *Faust* performance was. Smitty, who had seen a film adaptation, tried to help, but his memories from seeing it were more about the girl he had watched it with several years previously than the actual story. By the time they had found the river and made their way to the western part of the city, Taryn had given up trying to remember.

# Chapter 3

"I think we're going to need a cover story," Ozzie said, glancing in through the window of the jewelry store. "You know, just in case this sort of thing isn't done here. What if he doesn't usually take second-hand jewelry?"

"Second-hand?" Taryn said, raising her eyebrows at him.

Taryn had finally deemed a jeweler worthy of her necklace, an elegant little shop called Pierre's, and they were putting together a game plan outside of it. Inside, a portly man was standing behind the counter with a jeweler's loupe pressed to his eye.

"He's technically correct." Smitty said to Taryn.

She made derisive noise in her throat at that and turned back to Ozzie. She then unhappily admitted, "You're probably right."

"How about we're down on our luck travelers?" Smitty suggested. "We haven't eaten for days."

Taryn shook her head and replied, "No way. That's too desperate. He might lowball us and I don't want to take any chances. I have a better idea. Oz, make me cry."

"Seriously?"

"Yes, seriously! Lay the sadness on me."

Ozzie thought for a moment. This was actually going to be a little difficult. Taryn's propensity was to get angry, not sad.

"So I was driving down the highway on the way here, and there was this bunny in the road. I saw the car next to me heading straight for it. I was like *nooooooooo*, but there was no helping it. The bunny exploded. She probably had baby bunnies at home, waiting to be fed. They'll be eaten by dogs most likely. Sweet one-legged dogs with hearts of gold and indomitable spirits."

Taryn stared hard at him, her face flattened out into a scowl.

"You suck at this," she said flatly.

Ozzie shrugged, knowing it was true.

"Can I have a go?" Smitty asked.

"No," Taryn said. "I'll handle it."

Taryn then shook herself and took a deep breath, preparing for whatever it was she was about to do. Ozzie and Smitty followed behind her, trying to keep their faces closed. The man behind the counter looked up as soon as the bell over the door jingled, but his expression soured when he saw the three. These did not look like his usual patrons and he wanted to know why they were about to waste his time.

"May I help you?" he said, not quite sneering.

"That depends," Taryn said breathily.

Ozzie had to suppress a smile. This was kind of a perfect job for Taryn. He had an inkling of her plan, and she was already so upset over the idea of giving up her necklace that it was going to be easy for her to tug at this man's heartstrings…and his cash register, or whatever it was they had here.

"I want…rather, I *need* to sell an item," Taryn continued, "but I'm afraid we're not from this area. I don't know if your shop is of a satisfactory caliber for my business."

As she spoke, she fanned herself anxiously with one hand, took deep breaths, and for all the world appeared to be deeply emotionally distressed. Well, that wasn't far off, but the man didn't need to know why. A look that might have been close to admiration, or perhaps it was just plain arrogance, passed across the man's face. Was he proud of the shop, or perhaps he was keen on the idea of coming to this poor damsel's rescue. He seemed to relent ever so slightly. Ozzie then wondered if it was because Taryn had told him that they were not from the area. Maybe that explained their odd clothing and, with any luck, made them more desirable customers. Wait, he needed to focus! Ozzie had one of those faces that adjusted involuntarily to whatever direction his thoughts went. Overly curious lad from who-knew-where was not who he needed to be right now. Still, he could hope.

Bowing ever so slightly, the man replied, "I assure you, mademoiselle, there is no better purveyor of fine jewelry in all of France than Pierre."

Taryn's face turned desperately hopeful, and she asked, "Are you Pierre?"

"I am indeed," the man said with a sudden, wide smile. "So pleased to make your acquaintance."

He held out his hand, and Taryn smiled demurely in return. She placed her own delicate hand in Pierre's meaty one and didn't flinch as the man kissed it gently.

"Taryn," she said, batting her eyelashes, "and these are my escorts, Oswald and Loren."

Both boys had to restrain themselves from making faces at the sound of their proper names.

"So what is this fine piece you are interested in selling?" Pierre asked.

Taryn reached into her purse and gently pulled out the necklace. Pierre's eyes lit up when he saw it, and he handled it with as much care as he would a newborn baby. He said nothing until he began to examine it with the loupe.

"This is excellent quality. Why on earth would you want to sell it?"

Taryn's expression genuinely broke at that, which was perfect, and she was quick with her lie.

"He said he loved me," she huffed, letting tears well up in her eyes. "He is a liar."

"Ah, I understand," Pierre said softly. "He is a pig! Do not waste your tears on him. I feel for you, and the piece is exquisite. Give me just a moment."

Pierre then turned away to consult a large volume on the back of the counter, and Ozzie, Taryn, and Smitty resisted the urge to exchange nervous glances. Pierre turned back a few minutes later and spoke again.

"I will give you one hundred and fifty two gold pieces for it."

It was very difficult not to react. Though they couldn't be certain, that seemed like an outrageous sum of money. They succeeded, but Taryn had to blink more tears away. Ozzie couldn't be sure of the reason for it. Nevertheless, it seemed to garner them more favor with Pierre.

"I...perhaps..." she stuttered softly.

"It is hard to let go, mademoiselle, I know," Pierre said, placing a hand on hers, "but love is not a single, rare flower that dies forever when crushed. It is a phoenix that rises from ashes brighter and more beautiful that before. You must first let it be reborn."

Taryn smiled weakly at him and nodded, letting a single tear roll down her cheek.

"One hundred and sixty for your heartache, unless you would like to exchange it for a piece in my shop?"

Taryn batted her eyelashes at him again and said, "Thank you, but it is too soon."

"Of course. Allow me to draw up the ticket."

Ozzie, Taryn, and Smitty waited as Pierre went about his work. After ten minutes or so, they were bidding Pierre goodbye, Taryn letting him kiss her hand once more, and they were out the door with the money safely in Taryn's purse. As soon as they were some distance away, Ozzie began to clap mockingly.

"What a performance, Ryn," he said with a smile. He then mimicked, "He said he loved me!"

"Stop," Taryn said, pushing Ozzie lightly. "I did what I had to."

"Aw, I know, and we all appreciate it," Ozzie said, rubbing her back comfortingly. "Now we won't starve."

"Nice," Taryn said, rolling her eyes.

"I'm looking on the bright side!" Ozzie insisted.

"I'm a little scared of how well you did," Smitty commented with a smile.

Taryn shot him a look and replied, "I was just mad. I can do anything when I'm mad."

"True story," Ozzie said, and this he meant as a compliment.

Taryn looked at him and smiled, remembering everything she had actually been able to accomplish in Leleplar when her ire was up, though fighting an elf was probably not her smartest move.

They walked back to the Paris Opera House, stopping for a baguette along the way at a *boulangerie*, which was pretty easily recognizable as a bakery.

"Why are some words still in French when so much is in English?" Taryn asked as they walked with their dinner.

"Are you really looking for a sensible explanation for that?" Smitty said. "The fact that we're here, wherever *here* is, defies explanation."

"You're dealing with this pretty well," Ozzie commented. "Last time—"

"We don't need to go into details," Taryn warned. "I did just as well as could be expected."

Ozzie laughed loudly at that.

"I think I'd like details," Smitty said, smirking at Taryn, who rolled her eyes at him.

"She was a mess," Ozzie explained. "Every time something weird happened, *Oh no! We're all going to die! Everything is your fault, Ozzie! Why can't it all be normal and boring?*"

Smitty laughed with Ozzie at that, and Taryn snorted derisively.

"Oz conveniently left out the fact that the first thing I saw when I woke up in Leleplar was a centaur. And that we went searching for angry ghosts to fight. And that we were attacked by bandits. And that we almost died saving the world!"

"As it should be in any good adventure story," Smitty teased.

Taryn gave him a look, but said nothing.

"Which brings us back to our other task," Ozzie said more seriously. "We need to find out where we are...and maybe *when* we are. How do we do that?"

"Bookstore?" Smitty suggested.

"Have you seen any?" Ozzie asked. "I wonder what the literacy rate is here." His curiosity was going again.

"Not really," Smitty confessed.

"This is going to sound really weird, but what about going to visit the Phantom?" Taryn suggested cautiously.

"This isn't really the time to try and play out your fangirl fantasies," Ozzie replied.

"Shut up! It's not like that," Taryn insisted.

"Really?" Ozzie joked. "I've heard you rave about that book. I think you're a little excited to meet the *Phantom*." He said this last word very dramatically.

"You're ridiculous," Taryn told him firmly. "Yes, it's an amazing story, but being in it is completely different from reading it, as I know you know."

"What's the big deal?" Smitty asked. "He's just a semi-crazy, ugly guy with a mask who hides out in the theatre, right?"

"He's not crazy!" Taryn snapped. "And it's not his fault that he looks like a zombie! He was born that way, okay?"

"Doesn't he kill people?" Ozzie pointed out.

"Not for fun or anything. I mean…well…he doesn't really have much of a moral compass. Those people were a threat to him, though," Taryn insisted.

"Hm, yeah, great defense," Ozzie said with a smirk. "You're awfully tetchy about this guy."

"Okay, forget all of that," Taryn argued sensibly. "The reason I am suggesting this is because the Phantom has been all over the world. Think about it, no matter what the deal with this place is, there's no one we can really count on to give us the broader information we need. Remember Gyldain? He knew deeper stuff, stuff that we needed to know to get through Leleplar, stuff about Vurnal and the threat he posed. If the Phantom is familiar with the wider world, he can probably tell us more about this place than anyone else. Come on, he's the closest thing to a kind-of-but-not-really supernatural being that we know of."

There were a few moments of silence before anyone responded.

"Are you sure about this?" Smitty finally said. "I mean, we still aren't sure we're really in a book. He might not even be there and, if he is, he sounds dangerous."

"We have to try," Taryn said confidently. If I'm wrong, we start back at square one. If I'm right, I'm sure we'll be fine. I've read the book at least three times."

"And you're *not* a fangirling?" Ozzie asked.

Taryn hit him in the arm and he laughed, finally agreeing. They then set off again.


"So are we going to buy tickets or what?" Ozzie asked, looking up at the huge opera house.

"Um, I hadn't really thought about that," Taryn said. "We're not exactly dressed for a show."

"Maybe we should be snobby this time," Smitty suggested. "That should work at a swanky place like this, right? Plus, it's French."

"Don't be like that," Taryn scolded. "I'm sure real French people aren't stuck up. Books are hyperbolic and satirical, so you have to expect these people, if they are all book characters, to be exaggerated."

"That's very literary of you," Smitty teased.

"He's got a point, though," Ozzie said, thinking hard. "If anyone wants to give us a hard time about our clothes, why can't we just tell them we are dressed up? How would they know the difference?"

"Okay," Taryn agreed, "but let me at least do something with my hair."

"Really?" both boys said together.

Using the bobby pins and "hair diddies", as Smitty called them, from her purse, Taryn soon had her hair up in a simple, semi-braided up-do. She had Ozzie hold her compact up for her so that she could use the mirror as she worked, and there was much eye rolling.

"Don't ever say I never did anything for you," Ozzie said.

Afterwards, they headed up the stairs and Taryn took the lead again.

"Three for *Faust*, please," she said to the ticket seller.

The ticket seller said nothing, but looked over Taryn, Ozzie, and Smitty the same way he would a rotting fish carcass.

"Is there a problem?" Taryn snapped haughtily.

"We have certain…standards here, mademoiselle," the ticket seller replied superciliously.

"Standards about what?" Taryn demanded.

"Hmm, about the type of attire we expect our guests to wear."

"Clearly he hasn't traveled much," Smitty cut in scornfully, a slightly snooty affectation in his voice.

"Clearly," Ozzie agreed, copying Smitty's manner.

"Perhaps if you were better educated as to the ways of the world, you wouldn't be wasting our time. Now, three tickets, please. My *gold* is just as good as any."

The ticket seller didn't seem convinced in the least, but took their money anyway.

"You're lucky to get in," he said, getting one last shot in. "It's nearly a full house tonight."

"Must be all that talk about the Opera Ghost," Taryn replied waspishly.

The ticket seller went white.  Taryn just smiled wickedly.  The tickets cost two gold pieces, and Taryn and Ozzie both cringed at losing so much for a show.  They got more stares as they were led to their seats, but they ignored the looks and sat down confidently.

"Now what?" Smitty asked.

"Now we wait and see what happens," Taryn replied.  "I need to remember where in the story we are.  I think we're either in the very beginning or the middle."

"I don't know what Ozzie was talking about when he said you were freaking out," Smitty whispered, placing a hand on Taryn's.  "I think you're being really brave, and you've had the best ideas so far."

"You don't understand, dude," Ozzie whispered back.  "You didn't see it.  She was falling apart."

Taryn nudged Ozzie, but smiled.  She felt much braver than she had in Leleplar, probably because she was familiar with the situation they were in, as unbelievable as it was.  She hadn't known what to expect the first time; now she knew almost exactly what to expect…if she could only remember all the details.  Nevertheless, it made her feel in control.

During the performance, Taryn kept her eyes and ears open.  She saw two men up in one of the private boxes.  She, Ozzie, and Smitty were almost directly below.  She remembered that this was the Ghost's box and knew they must be the new managers of the Opera House, even if she couldn't exactly remember their names.  She heard whispers, gossip really, about Christine Daaé and Carlotta, and she filtered this out as unimportant.  By the end of the second act nothing had happened, and Taryn was thinking that she wouldn't glean anything helpful from the evening.  It would be a waste of precious money.  Then she heard it.  Like the calm before the storm, something very small and seemingly insignificant happened, but it set off a flurry of action.

Faust knelt down before Margarita, who was being played by the woman, Carlotta, that Taryn had seen mentioned in the advertisement outside.  While the prima donna belted out the melody of the song, she let out a dreadful *co-ack* to rival that of any bullfrog.  The color suddenly drained from Taryn's face.  She instantly stood up and tore down her row and towards the front of the theatre as quickly as she could.

"Taryn!" Ozzie called. He hesitated, not sure if he should follow.

Thankfully, the audience was so horrified with the croak Taryn's strange behavior wasn't much noticed. There was another *co-ack*, which only diverted everyone's attention further. Carlotta seemed unsure of what to do, but one of the mangers in box five called down to her to continue. She did so, but the horrible croaking only got worse. All the while, Smitty and Ozzie wondered what Taryn was up to. They could still see her. It was a good thing the entire opera house was watching Carlotta because Taryn looked like a lunatic, frantically running down the side of the audience, looking for something. Then came a sound so chilling that Ozzie and Smitty felt tension roll down from their necks to their arms and down their backs. It was very soft and came from the box above.

"She is singing tonight to bring the chandelier down!" came the disembodied voice.

They looked up just in time to see the massive chandelier that hung above the audience slipping from its hangings. At that same time Taryn's voice could be heard from somewhere ahead of them. Ozzie and Smitty looked down towards the front of the house and scanned frantically for Taryn's unmistakable red hair. There she was, running through the audience, fighting against other people to get somewhere, shouting at them to get out of the way. She stopped when she reached a rather hefty, unattractive woman dressed in black and a man in a large coat.

"TARYN!" Ozzie screamed, as the chandelier broke completely free of its rigging and began to sail straight down towards Taryn and those she had found.

# Chapter 4

"Ow!" Taryn cried angrily as Ozzie carefully pulled a splinter of glass from her arm. "That hurts!"

"If you would calm down for one minute and let me look at you, this might be easier for both of us," Ozzie told her firmly.

Taryn had narrowly escaped being crushed by the chandelier as she tried her best to save the concierge, her husband, and her brother. Taryn had been successful, but just barely. The group was convinced that Taryn was possibly a member of the Christine-Daaé-support camp and trying to trick them. It was in the last moments that Taryn had told them to look up, which they finally did, and all saw the massive chandelier about to fall right on top of them. Miraculously, Taryn had been able to half-run, half-leap far enough to avoid being crushed but had still sustained some minor injuries from flying shrapnel and the stampeding crowd that followed. Ozzie and Smitty had hurdled over the seats towards her, and all three got out safely, following close behind the mob.

Now, standing in dim gaslight on the street, Ozzie was attending to Taryn's various cuts and bruises as best he could. Taryn's fight reaction was running high, and she gave Ozzie a look of death when he scolded her, but he threw one right back. They stared one another down for a moment. It was Taryn who looked away first, knowing that Ozzie was angry with her for putting herself in danger. He couldn't hold it against her for long, though. She had been trying to save someone else's life.

"So...in the book...what happens now?" Smitty asked.

Taryn sighed angrily and closed her eyes to think, trying to ignore Ozzie's somewhat painful ministrations.

"I *think* the Phantom just kidnapped Christine."

"Do you still want to go look for him?" Smitty asked.

"Yes," Taryn said determinedly.

"Even though he's kind of a psychopath?"

"She's right," Ozzie said. "If he knows about this world, we need to talk to him. Ryn, how do we find him?"

"There's a secret passage somewhere," Taryn replied, "but I don't remember where. I also don't want to go that way."

"Why?" Smitty asked.

"Because somewhere along it is a torture chamber or something like that," Taryn explained.

"Wow, a torture chamber," Smitty quipped. "And you both think this is a *good* idea?"

"That's why I think we should take the underground lake," Taryn growled.

"Oh, well, why didn't you just say that?" Smitty asked.

"I was getting to it!" Taryn snapped. She then took a deep breath and said more evenly, "Sorry. Okay?" She waited, Smitty nodded, and she added, "It's not far. The entrance is around the back of the building. I think there are bars or a gate or something."

Ozzie, Taryn, and Smitty were headed down a short tunnel much sooner than any of them had expected. The gate had been easy to find and get through. It was not lit, however, so they had stolen a lantern, which was also easy enough to do. The Opera House was still chaotic.

"Old-timey France doesn't seem too concerned with security," Ozzie joked, trying to ease the tension that pressed in on them from the tunnel walls. "We should see what else we can get away with."

Taryn shushed him, not knowing exactly where the Phantom or the lake was. She just knew he wouldn't be happy about trespassers.

The lake was apparently no more than a stone's throw from the gate, and the sound of lapping could be heard as soon as they had slipped through. The light from their lantern reflected off the vast sheet of dark water and illuminated a myriad of stalactites reaching down from the low cavern ceiling. In the weak light of the lantern, these resembled sinister fingers reaching down to grasp intruders. A small boat was docked at the edge of the lake. Ozzie, Taryn, and Smitty cautiously approached it, Ozzie and Smitty taking the lead, and swept the lantern around as far as they dared reach. When all seemed safe, they climbed in, hung the lantern from the bow, and pushed away from the shore as quietly as they could.

"I think his house is just directly across," Taryn whispered. Despite her efforts, even that small noise echoed back uncomfortably loud.

There was only one set of paddles, and Smitty was in the middle, so the task of rowing fell to him. They tried to be as silent as possible as they went, which meant it was slow-going. The sound of the paddles dipping in and pulling out of the water masked the sound of the melody that crept through the darkness towards them. Ozzie, Taryn, and Smitty heard it before they realized it, allowing the mesmerizing resonance to seep into their ears, into their minds, and wrap around their senses.

Smitty stopped paddling, and no one complained.

"What is that?" he asked softly, leaning towards the edge of the boat.

"It's beautiful," Taryn murmured.

All three of them listened intently to the song, growing more attached to it as it grew louder. Then suddenly and without warning, the music stopped, allowing silence to come crashing back into their consciousness.

"Huh…" Ozzie muttered in confusion, coming out of his trance-like state.

BAM! The boat gave a violent lurch, threatening to overturn them all.

"It's him!" Taryn screamed.

Ozzie and Smitty each grabbed a paddle and held them at the ready as they waited for the Phantom to show his face. Everything was abruptly still again, however, and the three exchanged fearful glances. In that moment, a shadowy figure burst out from the lake behind Smitty and grabbed him around the chest. He was pulled back into the water, and the boat was completely tipped over in the process. As soon as Taryn hit the surface of the lake she began to sink. It was her purse full of gold pieces that weighed her down. It wasn't impossible to swim back up with them, but it was difficult, and she wasn't about to lose them to the black water. She was struggling and making slow progress, heading towards the faint light of the lantern, which was now bobbing on the surface of the water above. Suddenly someone was there holding her by the waist, pushing her up through the water. Taryn felt as if her lungs were going to burst. When her head broke through the surface, she gasped in fresh air. The capsized boat was right there beside her. She grabbed for it and caught a faint glimpse of Ozzie there helping her.

"Ozzie!" she cried frantically. "Where's Smitty?"

He didn't answer but dove back under as soon as she had a firm grip on the boat. Taryn called once after him and then grabbed for the lantern, which was quickly floating away. She held it high and looked down just in time to see something coming up nearby. She cried out in fear as it broke the surface and she could see Ozzie and Smitty struggling with the same figure that had attacked them. As soon as they had appeared, however, they disappeared again as the Phantom pushed them both back under.

"Ozzie! Smitty!" she screamed again.

Ozzie and Smitty surfaced again, closer to Taryn than before, clearly trying to escape to the safety of the boat. The Phantom laughed maliciously, which echoed off the cavern walls a thousand times. Taryn was suddenly filled with panic and desperation as she saw the ease with which the Phantom grabbed Ozzie and Smitty and shoved them below the surface of the water.

"Please! Stop! Phantom! Erik! Don't!" Taryn shrieked.

The creature that haunted the Paris Opera House suddenly looked up, and Taryn could see in the part of his face not covered by a mask a mixture of shock, anger, and wonder. This gave the two drowning boys an opportunity to get free, one that they immediately took. They resurfaced, but in the process Smitty knocked into Taryn and caused her to lose her grip on the boat. She sank fast and hadn't had a chance to take a breath. Her oxygen lasted but a moment, and she instinctively gasped, but only water came back to her. It burned in her lungs, and she coughed, only to take in more water. Taryn panicked, kicking her legs and flailing her arms as hard as she could, but it was too late. Her head began to pound, and her vision quickly grew dark. Then there was nothing.

Taryn opened her eyes slowly and tried to put her muddled thoughts together. She remembered the attack on the lake and a fragment of something after that, something that she associated with air, but she couldn't make sense of it. She looked around, hoping to see something that would help disentangle her memories. The first thing she saw was Smitty. He was sitting across the room from her, and she made a soft noise since she wasn't quite coherent enough to speak yet. Smitty heard her, though, and Taryn spotted Ozzie there with him a moment later. They rushed over to her, and, as things slowly came into focus, she could see that there was a large canopy of fabric above her, which meant she was on a bed. She felt the mattress move as each of her friends sat down on one side of her. They both were pale with worry.

"Are you okay?" Ozzie asked.

"How do you feel?" Smitty said right after him.

"What happened?" she groaned, the ability to form words and speech coming back to her slowly.

The boys exchanged looks, and Ozzie began to explain with a tone filled with what sounded like admiration.

"Well, I don't know. I didn't see it all, but the Phantom went down after you. You weren't breathing when he came back. He swam you to shore—that dude is fast! He gave you CPR or something. Do they even have that here? You started to breathe again and kind of woke up but then passed out. The Phantom told us to follow him, and he carried you inside and set you in here. When we asked if you would be okay, he just said that you would live and left."

"Are you okay?" Smitty asked again.

"Apparently I'll live," Taryn said with less difficulty now.

The two boys smiled and helped Taryn sit up after a little while. They propped her against the head of the bed, and from there she could see the room properly.

The room was very dim, lit only by sconces and candles and the fireplace at the other end of the room. Through the wild shadows, Taryn could see exquisite furniture, intricate architectural details, gilded décor, and all the things that spoke of wealth. A large waxed mahogany chair stood in front of the fireplace while others like it sat impressively around the room. A sofa was sitting between a wardrobe on one side and an end table topped with lit candelabras on the other. There were also a number of curious souvenirs scattered about the room, but their origin was impossible to guess. A set of double doors led out on the right hand wall, and those, Taryn noted to herself, seemed to be the only means of escape.

"This guy sure does have a nice place," Ozzie commented, looking around the room with Taryn.

"I think he built it himself, or designed it, or something," Taryn said vaguely. She was trying not to think too hard about anything.

The three sat there in tense but companionable silence for a while. Neither Ozzie nor Taryn were as afraid as they suspected that they should be, but they were safe and alive, and the Phantom had let them live. That provided more peace of mind than anything else. Had he wanted them dead—rather, *still* wanted them dead—they would be. Therefore, by that logic, he must want them alive, right?

What must Smitty be thinking now, though? What must he be feeling? He had nearly been killed on day one in this strange new world. By comparison, it had taken Ozzie and Taryn ages to actually have a run-in with anyone, and that was Tynx. He barely counted, if at all. Smitty was staring down at his hands at the moment. It was impossible to decipher his expression.

"Smitty," Taryn said gently. He looked at her sideways, and she placed a hand on his. "Are you okay?"

"What do you mean?" he asked.

"Are you scared?" she asked.

"Seriously?!" he replied, almost snapping. "Of course I am! That freak tried to kill us! He might be getting his torture chamber or whatever ready right now."

"Shhhhhh!" Ozzie hissed. "Keep it down, man!" He took a breath and added more calmly, "Now look, there's a reason he brought Taryn back to life and let us live—"

"Oh, Oz!" Taryn suddenly interrupted, looking horrified. "The drowning..."

All of a sudden, Taryn had realized what Ozzie had gone through that evening. How must he have felt nearly drowning a *second* time in his life? Was it that much more terrifying having lost his own father to it plus Kael, Taryn's little brother? She reached over and hugged him tightly, and Ozzie happily returned the embrace. She was shocked when she saw his *it's okay* expression on his face. It was the same expression he wore when they discussed his uncertain educational future. How did he stay so calm?! Then, not forgetting Smitty, Taryn reached over and hugged him, too. They both needed support right now, though hugs felt like a paltry means at the moment.

Just then, the door opened and all three looked to see a masked figure walk in carrying a tray.

The man was dressed in fine clothes—waistcoat, tailored trousers, crisp white shirt—and his hair was slicked back. He was the picture of calm gallantry, save for the unsettling mask that covered a good deal of his face. More frightening than even that, however, were the bright yellow eyes that burned out of black sockets from the eyes of the mask.

As the man walked in, Ozzie, Taryn, and Smitty could feel an aura of power about him, something that told them that this was not a man to be trifled with. The Phantom—Erik, Smitty and Ozzie knew now—walked over to the bed and set the tray in front of Ozzie. All three of them were trying to keep their eyes on their...host? Captor?...without staring or cringing or something equally offensive.

Erik looked at the three and waved his hand with stunning grace.

"Eat, I implore you."

That was what actually did make the three start. Despite his monstrous persona, his voice was smooth and perfect. It was low like the string of a finely tuned cello, and it sounded melodic even in everyday speech. They looked down at the tray and saw a very large silver teapot and three bowls with spoons. Obediently, they poured a dark, steaming liquid that was definitely not tea from the pot into the bowls.

"Beef consommé," Erik explained proudly like a maître d'. "It will restore your strength."

Ozzie, Taryn, and Smitty all nodded politely and began to eat the surprisingly delicious broth. Erik simply stood and watched them as they did so. They shifted uncomfortably beneath his gaze.

"This is really good," Smitty said awkwardly.

"Thank you," Ozzie added.

Erik didn't move or say anything in response.

"I appreciate you saving my life," Taryn tried.

The Phantom's face seemed to make some kind of expression at that, but it was impossible to tell what exactly it was. They all went back for seconds, but the rest of the meal was spent in awkward silence. Finally, as the bowls and spoons were gathered back onto the tray, Taryn spoke again.

"Erik…I know—"

"Yes, you seem to know quite a bit," Erik interrupted, cutting her off.

Somehow, his tone was sharp without being abrupt, commanding and beautiful at the same time, and Taryn felt her breath catch fearfully in her chest as she heard it. She was suddenly keenly aware that he could kill them at any moment, the inherent knowledge pressing on her heart, and she knew it was somehow through the power of his voice that made this possible.

"I saw you save those cretins this evening. I watched you fly to their rescue even before it happened. You know—much less are so bold as to call me by—my given name. What else do you know?"

"I…I can't really say. I just…"

"Answer my question!" Erik roared, causing Ozzie, Taryn, and Smitty to all jump.

They sat stock-still in fear. Erik's voice was having similar effects on them all. Taryn tried to think fast. She needed to diffuse this situation, to somehow give them an advantage. It was so difficult to think with the waves of dread rolling off Erik and resonating in her mind.

"You're in love Christine Daaé," Taryn began unsteadily. "I know the Persian saved your life. Your new opera is called *Don Juan Triumphant*. One of the pillars in Box Five is hollow!"

Taryn was ready to continue, but Erik held up a hand, and she stopped. She waited nervously as he turned away, looking thoughtful. Ozzie and Smitty were both taut with anxiety. Neither had any idea how these revelations would go over. Did Taryn have a plan? She was the only one really familiar with this character. They would go down fighting if it came to it, but down they would go nonetheless. They had experienced firsthand just how insanely strong Erik was on the lake, and, even two against one on land, they didn't stand a chance. Finally, after several tense minutes, Erik spoke softly.

"Tell me how you know all of this. Do not lie."

With that he turned his head back towards the three, gazing at them all with eyes that told them their lives were on the line. They exchanged fearful glances and swallowed hard.

"You're not going to believe us," Smitty said carefully.

"Tell me," Erik hissed.

"Well, you see, we aren't from this country," Ozzie said. "We're not from this world actually. We were kind of...dropped here."

"That does not answer my question," Erik said, his voice still dangerously soft.

Ozzie and Smitty each swallowed hard, neither of them knowing what to say next. Taryn opened her mouth to speak, but stopped. She took a deep breath to steady herself, knowing her friends needed her now. She wasn't even sure if what she planned on saying was exactly right, but she didn't think she could reveal that.

"Everything in this world is from books, *fictional* stories, in our world. You're in one of them. It's called *The Phantom of the Opera*."

Erik suddenly seemed amused, possibly even flattered, and he took several steps towards the three.

"And how does it end?"

Taryn hesitated for a second and asked, "If I tell you, will you help us...and promise not to kill us?"

He nodded and said with a smile, "I will do all in my power to help you."

The smile, of which only a fragment could be seen, sent shivers down Ozzie, Taryn, and Smitty's spines. It was even more unsettling coupled with those yellow, glinting eyes.

Seeing their uncertainty, Erik put his hand on Taryn's and said in a much graver tone, "On the other hand, if you do not tell me you will be very sorry."

Taryn swallowed hard, fighting the gasp that tried to escape her throat. Erik's hand was ice cold, and a smell of death came over her when he came near.

"Every...everyone does what you tell them to," she stammered.

Erik searched her face for any flicker of deceit, but there was none. He then moved back and motioned that they should follow him. He walked over to the other side of the room and took a seat in one of the chairs near the fireplace. Smitty, Ozzie, and Taryn all followed carefully and sat down on the sofa.

"Now, what is it that you would ask of me?" Erik asked smoothly.

"We need to know about where we are," Ozzie said. "I mean, information about this…country…land…place."

"And how to get home," Smitty added.

"Give me a moment."

Erik then left for a few minutes, closing the doors behind him—and was that the *shink* of a lock?—leaving the three to whisper amongst themselves.

"We need to get out of here!" Smitty hissed.

"Soon," Taryn whispered back. "We're close to getting some real help!"

"No! He's going to kill us!"

"He won't. We gave him what he wanted. He'll keep his word."

Ozzie shushed them both.

Erik soon returned carrying several very large rolled up maps. Spreading the maps out on the table before them, he spoke again.

"I do not know how your second request can be accomplished, but I believe I know who does. The country of England is a very strange one indeed. Wonderland is home to several mysterious beings, and there are other places filled with powerful magic. It is a very long journey, however. First you must go through the forest that surrounds Castle Rose. Be warned, there are legends of a curse in that forest. After that you will travel through the country of America in order to get to England. When you get to Wonderland, there are two beings that may be able to assist you: either the Cheshire Cat or the Caterpillar."

"Can we ask a few questions," Ozzie asked, raising his hand and trying to be as respectful as possible.

"Of course," Erik replied cordially.

"Is there anything else you can tell us that will help? Anything we should look out for? Allies? Anything?"

Erik chuckled sardonically and said, "As you may imagine, I have not made many friends in my life." He gestured towards his face. "The few allies I have made I do not wish to share. Nor do I believe my experience will help you; we are very differently gifted, I imagine. I can, however, provide you with some financial assistance. I have seen what you carry but will give you more in order to buy horses for the trip. Do not buy the horses until after you have made it through the forest of Castle Rose, for they will not go into the woods there. I believe I can also acquire a set of proper clothing for each of you. Look now; learn the lay of the land."

Ozzie, Taryn, and Smitty now looked from Erik to the maps spread out before them. They could hardly believe their eyes. On the largest map was what looked like a massive continent surrounded by water, much like Australia, but all of the familiar names on the map were not in the right places at all. Four main countries stretched around the borders of the continent. These were France, America, England, and Greece. In the very center was another, Germany, and several islands dotted the outlying ocean. Some of these were India, Never-Never Land, and Lilliput. The shape of each country and region was all wrong, as if they had simply been all mashed together. On the map were drawn several points of interest. Among these were The Mississippi River and the City of Oz in America. As Erik had said, Wonderland was part of the nation of England, as was Camelot. The city of Troy was in Greece, and Notre Dame and the Paris Opera House were in France. On the very top of the map were the words *The Continent of Terturelia*.

Each of the trio recognized a number of the places on the map, but none of them betrayed what they knew.

When Taryn looked at one of the other maps, however, she could not stop herself from exclaiming, "Ozzie! Look! It's Leleplar!"

She pointed at the second map, which showed Terturelia in relation to its known neighbors. Leleplar was yet another independent continent, smaller than Terturelia, but only separated by water. How much water was uncertain, but Taryn found herself desperately looking for some kind of legend to figure out how far apart they were.

"You know of the place?" Erik asked curiously.

"We do," Ozzie replied, but said nothing more.

Erik looked intrigued by this, but did not press the issue. The last map was simply of France and showed more specific details about that country. As they studied the maps, Erik went on to give the three what little advice he could for their journey, general things really. He told them that they would not have to worry about carrying very many supplies with them, for a number of inns were found all along the road they would travel—Taryn guessed Erik had not often made use of these establishments during his travels—and the money he gave them, in addition to what they had, would be more than enough to sustain them. He did advise them to carry a few non-perishables, though, just in case.

It was strange to see Erik's demeanor change so rapidly. He could be a completely different person now, the very picture of gentility. He was shrewd, yes, but not ten minutes ago he had been ready to kill them all, and before that he *was* trying to kill them. Now he was sitting and talking with them pleasantly and offering help.

Taryn and Ozzie knew they should be asking more questions—you can never be too prepared when setting out in a parallel world—but their brains just couldn't cooperate. It was likely a combination of anxiety, exhaustion, and sensory overload, but Taryn also suspected that peculiar power in Erik's voice was also keeping them fuzzy.

Finally, after sharing what advice he could, Erik stood up with his maps in hand and said, "You may rest here until I return with your provisions." He then began to leave, but turned back when he heard Taryn make a noise.

"Erik…" she stammered uncomfortably. "Thank you."

He bowed slightly to her and then was gone. No one said anything for a long time, as all three of them were trying to sort out their thoughts. They never moved from the couch and eventually fell asleep there.


Erik took the three back across the lake in his boat. He gave each one of them a parcel of clothes, a pack to share, and a pouch of money.

"Thank you again," Ozzie said sincerely.

"You've been very kind," Taryn added.

Erik nodded and replied, "I wish you all well. Perhaps we will meet again one day."

"Perhaps," was all Taryn said.

Ozzie, Taryn, and Smitty then began the short trek back up to the street. No one turned around to see if Erik was still there. Finally, after they had passed by the gate and were walking down the street in the safety of sunlight, Ozzie spoke.

"Well, that turned out well."

Taryn looked over and saw Ozzie grinning, obviously trying to lighten the mood. She allowed herself a chuckle and added, "*Eventually.*"

"He tried to *kill* us," Smitty said, not seeing the humor in the situation at all.

"Yeah, but look how it ended up. He was really generous," Taryn said defensively. "Look, the guy gets a really raw deal from life. It's hard to hold everything against him when you know his background."

"I have no problem with that," Smitty said flatly.

"Look at it this way," Ozzie said, trying to assuage Smitty's fears, "we're fine now, we're better supplied than Ryn and I ever were in Leleplar, and we know this place...sort of. Everything is looking up!"

Smitty sighed and said, "I guess that is good."

"Definitely!" Taryn said, joining Ozzie's little parade of happiness.

"So this is it, then?" Ozzie said, a smile suddenly spreading across his face. "We're off again!"

Taryn sighed and said, "I suppose we are."

"Cheer up," Ozzie said optimistically. "This is good for you. You can get firsthand experience with your major's subject matter. Plus, we're hardened adventurers now! Or two of us are. Smitty, let me get you up to speed on everything you need to know when questing..."

Taryn rolled her eyes and walked ahead as Ozzie began to expound upon the finer points of choosing a campsite, making friends and avoiding enemies, and anything else he could think of. Smitty looked as if he thought Ozzie might be a bit crazy, but listened patiently nonetheless.

*Something had changed. Balance had...shifted. The feel of it was jarring enough to wake her from sleep. The scrying spell showed nothing, but that could be a clue in itself. It was hard to say. No matter. She would dispatch her spies and watch. Such a thing couldn't hide itself for long.*

# Chapter 5

Ozzie and Taryn thought it was kind of amazing how quickly they fell back into the same routine they'd had in Leleplar. Their path took them west through the rest of Paris, and they stopped to get a few more supplies on the outskirts of the city: road food, a basic tent just in case, some extra clothes, etc. After stocking up, they would make their way through the rest of France towards America. It was a very long day full of walking, but Smitty seemed to manage it better than Ozzie and Taryn. Smitty was the most fit of the three, as he ran almost every day as a hobby, something that Ozzie had mocked on multiple occasions. All those past comments came back to bite Ozzie every time they had to stop and rest, as these breaks were mostly for his—and Taryn's—sake.

"What was it you once said?" Smitty goaded. "Running is an unimaginative person's activity."

"You win," Ozzie replied. "If we have to run for our lives, they'll get me first."

Smitty's expression soured at that, and he didn't respond. Taryn and Ozzie found this concerning, but couldn't talk about it since Smitty was right there. Their friend had run hot and cold since they had arrived in Terturelia. There were times where he had seemed able to accept everything almost as well as Ozzie did and others where he had retreated into himself. He was not angry and bitter the way Taryn had often been when she and Ozzie had first arrived in Leleplar, but cold and aloof. Ozzie knew Smitty very well and was surprised because his former roommate was generally pretty laid back. Then again, this was a situation that would test anyone. Ozzie tried pulling Smitty out of his shell by making more jokes about how much better Smitty was handling the situation than Taryn had in Leleplar. Taryn, knowing what Ozzie was doing, joined in, feigning offense. Smitty smiled and came back to them, but there still seemed to be some part of himself that he held back from his friends. Finally, Taryn asked Smitty something Ozzie never would have in a million years.

"What are you thinking?"

"Huh?" Smitty asked. "What do you mean?"

"You're not yourself," she replied simply. "What are you thinking?"

Smitty looked away from her for a few moments, studying the scenery around them.

They had entered the French countryside, which was breathtaking. The large cobblestone lanes had thinned out to a road of hard, packed earth. Vineyards flush with grapevines and fields full of lavender stretched out like green and purple oceans. Here and there, the occasional farmhouse or cottage could be seen, surrounded by overflowing gardens. Carts and riders on horseback had passed and tipped their hats in greeting to the group. It was a pastoral paradise.

"I'm fine," he said, turning back to her and shrugging.

Taryn raised a skeptical eyebrow at him.

"Shenanigans," Ozzie called back casually.

Taryn smiled at Ozzie and then turned back to Smitty before saying, "Whatever it is, we're all in this together. I mean, we literally haven't got any other choice, so you can tell us. You *should* tell us."

"Don't worry, I'm fine," Smitty repeated with a smile.

Taryn looked dubious, but dropped the subject.

They walked on, admiring their surroundings and around evening came upon a lovely chateau that had been turned into an inn. Flowering vines climbed up the grey stone building, while a lush garden buzzing with insects surrounded the outside. The innkeepers, Orville and Marie, were a kind, elderly couple with sweet, wrinkled faces. They asked for one room, but requested the largest one available.

"Where is it you three are headed?" Orville asked, getting them ensconced.

"Murica!" Ozzie said excitedly.

Orville and Marie looked somewhat confused at his enthusiasm and looked to the probably much more sensible Smitty.

"Do be careful going through the forest beneath Castle Rose, won't you, dear?" Marie said with concern. "It's a dangerous place and not worth the lives of you children."

"Is it really cursed?" Taryn asked immediately.

"It's wild, certainly," Orville said. "We've heard some mad tales, but most of our guests come through unscathed."

He winked at the three playfully. They three then got their key, and Marie led them to their room. As she was leaving, she took Taryn's hand and whispered quickly.

"Take this. My husband is afraid of losing business, so he does not talk about it, but the curse is real! I will pray to Saint Christopher for you; he will protect you."

Before Taryn could say a word, Marie hurried away. Taryn looked down and saw what Marie had placed there. It was a simple leather cord and small silver pendant with the effigy of a man embossed onto its surface. Taryn guessed this was Saint Christopher, but didn't have a clue as to who he was. She planned on telling the boys about it, but was immediately distracted by the room they had rented. Rather, a discussion that had already ensued about it.

The largest room, which Ozzie immediately started calling the penthouse, was all the way at the top of the chateau. It was essentially the entire attic, which was broad in both directions, but did have sloping walls. It also only contained one, albeit large, bed. Ozzie and Smitty were looking very uncomfortable and discussing whether or not there had been some kind of miscommunication downstairs. Taryn, however, started cracking up when she saw it.

"Oh, come on," she said once she was able to compose herself a little. "It's not that bad. Girls share their beds all the time."

"That is totally different!" Smitty said vehemently. "And how come I don't get invited to those slumber parties?"

"Tell you what, grin and bear it tonight, and you can come over next time Emily and I are cuddled up to watch a scary movie together," Taryn teased.

Smitty didn't respond, which meant he was considering Taryn's offer and only made her laugh again.

"What do I get?" Ozzie asked.

"Oh, you're fine. You've snuggled with Tynx before," Taryn said dismissively, trying to get her laughter under control.

"No, *you* snuggled with Tynx," Ozzie corrected. "I snuggled with you."

"Fine," Taryn laughed. "I'll be in the middle as usual."

Smitty looked as if he didn't quite know what to think of the current conversation, and Ozzie immediately explained to save his dignity or Taryn's honor or whatever was currently in question.

"It was strictly platonic, dude! We were in the mountains, and it was freezing, so we huddled together to survive. That's all!"

That seemed to appease Smitty for the most part, but he still looked as if he were seriously questioning what he had gotten into. Taryn insisted that one bed was totally normal for Europe, especially this time period, but Ozzie questioned her expertise on the subject, especially since they didn't seem to be in any specific time period. The debate continued all the way back downstairs for dinner.

The meal that night was excellent—homemade roast lamb, bread and butter, and greens. They spent dinner with Orville, while Marie served, and one other guest. He was a middle-aged man who was traveling to the city for business. He had traveled through the forest many times and secretly told the three that all the stories were just superstitious nonsense. Everyone there talked for some time and enjoyed the company. Ozzie, Taryn, and Smitty all immediately wished they could stay for a few extra days, but knew it would just be a waste of time and money. After dinner and back in the room, Taryn pulled the Saint Christopher pendant from her pocket and told Smitty and Ozzie about Marie's strange behavior. None of them were too worried after meeting the other guest, but Taryn tied the necklace around her neck anyway. Marie had been kind enough to give it to her; the least Taryn could do was wear it.

At bedtime, there was a little more awkwardness between Ozzie and Smitty. Taryn changed behind a screen and jumped into the bed, however, and patted each side of her playfully.

"Better get used to it," she said. "It's possible this is the way it is everywhere."

Ozzie sighed and went to change behind the screen, too.

"Okay, move over," he said, emerging a few moments later. "I hope you clipped your toenails. I don't want to get scratched by Sasquatch claws again."

Smitty finally followed suit, looking very uncomfortable, and eventually climbed onto Taryn's other side.

"Your chivalry does you great honor," she said formally, trying to make Smitty feel more comfortable about the very odd situation.

He smiled and said, "You are having way too much fun with this."

"It's only fun because you react so well," she teased.

With that, the three did their best to settle down for the night, knowing they had some serious traveling ahead of them.

Things were only slightly less awkward the next morning, but still more so for Smitty than anyone else. When he woke up next to Taryn, who was still sleeping soundly, he had to quickly remind himself where he was and what had happened the day before. Doubly so when he saw Ozzie there, too. After getting bathed—another difficult and uncomfortable situation, but one that Taryn and Ozzie had dealt with before—and changed, they headed downstairs for breakfast. They all felt very good about traveling after the hot meal of porridge that Marie had prepared and were soon out the door and heading down the road. The mood was light as they walked. It was hard to think of danger when there was so much sunshine and gorgeous scenery around them. Ozzie called for a lunch break on the side of the road around midday, and they got their first look at the forest just after. Cresting a tall hill with an easy slope, they all stopped and stared silently. Lumps formed in all three throats as the old growth forest loomed before them, about a mile down the road like a path into the underworld.

The huge trees grew so closely together that they blocked out the sunlight almost completely, blanketing everything in a false twilight. The tree branches looked gnarled and dangerous, as if they were threatening trespassers to stay away...or else.

There was a short discussion over whether or not to press on or make camp. Taryn wanted to make camp and take it easy for the rest of the afternoon and evening, but both Ozzie and Smitty felt it would be better to get through and beyond the forest as quickly as possible. The crux of their argument was that the forest didn't look all that big. It was early afternoon after all, and they could get through the whole thing and to an inn if they were quick and didn't take any breaks. Taryn, on the other hand, argued that it would be fine *outside* of the woods, and they would have all day the next day if they just waited to set off tomorrow. The vote was two against one, though, so Taryn finally agreed begrudgingly.

Ozzie, Taryn, and Smitty could see the path thin out, becoming less and less clear, as they approached the tree line. They had also seen a dark, crumbling castle at the top of a very tall, craggy hill near the center of the woods, which answered the question of just what Castle Rose was. Rosy it was not. It looked more like a skeletal bat perched on the rock. It was an unnerving feeling, having that great dark structure peering down on them as they drew near the edge of the forest. Thankfully, the leaf cover hid it from view as they entered.

# Chapter 6

Ozzie, Taryn, and Smitty trudged through the darkness with no idea how far in they were or how far they had to go. All three were edgy and felt as if they were being watched by a million invisible eyes. This had been a bad idea and they all knew it. Smitty was the first one to say so.

"You supported it," Taryn snapped.

"Well, now I'm un-supporting it," was Smitty's retort.

"Arguing about it won't help," Ozzie said, interjecting before his friends could really get into it. "Should we turn back?"

"Let's not," Smitty said, still irritable. "How about we just climb a tree and try to sleep?"

Taryn and Ozzie had to admit that they liked that idea better than tromping through a possibly cursed forest. This was a possibility that seemed more and more likely as the afternoon had worn on. The easiest explanation was that they had simply gotten lost, but how could they be lost?! They were still following the path, there hadn't been any forks down which they could have turned wrong, and they didn't seem any closer to the edge of the forest than they had several hours ago. Night had fallen and settled around them a while back, covering everything in a thick blanket of semi-solid blackness. Thus began the task of finding a suitable tree. This, however, turned out to be a fruitless effort. It was so dark now that it was nearly impossible to see. Some thin beams of moonlight managed to slip in through the few holes in the canopy, but this only provided visibility for a few feet. Ozzie tried using his cell phone as a light to help them see properly—the phones had been turned off since they were useless and to save the batteries—but it was no good. Getting soaked in the underground lake hadn't been healthy for the phones. Taryn's phone wouldn't turn on at all, and Smitty's wouldn't go past the loading screen. Ozzie's turned on but flickered now and again and the screen was a scrambled mess. Besides that, the trees were all so tall and so old that the lowest branches were all far too high to reach. As they searched, something caught Taryn's eye. It was different from the other shifting shadows of the forest. She stopped short to look at what it could be, causing Smitty to bump into her, smashing his nose against the back of her head.

"Ow! Taryn!" Smitty exclaimed.

"Smitty, shut up for a minute!" Taryn snapped back.

Ozzie had kept walking, but stopped when he heard his friends arguing. He turned to face them, though he could barely see them from this distance.

"Hey, chill out you two," he said, trying to keep his own fraying temper in check.

"Hush, please!" Taryn told him.

"What is it?" Smitty asked with obvious irritation.

"If you'd keep your mouth shut for one second, I could—"

Taryn never finished her sentence, as a deafening roar resounded from somewhere nearby. It had sounded like it had come from some sort of mix between a bear and a lion, and none of the three wanted to find out what could make that sort of noise. Ozzie, Taryn, and Smitty all broke into a run and were soon jumping over logs and crashing through brambles as they lost the path and stumbled in a panicked attempt to get away from the thing that they could hear tearing after them. Smitty and Ozzie both pulled ahead of Taryn quickly, their legs being longer than hers. A heavy, steady breathing of some sort of animal could be heard just behind them, and no one dared look back. That is, not until Ozzie and Smitty heard Taryn scream from behind them. They both skidded to a halt, Ozzie stumbling over a tree root as he did so, and looked back. Smitty, being the fastest one of them, could barely see anything back the way he had come, but Ozzie was only a few yards from Taryn, who was currently crawling backward away from a huge, hulking figure in the darkness.

"Ryn!" Ozzie cried, and got up quickly.

Smitty hesitated a moment, but saw Ozzie heading off, so he raced back the way he had come. He soon saw the shadow that cornered Taryn against a large rock and lunged at it. Both he and

Ozzie hit it full on at the same time, knocking the thing from its feet. All three tumbled on the ground, but the creature recovered first. It roared a thundering challenge and used one, massive paw to sweep the two boys away from it. The creature then turned back to Taryn, only to have the side of its face slammed with a large tree branch. The creature roared again angrily and lunged at Taryn. She held up the branch to protect herself. Her attacker simply grabbed it in its teeth and ripped it from her grasp. Ozzie and Smitty were dazed and came to their senses only just in time to see the creature attack Taryn and hurry away, carrying her in its jaws.

"Smitty, come on!" Ozzie cried. "We have to follow it! We have to help Taryn!"

Both of them got up and began to follow as fast as their protesting bodies allowed them. It was nearly impossible for them to follow the trail in the dark, however. Ozzie and Smitty didn't get far before they had completely lost track of which direction it had gone.

"Taryn!" Ozzie yelled desperately into the darkness.

There was no reply, and the two sank back against the trunk of a large tree, desperately trying to figure out what to do next.

"There's no use trying to find her tonight," Smitty finally said. "Let's wait until morning and then see if we can find the trail."

It was clear how badly Ozzie wanted to go blindly search for Taryn. He had an expression that said if he just knew which way to go, he'd be off in a heartbeat.

"We can't!" Ozzie insisted angrily. "We can't wait."

"Oz, we will never find her like this. In fact, we'll probably lose the trail forever if we try. We'll do better if we get some rest and wait for light."

Ozzie sneered at his friend in the darkness. It sounded to him like Smitty was just making excuses to avoid having to face the monster again. He shook himself. No, that wasn't true. Smitty wouldn't just abandon Taryn. He was right; they would lose the trail if they just tried to fumble their way around now. Ozzie agreed, and the two shared a sparse meal of bread and dried meat before drifting into an uneasy sleep. When they awoke, it was not because the sun had come up, though it just barely had, but because someone came stepping through the trees wielding a vicious looking axe.

Taryn awoke some time—she didn't know exactly how long—later and didn't move for many minutes, while her eyes focused on her surroundings. She did her best to remember what had happened. The memory of the attack in the forest came slowly back to her, and she swallowed hard at the thought of where she might be. A quick perusal of her surroundings made her feel slightly better, but not much.

She was a very large room, lit only by the weak early morning sunlight that tried its best to come through the thin gothic-arched windows. Everything about the room was magnificent, including the bed that Taryn was laying on now. The exquisitely carved stone of the room's architecture was painted with stylized flowers and vines and shapes. The furniture shone as if it had just been polished and was covered in colorful hand-embroidered patterns. The bed Taryn was lying on was a lovely four-poster bed with deep green curtains and roses carved into the posts. There was also a marble fireplace against one wall, but it looked unused at the moment.

Taryn sat up slowly, unsure whether or not she was glad she always seemed to wake up in nice bedrooms whenever she was in trouble, and then worked on standing. She noticed a pitcher with what looked like water in it and a glass on the nightstand and immediately rejected it. She wasn't about to drink anything here just yet, despite the fact that she was parched. She then walked over towards a set of double doors and, much to her surprise, found them unlocked. Obviously, whoever had captured her either wasn't very smart or wasn't trying very hard to keep her captive. Cautiously, she poked her head out of the room and looked around. There was no one about and all that stood outside of her room was a long dark corridor.

The corridor was lit by a combination of dim sunlight from more arched windows and wrought iron candelabras, which ran all down the hall. The walls on either side exhibited more exquisite architecture, but the painting was less prominent out here. An intricately carved rail ran along the length of both walls and, once in a while, a buttress ran up to support the high ceiling. The flat grayness of the stone walls was occasionally interrupted by tapestries so bright that the characters and animals in them looked ready to jump out.

Taryn left her room, began down the hall, and wandered around in the hopes of finding the exit...assuming there was an exit to this maze. All along the way she saw more and more amazing art and architecture. Had she not been so nervous, she might have been able to appreciate it. She finally came to another set of doors that looked promising. So far, every other set of doors she had seen were open and looked to go nowhere she needed. These were closed and looked important, though Taryn couldn't quite put her finger on how. She thought they might lead to a great receiving hall and was just reaching to open them when a shadow passed over her and onto the doors. She swallowed hard, determined not to panic, and turned to see an inhuman creature towering over her.

Ozzie and Smitty were on their feet at once, though their bodies protested loudly. The man that stood before them was taller and wider than them both, and the axe he carried looked sharp enough to easily split them in half. Both of them knew if he really put up a fight neither of them would have a chance, but they weren't about to show that. Ozzie and Smitty stared at the man warily, not moving. After a moment, the man's stern, bearded face broke into a broad grin, and he laughed heartily.

"Puss," he said jovially, "have you ever seen such a pair of scared rabbits before?"

Suddenly, a slender cat with bright, inquisitive, green eyes slunk out from behind the man and inspected the two boys carefully. Ozzie and Smitty both found it very strange that the cat was wearing a tiny pair of leather boots.

"No," the cat said slyly, making both Ozzie and Smitty jump back. "They are lost, yes?"

"No!" Ozzie said quickly. "Yes. I mean, sort of. See, we were traveling through these woods."

"That was your first mistake, monsieur," the cat quipped.

"Thank you," Ozzie continued, quickly losing his patience. "Well, we were attacked by a...a...an I don't know what. Some sort of monster, and our friend, Taryn, was taken."

"And you are afraid for her," the man with the axe said, softening at the news.

"Yes, we are," Smitty admitted. "Can you help us, please?"

The man and the cat exchanged glances and then turned back to the two boys.

"I think it would be best if you two followed us back to my cabin," the man said. "You are both tired and look like you need a proper meal."

"But Taryn—" Ozzie began.

"He's right," Smitty said firmly. "If she's even alive…"

Ozzie was tempted to argue, but decided getting some answers would be more helpful. Even so, he wouldn't stay any longer than necessary. He and Smitty began to follow the strange pair through the woods.

"By the way," the man said back over his shoulder, "my name is Bernard, and this is my friend, Puss."

"At your service!" the cat announced proudly.

"Okay, Puss in Boots," Smitty whispered to Ozzie, "and what? Token woodcutter?"

"I think so," Ozzie said, though his mind was elsewhere.

After a little while, a simple log cabin came within sight, and all four headed inside. The cabin was just one, large room, but it was safe and comforting. Ozzie and Smitty took seats at the table, while Puss simply jumped up on top of it. Their host went over to the fire and filled two bowls with a thick, unidentifiable gruel. He served the two boys and then sat down across from them.

"Eat," Bernard instructed. "You both need a hot meal, I think."

Ozzie and Smitty obeyed, and, though the food did make them feel better, it wasn't the best stuff they had ever tasted. Nevertheless, they were grateful.

"So," Ozzie began, before shoving another spoonful into his mouth, "what about this monster thing? What can you tell us about it?" He had also wanted to ask if there was any chance that Taryn was still alive, but was too afraid to hear the answer.

"Oui, the Beast…" the man said gravely. "He has terrorized this forest for years. He usually attacks small groups. You would have been better traveling with a caravan."

"So how is it that you can live here?" Smitty asked.

"Because I only leave my cabin during the day, and the creature does not come out of his castle except at night."

"That still doesn't explain why you haven't been attacked," Smitty said skeptically.

Bernard laughed and, gesturing at his axe, said, "Oh, I have been, but I bit back. Since then, I leave the Beast alone, and he returns the favor."

Ozzie suddenly saw Puss smirk slightly, but he couldn't guess why.

"You mentioned a castle?" Ozzie said, turning away from the clever feline. "Do you mean Castle Rose?"

Bernard nodded and Smitty asked, "Why is it called that anyway?"

"It has always been called this. Legend says a garden full of the most beautiful roses grows all around it. At least it did before the curse. There's no way to know now."

The more Ozzie heard, the more fearful he grew for Taryn, and he finally asked the crucial question: "So what do we do now? To save Taryn, I mean?"

"Nothing," the man said, shaking his head. "I'm afraid your friend is as good as dead."

"No!" Ozzie cried angrily, jumping to his feet and pounding the table with his fist, making Smitty jump. "She *could* be alive. We can't just leave her!"

"I am sorry," Bernard said evenly.

Ozzie looked frantically from Bernard to Smitty, waiting for someone, anyone, to agree with him. Neither did. Puss, however, suddenly cleared his throat and spoke.

"If you don't mind, Monsieur Bernard, I could take them to try and save their friend, if it is that important."

"It is!" Ozzie insisted.

"Very well," Bernard agreed easily. "If anyone can help them, it is you, Puss."

"Ozzie, are you sure about this?" Smitty asked suddenly, giving his friend a look.

It all seemed too easy to Smitty, and he had seen the cat smirk, too. He sensed that something wasn't right about the whole thing.

"Smitty, we have zero options here," Ozzie said determinedly, "and I am *not* about to abandon Taryn to that thing. You can stay here, but I'm going."

"Okay, okay," Smitty said, backing down. "I'm coming."

"We had better go now," Puss suggested. "It will take some time to get to the castle, and you will want to get there before the sun goes down."

Ozzie and Smitty thanked Bernard and bid him goodbye. Bernard in turn wished them luck and watched as the three disappeared back into the trees.

Taryn barely suppressed a scream as she looked before her and saw what could only be described as a monster standing there. Bird, fox, ox, cat, and human seemed to have all been mashed together into something that wasn't any of those things. Fingers melded into paws, legs into hooves, ears into hair all so seamlessly that Taryn's brain almost refused to believe it could be real. It wasn't the inhumanness of the creature that terrified her, however, as how much it reminded her of Vurnal's shiftlings in Leleplar. The shiftlings were elf-Shifter hybrids that Vurnal had created to be his servants. Unlike the creature before her, however, each shiftling had borne the traits of a single animal, but that distinction didn't matter to her much at the moment.

Taryn's voice caught in her throat as she tried to speak and all that came out was a tiny whimper. The creature blinked its large, owl-like eyes at her and said nothing at first. Finally, when it spoke, its voice was surprisingly soft and meek, but very low.

"It would not be wise to enter the master's domain."

"An...and who is your master?" Taryn barely squeaked.

"He is the master," the creature replied simply.

This did not bode well. The shiftlings had been drones for Vurnal, and this creature seemed to be of the same ilk for his mysterious master.

"Is there anything you can tell me about him?" Taryn asked carefully, hoping that maybe the creature wasn't very bright.

"This is his kingdom. Anyone who enters belongs to him."

"Look, I realize I was on his land, but I didn't mean to be," Taryn begged, giving up on information gathering. "Please, can you help me get out of here?"

"You belong to the master now," the creature said, shaking his head.

Taryn felt any hope that had remained inside her fading away, and she barely kept a hold on her limited resolve when she spoke again.

"What should I do?" she asked.

"Obey the master," the creature said, "and do not enter his domain."

Taryn looked back at the doors and, for the first time, noticed that the doorknobs were in the shape of a horrid beast's head. From the creature's warnings, she suspected that these doors led to her captor's rooms, somewhere she had no desire to be anywhere near. She then quickly swept around the creature and began her way back down the hall. As her fear increased, so did her desire to find an escape. She tried to think of what usually kept her from being afraid and remembered that it was her temper. She tried to think of something to make her angry, but there wasn't really anything to be angry at just now. The strange drone-creature unnerved her more than anything, and his talk of his master made her imagination run wild with what this thing might be to have such power.

Suddenly, a thought so terrifying gripped Taryn that she had to lean against the wall and steady herself. What if Vurnal was still alive?! What if that was why they had been brought here? Was it possible Ozzie hadn't actually killed him? What if this was his castle? Taryn forced herself to slow her breathing. No, she had seen Vurnal die with her own eyes. He was gone forever. Wherever she was, whatever was in this castle, it was something different.

Taryn did her best to remember where she had already been and made it a point to avoid heading back towards what was known as the master's domain. She saw no other creatures like the one she had just met and for that she was thankful. No matter how long she walked, however, no matter how many different corridors and rooms she found, she failed to find an exit. As strange as it was, she began to think that perhaps none existed.

As Ozzie, Smitty, and Puss made their way through the trees and undergrowth of the forest, Smitty eyed the feline suspiciously. He didn't trust Puss very much, and decided to question him a bit.

"So, Puss, how did you come to be here?" he began.

"It is a very long story," the little tabby replied with a smirk.

"We've got time," said Ozzie, who was desperate for anything to keep his mind off what might be happening to Taryn.

"Very well," Puss said, sensing Ozzie's anxiety. "I grew up with a poor family. When the father died, I was given to his youngest son. I promised to help the boy in exchange for my fine clothes. He granted my wishes, and, due to some very impressive planning on my part, I helped him to marry well and become wealthy."

"So what happened to happily ever after?" Smitty asked.

Puss sighed and explained, "After a few years of royal treatment, I began to grow bored, so I went off in search of adventure. That is when I found Bernard."

"So where's the adventure?" Ozzie asked.

"Helping lost strangers such as yourself," Puss said with another smirk. "The Beast provides quite a lot of adventure."

"So does that mean you're going to charge us?" Smitty asked skeptically. "Will we have to buy you a hat or something?"

"Monsieur!" Puss said, looking scandalized. "The life of an innocent girl is at stake. Do you think I would try to profit from such a horrific event?"

"I guess we'll find out," Smitty said with finality.

The three continued to walk on for most of the morning until about noon when they came to a steep, jagged cliff face.

"Come," Puss told them, adroitly bounding up to an outcropping of rock. "Castle Rose is just on top of this mountain."

Ozzie and Smitty looked up at the great climb that lay before them, exchanged a look, and shrugged. There was nothing else for it. They could either go up or go back; there was no other way.

Taryn searched for what must have been hours, but found no way out of the labyrinthine castle. Every door she found simply led to another maze of rooms and hallways, and all the windows were either too high up to reach or too narrow to climb through. Strangely, some rooms she came upon were uncannily timed in their appearance. A water closet, for instance, came across her path just as she was awkwardly wondering where she might find a toilet. Eventually the smell of food began to drift her way and, although her brain told her not to eat anything here, her rumbling stomach overrode her common sense. Taryn followed her nose all the way to what looked like a simple sitting room.

There was a fireplace at one end of the room and a large armchair sitting in front of that. Other chairs and couches were strewn about the room, as well as end tables with lit candelabras atop them. Various paintings scattered about the wall, some depicting gorgeous landscapes, others portraying animals, and a few containing portraits of unidentifiable people.

Taryn carefully entered the room and edged around to see if anyone was sitting in the big armchair. She released an anxious breath when she saw it was empty and approached. There, on the table next to the chair, was a large platter with a silver cover over it. A silver goblet was there as well, filled with what looked like wine, and a set of silverware rolled up in a napkin, secured with a silver napkin ring.

Taryn tentatively sat down in the chair and removed the cover on the platter. She tried not to drool when she saw the exquisitely prepared meal there. It looked like a dish she might get from a five star restaurant. Despite being famished, however, she remained wary and was very careful as she cut a tiny piece of meat for herself. She sniffed it and then tasted it with a flick of her tongue. Nothing seemed out of the ordinary, and she decided that it was safe to eat. Before she knew it, she had cleaned the plate and nodded off, despite telling herself that she was just going to shut her eyes for a minute.

By the time Ozzie, Smitty, and Puss reached the brow of the hill, Ozzie and Smitty were both drenched in sweat and panting in exhaustion. Puss, however, looked as if he had just finished a light jog.

"As soon as we get back, I'm going start working out," Ozzie told Smitty, kneeling down on the ground to catch his breath.

"For real this time?" Smitty asked.

"Shhh," Puss hissed suddenly. "It would not be wise to tell the Beast that we are here."

They didn't reply and very carefully set off across the hilltop.

A gaunt, crumbling castle rose up in the distance. It was surrounded by a high stone wall, and a vicious-looking, rusted metal gate was set into the wall at what used to be the front entrance. All around the gate and the walls and just beyond were thorns and brambles topped with perfect red, pink, and white roses.

Ozzie and Smitty picked their way carefully through these, acquiring a good many cuts along the way. Finally, they reached the gate.

"Great, just what we need," Ozzie said bitterly, "a good case of tetanus."

"How do *we* get in?" Smitty asked, looking down at Puss, who had easily slipped through the bars.

The cat silently cocked his head towards a set of bars in the gate that looked a little crooked. Smitty took a hold of one and found that it had come loose from the bottom crossbar. The bar had moved just enough so that he could almost fit through it. Ozzie helped Smitty push it far enough to the side that they could pass through the gap. As they drew near the castle, however, they came upon a bigger problem: There was no entrance. They were approaching a solid wall of stone.

"Puss, this is really not looking good," Ozzie said, feeling desperate.

"Watch and learn," the cat said cockily.

With that he ran up to where the front entrance should have been and, impossibly, walked right through the stone. Ozzie and Smitty stood there staring in shock until Puss reappeared, the front half of his body sticking out of the building.

"This is an enchanted castle, if you did not notice," Puss said with a tone that suggested that he thought the two boys were rather slow.

Ozzie and Smitty exchanged looks, and Ozzie took a step forward. Smitty grabbed his arm before he could go any further, though, and spoke quietly.

"Oz, something's not right here. How does he know so much about this place?"

"I don't know the answer to that, and you might be right, but we can't just leave Taryn to whatever fate that thing has planned for her. We don't have any choice."

"And what if she's already dead? Huh? What then? We might be walking into a trap right now, and it'd be for nothing."

Ozzie leveled his gaze hard at Smitty and replied, "We don't know what's happened. While there's still hope for Taryn, I refuse to give up on her. You do what you want."

With that, he ripped his arm out of Smitty's grasp and followed the cat through the wall. Smitty growled and followed a moment later. It was cool as they passed through, and they almost felt as if something pushed them along as they went. As soon as they were inside, their eyes began to adjust to the serious lack of light inside.

"Look, man, don't think I don't want to help Taryn," Smitty whispered. "Believe me, I do. I just don't want to be stupid about it."

"I get that," Ozzie said, looking around instead of at Smitty, "but we can't take chances by being too careful."

"Sure, but don't go thinking—"

Smitty was interrupted by a hiss from Puss as he motioned for them to remain completely quiet. He scowled at the cat.

Taryn thought she was dreaming when she first heard the sound of Ozzie's voice. She opened her eyes and shook her head to clear it.

"Oz?" she whispered vaguely.

She heard the sound again and shot up from her chair.

"Ozzie!" she cried frantically and she sped off without another thought in the direction of the voice.

Puss, Ozzie, and Smitty hadn't made it very far into the castle before they were spotted by a creature similar to the one that had approached Taryn. The creature let out an angry cry when it saw the intruders, which was answered by many others throughout the castle. The group was now running as fast as they could up stairs and down corridors to escape from the pursuing creatures. The two boys yelled randomly for Taryn, not knowing whether or not she was even alive. Their spirits lifted as they heard the girl's voice calling back to them from somewhere. It spurred them forward, which was very good because the creatures were gaining despite their awkward, lumbering gaits.

WHAM!

Ozzie and Smitty had just turned a corner when something solid flew right into them. Everyone there—except for Puss, of course—tumbled down in a mass of arms and legs. The cat had jumped out of the way just in time. Ozzie was the first one of them to look up and recognize the head of fiery red hair.

"Ryn!" he cried, and then looked back to see their pursuers catching up. He then commanded, "Come on! We have to go!"

They all got up and began to run again.

"Okay, Puss, lead us out of here!" Smitty told the cat. "Where's the front door?"

"There is none," the cat called back. "Like the forest, the castle does not provide an exit to those the Beast has not permitted to leave."

"What?!" Smitty screamed. "You liar! You left!"

"What does he care about me? I am a cat."

"Taryn, do you know how to get out of here?" Ozzie cut in.

"No," she said. "Follow me."

"What?" Ozzie said in confusion.

Taryn led the group down a few more corridors that she barely remembered, but she knew that they would be useful in losing the creatures that were tailing them. The creatures were slowed up by the maze and, after turning a very sharp corner, Taryn led them through a set of large, promising looking double doors. Once all four were inside they shut the doors as fast as they could and shoved a candlestick through the handles to bar them. They then listened hard and heard nothing for several minutes. Satisfied with their temporary evasion, Ozzie, Taryn, and Smitty leaned against the door, breathing hard.

"So…who's your furry friend?" Taryn asked after a few minutes.

"Ryn, this is Puss in Boots," Ozzie said with a relieved grin. "Puss, meet the damsel in distress, Taryn."

"Bonjour, mademoiselle," Puss said with a bow.

"It's very nice to meet you, Mr. Puss," Taryn replied with a nod, very amused at meeting the fairytale cat.

"Thanks for the warning on that one-way door, cat," Smitty said angrily.

"It is part of the enchantment," Puss said with a shrug.

Smitty growled to himself and said to his friends, "I say we feed the fur ball to those things out there."

"He's fine," Ozzie said distractedly. He was just happy that they had found Taryn safe and sound. "Let's see where we can go from here."

They began to look around and found that they were in some sort of receiving parlor. Another set of doors led out on their left, while all sorts of furniture stood ready for guests. Directly across from them was a set of glass doors that led out to a balcony.

Ozzie and Smitty made for the balcony doors and found them locked tightly. They picked up more candlesticks to begin breaking the windows. Meanwhile, Taryn headed for the other doors and opened them up wide. She was surprised to find that this next room was a grand set of bedchambers in shambles. It was as if a tornado had run through the place. And, even more shocking than that, was the enormous Beast that was currently chewing on an armoire. Taryn let out a terrified scream and then immediately covered her mouth, wishing she could take it back. The Beast's gaze snapped to her, and Taryn pulled the doors closed as fast as she could and began to run. A split second later, the Beast exploded through them. Ozzie and Smitty were suddenly at Taryn's back, staring in horror at the Beast. It roared, and they all covered their ears. They headed for the door, but the Beast was bounding towards it before they could even get close. They headed for the balcony next, but the Beast cut them off there, too. It didn't take but three strides for it to cross the room, and Ozzie, Taryn, and Smitty were soon cornered against the wall.

The Beast was a horrifying patchwork of all kinds of animals. Its front paws were nimble like a raccoon's but had a long, sharp claw on the end of each digit. The back legs were large and powerful, which explained how it was able to bound so far so fast. Standing up, it would have been ten feet, and its horse-like tail would drag on the ground. There was a ridge of stiff hair down its neck and back, and it had a set of small velvety antlers protruding from its head. The huge fangs and intense yellow eyes did nothing to help its terrible appearance.

Ozzie, Taryn, and Smitty cowered together, the boys holding their candlesticks as if they might actually provide some kind of defense. None of the three dared speak, but Puss' small fearful voice suddenly resounded from behind the creature.

"Master—" he began softly.

The Beast suddenly turned towards Puss and roared angrily, making everyone—including Puss—jump, and it leapt towards the cat. The cat yowled in fear and jumped to the top of an overturned chair. The Beast brought his face very close to the cat, breathing hard with rage, as Puss tried to make himself as small as he could.

"You betrayed me!" the Beast said in a very low, guttural voice. "Why did you bring them here?"

The trio was carefully edging its way around the room towards the balcony. Puss and the Beast were closer to the door that led back out to the castle, so maybe—provided they had a lot of luck on their side—they would be able to escape down some trellis or vines or something. As they listened to the conversation between Puss and the Beast, they assumed that the Beast was referring to Ozzie and Smitty.

"I thought you could turn them into servants for yourself," Puss said quickly. "Then your chosen and her friends won't have to be parted, and that should make them happy, yes?"

"Chosen what?" Smitty hissed to Taryn and Ozzie.

Neither was brave enough to venture a guess at that moment, but Taryn thought hard to try and figure it out. Whatever *it* was, she was it. Suddenly, things began to fall into place, though there was something wrong. She thought they might be sitting in the story of *Beauty and the Beast*, but, as far as she could remember, the original tale didn't mention anything about creepy servants. They had probably wandered here and been changed against their will. If she was right, she suspected she was also meant to play the part of Beauty.

The Beast growled low and took a swipe at the cat, who jumped away just in time. The Beast seemed to think on this for a moment and then said, "Perhaps...I knew there was a reason I allowed you to stay in my forest. Bernard knows of this as well?"

"He did not question me, but I believe he can guess."

Smitty, Ozzie, and Taryn all exchanged fearful glances. They had been doomed every step of the way in the forest. The Beast then turned back to the three, killing any current escape plan, and looked at Taryn with care. He took a step towards her, and she shrank back against her two friends.

The Beast's expression then changed to one of stern determination, and he said firmly, "You need not fear me. I will not harm you."

"I don't think so," Ozzie said protectively. "In case you forgot, you attacked us last night and almost ate Taryn."

"Do you see a mark on her?" the Beast asked.

"Doesn't matter," Ozzie countered. "She stays with us."

The huge creature growled and said dangerously, "Give her to me, or I shall take her by force."

"What if we—" Smitty started.

"I want them with me!" Taryn interjected suddenly.

"As you wish," the Beast replied calmly, nodding his head.

With that he began to walk out, the door opening all by itself as he approached. Puss zipped towards the balcony doors and through one of the broken windows. Smitty tried to grab him as he went, but the cat was too quick. Just like that, he was gone. Ozzie, Taryn, and Smitty all looked at each other and followed the Beast. When they reentered the corridor, there was no sign of the strange creatures that served the Beast. They only walked a minute or so before they were back at the room in which Taryn had woken.

The Beast sat down in front of the door like a docile housecat and said, "This is your room. I hope you like it."

Taryn swallowed hard and replied, "It's lovely. Thank you."

The Beast nodded and then said evenly, "Very good. I will see you all at dinner."

He stalked away without another word. Ozzie, Taryn, and Smitty all watched him leave. As soon as he was gone, they hurried into Taryn's room and closed and locked the door behind them.

# Chapter 7

"So now what are we going to do?" Smitty asked, dropping his pack onto the floor.

"I know what we're not going to do," Ozzie replied adamantly. "We are *not* staying here."

He then headed over to the windows and began to look for a way to escape.

"Ozzie, stop," Taryn said worriedly. "Think about what you're doing."

"I am. I'm thinking about a way to get out of here!" Ozzie said angrily.

Taryn headed over to her friend and took his busy hands in hers. He looked at her with a mask of determination, but underneath it she could see fear and worry.

"Ozzie, look," she told him sternly. "This is not a movie where the worst the Beast will do is lock you up and leave you to die. He will kill you, and I am not about to let that happen, but I need your help. I don't know what he plans on doing with you two, but he's letting me keep you with me. I don't want to endanger that, so let's not rock the boat until we put a plan together. Okay?"

"Wouldn't that be 'poke the bear'?" Smitty muttered unhelpfully.

When Taryn and Ozzie looked at him, he was brooding. Taryn looked back to Ozzie plaintively, and he nodded in agreement. They went and sat down next to Smitty to try and figure out their next move. It was Smitty who spoke first.

"So what are we in now and how does the story go?"

"I'm pretty sure it's *Beauty and the Beast*," Taryn explained. "You guys know it, right?"

In response, both and Ozzie and Smitty waggled their hands uncertainly.

"Okay, well, the original story is kind of vague and has a lot of paraphrasing. Basically, Beauty's father comes here cold and hungry. The Beast takes care of her dad without letting daddy dearest actually see him. Beauty had asked for a rose, so Beauty's father ends up picking one from the garden outside for her. That really ticks the Beast off and he threatens to kill Beauty's father. The Beast changes his mind, though, when daddy explains the situation. The Beast offers the dad a deal: either one of his daughters willingly comes back to die in his place, or, if they won't, dad comes back to meet his death. Beauty agrees to come, but the Beast doesn't kill her. She becomes less afraid of the Beast over time and is provided with anything and everything. After a while, she tells the Beast that she misses her father, so the Beast sends her home, but Beauty promises to come back. Back home, her sisters are jealous of her nice things, so they convince Beauty to stay longer than she planned. When she does go back to the Beast's castle, the Beast is dying. She says I love you, he turns back into a human, the end."

"A bit milder than our friend here, yes?" Ozzie said.

"I know. That's what's so weird." Taryn agreed. "Why is it different?"

"Well, you said the original story was really vague," Smitty said. "Maybe this is the part that was left out."

"Or maybe it's like some kind of crazy time travel loop!" Ozzie chimed in. "Maybe we're part of the original story. Maybe the story ends up being the way it does because of something we do here first!"

Smitty looked dubious, while Taryn opened and closed her mouth several times. She was confused because she was trying to both understand Ozzie's idea and find an argument against it.

"The concierge at the opera house died in the book," she finally said.

Ozzie shrugged, clearly unaffected by this blow to his logic, and said, "Okay. Well, we'll think of something."

The other two nodded, and the three spent much of the rest of the afternoon alternatively looking around the room for some way out and resting. Fear was a very draining emotion. They could not find any sort of escape, despite some of Ozzie's crazier ideas, but, as the afternoon drew on and relief began to settle over them, they were thankful to just be together again. They only became anxious again later when one of the servant creatures knocked on the door to inform them that supper was ready. The three apprehensively followed it to a massive dining room. The Beast was there already, lying on a rug in front of the fire like a monstrous hunting dog. Ozzie, Smitty, and Taryn all went to sit down at the table, but the Beast snarled angrily and made them stop short.

"She sits," he growled. "You two serve."

"I would like their company," Taryn protested carefully.

"They will be by," was the Beast's simple answer.

The three exchanged glances, and Taryn sat down. Meanwhile, Ozzie and Smitty followed one of the creatures back to the kitchen, wherever it was, and reappeared a few minutes later with platters of food. They set the food down on the table and served some to Taryn.

"Thanks, you guys," she said smiling uncomfortably at them both.

Afterward they stood back by a small table while Taryn ate. Their stomachs growled as they smelled the food, and Taryn felt incredibly awkward. She wanted to make conversation with her friends, but what could she say while the Beast was sitting there? She was in no joking mood and she wasn't sure if they would be willing to talk either. So the only sound heard in the massive dining room was that of clinking dinnerware.

After Taryn had finished, the Beast, whose eyes had never left her, asked, "Would you care to join me for a walk?"

Taryn felt her mouth go dry. The very thought terrified her, and she found that her voice had left her. She nodded dumbly in response. The Beast looked pleased.

He then turned to Ozzie and Smitty and growled, "Stay with my servants; they will show you what to do. Only after you are finished will you eat with them."

The two nodded, though it was clear that this was the last thing they wanted to do.

"Where can we meet you afterward, Taryn?" Smitty asked casually.

"The courtyard. The one you can see from my room window," she replied as steadily as she could.

She wasn't familiar enough with the castle to actually know how to—much less even if she could—get to that particular area, but she figured the Beast would say something if it would be an issue. She was testing him, but he said nothing as he sat and waited silently for her.

The two boys nodded and went to their work. Taryn then looked at the Beast, who bowed to her and spoke kindly.

"This way, if it pleases my lady."

Taryn followed as the Beast led the way out of the dining room, her breath coming quick and shallow. They walked somewhat aimlessly down hallways and corridors, though the Beast seemed to know where he was going. They eventually came down to a set of double doors that looked suspiciously like they led somewhere special. Taryn, who had silently walked as far from the Beast as she could without being what might be considered rude, stopped and stood nervously. The last special-looking doors she had walked through had led to the Beast's chambers. The doors opened on their own when he padded towards them, and Taryn could see a grassy courtyard with a high stone wall surrounding it beyond.

"This is my personal garden," the Beast said.

"Um, thank you," Taryn mumbled.

They walked on. For a moment, Taryn felt a bit like she was on an incredibly awkward date. She knew the story and what the Beast wanted. She was actually waiting for him to ask her if she would marry him. The thought might have actually made her laugh if she wasn't so scared for her life. They finally stopped near a bench, and Taryn sat down and looked around. She noticed that the stone walls were all lined with thick, vicious looking brambles, which were in turn topped with gorgeous roses. These were the same plants that Ozzie and Smitty had seen around the castle exterior.

"They're lovely," Taryn ventured. "Your roses, I mean."

"Thank you. They are precious to me."

Taryn didn't know what to say to that, so she just made a noise of acknowledgement.

"Your companions, who are they to you?" the Beast then said to her.

Taryn swallowed hard. She knew her answer might determine Ozzie and Smitty's fate, or hers for that matter. Taking a deep breath, her heart pounding in her chest, Taryn looked straight at the Beast and spoke simply.

"They are precious to me."

It was now the Beast's turn to make a noise of acknowledgement, and Taryn's heart skipped a beat. She didn't know what that meant and considered asking. Would that betray weakness in her, though? She had already told him what Ozzie and Smitty meant to her. Would it be detrimental somehow to make demands of the Beast? Probably. She had gotten into trouble too many times before by being impulsive, so she decided to keep her mouth shut...for now.

Taryn and the Beast sat in the courtyard in silence for the rest of their time together. Taryn was on edge the entire time, waiting for the Beast to move or speak or do anything the entire time. Despite her anxiety, nothing happened. He simply sat by her like a sentinel. Finally, he spoke again.

"I bid you goodnight, my lady."

With that, he padded away, back through the doors and into the castle. Taryn waited a few minutes until she felt confident that the Beast was really gone. She then stood and hurried back inside, turning her thoughts onto how to find the courtyard outside of her window. She hadn't been searching for more than a minute before she saw a set of stained glass doors standing open. Beyond, pacing anxiously, were Ozzie and Smitty. Taryn practically ran to them and, just for good measure, hugged both of them in relief.

Ozzie held her for a moment longer and asked, "You okay?"

"Yeah," Taryn replied, "I'm okay. I don't think he wants to hurt me."

"That doesn't mean he won't," Smitty said darkly. "What did he say?"

Taryn then told them about her pseudo-date with the Beast, which didn't take much time at all and led to a discussion about their current state of affairs.

First of all, it seemed that Ozzie and Smitty were now Taryn's personal servants, which she hated. It was awkward and wrong, but she was afraid to go against the Beast's wishes. She told Ozzie and Smitty that, if she could swing it, she would try to keep them with her most of the day. It was impossible to tell what the Beast would allow, though. As for escape, well, that was going to be even more difficult. They'd have to do it during the day, as Ozzie and Smitty had told her how the Beast only left his castle at night. Why? They didn't know, but they were grateful anyway. They also revisited what Puss had said about people the Beast didn't permit to leave not being able to. Both Taryn and Ozzie were adamantly against this idea, insisting there had to be a way around that little detail.

"If we manipulated the Creation Stones to spit out basic elements and dehydrate Vurnal to death, we can escape from a castle and a forest!" Taryn hissed.

That being said, this courtyard or another one like it was probably their best bet.

"What about the servants?" Smitty suggested. "Do you think we could get any of them to help us? We tried talking to them tonight, but none of them really seemed with it, if you know what I mean. They're kind of dazed or something."

Ozzie shook his head and said, "They're probably bewitched by whatever changed them. They may or may not be dangerous, but I don't think they'll be any help either."

"I still don't understand why the Beast needs to kidnap and enslave people. In the fairytale, there was some kind of invisible power. I don't know if it was invisible people or what, but something took care of the castle automatically. I think that power is here too, but he's adding those…creatures to it. Why? Just to be cruel?"

"Who knows," Ozzie said. "Come on. Let's take a walk."

Both Taryn and Smitty knew "let's take a walk" was really code for "let's look for an exit". Ozzie was still anxious about them being there and he wanted to be busy. They then began to walk around the courtyard, strolling slowly, pretending to unwind as they walked, looking at everything and nothing in particular. In reality, Taryn was trying to figure out the best way to circumvent the curse, Smitty was thinking about how much time the Beast might really allow them to spend with Taryn, and Ozzie was groaning to himself about how boring and useless this garden really was and what he could do if he just had a good grappling hook. Ozzie's wishes doubled when, after walking all the way around the perimeter of the courtyard, they had only discovered a very tall stone wall. Despite the castle's crumbling exterior, it could not be climbed without risk of falling to one's death.

Maybe, Ozzie thought, he could find things in the castle that would help. It wasn't as quick a fix as he would like, but it was something. Having finally formulated a framework for a plan, he could relax a little. He then suggested they go back inside.

Smitty, Ozzie, and Taryn were barely through the stained glass doors when one of the servant-creatures appeared and stopped them. The three immediately assumed defensive positions before they even realized what they were doing and waited.

"The master commands that the two young men leave the lady to her rest," the creature said.

"I was hoping that they could stay in my room," Taryn replied immediately. Then, realizing how bad this might sound, she added quickly, "I'm still frightened of being in a new place and I feel better with them nearby. I just don't know what I'll do without them."

Taryn's insides were twisting around anxiously, but she couldn't be sure if it was because she hated coming off like such a scared, needy damsel or because in that moment she really was.

Without skipping a beat, the creature replied, "The master says that you will see them tomorrow."

Taryn felt better at that assurance, but still didn't trust the Beast or his servants.

"When?" she asked immediately.

"He is aware of your wish to keep these two close. They are yours after completing their tasks."

Taryn had to take a breath to calm herself. Her fuse was running short, and she was in danger of snapping and saying something stupid. She knew the castle could take care of itself, so why did Ozzie and Smitty have to be taken away from her? Why did they have to be out of her sight where she couldn't know they were okay? Her fear for her friends was overtaking her good sense, and it was Ozzie's offhand comment in the end that brought her back down.

"They are standing right here."

Taryn smiled at Ozzie and finally said, "Very well. Please tell the master thank you on behalf of all of us."

The creature nodded and then waited. Ozzie and Smitty bid Taryn goodnight before leaving and then followed the creature through a number of corridors back down towards the kitchen. From the kitchen—a large open room with a huge fireplace and brick oven and countless long preparation tables—they headed down another flight stairs. These stairs were in the same terrible shape as the outside of the castle and clearly only used by the servants. Ozzie and Smitty were led down into something like a large dormitory where a number of the inhuman servants were already settling down for the night. Every single one of them looked as depressed and submissive as abused dogs. It was clear they were prisoners here.

"You sure there's no chance of getting them to revolt?" Smitty whispered to Ozzie.

"Not likely, Spartacus," Ozzie replied. "They'd have no hope even if they did rebel. They're still under the curse. This way they at least have something to do. We don't know what would happen if we killed the Beast and there's no way we could contend with him anyway."

Smitty nodded, seeing the logic of his friend's argument. The two then found some unclaimed pallets on the floor and lay down to sleep.

Taryn was pacing her room. It was mid-morning, and she had been up for several hours now. Anxiety and worry hadn't allowed her a good night's rest, and she had barely touched the breakfast that was waiting for her when she woke up. Needless to say, she was not in a good mood now as she was frantically wondering where Ozzie and Smitty were. She had walked around for a bit trying to find them or anyone else so that she could find out what was going on. Unfortunately, there was no one to be found. Finally, a knock resounded at her door, and she turned to see Ozzie's tired face poking through the gap between the doors.

"There you are!" she exclaimed.

Both boys looked exhausted and were carrying trays replete with a full afternoon tea service, presumably for Taryn. After setting the trays down, Ozzie and Smitty collapsed wherever they could.

Closing the door behind them, Taryn asked, "Where have you two been?"

"We were up before dawn," Ozzie explained.

"We did get a good breakfast," Smitty interjected.

"*Before dawn!*" Ozzie repeated. "So that we could do laundry and fix breakfast and clean."

"We're free till this afternoon. We have to keep you fed and clean up in the meantime. That's for you, by the way."

Taryn looked at the tray, immediately decided that she wasn't going to be able to eat everything there, and offered to share with her friends. They accepted the offer gratefully. It actually ended up that she and Smitty ate, while Ozzie, who had crashed on the bed, was fast asleep and snoring away. Smitty later fell asleep in a chair and Taryn on the couch. Ozzie ate the leftovers later after he woke up and then fell back asleep. A knock on the door awoke them later to inform the two boys of their afternoon duties. Both went away muttering under their breath, and Taryn went exploring again a little while later.

It wasn't till that night at dinner, after Smitty and Ozzie had been able to catch up on a little more sleep, that they saw the Beast again. Once again, he was reclining on the rug in front of the hearth, watching the two boys with malevolent eyes. He greeted Taryn, however, with gentility.

"Good evening, my lady," he said with a little bow.

"Good evening, my lord," she replied stiffly with an awkward little curtsey.

"How did you enjoy your first day here?"

Taryn thought carefully for a split second before replying and said courteously, "It was very nice. Thank you for allowing my friends to spend part of the day with me."

Now it was the Beast who seemed to stiffen as he replied, "Anything to please you, my lady."

Taryn somehow doubted the complete sincerity of this statement, but said nothing. Dinner was served, and the girl thanked her friends profusely, still feeling very bad that they were forced into this position of serving her. Besides that, dinner was silent and awkward for Taryn, followed by yet another silent and awkward walk with the Beast to his courtyard of roses. The only difference tonight was that there was less talking.

"I wonder if it'd be possible to get up to the top of the wall and climb down," Taryn whispered to Ozzie and Smitty later in her room.

"Oz is already on that," Smitty replied.

Ozzie had shared his idea with Smitty earlier that day when they were left alone for a few minutes.

"Oh good," Taryn replied. "Tell me what you're thinking."

Ozzie then shared his idea from the night before about building a grappling hook. So far, he was thinking he could use a candelabra as the hook, and he was sure he could find rope somewhere. Taryn's expression had turned dubious.

"While I appreciate your MacGyver spirit, Oz, I'm just not sure that's going to work."

"Why not? What did you have in mind?" he asked.

"Sheets, like you see in movies."

Smitty and Ozzie couldn't help but nod at the plausibility of the idea.

"We would still need to get up there first," Smitty said. "Let's all keep our eyes open and see what we can find."

The three agreed on the plan and then spent the rest of the night happily enjoying one another's company. One of the servant creatures came by sometime later to fetch the two boys to bed, and Taryn gave both Ozzie and Smitty hugs before they left.

The next day, the three met up after Smitty and Ozzie were done with chores. They rested and shared tea again and then headed out to examine the walls once more. No matter where they went, the walls were impossible to climb. Nevertheless, they looked for ways onto the top of them. The only options appeared to be either climbing to the top of a turret and then climbing down from there, or Ozzie's grappling hook idea.

The turret idea had a few issues. It wasn't flat-topped like some they had seen, but conical and closed off at the top. Then there was the extreme height to contend with. Ozzie turned a bit green at the mention of this, and Taryn took his hand comfortingly.

She knew about Ozzie's fear of heights and how hard this was going to be for him.

Then again, he would still have to deal with the height of the walls even if he was able to build a grappling hook. Taryn had come around to the idea a little more, especially when Ozzie mentioned that he was eyeing some of the less decadent candelabras in the castle for his invention. Even if he built one, though, they would have to get it attached *securely* to the top of the wall before they could do anything with it...and probably pray that it was reliable.

It was agreed that Taryn would be responsible for reconnaissance since she would be far less suspicious walking around by herself than all three of them. Ozzie and Smitty would keep their heads down and do their chores, but they too would keep their eyes open.

The days that followed passed in pretty much the same pattern each day. Ozzie and Smitty were forced to get up before the sun to do various chores before they brought Taryn her tea around mid-morning. The three then spent their time together catching up on sleep and talking about their escape plans. It was only going marginally well.

Thanks to whatever strange magic existed in the castle, Taryn was usually able to find any room she wanted easily and quickly. She had already found her way up to all the turrets, but, like the rest of the castle, there was no easy means of getting out of the towers. The windows there were just wide enough for her to get through, but it was unlikely someone Smitty's size could. Taryn had noticed that the roof was wood, however. That gave her an idea, albeit a dangerous one. Besides that, she had explored the various other bedrooms and found all the beds dressed and ready to accept guests. If she needed to, she now knew where to find plenty of sheets. She had not been successful in her attempts to find candelabras suitable for Ozzie's grappling hook, as all the little ones she saw were made gold or silver. There were some tall but very heavy floor candelabras in the hallways, however, made of wrought iron that Taryn considered.

Ozzie and Smitty listened to her reports with interest, but couldn't contribute much. They were watched nearly all the time, and the few minutes their overseers, as they called them, left them alone weren't enough to do anything. There was always someone watching, even at night. The only exception was when they were with Taryn, and they couldn't help but wonder if there was someone observing them even then. The Beast had to have ordered the surveillance. He had to know they would try to escape. Ozzie was more frustrated than Taryn had ever seen him, and Smitty soon started to offer less and less in the way of escape ideas. Ozzie and Taryn were very concerned that he was giving up.

Taryn's dinners and evening strolls with the Beast continued, though not much changed. He still said nothing to Taryn each night as they walked and sat together, and Taryn said almost nothing to him. She tried to think of clever things to say, but nothing ever came to her. What did one say to a captor that doesn't do anything except keep you captive? The only things Taryn ever asked were questions like, "Can I touch your fur?"—it was surprisingly soft—or "What do you do all day?"—sleep. These were questions a child would ask out of curiosity, and that was all Taryn had besides her fear. She had wondered early on if she might eventually develop some kind of friendship with the Beast. It was not because she thought she was going to become some kind of Stockholm syndrome victim, but because that was what happened in the story. That didn't happen. The only feeling that changed for her was her fear. Taryn became accustomed to the Beast's presence and, while he still made her nervous, he didn't frighten her the way he had before.

The Beast, on the other hand, had initially seemed confused and even wary of her odd questions. Taryn would then candidly explain her reasoning for making such a strange request—it was usually a shrug and, "I've never met anyone like you; I'm curious"—and he would usually relent and grant it. After a while, he seemed more open to her inquiries and stopped questioning her, but that didn't fool Taryn. She wasn't so stupid as to let her guard down around the huge creature just because he was starting to trust her.

The only thing that really seemed to be in Ozzie, Taryn, and Smitty's favor was the castle's magic, which provided Taryn with anything she wanted. She mentioned that she remembered something in the fairytale about Beauty being provided with whatever she wanted too, but she couldn't remember if there was a way they could use it to their advantage. They did give it a try, but to no avail. Taryn said to the air on numerous occasions how nice it would be to have a grappling hook, a rope, a ladder, and even a sledgehammer. Nothing worked, and the three guessed the castle could sense the intention behind each request. On the other hand, the castle did provide Taryn with all the entertainment she could ever need. Anytime she found herself or Ozzie or Smitty bored, the perfect fix would appear as soon as they weren't looking. She eventually willed a few books, several games, and materials for drawing, amongst other things within reason, into being. This kept the three from completely dying of boredom, though they most enjoyed just sitting and talking of the time. It was in the company of each other that they found the most comfort and enjoyment.

# Chapter 8

Taryn was frustrated and worried. It had been a few weeks since coming to Castle Rose, and Ozzie and Smitty were running late…again. It had only happened a few times, but that was too much for Taryn. Something was wrong and it scared her, and being scared made her angry. Last time they had been late, Ozzie had apologized, but Smitty hadn't seemed concerned in the least. Their reasoning was some flimsy excuse about having gotten caught up in their chores.

"Caught up in your chores?" Taryn had snapped. "Since when do you care about the quality of your furniture polishing?"

They had also left to do their afternoon tasks yesterday without having to be summoned.

"It's habit by now, Taryn," Smitty had said when Taryn complained about them leaving early. "It's just easier to get them over with."

"They're not over with until after dinner, which comes at the same time every day," Taryn had said, "so there's no point in going until you're called."

"We love you too, Ryn," Ozzie had said with an easy smile. "I guess I should go with him. We'll see you tonight."

Taryn had growled at them, but said nothing more. Now she was fuming and planning all kinds of things to say to them. They hadn't discussed escape plans in a few days either. She'd bring that up, too. Ozzie and Smitty showed up not long after with her usual tray of tea, and Taryn laid into them.

"Nice of you to show up," she snarled. "What happened? Did you stay behind to admire your handiwork on the silverware?"

"Geez, Taryn," Smitty replied in annoyance. "What's your problem? Are you PMS-ing or what?"

Dana Fraedrich

"Hey, man, cool it with the attitude," Ozzie interjected.

He had learned by now that stressful situations made Smitty snarky, but that was over the line for him. That, and he knew that Taryn wasn't just angry for the sake of being angry. There was a reason for her vehemence.

"What's wrong?" he said, turning to Taryn. "Why are you so upset?"

"Because you two think it's more fun to dust and mop than come see me, the only other friend you have in this whole ridiculous country!"

"Someone thinks she's the center of the universe," Smitty muttered.

"Just what is wrong with you?" Taryn demanded. "Are you suddenly excited about being a slave the rest of your life? Excuse me if I cherish what little time we have together. Ozzie, I need to know why you're both so..."

Her voice trailed off when she noticed something very, very wrong with Ozzie's grey eyes. She swept over to him and stopped not an inch from his face, studying his eyes intensely.

"Ah, Ryn, this is kind of awkward," Ozzie joked. "I love you and everything, but don't you think Tynx will be a little jealous?"

"Stop talking," she said firmly.

Ozzie was about to make another joke, but stopped when he saw Taryn go pale. She moved from his eyes to his teeth and then to his ears.

"Okay, this is making *me* uncomfortable," Smitty said from his chair. "Should I leave you two alone?"

"Don't you dare," Taryn said, moving over to Smitty quickly and examining him in the same way.

"Oh, well, *hey*," Smitty teased. "This I can handle."

"What did I say about talking?" Taryn said.

"Yes, ma'am."

"You're reaching new heights of weird," Ozzie told her after a moment. "You mind telling us just what you're doing?"

"Go look in the mirror," she told them suddenly. "I mean, really *look*."

Both Ozzie and Smitty saw just how serious she was and obeyed. They crowded in front of Taryn's little vanity and examined their reflections. At first they didn't notice anything, but then they caught sight of their teeth. It took both of them a few moments of hard staring to really believe it, but it couldn't be denied: their teeth were definitely pointier, unnaturally so. From there they began to examine the rest of themselves frantically. Ozzie found that his stormy eyes now carried a very distinct yellow hue, while Smitty's pupils were longer now and had begun to stretch along the center of his eye. Likewise, both of their ears were longer than they had been.

"I'm not imagining it, am I?" Taryn said from behind them.

Ozzie and Smitty turned towards her, and they all exchanged frightened looks. Then, all at once, they flew into action.

"Taryn, we have to get out of here *today*," Ozzie hissed.

He had to be quiet, lest they be overheard.

"I know," Taryn replied, matching Ozzie's volume level. "How do you want to do it? We don't have your hook."

"We'll have to make do with what we do have and we'll need a distraction. We need to gather as many sheets as possible. You and Smitty go get them and meet back here in ten minutes."

Ozzie then headed over to the bed and began tearing the bedclothes off of it. Smitty said nothing and rushed out to do as Ozzie had said, followed closely by Taryn. Ozzie then began to furiously tie together the ends of the sheets that were hurriedly delivered to the room. Within the ten minutes, they had a sizeable pile, but no way to know whether or not the sheet-chain was long enough or secure. Taryn and Smitty helped tie the rest of the sheets together while Ozzie explained the rest of his plan.

"I'll need help getting these up to the tower, but, as soon as we're up there, you two head down to the wall below."

"What are you going to do?" Taryn demanded.

"I'm going to create our distraction," Ozzie answered simply.

"We are *not* leaving without you!" she snarled, grabbing his arm fiercely.

"We don't have time to argue!" Ozzie snapped back. "That's not what I'm thinking anyway."

"That's hinging a lot on a slapped-together plan," Smitty said darkly.

"Just finish with the sheets," Ozzie said.

They did so in almost no time and made their way as carefully and quickly as they could up to the nearest turret. Ozzie, Taryn, and Smitty prayed they wouldn't be seen. There was no way they could explain away the connected bundles of sheets they each carried. Once up the tower steps, Ozzie ran back down and grabbed two of the tall, wrought iron floor candelabras from the lower hallways. He didn't notice the protests from his arms and shoulders as he hurried back up the steps, spurred on by adrenaline and fear, but he was careful to make sure their flames didn't go out. Even if the torches in the tower were lit during the day—they weren't because the thin windows there let light in from three hundred and sixty degrees—he didn't think a torch would be tall enough for what he was planning. As soon as he was back, he began tying the end of the sheet-chain to one of the candelabras and issuing orders again.

"I've got this. You two, head down." Taryn hesitated, and Ozzie nearly yelled at her, "Now!"

"Come on, Taryn," Smitty urged.

Taryn ignored him and knelt down next to Ozzie.

"I just want to say if you don't show up down there and escape with us, I will kick the ever-loving snot out of you, Ozzie Thomason!" she growled.

"Don't worry, Ryn," Ozzie said, giving her a kiss on the forehead and a quick smile. "I'll be there."

She didn't take her eyes off of him and only moved when Smitty took her hand and pulled her to her feet. Then they ran as fast as they could down the stairs, down the hall, and down to the door for the courtyard. It took far longer to find than usual, and Taryn couldn't help but wonder if the castle was working against them.

As soon as Ozzie had everything in position, he made sure all the candles on the candelabra he had left free from the sheet-chain were lit and carefully lifted it towards the ceiling. It wasn't tall enough. The candles were still more than a foot away from the wooden roof of the tower. Ozzie swore. He hadn't wanted to have to go with plan B, as it was more difficult and dangerous. It had to be done, however, so he lowered the candelabra and placed it next to the nearest window. He then began to carefully climb up into the thin slot of a window, doing his best to anchor himself in place. It was tricky because the stone walls were thick, which made it difficult to find handholds, and he was already just barely fitting himself into place. Chances were, he would fall forward and possibly injure himself. He managed to press his hand against the top of the window and his feet against the sill, leaving his other hand free to grab and lift the candelabra.

It was heavy, and Ozzie was already sweating and getting tired. His mind began to panic, thinking that whatever power had begun to transform him was also draining him now, too. No! He wouldn't become a mindless, misshapen drone! He couldn't! He had too much to lose! Forcing the weakness to the back of his mind, Ozzie pressed his hand more firmly against the stone and lifted the candelabra with the other, grabbing it as low on the stem as possible. He forced his arm as high as it would go, forced it to remain steady, forced himself to ignore the burning of his muscles as they strained. The candles touched the roof, which began to smoke as the flames licked at the wood, but that was all. Sweat broke out on Ozzie's forehead as he fought to keep the candelabra upright. His arm shook. He willed himself to remain steady, but his strength gave out, and his arm drooped and then dropped. Ozzie didn't let go of the candelabra, however, and down he sailed, pulled after it out of the window and onto the unforgiving stone floor. Ozzie swore again as pain shot through his hands, wrists, elbows, and knees. The candles had gone out, and most of them were broken now. Ozzie looked to the other candelabra, immediately thinking that he would have to use it instead. Then he saw them: the flames, small and weak, but growing slowly. The roof had lit! Soon it would spread, and the servant-creatures would have no choice but to focus all of their attention on putting out the fire, lest it spread all over the castle.

Ozzie jumped to his feet, suddenly elated that phase one of his plan was complete. He found new energy for phase two, which was much easier, but had to be completed *very* quickly.

Taryn and Smitty squatted back to back behind a bush, keeping their eyes peeled for trouble. There was almost nowhere to hide. The rose brambles grew just as thickly along this stretch of wall as everywhere else, but not thickly enough to hide them. Besides the brambles, there was just grass and the occasional bit of overgrown garden plant, left to whatever fate the elements allowed it when the outside of the castle was abandoned. Whether the Beast's private garden was tended to by the servants or the castle's magic was unknown, but, whatever it was, that care didn't extend to this courtyard. Smitty and Taryn knew better than to think their scrubby, little bush would hide them if anyone came out to search for them in earnest, but Ozzie was taking care of that…hopefully. They had arrived just in time to see Ozzie standing in the window and then fall out of it back inside the tower.

"That's not that bad," Smitty said immediately, though unconvincingly. "He might have actually jumped down."

Taryn said nothing, and they waited to see what would happen next. They each let out an anxious breath when they saw the end of one candelabra poke through the window and float down the side of the turret, followed by a chain of sheets. Once the candelabra was out, it made its way down to the wall quickly, slowing only once it was close enough to maneuver into place. Taryn and Smitty watched as Ozzie carefully swung it so that it sat evenly between two teeth of the battlements. The rest of the sheet-chain followed quickly until the end was reached, and they saw Ozzie's arm fling it as hard as he could towards Taryn and Smitty's side of the wall.

"Great job, Oz," Taryn muttered. "Now get down here!"

They saw nothing of Ozzie after his arm had disappeared into the tower again, but they did see the smoke. It had begun to lazily curl out of the window while the candelabra was making its journey down the castle wall. Now it was streaming out steadily, and flames could be seen licking around the edge of the roof. There was no way to know if any of it had begun to collapse, which was Taryn's biggest fear at the moment.

"Come on!" Smitty said after checking that the coast was clear.

He ran towards the sheet-chain and found the end just beyond his reach. He jumped and grabbed the end, pulling the chain down and scratching himself on a few thorns as he did so. There was more slack gathered on the wall, and Smitty pulled until the chain was taught. This caused several of the sheets to catch on the thorns and snag, but most of the thorns broke off their vines before much damage could be done. Still, Smitty and Taryn exchanged a nervous look, hoping none of the tears were worse than they appeared. All that done, the chain now came to the ground and then some, which was lucky. Their escape method was in place, and Taryn looked desperately across the courtyard for Ozzie to appear.

Ozzie ran faster than he ever had in his life. He had never been affected by the castle's magic the same way that Taryn had, so finding the doors out to the courtyard was easy because they stayed put. The servant-creatures were on the move, however. He could hear them calling to each other. Some of the cries came from the burning turret, while others came from below or across the castle. One suddenly resounded nearby, too near, and Ozzie threw himself into the nearest room. He peeked out through a crack in the door and watched as one of the creatures ran by. He waited a moment and then slipped back out. Continuing his run, he turned a corner and nearly ran into another creature. It grabbed at him with its long, feathery fingers, and he dodged, but just barely. The creature squawked an alarm, and Ozzie knew it was calling more of its comrades to it. He didn't think as he grabbed for whatever he could and laid his hand on yet another floor candelabra. He swung it wildly and hit the creature squarely in the side. It stumbled, and he ran. He didn't know if he had injured it, but he didn't dwell on that thought long. He would get out of here or die trying.

Taryn let out a cry of joy when she saw Ozzie burst through the doors and out into the courtyard. She hopped up and down anxiously as he made his way across the lawn to them.

"Go! Go!" Ozzie yelled to them as soon as he saw them.

Taryn, having seen Ozzie safe and sound, did as she was told and began to climb up the rope. She had never been able to complete the rope climb challenge in gym class, but that didn't seem to make as much of a difference now as she thought it would. She used the wall for support, walking up it as she pulled herself up, wrapping the sheets around her arms for support. It was slow going, and Smitty and Ozzie remained below, ready to catch her if necessary. She eventually made it up and climbed over the top of the wall, all too aware of the animalistic cries from the turret above her. Ozzie practically pushed Smitty up the wall next. Being athletic, Smitty made it up faster. Then there was just Ozzie.

When he tried to climb, his body refused to cooperate. His arms were like jelly by this point, and pain shot through his hands.

He might have broken something when he fell from the tower window. He had certainly done something bad. He tried to force himself up, but ended up falling from only a few feet up.

"Ozzie! Ozzie! What's wrong?" Taryn called down frantically.

"I just...I..." Ozzie stammered.

He didn't know what to do. He couldn't make it up, but Taryn and Smitty couldn't wait for him forever. They couldn't wait an hour for him. It'd be too late for them to get away by then. He...he wasn't going to make it, but how could he make Taryn leave him behind?

"I..." he began again and steadied his voice. "Taryn, I'm not going to be able to go with you." Taryn opened her mouth to protest, but he cut her off firmly. "No! You two need to pull the sheets up and climb down the other side. Smitty, make it so."

Smitty stared in disbelief down at his former roommate. He wasn't saying...he couldn't be. No, he couldn't give up. They couldn't survive here without Ozzie. He had to make it! He snapped out of his shocked stupor and realized that Taryn and Ozzie were arguing.

"You stupid git!" Taryn shrieked, tears beginning to stream down her face. "You're out of your mind if you think I'm leaving you here!"

"We don't have time for this, Taryn! Just go!" Ozzie yelled back furiously. "Think of your family! They've already lost one child; they don't need to lose another!"

"Oh, you're one to talk! You'd leave your mum all alone, just like that?!"

"Shut up!" Smitty cried. "Ozzie, tie the sheet around yourself like a swing. We're going to lift you up."

"You don't have time—" Ozzie insisted again.

"Do it now, or I will set Taryn loose on you!"

Ozzie scowled at him, but knew he wasn't bluffing. He then hastily began to tie himself into the sheet-chain, looping it underneath himself for a seat. As soon as he had done so, Smitty told him to hold on and use his feet to climb. Then began the painstaking task of lifting Ozzie up the side of the wall. Taryn and Smitty both pulled, hand-over-hand, bit by bit, trying to avoid the thorns as much as possible, as Ozzie held on and walked up the wall inch by inch. Taryn ventured a glance upward as they pulled and saw the smoke had lessened. Her heart quickened. The servants were getting ahead of the blaze. It wouldn't be long before they were free to pursue the escapees.

*Just a little more*, she told herself. *Just a little further and the hard part will be over.*

She actually had to restrain herself from throwing herself at Ozzie in relief when she and Smitty finally pulled him over the edge of the wall. Instead, she settled for anxiety-fueled rage.

"Don't you *ever* do that to me again! You hear me! Don't you ever give up and leave me!"

"Stay in your sling," Smitty cut in. "We're lowering you down now."

They quickly adjusted the position of the candelabra, bracing it against a set of the outside battlement teeth, and got into position to lower Ozzie down.

"Hey, Ryn," Ozzie said, looking at her as he adjusted himself against the wall.

"What?" she snapped.

"You're the best." And he winked at her just before starting down.

"I hate it when I'm angry and you're nice to me!" she called back. "And I'm sorry for calling you names."

Getting down was much faster, as Ozzie was able to repel off the wall while Smitty and Taryn kept a hold on the chain, letting it run through their hands at a nice, safe pace. It burned their skin, but they didn't care.

"I know," Ozzie called up to her. "I'm sorry for trying to guilt you away."

"I understand."

"I'm not sorry for anything I did and I'd do it again!" Smitty broke in.

"You're a good man, Smitty," Taryn said.

Ozzie made it to the ground without incident, and Taryn followed quickly, trailed by Smitty. This time, they didn't wait and take turns. Taryn was making it down so fast, it was probably safe for Smitty to start down, too. He climbed over the edge and began to rappel down. There was a disturbing ripping noise coming from the sheets now, and Smitty climbed more quickly. If he could just make it down to a safe distance, they would be fine.

Taryn heard the noise too and tried to speed up, but she was already going as fast as she could. Smitty was gaining quickly, though, so that was good. As soon as her feet touched the ground, however, there was a new noise: a monstrous roar from somewhere deep in the castle. It was so loud, it sent birds fleeing from the trees all around, and panic set in. Smitty forewent climbing altogether and jumped down the rest of the way to the ground. Thankfully, he was close enough to avoid any serious injury. He was steady on his feet again in a moment, and all three were suddenly running pell-mell across the hilltop. Bramble thorns caught and nipped at their pant legs and skin while rosebuds were smacked and struck violently, sending rose petals flying and snapping stems. It was a small war being waged by the castle, its last defense against the three. As soon as they reached the edge, they stopped and looked down.

"We have to climb this?!" Taryn demanded.

Ozzie looked down, down, down past the rocky outcroppings to the ground so very, very far below. His mind began to imagine what it would be like to fall from such a height. Would it hurt when he hit the ground? He felt himself sway and then the feel of someone grabbing him and holding tight. Eyes. Bright green eyes were suddenly there, blocking his vision.

"Oz, it's fine. You're not going to fall, but you have to keep it together," Taryn said firmly. "We're going to start climbing down, and I want you to *only* look at the spot you're putting your feet. Okay?"

He swallowed hard and nodded. They began the climb down as quickly as possible, Taryn coaching Ozzie through it the whole way. The wall had been one thing. They had been panicked, and Ozzie thought he was going to die. Looking down from a small, steep mountain was entirely another.

"Do you think the Beast might actually be able to come out during the day?" Smitty asked as they climbed.

"Bernard the token woodcutter said he only comes out at night," Ozzie said, looking for anything to fixate on besides the open air just beyond his back.

"Better for us," Taryn said, though she was not convinced.

She was thinking about the conversation she'd had with him where he'd said he slept during the day. That roar they'd heard...he's definitely not sleeping now.

It was mid-afternoon by the time they reached the bottom of the hill, and all three were exhausted and starving. They had brought their packs with them and, as the Beast showed no signs of having emerged yet, chanced pulling out some food. Taryn had nicked what she could from her tea trays—mostly biscuits, but anything with a long shelf life really—and stashed them away. That, along with the other food they already had packed, gave them more than enough for the moment. They walked as they ate, however, wishing to waste no time. Running wasn't an option for any of them just now anyway; they were all too worn out. They took only a moment to orient themselves before setting off again with snacks in hand. Smitty and Taryn had looked out during their climb to locate the closest edge of the forest. Close was a relative term, but it was their only choice. No one bothered to ask what would happen if they didn't make it out by nightfall, or, if they did, what would happen with Smitty and Ozzie's transformations. Could the Beast find them beyond the border of the woods? And what about the curse? No one had really figured out a way to work around that. It was fruitless to give voice to these fears, as they could only continue to flee.

Ozzie, Taryn, and Smitty strode in one direction determinedly, saving the majority of their strength for running in case it came to that. An hour passed and then another. It was impossible to tell if they were making any real progress. A few times, Smitty and Ozzie had cheerleader-lifted Taryn up to one of the tree branches none of them could reach on their own so that she could climb up and make sure they were still on the right track. Each time was more disheartening than the last. They didn't seem to be making any progress at all! They lifted Smitty up once when he refused to believe what Taryn was telling them.

"There has to be something we can do!" Ozzie said.

"What?" Smitty demanded, back down on the ground now. "We have literally nothing but ourselves and what we're carrying!"

"Can we make the Beast not want to keep us somehow?" Taryn asked.

"Can you make yourself less desirable?" Ozzie asked.

"I don't know how, but I have another idea," Taryn said, a mad gleam in her eye. Then, turning back the way they had come, she began to shout at the top of her lungs, "Hey! Beast! I'll make you a deal! Let them go and you can have me all to yourself! No strings attached, just let them go!"

"Taryn, what are you doing?!" Ozzie demanded, grabbing her arm fiercely.

"Trying to get you two a Get Out Of Jail Free card!" she snapped.

"No way!"

"Ozzie, he is going to *kill* you!" she cried desperately. "We are *trapped*, and he is going to come down here and kill you both, and I *cannot* let that happen! Not when I have the power to stop it!"

"Not at the cost of you!" Ozzie shouted back.

"Guys! Shut up!" Smitty commanded, adding his own voice to the argument. "Look, what if we can get all of us up a tree? I can pull…"

Smitty trailed off as Taryn began shaking her head. "He will work at clawing any tree we climb until we all come crashing down. Please, both of you, let me do this. It's the only way to save all of us."

Ozzie opened his mouth to protest again, but stopped when another roar sounded from the hill. The Beast's roars had continued to resonate periodically from the direction of the castle all afternoon, but they had remained at a constant level…until now. This one was definitely louder and closer. They all looked up to the canopy to look for signs of dusk. It was impossible to tell, but then another roar came racing across the air towards them. The Beast was out of the castle, and he was catching them up quickly.

"Come on!" Smitty said urgently. "Run!"

All three took off again, but not as fast as they willed their bodies to go. They were still fatigued, and walking hard for several hours hadn't really helped. Another roar. It was so much closer now! The Beast would be on them in minutes. *Faster, have to go faster*, ran through all three heads as they pumped their legs desperately. Adrenaline was only getting them so far; it couldn't outrun a curse. Then he was there, the Beast, through the trees beyond, glaring at the group murderously. Ozzie, Smitty, and

Taryn all screamed and veered, Taryn in one direction, Ozzie and Smitty in the other.

Ozzie was the first one to realize they had been separated and started calling for Taryn. His usual fear for her safety was now coupled with the fact that she might strike a deal with the Beast, one that would take away her freedom forever. He knew she would do it. He had been willing to lay down his life earlier that day, and she would do the same. He hoped his calls would alert the Beast to his location, bring him closer and away from Taryn. He couldn't lose her, not again. Taryn called back. She wasn't far away, and Smitty joined in, too. Suddenly, the Beast came bursting out from the trees behind them, overtook them, and turned mid-run to face the two boys. Ozzie and Smitty stopped short and tried to back up. They tripped over each other, however, and went tumbling to the ground.

"I will eat you both alive!" the Beast roared.

"NO!" came Taryn's terrified scream.

Then she was there, leaping into the space between the Beast and her friends, arms outstretched to protect them. The Beast roared in her face and, shockingly, Taryn roared back! It was a desperate, furious war shriek, and Ozzie and Smitty both jumped as it pierced their ears.

"I told you they were precious to me!" Taryn shouted at the Beast with her next breath. "You'll have to kill me to get to them."

"I can remove you easily," the Beast snarled.

"No! I offered you a deal, me for them—"

"I do not suffer insolence from my servants. They will die!"

"And what would that do to your chances of getting me to marry you?"

The Beast opened his mouth to say something, but no words came. He shook his head, looking frustrated somehow, and roared again.

"Look, I'm sorry, but you can't force someone to love you. You tricked me, hoping that I would end up with nothing so that I would just run to you. That's not love. That's manipulation, pure and simple. No woman in her right mind is going to love that kind of treatment, especially not if you keep on the way you are, kidnapping people and transforming them against their will. How long will it continue? What do you think anyone would think of what you're doing? A girl will only go for you if she sees you're the kind of person she wants to be with. Yes, it sucks to be trapped like you are, but you know the curse will only lift if she *chooses* to be with you."

The Beast narrowed his eyes at Taryn and hissed, "Who are you? How do you know all this?"

Oh no. In all of her fear and anger and desperation, Taryn had shown her whole hand. The Beast couldn't talk about the curse, but she knew the details and had spilled them all. Taryn swallowed hard. She couldn't undo what she had done, so she pressed on as best she could.

"Does it matter? I'm right, aren't I?"

The Beast growled in frustration and shook his head again.

"How long?!" he managed to say.

"I don't know," Taryn said as firmly as she could.

If she was lucky, the Beast would think she was something magical and let her be, but she could tell he wasn't yet convinced. If she misspoke, he might lash out and kill Ozzie or Smitty or her.

"You have to be patient," she continued. Unconsciously, she began to stroke the fur on the Beast's neck the same way she would a dog. "I promise, one day you will cross paths with a beautiful girl, and she will see the good heart within you and lift the curse, but only if you let her see it."

She then seemed to realize what she was doing and pulled away awkwardly. She did her best not to rip her hand back, but she was not smooth about it either. The Beast had to have noticed.

The Beast said nothing for several minutes, looking Taryn up and down. He was warring against himself, and Taryn, Ozzie, and Smitty prayed his anger didn't win out. Finally, the Beast spoke.

"I do not know what you are. I do not know if you speak the truth, but you have spoken enough to convince me that you are worth listening to. Very well, I will release you and your friends. I do hope I am not making a mistake."

"Believe me, you're not," Taryn said sincerely.

The Beast nodded and said, "You three are free to make your way through my forest. Your friends will return to normal soon."

Now it was Taryn who nodded and said, "Thank you."

The Beast did not respond and simply walked away, disappearing through the trees. Silently but swiftly, Taryn helped her friends up, and they began walking in the opposite direction the

Beast had gone. No one said anything until they were out of the forest, away from the edge, and had made camp. It was Ozzie who spoke first.

"Little Fire Warrior of the Irish Hills."

"What?" Taryn said absently. Then, "Wait. Why are you calling me that?!"

"Little Fire Warrior of the Irish Hills," Ozzie repeated.

"What does that mean?" Smitty asked curiously.

"That's Taryn's name, her *true* name," Ozzie gloated. "Pretty fitting, don't you think?"

"How…how do you know that?" Smitty asked, confusion replacing curiosity.

"A unicorn told us," Ozzie replied easily, still grinning at Taryn.

"I was just trying to save your crazy tails," Taryn said, waving Ozzie away.

"I'm back to not understanding what's going on," Smitty said.

"Don't worry about it," Taryn said. "Ozzie's just being ridiculous."

Smitty shrugged and accepted that. He was too tired and hungry to pursue the question, as was everyone else.

*Impressive. They had actually escaped from the Beast's castle. As soon as the girl had been taken, she had written them off as done for. The boys should have abandoned her but they had shown incredible fortitude and pursued. And then to actually get away! Long ago, when she had seen how dark the creature's heart became after she turned him, she was certain anyone who crossed his path was as good as dead. Not them. It was incredible and intriguing and disconcerting all at once. How had they convinced that heartless creature to let them go? They could no longer be ignored.*

# Chapter 9

Ozzie, Taryn, and Smitty only broke camp the next day so that they could get to an inn and recuperate properly. They were exhausted from their ordeal and none of them liked the idea of traveling again so soon. Even as far as they were from the border of the forest, however, they couldn't relax. No one slept well and they hated being so exposed. True, the Beast had said he would let them go, but they couldn't help but wonder if he would, if he *could*, change his mind.

Ozzie speculated that they were probably okay because, the way he figured it, the Beast probably thought Taryn was some kind of powerful being not to be messed with and had therefore decided it was best to set them free. He didn't object to hightailing it as soon as possible the next day, however. Taryn had hoped for something of the same ilk, but couldn't quite believe it might have actually happened. Then again, the Beast had been cursed by magic, so those odds were in their favor. Smitty refused to guess about the Beast's reasoning and instead focused on getting away from the forest as quickly as possible.

They stayed at the first inn they found for several days. Fortunately, it was a pleasant little place located just before where the forest road and another created a fork. All three were suddenly quite content with sharing close quarters. There were apologies for poor behavior and angry words and a lot of relieved hugging. It was all happily chalked up to the castle, the curse, and the situation. In addition, Ozzie, Taryn, and Smitty were quieter than was their custom. They were grateful, *really* grateful, just to be alive, and it took a few days for the sobering effect of that knowledge to fade. The majority of their time there was spent either relaxing sedately in their room or taking leisurely strolls around the inn. They never strayed far, however, especially when one of their number remained up in the room, though no one actually mentioned this little fact out loud.

Ozzie's injuries were of the most concern, but they didn't get worse, which was good. Taryn and Ozzie felt Tynx's absence on this trip most poignantly as they tended to their wounds. The half-elf had been very good with herbalism and healing and had saved them more than once with those skills. Without him, they realized just how ill-equipped they were to deal with even the smallest of hurts. Still, they did their best and, thankfully, the worst Ozzie had to contend with was some extreme soreness, stiffness, and bruising. If something was broken in his hand, it wasn't bad enough to be certain. Similarly, the other injuries—cuts and rope burns mostly— seemed to be healing well without any signs of infection thanks to some meticulous cleaning and monitoring.

The signposts along the road on the way to the inn had read that America was still over fifty miles west of them, which meant a few solid days of walking. Ozzie, Taryn and Smitty decided that it would be wise to buy a good map, which they were able to do in the next town. "Good" might have been an overstatement. They discovered very quickly that a sturdy map was pricey, and they weren't sure if they could really afford one of those. Therefore, Ozzie, Taryn, and Smitty were forced to buy one—drawn by hand, of course—on thick paper, which, to their memory, looked somewhat different to the one they had seen in Erik's house.

"Why would we buy a map that's wrong?" Smitty objected when they realized this.

"It's not completely wrong," Ozzie argued. "It's just a little off, and a map that's a little off is better than no map at all."

No one could really dispute that point, but there was still some objection to the purchase. The argument was quickly shut down by the point that they couldn't be completely sure of the accuracy of anything they bought. After all, the Google Maps hadn't really made it to Terturelia yet. In the end, they bought the paper map, flaws and all.

The road through France continued fairly easily, despite a light rain shower or two. They continued to stay at inns, which made the traveling much easier, and Ozzie and Smitty returned to normal within a week. It was an odd feeling for the three when they crossed the border into America because it was their country they were entering, yet it absolutely wasn't. Mississippi was the first region within America, according to the map, and it was at this time that Ozzie made an observation.

"Do you think Mississippi belonged to France at one point? The ones here, I mean."

"What?" Taryn and Smitty asked at once.

"Think about it. Mississippi here is right next to France. Mississippi back home used to belong to our France. Maybe a Louisiana Purchase happened here, too."

"I suppose," Taryn replied. "But what's your point?"

"I don't know, just thinking. Maybe, if that's the case, it means more here will be familiar to us than we expect."

Taryn said nothing, but smiled. She liked that kind of thinking.

Now that they had left France and all the scary things there behind, the next order of business was to buy some horses. Smitty was especially enthused about this idea, as it meant they'd be traveling at a faster pace. He and Ozzie started a lively conversation with that evening's innkeeper, a sweet but tough woman by the name of Anna, on the subject, while Taryn was content to be quiet and gaze out the window.

The next morning, Smitty happily volunteered to do the talking when horse shopping, saying that these were "his kind of people". Smitty was a proud Virginian back home and felt a certain kinship with the people of the "southern" state of Mississippi...even if it wasn't the same state or even in the southern part of the country. Ozzie and Taryn thought he played up his accent a little when they arrived at the livery stables, but they just smiled and said nothing. The owner of the stables was a congenial sort, so they couldn't tell if Smitty's charm actually did anything, but at least they didn't offend anyone. Smitty explained that they were traveling to England and would need some tough, reliable horses. When the stable owner asked about riding experience, Smitty just laughed and said that they didn't have as much as he would have liked. After that, the owner left with a stableman to go gather the animals. Smitty, feeling very pleased with himself, turned back to his companions only to see Taryn hanging back and looking uncomfortable.

"Hey, what's wrong?" Smitty asked with concern.

"I…I don't like riding," she said quietly.

"Really?" Smitty asked.

"The closest I've been to a horse was the pony rides when I was four."

Suddenly, Ozzie began to laugh as he said, "Oh, yeah! Half way through you got so scared that the pony was going to bolt, you started crying and wanted to get off." Taryn shot him a withering glare, and he said more soberly now, "Yeah, I remember that. Traumatic."

"Don't worry, Taryn," Smitty said encouragingly. "They're like big dogs. I'll teach you."

With that, the two boys told Taryn all they knew about riding, which was relatively impressive considering that both of them had only had smatterings of experience. The horses were brought in a few minutes later and secured to cleats on the walls. Ozzie, Smitty, and Taryn were then allowed to inspect them.

"Best horses in the whole country," the stable owner boasted. "Resilient, brave, and they'll get you where you need to go."

The horses seemed to be in good shape—not that any of the three could really tell—and stood calmly as their would-be owners looked them over and petted them. Taryn gravitated towards the smallest of the three, a little palomino mare called Honey. She was thankful that the horse didn't start or jump or whatever it was that bad horses did, but that didn't mean she wouldn't later.

Ozzie, Smitty, and Taryn agreed to buy the animals and left with their purses much lighter after that, plus the purchase of tack and brushes and all the other equine accoutrement. It was a little overwhelming how much was required, and they couldn't be sure if they hadn't overbought, but they had to take the stable owner at his word. Smitty ended up with a chestnut named Ember, and Ozzie's was a handsome bay called Shadow. Taryn was tenser than ever as they got back on the road atop the horses, but Smitty stayed by her side and coached her, and they didn't exceed a trot that day. Thankfully, the horses seemed understanding towards their inexperienced masters and didn't do anything "too scary", as Taryn put it.

The road took Ozzie, Taryn, and Smitty a little further west before eventually bending north. The weather stayed fairly good, but it was warm. Any time spent riding out in the open became uncomfortable under the persistent sun. Mosquitoes became more prevalent, which was maddening, and all three got sunburned, Taryn worst of all. Surprisingly, Smitty was optimistic despite these circumstances.

"It could be worse," he said. "It could be the height of summer, and then we'd really be suffering."

Taryn, whose sunburned scalp had begun to flake like a severe case of dandruff, was less than amenable to Smitty's logic. She said nothing, however, knowing the negativity wouldn't help anything. Something that bothered the three more than anything else, however, was something they hadn't considered at all. The first time Ozzie, Taryn, and Smitty rode past a field full of slaves, they actually didn't believe what they were seeing. It was a jarring sight, to be sure, and it incited a heated debate between Ozzie and Taryn, which Smitty was content to sit out.

"Oz, we have to do something," Taryn insisted. "This is *wrong*!"

"We can't. Slavery is legal here, and you're not about to change that," Ozzie replied. "We'll only be putting ourselves in danger if we try to get in the middle of it. Besides, we both know it'll be outlawed eventually."

"Do you really think it's okay to just stand by and do nothing?"

"It's not safe, Taryn," Ozzie said. Taryn winced at his use of her full name; she knew that meant he was really serious. "We've almost died at least twice now. I know it sucks. Sucks doesn't even begin to describe it, but it doesn't do any good to go picking fights you won't win."

Taryn was more surprised than anything. Ozzie had been the one excited about their circumstances when they were in Leleplar. Okay, maybe he wasn't completely excited, but he had always been open to the possibilities that world offered. Now he was the one telling them not to take chances, exactly what Taryn had done in Leleplar. She wondered if their experience there had sobered him up, or if he was taking things more seriously here because Terturelia had elements of their world in it.

*Heroes, Legends, and Villains*

# Chapter 10

Taryn and Ozzie couldn't believe their luck. They had made it over halfway through America, following the signs for England, without incident. Smitty hadn't been through what they had, so he didn't have the same perspective, but he listened with interest as Taryn and Ozzie discussed points of interest from their last journey. From what he heard, it seemed as if a day didn't pass during that time where they weren't running from danger, meeting some new friend or foe, or almost dying. Well, they had done the almost dying thing here early on, so maybe that was it for them. He certainly hoped so. The trip was quiet, the horses weren't overworked, and the trio had fallen into a routine.

Ozzie, Taryn, and Smitty would generally roll out of bed whenever the sun or inn noises woke them, eat a hearty breakfast where they could get it, and would then get back out on the road and ride until about sundown, or as close to it as they could get. Road trip games were played—and altered or intensified when they got boring—which led to more than one accident-near-miss. This was usually due to Ozzie and Smitty egging each other on to try and make the game "the most epic ever!"…so far. Taryn played the voice of reason in these scenarios, usually insisting the game be taken back down a notch. Ozzie, Taryn, and Smitty learned more about one another during this time as well because, well, besides games, talking was really the only other thing to do. Taryn and Ozzie already knew each other so well it was more the two of them learning more about Smitty and vice-versa.

Smitty, it turned out, was handier with the horses than he had initially let on. His sparse experience had taught him enough to know that training was a continuous process—he cited the training he had given his dog more than anything, but the principles were the same. Therefore, he encouraged Ozzie and Taryn to never let the horses graze while they were mounted, lest the horses think they can do it whenever they pleased. He also suggested that they help the grooms at the inns put the horses up for the night. That way, they would learn more about caring for them and build trust with their horses at the same time. This was especially good for Taryn, as she remained nervous about Honey for a long time. Smitty was always patient with her, however, and did his best to put her at ease. This unexpected knowledge or instinct or whatever it was turned out to be quite a boon, as Ozzie and Taryn were nearly inept in this department.

The peaceful nature of the journey caused Ozzie some consternation, though, despite the fact that he knew it was better, *safer*, this way.

"It just…I just don't understand the point of getting dropped here if this is all we do," he explained after Taryn had questioned him about his strange mood.

"You really think there has to be a…" Taryn began, but let it drop when Ozzie smiled knowingly at her.

She tried to scowl at him, but couldn't help smiling. Ozzie's itch for adventure was finally relieved, however, as it eventually had to be. The three were making their way through the land of Oz when it happened. Taryn, who had been pretty relaxed thus far—barring her fear of Honey turning on her—through the real-world settings around them, had begun to grow nervous because Oz was, in fact, a fantasy land. Ozzie's spirits, however, lifted like a helium balloon set free, which only thinned Taryn's patience, as cheeriness is wont to do to cynicism. When Ozzie tried to encourage her, her bitter retort only served to start a debate.

"How on earth is a world with magic in it better than one that's based on our own, even loosely so?" Taryn asked. "You can't count on a world like that."

"True, but you can't exactly count on the 'real' world either, can you?" Ozzie countered. "Most fantasy creatures are bound by some kind of honor. A lot of the people are, too. People in our world aren't bound by anything. A lot of them are terrible without even realizing it."

"When did you get so jaded?" Smitty interjected.

102

"My mom's been screwed over by Corporate America more than once," Ozzie replied with a shrug. "Given the chance, most people won't look beyond their own nose."

Taryn wondered if this was a point for cheeriness or cynicism.

"Nevermore!"

Ozzie, Taryn, and Smitty stopped their horses and looked around. They were on the yellow brick road in some kind of forest, but the road was broad enough and the trees spaced far enough to allow wide swaths of sunlight to spill down from the sky. They looked up and down the road and through the trees on either side of them, but there was no one as far as they could see.

"Hello," Ozzie called. "Anyone there?"

There was no answer. The trio looked at one another and shrugged and then started off again.

"Nevermore!"

Smitty whipped around in his saddle and looked behind them.

"Nevermore!"

It was then that they spotted it: a large raven sitting on a tree branch nearby.

"Hey, I get it!" Smitty said. "It's the raven from Poe, right?"

He looked back to Taryn, who was staring at the bird with her lips pursed into a hard, thin line.

"Taryn?" Smitty said. "What's wrong?"

"I don't want to be here," she replied quickly. "Let's go. Really, Ozzie, how can you like these kind of places?"

"Dude, I thought Poe was your boy," Ozzie said, turning Shadow to follow Honey.

"He is, but people *die* in his stories," Taryn replied. "Like, a lot of people."

"No one dies in *The Raven* do they?" Smitty said.

"No, and I don't care," Taryn said firmly. "One raven could mean more Poe characters."

"Nevermore!"

The three stopped and turned again to see the bird had followed them.

"Hey! Get out of here!" Smitty yelled, waving towards the bird. It simply sat there staring blankly at them. He turned back to Taryn and said, "I'm sorry, I tried."

Taryn raised an eyebrow at him and then proceeded to guide Honey to the nearest tree. She broke off the end of a smallish branch and hurled it at the black bird. The raven easily flew out of the way before the stick came near, though it wouldn't have mattered anyway. Taryn missed the bird, and the branch struck the tree trunk instead.

"Nice shot," Ozzie quipped, watching the bird settle back down on its perch.

"Shut up," Taryn replied shortly, reaching for a new projectile.

She suddenly heard a great creaking sound and looked up to see the branches of the tree coming down towards her, reaching for her with long, spindly, leafy fingers. Taryn screamed and jerked Honey's reins away from the tree. Shadow and Ember shied away from the trees, all of which were now reaching towards the trio.

"Run!" Smitty cried, and urged Ember into a gallop.

Honey and Shadow immediately followed. It was only the death grip that Ozzie and Taryn had on their saddles that saved them from falling off. The horses ran down the road staying in the center away from the reaching trees. Smitty, Ozzie, and Taryn could only hold on for dear life and try to keep them on a steady path.

The horses drank from the stream greedily, while Ozzie, Taryn, and Smitty were scattered across the grass. They didn't know how long they had run, but they knew they hadn't stopped until they were well beyond the woods and their reaching branches. They had left the yellow brick road somewhere along the way as well, but the track they followed looked used enough to at least be a secondary road, or so their logic went. Besides that, Ozzie, Taryn, and Smitty had come out well considering the circumstances. The trees had only been able to reach them when the horses veered to one side of the road or the other. Their thick boughs and trunks prevented them from reaching very far, but all three got snagged more than once along the way.

"People who travel in fantastical lands shouldn't throw sticks," Ozzie finally said, looking at Taryn.

"I know," Taryn groaned, keeping her head between her knees, "I'm sorry."

No one said anything more for a long time. The horses were cared for and camp was set up in the interim. Finally, as the three settled down for dinner, Ozzie spoke again.

"This is going to be like last time, isn't it?"

"If Taryn keeps on freaking out, it looks like it," Smitty snipped.

"I'm really sorry, guys!" Taryn insisted. "I got scared. I thought if Poe's raven was there, worse things would start showing up. Most likely crazy people."

"If they freak you out so badly, why do you like his stories?" Ozzie asked.

"Because reading them is completely different from participating in them! Did you like running for your life from and fighting Vurnal? No! But you like reading about other people doing stuff like that."

"That's fair," Ozzie replied evenly.

"That doesn't help us now," Smitty said. "We can't go back that way and we have no idea where we are."

"We can look at the map tomorrow," Ozzie said reassuringly. "Let's just all take it easy for now since—"

"Don't!" Taryn interrupted. "You *have* to choose a new theme song this trip."

Ozzie stared at Taryn for a moment, a smile playing at both their lips.

"It's a small world after all…"

"Great!" Smitty exclaimed, unable to keep from smiling now as well.

The three all laughed for a moment before Taryn spoke again.

"Seriously, guys, I am sorry for pissing off the trees back there. Please say you forgive me."

Ozzie reached out and grabbed Taryn's hand. He knew that Taryn was really concerned by the fact that she had brought it back up. She wanted them all to be okay; her past with Ozzie had taught her how badly unforgiven grudges could fester. He smiled at her, remembering how much trouble he had gotten them into in the past.

"No worries, Ryn," he said. "We're okay."

She smiled back at Ozzie and then looked to Smitty, her eyes still filled with concern. Smitty didn't say anything for a moment. When he finally did, it was clear how he really felt.

"Sure. Whatever."

Taryn continued to look at him pleadingly, but he wouldn't look back at her. The rest of the evening was spent with Ozzie and Taryn going about their business together and Smitty fuming silently to himself. Several hours later, after Taryn had fallen asleep on her bedroll, Ozzie pulled Smitty aside.

"Dude, you have to give Taryn a break," he said. "She's your friend."

"She could have gotten us killed!" Smitty hissed.

"Yeah, and she's saved our lives a few times, too. We didn't die, and it was an honest mistake. Okay? Things happen in these places that you don't expect, things you can't predict. More stuff is going to happen, and we can't do anything about it, so put your big boy pants on and stop pouting."

Smitty was visibly taken aback, while Ozzie was staring daggers at him. Ozzie then left him with his thoughts.

The next morning, Ozzie pulled out the map for them all to look over. This was the point where not springing for a better map came back to bite them. The fighting forest was but a blurry clump of trees, and they couldn't be sure where they were in relation to it now. Even knowing that might not have helped, as there weren't very many major landmarks in the area, just roads. Anxiety grew thick in the air when this was realized.

"We're on a road," Ozzie said, trying to be optimistic. "It has to go somewhere. We'll just follow it until we find where that is."

"What if we go back and go around the trees?" Taryn suggested.

"I really don't know if we can find our way," Ozzie replied. "Even if we can, I don't think it's a good idea to leave the road."

"I'm with Ozzie on this," Smitty said simply.

It was agreed, and they broke camp quickly, eager to find Ozzie's somewhere. Everything seemed fairly normal again—not counting the constant undercurrent of worry—as if the arguments from the night before had never happened. This made Taryn uneasy and she kept stealing worried glances at Smitty, who would smile at her when he caught her.

"Are we okay?" she eventually asked.

"Yeah, sure," Smitty replied with a smile. "Don't worry about it."

"Don't lie to me, Smitty," Taryn said firmly. "If you're still upset, I want you to tell me. I don't want you to stay mad at me, only to later have it come back worse than it started."

"I'm not mad anymore," he said.

"Really?"

"Really."

Taryn let it drop then, and Ozzie snuck a glance back at Smitty. The scene looked innocent enough, so he also let it go.

Eventually, around midday, the three came upon another road, which was a relief. It ran almost perpendicular to the way they were headed, so they turned down it towards the direction they had come from the previous day. The direction the sun had set in and then risen from thankfully gave them some idea of where they needed to go. They never came back upon the yellow brick road, however. The hard packed earth just went on and on. There were no signposts, no mile markers, no nothing. At first this seemed perfectly fine to the three. They had run the horses hard for a long time the day before, but, as evening drew near, they were all beginning to get worried again. They were all wondering just how far off course they had actually gone and, more importantly, if they'd be able to find their way back. Taryn was the first to say what they were all thinking.

"Guys, I think we might be lost…"

Both Ozzie and Smitty stopped their horses and turned back towards her. They exchanged worried glances and Smitty responded.

"Maybe. What do we do if we are?"

"I think we need to ask for directions," Taryn said firmly.

Ozzie smiled at that and said, "No, Ryn. Don't you know? We're men. We don't ask for directions."

Leave it to Ozzie to find humor in any situation.

"Dude, get serious," Smitty said. "She's right."

"We're working on it. If there was someone here to ask, we might, assuming they didn't look like a serial killer. This road has to lead somewhere. Let's just keep going."

"What if we're going in the wrong direction?" Taryn asked.

"Then we'll deal with that when we get there," Ozzie said. "Better to stay on the track we're pretty sure about than to turn around, lose time, and go in the direction we don't have a clue about."

He was clearly not as concerned about their predicament as Taryn and Smitty. No one could really argue his point, however, and they pressed on. It was two days and a lot of frayed nerves later that they finally came upon some semblance of civilization again. They had apparently been on a back road that was mostly used by travelers—travelling entertainers or merchants or something like them was what Ozzie, Taryn, and Smitty thought this must really mean—in the winter.

Ozzie, Taryn, and Smitty spotted the village from far off and their hearts soared at the sight of it. It wasn't just because it was the first sign of other people in over three days, but also because it was gorgeous! They got their first glimpse as they crested a lush, green hill. Spread out below them in the valley were fields fat with crops and houses that looked so perfect they might have been pieces in a model. Anywhere they could get help and a decent place to sleep would have been great, but to find such a pastoral paradise was joyously unbelievable. That is, until they saw the sign showing the name of the village.

"It's fine," Taryn said, clearly not fine. "It's fine. We'll just make sure to stay inside at night. Okay? No one steps foot outside after dark."

"That seems fine," Smitty agreed soberly.

Ozzie wasn't sure what to say at first and only looked at the sign for Sleepy Hollow.

"Have either of you actually read this one?" he finally asked.

"Um…" was Taryn's response. "Maybe. If I did, it was a long time ago, and I don't really remember."

"I don't read all the books for our classes," Smitty confessed. "I watch a lot of movie versions."

"That's why I get better grades than you," Taryn said, though she was still staring at the sign.

Apparently, Taryn and Ozzie had seen at least one film adaptation of the book as well, which didn't help. Thus, the idea to stay indoors at night was a popular one. They soon found a cozy tavern, which served as an inn as well, and settled in. They looked for Sleepy Hollow on their map, but it wasn't marked. Ozzie cautioned against asking for directions until they were sure the people here were trustworthy, but even he couldn't insist on that too strongly. Everyone they had met so far was just the epitome of kindness.

# Chapter 11

Ozzie, Taryn, and Smitty sat in the tavern by the window watching the sunset. It was the evening after they had arrived in Sleepy Hollow, and they felt happy and languid. They weren't talking, lest they have to talk about when they would leave. It was an unhappy thought after the stress of the last few days, and silence was easier. They'd get to it; they just didn't have to yet. Dinner was ordered, and the serving woman, a sweet, plump matron called Gertrude, asked if they needed anything else.

"No, thank you," Taryn said with a smile. She then pointed out the window and asked, "There are a lot of people heading up the road. Is something going on?"

"Oh, there's some merry night happening at the Van Tassel castle," Gertrude said in a jolly, almost singsong kind of way. She looked for all the world like she might pinch Taryn's cheek in that moment. "It surely would be nice to go, but someone has to be here to look after things. It will be a quiet night."

After that, Ozzie, Taryn, and Smitty ate their dinner and then moved to the fireplace to chat. Apple cider was brought to them, and the idea of when they would leave, as well as the distaste for it, came back. The subject was avoided.

"I think it's fall here," Smitty commented, looking at his cider.

"Oh?" Taryn said lazily.

"Yeah, it kind of looks like it."

"So?" Ozzie asked. He didn't really care about the answer. He was just flowing along with the conversation.

"Just trying to get some bearings on things. Is it possible the seasons are different depending on what country you're in?"

"I don't know," Taryn mused. "To be fair, we've been speeding through regions. I mean, we were in the deep south/not

110

actually south a week ago, which is hot even in the fall, right? We were in France before that. I'm not a hundred percent sure of where we are now."

"Somewhere up north, I think," Ozzie said.

The conversation died there. They knew they wouldn't really figure it out and so couldn't be bothered to ponder the question further. They sat in companionable silence for a while, just being content. Crickets were chirping outside, Gertrude was tidying up, the fire was crackling, and the dining room was empty. It seemed almost the entire village had taken the Van Tassels up on their hospitality. Ozzie, Taryn, and Smitty each spoke intermittently in their turn until Ozzie finally broached the subject they were all avoiding.

"So when are we going? I think it should be tomorrow."

They hadn't asked for directions yet, but now it was only because they hadn't wanted to. All thoughts of being in danger of being taken advantage of were gone now.

Taryn sighed and conceded, "I suppose we should. Smitty, do you mind going to get the map?"

She tapped his cider mug, which was empty, to indicate her reasoning. She smiled prettily at him to put a bow on her request. Smitty smiled back and stood silently, setting his mug on a table as he went. He strolled up the steps, letting his mind wander as he went.

After he was gone, Taryn spoke to Ozzie hopefully.

"He seems better, doesn't he?"

"I think so. It's hard to tell," Ozzie replied.

"I know it's difficult. I'm the least shining example of good alternate-universe-behavior, but I'm worried about him."

"I know," was all Ozzie said.

He thought back to his conversation with Smitty the night they had gotten lost. He knew Smitty well enough to know he had still been angry that night, and Ozzie's words may or may not have added fuel to that fire. It had needed to be said, though; they couldn't afford to be petty or unforgiving here. Smitty did seem better now. Maybe he had taken Ozzie's advice and had toughened up.

Ozzie looked back to Taryn and saw her looking curiously at him. She knew there was something he wasn't saying. She always did. He gave her the most encouraging smile he could.

"Don't worry. It'll all be fine."

Taryn smiled back and said, "How can you always be so positive?"

"We've talked about this. Heavy medication, remember?"

Smitty was back downstairs a few minutes later with the map in hand. They gathered at the front counter before Gertrude and began to ask their questions. She was a great help in providing advice for getting back on track. It was several days' journey back to the main road, but it was an easy one. There wasn't a lot out this way, but they would have to beware of wild animals. It was decided they would leave early the next morning and just hope to find an inn before nightfall. Taryn still expressed concern about what they might find, even in the daytime, but there was no helping that. They would just have to be careful.

"Should we buy some weapons?" Smitty asked that evening as the three got ready for bed.

"We can see what we can find," Ozzie said, "but I don't know if Sleepy Hollow has much in the way of swords."

That night, as Ozzie, Taryn, and Smitty slept, they were wakened suddenly by the sound of a horse's terrible scream, followed by a thundering tattoo of hoof beats. They all clung onto each other, listening to the noises pass by outside the window, and were suddenly very glad to be leaving tomorrow. They were keener to buy some kind of weapons the next day too, but all they could find were some hunting knives.

"It's just as well," Taryn said, as they walked the horses down the lane and made their way out of Sleepy Hollow. "Ozzie and I were never that good with weapons anyway."

"The irony of our crude weaponry isn't lost on you?" Smitty teased. He seemed much happier now with a blade strapped to his belt.

Taryn smiled, and they mounted the horses to head out properly again. Gertrude had been right. The road was easy with gentle slopes and a babbling brook that ran parallel to the road to keep them company, but the horses were uneasy, and not even Smitty could figure out why. Ozzie, Taryn, and Smitty had to camp that night; there hadn't been any villages, towns, or inns all along their path that day. As they ate dinner that night the horses kept looking around nervously, their eyes rolling back and forth. It didn't help to put their human masters at ease, and Ozzie finally said they should assign watches for the night. Taryn would take the first—"Since you're the crankiest without sleep...ow!"—Ozzie would take the second since falling back to sleep was easy for him, and Smitty would take the third.

The horses were their barometer that night, as they would be able to sense danger long before Ozzie, Taryn, and Smitty could. As Taryn sat gazing out into the darkness, working to get her temper fired up just in case, they *whuffled* and pawed the ground anxiously. While Ozzie was tending the fire and sweeping his gaze left and right or miming what he thought could be attack moves with his knife, the horses were stepping back and forth and occasionally pulling at their ties. By the time Smitty's turn came around, Ozzie couldn't go back to sleep. He didn't know if whatever was spooking the horses posed an actual threat—Gertrude had mentioned wild animals—but he couldn't take a risk by sleeping. Ozzie also wasn't sure if he should wake Taryn. He didn't want to worry her in case it wasn't anything serious, but he didn't want her to be unprepared in case it was. In the end, he told Smitty they would let her be. Ozzie saw her hunting knife next to her and trusted her. Besides, the horses might wake her up anyway.

He and Smitty spent a lot of time trying to keep them calm. The last thing they needed was for the horses to break free and run off. They could also hurt themselves or each other if they got too riled up. If only they had a more defensible position, but it was open plains all around them. Being tired wasn't helping either. Both boys were getting paranoid, and Ozzie could only think about the brook next to them and hope it would protect them if their pursuers were undead.

Taryn started from sleep when Ember finally reached her breaking point and began to whinny, rearing up onto her hind legs. She was awake in a second—some habits learned in Leleplar had come back as if they'd never gone—and saw Smitty running beyond the horses, while Ozzie fought to keep Ember down. Smitty began shouting for Ozzie and then Taryn too as he looked out into the darkness. Then there was a large streak of fur. Smitty went down.

"Smitty!" Taryn and Ozzie cried together, and they ran, knives in hand, to rescue their friend.

There was an animal's noise of pain, a strange chirpy sort of yip, and Smitty was crawling backwards as the animal retreated a step. Ozzie reached him first and helped him to his feet, brandishing his knife in the animal's direction as he did so. Taryn was on her way, but the animal leapt between her and the boys before she could get there. Taryn jumped back, ready to attack, but the creature already had its back to her. It was too dark this far from the fire to make out much. Ozzie and Smitty were but dim figures beyond, but Taryn could make out the animal's lanky rear end. It told her wolf, but there was something wrong. If this was a wolf, it was enormous. Then she saw them: The claws as the creature scratched the ground with its front feet. Its large, bird-like talons glinted in the weak firelight. But what had claws like that? A griffon? No!

"Heinz!" Taryn cried.

The creature turned its head towards her just enough to look at her while still keeping an eye on Smitty and Ozzie. It was indistinct, but Taryn could see the outline of her faithful enfield's face. Taryn's face broke into a huge grin before she realized what Heinz was doing.

"Oh, Heinz, baby, it's okay," she cooed, throwing herself onto him—someone made a noise of protest—and scratching him behind the ear.

"Is it really him?" Ozzie asked. His tone was hopeful but careful.

Even if it was Heinz, he knew the enfield would defend Taryn fiercely if he sensed a threat, so Ozzie erred on the side of caution for the moment.

"Of course it is!" Taryn replied. Her voice was taking on a distinct baby-talk quality. "Come on, sweetie. You remember Uncle Ozzie, don't you?"

Taryn led Heinz over towards Ozzie and Smitty, causing Smitty to skirt around back towards the fire, and she wrapped her arms around Ozzie in a gleeful hug. She was practically bouncing. Ozzie held his hand out and waited for Heinz to sniff it. It wasn't a full moment before Heinz recognized his scent and had begun to chitter excitedly. Thankfully, Heinz did not jump up like most canines and risk slicing someone open with his claws, but instead wagged his tail and turned in circles.

"Come on, Smitty, your turn," Taryn called. "Smitty?"

She turned and saw her friend standing back at camp looking furious and scared.

"Yes, I'm still here, in case you care," he snapped at her. "What is that thing?!"

Taryn, almost literally, bit her tongue. Smitty's reaction was making her angry, but she forced herself to look at things from his perspective. He had never seen an enfield, probably didn't make the connection between the creature before him and what she had told him about Heinz, and, oh yeah, had been attacked as well. That softened her up quite a bit, and she approached Smitty, reaching out to him. She took his hand in hers and put on her most comforting smile.

Pulling him towards her gently, she explained, "This is Heinz. He's my enfield. You remember me telling you about him?"

"*That's* your guard dog?! You didn't tell me what a beast he was."

Taryn's smile instantly vanished, and she bit back a nasty retort. "Do you want to make nice with him or not?" she instead asked through gritted teeth.

"Do it, dude. Are you really going to choose to be his enemy?" Ozzie prodded.

Smitty looked down at Heinz and locked eyes with his yellow ones. Heinz growled deep in his chest, but stopped as Taryn wrapped an arm around Smitty.

"Heinz, baby, this is Smitty. Smitty is our friend…even if he does call you names. You have to be nice to him."

"Really, Taryn? You're siding with him?" Smitty said, still clearly upset.

"Look, I'm sorry he attacked you," she said, pulling away from him now, "but he was trying to protect me. That's his job."

"Protect you? From me? Because I'm such a threat."

"He doesn't know you! Look at you. You're fine, so let it go."

"Heinz isn't," Ozzie broke in.

Taryn spun around to look at Ozzie and Heinz and saw Ozzie examining Heinz's leg. Taryn knelt down and saw that the back of Heinz's front leg was bleeding. It wasn't bad, as the tough, scaly skin had protected him, but it was still enough to set Taryn off.

"You stabbed my enfield!" she yelled angrily at Smitty.

"He was going to tear my throat out!" Smitty shouted back.

"No wonder he doesn't like you! You could have killed him!"

"Not likely! And just what else was I supposed to do? He attacked me!"

"Enough!" Ozzie bellowed over them. Both Taryn and Smitty turned and scowled at him. In a more normal tone now, Ozzie continued, "Smitty, sorry you got tackled, but Taryn's right. It's in an enfield's nature to protect their charge, and you are fine. Taryn, have a little compassion. The guy thought he was going to die. Heinz, over to the fire with you so we can look at your leg."

Heinz looked to Taryn for permission or clarification or whatever it was that he needed. She nodded and gestured towards the camp tiredly. Heinz began to head over, causing the horses to all whinny and rear up in fear. Heinz then gave one crisp, short bark, and they stilled. Taryn and Ozzie exchanged a look of surprise at that, but said nothing. They then followed, trailed uncertainly by Smitty. Ozzie couldn't see anything else to do but wrap the leg in a bandage, so he did. That didn't last. As soon as he had it secure, Heinz started pulling at it with his teeth.

"Can we make a cone for him?" Smitty suggested.

"No, we shouldn't need to," Taryn said. "Heinz, stop."

The enfield looked at her and made a noise of protest. Taryn gave him the same look she would to a small child testing his boundaries.

"I mean it. Leave it alone."

Heinz whined in defeat and lowered his head to the ground. Taryn leaned on him, stretching her arm across his massive body and breathed contentedly. For the first time in a long time, she felt truly safe again.

Smitty sat by Ozzie, being careful to keep one eye on Heinz at all times.

"Are you okay, man?" Ozzie asked, trying to get settled again.

"Yeah, I'm fine," Smitty replied.

Ozzie gave Smitty a look, which Smitty refused to return, and Ozzie let it drop for the moment. They eventually all fell asleep again until about dawn. That was when Heinz stirred, walked to the edge of camp, and started barking.

"Are. You. Freaking. *Kidding me?!*" Smitty demanded angrily exactly one second after waking up. "What now?"

It was apparently hunting time, and Heinz took off. Taryn called after him but stopped when she saw him turn and snatch a hare out of the grass. He returned a minute later and dropped the fresh carcass at Taryn's feet.

"Good boy!" Taryn gushed. "Ozzie, can you dress it? We can fry it for breakfast."

"Sure!" Ozzie said, thrilled at the prospect of such a good meal after such a trying night. "Smitty, want to learn the manly art of gutting?"

"Why not?" Smitty said tiredly.

He was still pretty annoyed, but this was good news even despite that.

"Best puppy ever!" Taryn cried excitedly, hugging Heinz around the neck. "Be sure to save the gizzards for him."

Her outlook on this trip had turned around quite literally overnight. With her faithful protector back, they could handle anything the literary world had to throw at them.

# Chapter 12

Their path led them northwest towards England. With some help from some kind locals, the group was able to trace the exact path they had taken thus far. Had they not been detoured at the fighting forest, their path would have been a straight shot north into England. They had gone west instead to Sleepy Hollow and west again out of it. Because of that, they would travel towards the coast and then work their way up it. Despite this fortunate turn of luck, things were not ideal.

Taryn was in brighter spirits than she had been the entire trip, and Ozzie too was more optimistic, if that was even possible. Smitty was still clearly uneasy about being around Heinz, but he made an effort to get to know the enormous enfield. He would come and sit with Taryn and speak to Heinz like he would any other strange dog and ask about him. Taryn was more than happy to help during these times because, one, she adored Heinz and was beyond proud of him, and two, because she really wanted Smitty to be happy and comfortable. Heinz clearly still had his reservations about Smitty as well, which Taryn couldn't understand, but he was obedient and tolerant for his mistress.

"I wonder how he got here," Ozzie said at one point. "Could he have swum across the ocean?"

"Yes, Oz, he swam across the ocean," Taryn teased.

"I don't doubt his determination," Smitty said. "I'm sure he would if he could."

"Guys, come on," Taryn said. "That's crazy talk."

"Then how did he get here?" Ozzie pressed. "I seriously doubt he just strolled onto a ship without incident. He'd have to have someone there to vouch for him like we do."

This had been the one disadvantage of having Heinz with them: no innkeeper had let them stay without making them prove Heinz wasn't dangerous and completely under Taryn's control. Even after they did so, much to Heinz's chagrin—even enfields didn't like to be made to roll over, beg, and play dead—most establishments still turned them away. Loaded with gold or not, the group was traveling with a "wild beast". Once or twice, after being turned away by the local inn, they'd asked the nearest farmer if they could sleep in the barn or some other smelly but sheltered place. The farmers, however, were less than inclined to allow the wild beast anywhere near their precious livestock. Thus, the group ended up camping as many nights as they didn't. Thankfully, no one outright panicked at seeing Heinz. Plenty stopped and stared and pointed, but no screaming or anything. This could only mean that there were fantastic creatures somewhere within Terturelia, or that the creatures of Leleplar were common knowledge, or both. Either way, it made Ozzie excited.

Taryn didn't answer Ozzie's question. She knew what he was getting at and she wasn't about to let herself think about the possibility. The issue was dropped like a hot rock and was shot down as soon as it was broached again.

Despite being turned away from less woodsy accommodations here and there, the traveling was easy. Ozzie, Taryn, and Smitty could sleep easy knowing Heinz was there to protect them no matter where they were. The land around them remained fairly constant now, and they even discovered that they had dodged a bullet by being detoured. Had Ozzie, Taryn, and Smitty remained on their original path, they would have had to ride through Alaska. Granted, the Alaska of Terturelia was nowhere near the size of the real Alaska, but it still would have been treacherous. Instead, the last state they passed into before hitting the border of England was Massachusetts, which was chilly but very picturesque. Here, the flatlands turned to dense, vast forests with leaf cover so thick it made everything dusky even when the sun was shining brightly overhead. Since it was fall, the leaves were all starting to change, so the canopy above was a dazzle of red, purple, green, yellow, and orange, and the path was littered with the brown ones that had already given up. Civilized places were few and far between, extra layers of clothing were put on, and the group started camping overnight more often than ever. The terrain grew wilder and signs of other travelers less frequent. When they finally reached the border of England, there was barely a sign for it. It was just a rock, about the size of a basketball, with "England" carved into it. That was slightly disconcerting, not to mention anticlimactic for Taryn and Smitty who were both excited about seeing the literary version of that country. There was nothing else to be done for it, though, so on they went.

Nothing about England so far was as Ozzie, Taryn, and Smitty had expected. Ozzie, who had never been, basically expected it to be a big, old-timey version of London. Taryn and Smitty had expected it to be all small, medieval towns and castles and 19th century people. Instead, it was all trees. They had been riding for days at a slow pace surrounded by nothing but forest. The path was skinny and turned often, and the leaf litter hid rocks, roots, and other treacherous obstacles, so it wasn't safe to go any faster than a walk. Ozzie, Taryn, and Smitty ended up leading the horses on foot half the time now just because any light that managed to penetrate the leaf canopy was pathetically weak. It was as if they were always walking in twilight, and dark came much earlier. Rain came more often now too, which didn't help anyone's mood. There was talk that they were lost, but they had been following a stream, and nothing was repeating. The animals were calm, though, and Heinz was quick to either scare off or kill any creatures that came near. Since they had food and shelter and water, the biggest concern was that they would never escape the dark, cold, rainy monotony of the woods. Ozzie was the most frustrated by this, but Taryn and Smitty kept on reminding him that, while it was disconcerting, it was far better than running for their lives.

"Didn't I tell you wandering through the woods was better than this?!" Taryn cried.

Ozzie, Taryn, and Smitty were all running pell-mell down the path without much hope of safety. Nothing around them indicated an end to the forest, and their pursuer was surely better at navigating the trees than them.

Ozzie didn't answer. He was too busy thinking up contingency plans in case they were caught. Nothing would be worse than that, and blind panic was preventing him from thinking clearly.

It had all started so innocently. The horses were nervous, and Heinz had been restless, watching the trees and growling. This had all happened before when the occasional wolf had trailed them, though, so nothing much was thought of it. Then the spider came crawling across their path. It looked like a tarantula, and Ozzie had screamed in a way he wasn't proud of, which made Shadow jump. Taryn stomped the thing with her foot. She was aggressive about it, as she was with all spiders now. She never said so, but Ozzie believed it was because Vurnal was in the form of a spider when they first met him in Leleplar. He figured Taryn was taking out some feelings she hadn't worked through on the little arachnids, and he was totally fine with that. When the tarantula was crushed beneath her boot, there was a horrible, dry, clicking shriek from the forest, followed by the sound of undergrowth being trampled. The noise came towards them fast. Shadow and Ember reared up, ripping the reins from Ozzie and Smitty's grasp, and followed after Honey, who had bolted back the way they came.

"Run!" Ozzie screamed, and they all took off.

No one had seen their pursuer, but they could hear it in the trees. It sounded big. Big enough to eat them? Big enough for Heinz to fight? None of that was certain, and they didn't want to find out. The noise in the woods stopped, but on they ran. A few moments later, the mother spider came flying out from the trees and landed on the path before them. Ozzie, Taryn, and Smitty screamed and retreated. Heinz took the position in front and barked threateningly at the nightmarish creature.

The spider was half the height of a man with multiple, glassy, black orbs for eyes. Spiny hairs covered its impossibly spindly legs, which looked as if they should collapse under the weight of its bulbous body, the back of which was thickly covered in a clutch of plum-sized, slimy spheres. The spider also had massive fangs that looked far too big for its face and protruded down past what would have been its chin.

Taryn was torn. The giant spider terrified her, but she couldn't leave Heinz. It would surely kill him, but it would surely kill her, too. Their hunting knives were no match for the spider. What she wouldn't give for a flamethrower right now! Wait...

She grabbed a fallen branch from the side of the path, thrust it at the boys, and said, "Make a torch! I'll distract it!"

"Taryn, don't!" Ozzie cried.

He was sick with horror. Everything in his body was telling him to run screaming, but he was just barely holding it back. What Taryn had said made sense. Fire should scare the thing away. He just had to make himself do it.

"Help me," he said shakily to Smitty, who looked just as ready to run.

They ripped their steel and flint out from the nearest pack, laid the branch on the ground and furiously began trying to light the leaves on the end. The leaves were thankfully dry, but it was still really difficult to get them lit.

Meanwhile, Taryn had joined Heinz and was brandishing her knife and screaming as frighteningly as she could. She was only semi-successful in this last effort, as she was praying frantically that the thing wouldn't lunge and kill her at the same time.

"Agggggghhhhh! Do not kill me! Ack! Don't you take one step near me! Stay back! Aggghhhhhhhhh! I do *not* want to die like this!"

She was hoping the spider would decide she and Heinz were too much to handle and retreat. It looked furious, however. That was understandable since Taryn had smashed its baby to a crunchy pulp. Thus began a terrifying stalemate, wherein the spider would advance, Taryn would retreat, Heinz would leap and snap and dodge, and the spider would retreat again. Heinz would then snap again, the spider would retreat, try to attack, and the cycle would begin again. This clearly annoyed the spider, which continued to chitter and click and hiss grotesquely.

"Guys!" Taryn screamed back behind her. It was taking every ounce of effort she had to make herself stay put and avoid being killed. She honestly didn't know how long she could keep it up before something gave out. "What's taking so long?!"

"Almost there!" Ozzie shrieked.

His heart was beating out of his chest. Giant spider, Taryn in danger, pressure to light a fire...it was getting close to being too much to handle.

"Got it!" both he and Smitty cried together a minute later when the leaves finally caught.

They had eventually decided to bunch the leaves all together to make a larger surface for the sparks to catch on, as opposed to just striking the flint like a maniac and hoping one of the leaves lit. A small part of the back of their minds thought they should have thought of that a lot earlier, but…panic and everything.

The fire spread quickly, but they didn't wait for it to finish. Ozzie grabbed the impromptu torch and ran forward. Smitty followed with his knife. He gave Taryn and Heinz a wide berth, lest he light them on fire, and shook the flaming branch at the spider. The spider shrieked and retreated, but it clearly had no mind to leave. It was still too angry. What was worse, the leaves were burning up quickly. Some had already been completely eaten up by fire, and the rest were following quickly. The wood was not catching well, and the torch was dying faster than it had been born. The spider was desperate by now and, seeing this flaw in the human's plan, it lunged and lunged again. Ozzie, Taryn, and Smitty screamed and jumped back. They were out of ideas, and their resolve was slipping fast. The spider lunged closer. Taryn screamed when she thought it bit Smitty, but he had moved his arm just in time. It reared up again to attack. It was going to get one of them this time. Then came arrows whizzing by their heads and shoulders and bodies. One buried its head into the back of Ozzie's calf. Ozzie screamed and went down.

"OZZIE!" Taryn shrieked, running to him.

The spider would get to him first—it was in midair just then—but she would take it out anyway. Even if she had to jump on its back and stab it in the head, maybe they could find a town and save Ozzie before it was too late. Heinz was leaping forward. Taryn hesitated a split second before pressing on, knowing now Heinz would take the fall for Ozzie. Smitty was out of her line of sight, but that probably meant he was safe. All of this happened within a few seconds. Taryn reached Ozzie and saw that he was okay except for the arrow in his leg. He was swearing but trying to crawl away. Taryn grabbed his arm, hooked it over her shoulders, and looked back to see where the spider was. Surely, as tough as he was, Heinz could last just a little longer before it killed him. When she looked back, however, the scene was calm. Heinz was standing on top of the overturned spider's belly. He was watching its teeth for any movement, but it was dead. There was an arrow sticking out of its head and several more from its body. She looked back and saw Smitty standing completely still on the path. Beyond him, in the woods, she could just make out slender figures, but they could be more trees as unmoving and well camouflaged as they were. Only the bows and nocked arrows betrayed them for people.

"We don't want any trouble," Taryn called immediately. "We just want to go on our way and find a doctor for our friend."

"Also, thank you for helping us," Smitty added. "Please don't think we're ungrateful."

"We will take care of your friend," one of the figures called back.

Smitty looked to Taryn and Ozzie, who shook their heads almost imperceptibly.

"Thank you," Ozzie called, gritting his teeth through the unbelievable pain in his leg. "That's very kind, but we'd prefer to manage on our own."

Suddenly, all as one, the figures began to stride forward. Ozzie and Taryn groaned inwardly and none of the three moved. They were outmanned and outgunned, so to speak. If these people were looking to take them prisoner, they had no choice in the matter. When they came closer, the three could see their would-be saviors were not human at all, but elves, and all of them were keeping their arrows trained on the three and Heinz.

"These guys again?" Taryn growled under her breath.

"Again?" the one who had spoken before asked.

He was tall and slender with graceful features, just like the elves Ozzie and Taryn had met in Leleplar.

Taryn rolled her eyes. Of course they had heard her; they were elves.

"It's a bit of a long story, and he's bleeding," Taryn snapped. "We really need to get him a doctor."

"We will take care of your friend," the elf said again. When Taryn opened her mouth to object, he cut her off and added more sternly, "I am not asking."

Taryn made a noise of annoyance more than defeat.

"Hate it when you're right?" Ozzie asked.

"Hate it when I'm right," she confirmed.

Several of the elves stayed behind to take care of the mother spider. They had eliminated the nest and all of the other spiders, but this one had escaped, and the elves had been tracking it for some time. The spheres on her back were her eggs, which could have hatched at any time. The one Taryn had killed was likely one of the first, and the elves would have to send out another party to search for any siblings. Those that had stayed behind would destroy the remaining eggs. All of this made Ozzie, Taryn, and Smitty's skin crawl.

"You should be thankful," one of the other elves said. "Had the spider not been carrying her young, you would have all been dead within minutes."

"Small mercies," Smitty said.

The three were relieved of their weapons, and Ozzie's leg was attended to right then and there in an incredibly efficient manner. The first thing to do was to remove the arrow, which was the worst part. Taryn and Smitty were instructed to hold his arms while Ozzie knelt on the ground. The elves would then make a small incision in his leg to give the arrow a path out that didn't involve taking a chunk of Ozzie's flesh with it. Thankfully, the arrowhead was small and very sharp, so it had entered fairly cleanly.

"Aren't you supposed to push it through?" Smitty asked.

"You're not helping!" Ozzie yelled. He then screamed again as the arrow was carefully pulled out.

The elf attending to Ozzie either didn't respond or was drowned out.

"How could you have missed so badly?" Ozzie cried. "You're elves!"

"You jumped in the way," the elf replied calmly between Ozzie's exclamations.

A numbing agent was then applied to the wound in the form of a chunky, white paste made from some kind of berry and dark green leaves. Ozzie sighed in relief as the paste sent a wave of cold through his leg, and the pain began to ebb instantly. The whole thing was then wrapped in a bandage.

"This will not last the entire way," the elf said. "Tell us when the pain becomes too great."

Ozzie thanked the elves and was shocked to find he could walk without too much difficultly. He could feel pressure where there used to be pain and was reminded of a trip to the dentist.

Ozzie, Taryn, and Smitty were not restrained, probably because they were being so compliant, and they followed the elves slowly through the thick trees and underbrush. Both Ozzie and Taryn were silent, observing their captors and wondering why they weren't acting like the elves in Leleplar. Those that they had met in the village of Nerlua were incredibly arrogant and had only given Taryn and Ozzie the time of day because of Heinz. These elves seemed fairly even-keeled. True, Ozzie, Taryn, and Smitty were their prisoners, and there was no mistaking who was in charge, but they were surprisingly kind...for captors. The little they did say to Ozzie, Taryn, and Smitty was with an even tone, and when the terrain got rougher they were patient with their human prisoners, even helpful. Ozzie had to be assisted quite a bit because of his leg, as the pain would return sharply if he pushed it too hard.

Taryn kept looking to Heinz as they walked, and he wagged his tail at her. She dearly wanted to ask him what was wrong with him, but obviously couldn't without the elves hearing. Shouldn't Heinz have tried to rip someone's arm off by now? Why wasn't he freaking out? The fact that he wasn't actually made her and Ozzie feel marginally better, but that didn't change the fact that they were captives.

It was several hours' walk, mostly due to Ozzie's leg slowing them down and having to be redressed a few times, but the elves finally led Ozzie, Taryn, and Smitty to the most beautiful city they had ever seen. It wasn't massive like Sunrise Tower in Leleplar, but it was bigger than Nerlua. Maybe it was a town. None of the three really understood what the difference was except for size...doubly so for elven settlements.

The city was entirely housed within a steep valley, the walls of which sloped down to meet the focal point of that place: a gigantic tree that towered over everything. If one could climb to the top of it, America could be seen beyond the forest. The architecture of every building was curving and graceful, intricate, as if every beam had been individually bent and carved by hand, which it might have been. Pools dotted the basin of the valley, over which spanned beautiful bridges and more trees and verandas of houses. It was stunning enough to make Ozzie, Taryn, and Smitty forget for a moment that they were prisoners.

They were led down, down, down into the valley to the colossal tree, before which was the royal palace or head lodge or whatever was applicable to these elves. A considerable entourage was waiting for them outside the building on an exquisitely carved, round platform. It was hard to tell who was in charge here since all the elves dressed similarly. Several of them, however, were wearing delicate looking crowns, so it was probably one of them. Beyond the platform, Ozzie, Taryn, and Smitty could see other elves watching them from the houses. This was even more disconcerting, as there must be hundreds, if not thousands, of elves surrounding them.

"Welcome to Arbor Glen," one of the crowned elves said. His voice was kind, but, like their captors, it was clear he did not fully trust the humans. "I am Erandiar Pallanen."

Ozzie, Taryn, and Smitty remained silent.

"I trust you were treated well on your journey?" Erandiar continued.

"Yes, very well," Ozzie finally replied. "Thank you to you and your people for taking such good care of us."

"And thank you for saving us," Smitty added.

Erandiar nodded and looked to Taryn.

Taryn took a deep, calming breath. Their situation was precarious despite what all the niceties said. She tried to focus on the fact that Heinz was calm. That meant they weren't in danger, right? So she didn't need to make it worse by shooting off her mouth. She did her best to smile, though it was tight and nervous.

"Thank you to you, sir, and to your…soldiers very much for treating Ozzie and killing the spider and not killing us. We are really happy about this, I promise." Taryn paused. This wasn't coming out the way she wanted. "I admit I don't know whether we are guests or prisoners. Still, we are very thankful to be alive and well, so, um, thank you." She then ended by mumbling awkwardly, "I'm repeating myself now."

Erandiar didn't smile, but he looked somewhat amused. If the elves thought these three humans were a threat, that suspicion had to be dissipating fast.

He then replied, "May I have your names?"

"Taryn!" someone shouted from below the platform. "Taryn! Ozzie!"

Everyone turned towards the voice and saw someone running towards the platform. He was still a way off, but Taryn and Ozzie couldn't mistake what they saw as the figure approached. It was the telltale, elongated, graceful features, muted though, as if they weren't quite all that they could be, that gave it away.

"Tynx!" Taryn cried, and she went running towards him.

"Don't shoot her!" Ozzie called to the soldiers, who were still standing by. "We know him!"

The elves apparently weren't threatened by this odd turn of events since none of them moved except to get a better view of what was happening.

Taryn collided with Tynx as she threw her arms around his neck. Tynx caught her and wrapped his arms tightly around her, spinning her around and around and laughing. Taryn was laughing too and squealing. Ozzie stood back, watching the two and smiling broadly. Smitty was suddenly beside him, looking at Taryn and Tynx with an uncomfortable expression.

"Um, shouldn't we…" he began.

"Nah, just give them a minute."

When Ozzie's voice finally broke through to Taryn's ears again, she was leaning into Tynx, hugging him tightly with her head on his chest. His head was on top of hers as he basked in the joy of seeing her again.

"Hey, Ryn, you mind joining us back up here? We're kind of in the middle of an interrogation. Ours, that is."

"Oh…right." Taryn said uncertainly.

Where exactly did they stand in the elves' eyes now? Did they think more of their prisoners? Less of Tynx? She suddenly felt very stupid and self-conscious, but, to be fair, Tynx had started it. Yes, that was what she was going with. Right.

Tynx broke away from her and dashed up to the platform. He bowed deeply before Erandiar.

"My lord, please forgive me," Tynx began sincerely. "These are dear friends of mine for whom I have long searched. I was overcome with joy, but that is no excuse for interrupting. You have my deepest apologies."

"Tynixenal Delalewyn, I know of you and your search," Erandiar said with a tone none of the humans quite understood. It sounded like respect, but it went deeper than that somehow. "Are these truly the companions with whom you traveled before you came to our land?"

"Two of them, yes," Tynx replied, gesturing to Ozzie and Taryn.

Pointing to Smitty, Ozzie interjected quickly, "He's with us."

"Very well," Erandiar said with a nod. "Tynixenal, I entrust them to your keeping."

"Thank you, my lord."

Erandiar then bowed to Ozzie, Taryn, and Smitty and left, his court following behind. They bowed in return and then watched as the soldiers that had escorted them also dispersed, leaving them alone on the platform with Tynx.

"What just happened?" Smitty asked after they were all gone.

Ozzie laughed and replied, "Let's talk about it later." He then turned to Tynx, and said, "Fancy meeting you here. It's good to see you, man."

Tynx reached out to embrace Ozzie, returning the sentiment.

"And this is our friend Smitty. Poor guy got dragged along with us this trip," Ozzie went on to explain. "Smitty, the famous Tynx."

"Very nice to meet you," Tynx said, shaking Smitty's hand. "A friend of Taryn and Ozzie's is a friend of mine."

"Uh, likewise," Smitty said awkwardly. "Nice to meet you, too."

"Is there somewhere we can go?" Taryn asked. "Ozzie needs something more permanent for his leg and, um, yeah, we've got some catching up to do."

Despite the seriousness of the situation, Taryn couldn't help but smile at Tynx.

He smiled back at her and said, "Absolutely."

# Chapter 13

The obvious first order of business was attending to Ozzie's leg, but everyone was distracted. Ozzie could feel pain coming back and was trying to get Tynx to hurry up, but Tynx kept on looking at Taryn, who kept on looking at Tynx and then looking away, and they both kept on smiling. Meanwhile, Smitty still didn't have a clue as to what was going on. To try and make everyone happy, they talked as Tynx worked.

"I'm glad Heinz found you," Tynx said, cutting a length of thread for Ozzie's wound. "I was a little worried when he left."

"Should he be doing that?" Smitty asked. "Are you qualified?"

"He's fine," Taryn replied. "You mean Heinz has been with you this whole time?"

"Ozzie, this is going to hurt," Tynx said. "Mostly. He left a while back. He just got up one day and trotted out into the wilderness. I tracked him for a while, but after about a day or so—"

"Ow! Holy crap, dude! What did I ever do to you?!" Ozzie yelled.

Ozzie was currently lying on his stomach on a sofa in a cozy little cottage that presumably belonged to Tynx. He was already feeling pretty silly about his position when Tynx had added insult to injury by pouring a clear liquid into the arrow wound that made Ozzie's leg feel like it had just been lit on fire.

"It will prevent against infection," Tynx said firmly. "After a day or so, I decided Heinz knew what he was doing, so I left off. I think he only stuck by me because he didn't know what else to do. An enfield's bond is only broken when their charge dies. You weren't dead, though, just…gone. There, it's clean. I'm going to start stitching now. That's going to hurt, too."

Ozzie growled as he bit a throw pillow.

"I'm so sorry we left the way we did," Taryn said, taking a hold of Tynx's hand. "I can't explain it. We just woke up in our own beds."

"Gyldain thought something like that had happened. 'Spirited away most likely' he said."

"That sounds like him," she replied, rolling her eyes.

Tynx gave Taryn's hand a squeeze and smiled at her again.

"Ryn, I'm super-happy for you right now, but Tynx is my half-elf right now. Give him up," Ozzie interjected.

"Sorry," they said together.

Tynx then began the delicate process of stitching Ozzie's flesh back together. No one said anything for several minutes, save for Ozzie who had buried his face into the pillow and was yelling indiscernibly into it.

"Isn't...Leleplar?...really far away?" Smitty asked finally, breaking the silence. "How did you end up here?"

"After things settled down, I returned to Nerlua for a time and studied under the healer there. It was during that time I learned America was here and was fortunate to find a ship that would take me in exchange for working as a crewman."

"Wait, you mean you're not rich?" Ozzie said incredulously. "Weren't you showered in gold for helping defeat Vurnal? Agh! Be gentle!"

"You're done!" Tynx declared. "You'll have to keep it clean and take it easy, but you should be fine. I'll keep an eye on it."

"Thank you!" Ozzie exclaimed. "Do you have any more of that numbing stuff?"

"It won't do much good now, but it'll soothe the surface of the wound."

Tynx then fetched a small pot of the numbing cream from a shelf, which held the rest of his herbalism supplies, and began to apply it.

"So why aren't you rolling in it?" Ozzie pressed.

"No one knows what we did," Tynx explained, giving Ozzie one of those looks that meant he didn't understand where he got his ideas. "I mean, the elves did, which was the only reason they accepted me back. Accepted might be a strong word, but they weren't horrid and they taught me a lot. That's a reward in itself."

"Oh…" Ozzie's face fell.

"So you went to America to find them. That still doesn't explain why you're here," Smitty said, prompting Tynx to continue.

"I had no money and no idea where to go, so I plied my trade where I could to support myself and traveled from place to place. No one could help me. Most of them looked at me as if I was mad when I asked after you. America was not how you described it. Did I misunderstand?"

"No, you definitely did not," Taryn said. "It's not our country."

"I thought you said that's where you were from," Tynx replied, looking confused.

"Yes, but this land's America isn't ours. We got dropped here. Well, in France actually," Taryn explained. "The countries here have the same names as ours, but, as far as we can tell, they're full of characters and places and whatnot from books."

"There's a point," Ozzie said, gingerly testing out his newly mended leg. "What book are we in now?"

"Wait, books?" Tynx said, more confused than ever now.

"Not a clue," Taryn said, throwing up her hands. "Smitty, ideas?"

"I still don't understand how any of us ended up here!" Smitty cried in exasperation.

"Okay, one thing at a time," Ozzie said. "Tynx, finish your story."

"There's not much more to tell. I eventually crossed paths with Roelrhir and Nariel—they're two of the scouts that found you—and they invited me to come here with them. I was hesitant at first because, well, you know, but this community has very different ideas about my…heritage. I didn't know what else to do after running into nothing but dead ends, so I stayed and began to work with the healers. I've been trying to find answers in the records here, but I never found anything helpful. I guess I know why now."

"Erandiar said he knew of you," Ozzie said. "Do you think he knows what you did in Leleplar? Do you think that means he knows our part in it, too? Is that why he let us go so easily?"

"There's no way to know, but I think he somehow has an inkling," Tynx replied. "I don't think you were ever in any real danger. Roelrhir and Nariel had to have recognized Heinz. They know he wouldn't travel with you without good reason. They have to be cautious, though, with the way things have been of late."

"What do you mean?" Taryn asked.

Tynx sighed and said, "Why don't we talk more after dinner. You all must be famished."

"Good idea!" Ozzie said enthusiastically. "Just point the way."

Tynx put out rolls, cheese, and fruit to tide his guests over until he could get a simple fish dinner put together, for which Ozzie, Taryn, and Smitty were infinitely grateful. After the fight with the spider, the journey to Arbor Glen, and the excitement of finding Tynx, they had completely forgotten to eat and were starving.

Over the next few hours, Ozzie, Taryn, and Smitty regaled Tynx with the tale of their adventures thus far. Tynx was horrified when he heard of their run in with the Beast at Castle Rose, having heard awful tales about the place. He also promised to enlist help the very next day when he learned about the loss of Honey, Shadow, and Ember. Tynx had more trouble believing that everything in Terturelia was based on stories from his friends' world. It made him feel...odd. What did that mean for Leleplar? Did that say something about him and his role in their lives? Tynx was not able to articulate most of these thoughts, but he chose to simply accept it at face value in the end...as best he could anyway. He seriously doubted that he could untangle these philosophical enigmas in a single evening and so eventually put these ideas to bed in his head for the time being. When they were finally done, Tynx looked pensive.

"Do you know why you were brought here?"

"No!" Ozzie exclaimed in frustration. "Our only goal right now is to make it to Wonderland and find out how to get home. Lame!"

"I have a feeling there is more for you to accomplish here than just that."

"Why?" Taryn groaned. "Don't get me wrong. I'm *thrilled* that we saved your world, really and truly, but how many times did we almost die in the process?" Her voice then cracked when she added, "How many times have we almost died here already?"

Ozzie and Tynx fixed her with matching looks, and she sighed and looked away. Taryn wasn't trying to be selfish or cowardly, but just thinking about all the fear and danger and heartache from their time in Leleplar had set her sobbing on Ozzie's shoulder more than once over the last two years. She sincerely wondered if she hadn't developed some kind of mild stress disorder due to the experience, but there was literally no one to talk to about it besides Ozzie. Any mental healthcare professional would write her off as crazy. Why Ozzie didn't have any issues was beyond her. Now they were back to face who knew what death-defying peril, not to mention what they had already endured. She didn't know if she could go through all that again.

The only saving grace was that she wasn't alone. Having Smitty there to deal with the horses had proved to be helpful, even if he did close himself off and retreat mentally and emotionally. Ozzie was so eager, which *still* annoyed her to some extent, but he was wiser now and more cautious than he had been in Leleplar. He had also been the glue that held her and Smitty together this whole time. He was their leader, so to speak, and, for all his limited hands-on experience, he was pretty good at this adventuring thing. Heinz had made it better, and Tynx was here now, too! They were actually in a better place now than they had ever been. Tynx and Heinz knew what they were doing and had the strength, experience, and skills to get them through this. Despite all of that, however, a small part of her brain still screamed in terror while hunching down into the fetal position, begging to just go home.

Tynx fixed Taryn with that intense gaze she knew meant he was searching her feelings. Being half-elf, Tynx was hypersensitive to the emotions of others, almost like a sixth sense. Taryn saw that glint of light in Tynx's eye, the one she knew was hers, and couldn't help but wonder if he could sense hers even more clearly because of what they had been through and the bond it had created. Unsolved mystery, she knew, but, nevertheless, she smiled at him when she saw it. Tynx put a hand on hers and spoke encouragingly.

"Try not to fret. I won't let anything happen to you." He had said *try* because he knew Taryn well enough to know that she would anyway.

"Plus, you know Heinz will bite the face off anyone that tries to mess with you," Ozzie added.

He too knew how Taryn felt and he wanted to be there to support her. Smitty, who was feeling more like an outsider than ever, used this opportunity to ask what kind of protections or defenses or whatever Tynx and Heinz could provide. This began an encouraging discussion about what Tynx had learned during his time with the elves in Nerlua and Arbor Glen.

His herbalism had improved remarkably. The elves of both lands were masters of the art, and Tynx had been an eager student. He had also learned to fight better, which was apparently due to formal training and as well as a few unintended altercations with other elves. That hadn't happened often, only a few times, but, as Tynx had said, accepted was a strong word for his homecoming to Nerlua.

After that, Tynx related what he had heard about the current state of affairs in Terturelia. He didn't know much, save for what Roelrhir and Nariel told him when they were home from their scouting missions, which was less and less often of late. The elves were preparing for something. Some of them were mobilizing, while others were leaving for an undying land in order to leave the realm forever.

Smitty jumped up in his chair while Ozzie choked on his water at hearing that. They stared at one another in shock for several moments before exploding.

"I know where we are!" Smitty cried.

"So do I!" Ozzie replied.

"Yes!"

"It could be anywhere! Any time, I mean!"

"We're talking about centuries, millennia even, of history here."

"Help?" Tynx said.

Ozzie and Smitty then gave a patched together synopsis of their thoughts, but their memories were fuzzy on many of the names and details, so they kept on correcting each other or backing up and rehashing what they had already covered. By the time they were done, neither Tynx nor Taryn had gained any additional knowledge on what the boys were talking about. To Taryn, though, it sounded like every fantasy-fiction story she had heard Ozzie talk about.

"You know what?" Taryn suggested. "Let's just not assume anything. It sounds like this place has had its share of trouble, so we should just focus on avoiding that."

The look that Ozzie and Smitty shared said that they weren't done debating the subject, but they would put it aside for now. Exhaustion finally kicked in after that, and Ozzie, Taryn, and Smitty ended up passing out on Tynx's furniture before he could even finish considering the best arrangements for everyone.

The next day, Ozzie, Taryn, and Smitty all woke up sore but happy. Ozzie's leg hurt again, and Tynx checked it for any signs of infection. He also asked Ozzie some questions about the injuries he had sustained to his hands during the escape from Castle Rose and did a quick examination just to be safe. Thankfully, Tynx said everything seemed to have healed just fine. As promised, Tynx arranged for a small party to go out and find the missing horses. What he hadn't said was that he planned on going with them.

"You can't leave us here!" Taryn protested. "We don't know where anything is. We don't know if they'll take our money. We just found you again, for goodness sake! You can't risk going out there and something happening!"

Tynx said nothing at first, but wrapped his arms around Taryn and held her tightly against him. Taryn returned the embrace and fought against the tears that were trying to eke out of her eyes.

"I cannot ask this of the others if I'm not willing to go myself," he finally told her. "I promise I'll be careful."

"When will you be back?" she whispered.

"Soon."

Tynx headed out with the search party the next morning, but not before personally taking Ozzie, Taryn, and Smitty around and introducing them to everyone they would need to know. This was mostly so the humans would know where to go to get food, but there was also the healing house, which Ozzie was instructed to visit every day. They were also assured that their money was good here.

Taryn tried to be strong when Tynx left. She put on a good show, but both Tynx and Ozzie knew the truth. Smitty could tell too after he found her crying by herself in the garden later on that day. He tried to encourage her, reminding her that Tynx was out with a team of super-fast, super-skilled elves, which helped a little, but he could see she wouldn't be okay until Tynx came back.

"Dude, why's Taryn so into the elf?" Smitty asked.

Ozzie was in the kitchen looking for something to fix for dinner. They would need to go shopping tomorrow. It was later on that same day, and Taryn was still in the garden. Smitty had sat with her a while but left Taryn to her thoughts after seeing that he wasn't going to make any more progress.

"What?" Ozzie asked in surprise, picking up an apple from a basket. "You mean Tynx? He's only half-elf."

"Whatever, you knew what I meant," Smitty insisted. "She's falling apart over him."

"You have to understand, they have a history, a pretty major one. He's the guy who saved the world with us last time and almost died with us and saved our lives…a couple of times. Like I said, there's a history there."

"I just don't see the point. It's not like anything can happen between them."

Ozzie stopped and turned towards his friend, looking at him curiously.

"Smitty, why are you bringing this up? Do you have a pony in this race?"

"She's my friend. I care about her," Smitty replied with a shrug.

"You have a thing for her!"

"No, I don't!"

"Yes, you do! You did the same thing with Liz and then Annie. You always oversell how much you don't care. Why do you do that with girls you're into?

Smitty sighed in frustration and confessed, "I don't know. I mean, she can be really fun and she's pretty."

"You've really thought this through."

"I don't know, Ozzie! Is this really the time to worry about that?"

"Dude, calm down. I'm sorry, but you are the one who brought it up. You're right, nothing can happen between them, but whatever they built in Leleplar obviously hasn't gone away despite being separated all this time. More importantly, no matter what happens, we're stuck together here and we're stuck with him for the foreseeable future. Are you going to be okay with that?"

"Yeah, yeah, I'll be fine," Smitty said, shrugging off the question like a jacket. "Don't worry about it." He hesitated a moment before adding, "You're not going to tell Taryn about this, are you? I know how you two are."

"You can trust me, man," Ozzie said sincerely. "I won't tell her."

Ozzie had already decided not to tell Taryn for several reasons, the main being the good of the group and success of the mission. Awkwardness and discord, especially over feelings he knew Taryn didn't reciprocate, between his friends wouldn't help anything.

Tynx and his party didn't return for over a week. By the end of it, even Ozzie was concerned. Taryn was fretful and snappish until Ozzie finally had to confront her and tell her she wasn't being fair to anyone, at which point she apologized and started crying. At this, Smitty motioned to indicate that he thought Taryn was being crazy. Ozzie waved him off as he held Taryn. He knew this was far better than how Taryn would have reacted two years ago. Back then, she would have closed off and stonewalled Ozzie. He knew she wouldn't be at peace again until Tynx came back, despite the way she tried to act like she was back to normal after this mini-breakdown.

Smitty was keenly interested in Arbor Glen, and he and Ozzie handled the business of keeping the larder, as Smitty took to calling the kitchen, stocked. They both loved getting to know Tynx's neighbors and the various merchants around and peppered them all with questions in order to figure out where in story-time they were. They had to be careful, though.

"If we reveal too much, we might clue someone into the future, which could change it!" Ozzie explained. "What if we end up destroying the world?!"

Smitty wasn't as concerned, but saw Ozzie's point. Even with all of their carefully worded questions, however, they weren't able to glean anything.

"Or being smashed together in an alternate reality has altered the storylines from what you know," Taryn suggested.

The three were scattered around Tynx's sitting room while Heinz gnawed on a deer skull, which he had managed to charm from a hunter. Taryn had ventured out with Ozzie and Smitty that day—part of her everything-is-fine-with-me-now act—and had listened to them debate the subject for most of the afternoon.

"Are you suggesting a crossover?" Ozzie asked. "Is James Bond going to show up with a battalion of elves behind him? Actually, that would be really cool!"

"No, that's dumb. I'm saying it's really unlikely that every story will play out exactly like the original version. Being in the same geographical region, they're going to bleed into each other and influence events. Heck, we've already influenced a handful without even trying."

Smitty and Ozzie exchanged looks and shrugged their shoulders. That was as good a thought as any they'd had so far.

"Or this is just an *untold* story!" Smitty suggested a moment later, and on the debate went.

Ozzie was good about making trips to the healing house, but quickly had to get used to the pain of his injured leg. The winterberries, as they had learned they were called, were apparently somewhat rare. They only grew at the height of summer and were a much sought after treat by many creatures, so the elves had to collect as many as they could in a very short amount of time. The healers didn't deem Ozzie's wound serious enough to waste the precious supply they had since he had a comfortable place to rest and heal now. Thankfully, however, there were no signs of infection. Ozzie had to admit it was tough at times, especially after his outings, but he pushed through the pain until Taryn or Smitty told him to sit down and rest.

The search party returned in the evening during a rainstorm, which Ozzie, Taryn, and Smitty all thought was far prettier here under shelter than out camping. Tynx called out as soon as he was through the door.

"Thank goodness you're okay!" Taryn gushed, giving him a huge hug. "And you're soaked."

Despite getting the front half of her body wet, Taryn was smiling brightly.

"Hey! Welcome back!" Smitty said, strolling after Taryn. "Did you find them?"

Tynx frowned and shook his head. "No. We tracked them for a few days, but the trail eventually went cold. I'm afraid they're gone."

"That sucks," Taryn sighed.

"You didn't even like the horses," Smitty pointed out.

"I liked having them," Taryn retorted. "I mean, they were fine and everything. They just...take Heinz for example. Heinz communicates."

"Horses communicate, too. You just don't understand them."

"I *know* Heinz will never hurt me. He'll never freak out and trample me or run away."

"You have to admit, Heinz is a very special case," Tynx said.

Taryn stuck her tongue out at Tynx and made a face. Tynx returned the sentiment, which made Taryn laugh.

"Where's Ozzie?" he then asked.

"Sleeping," Smitty replied.

"How is he faring? Is his leg healing? Did he go to the healers like I told him?"

"Look at you, so worried about your patient," Taryn teased. "Oz will be flattered."

"He's great," Smitty added.

"Good to hear," Tynx said. "Well, if you will excuse me, I'm going to go change into some dry clothes."

"Dinner will be ready within the hour," Taryn called after him.

"You're a miracle!" Tynx called behind him.

Taryn and Smitty then headed into the kitchen to work on the promised meal. Cooking was certainly a challenge in Arbor Glen without any modern conveniences. Of the three, Ozzie had the most experience, followed by Taryn and then Smitty. They had all done reasonably well with soups and stews in the pot that hung over the fire, though. Many of the ingredients were strange to them, so some of their meals had ended up with unusual flavor combinations, but they were learning.

Unsurprisingly, Ozzie emerged for dinner, and Tynx was very glad to have a hot meal so soon after coming home, even if the rabbit stew was overly sweet. Thus began the weeks Ozzie, Taryn, and Smitty spent in Arbor Glen. They couldn't go anywhere until

Ozzie's leg had completely healed. They used the time wisely, however. The first thing they had to do was replace some of their gear that had been lost with the horses. It had been previously agreed that Ozzie, Taryn, and Smitty would carry what they absolutely could not do without just in case a situation like this arose. That meant food, money, basic tools, blankets, and an extra set of clothing were in their packs. Everything else—the tent, pallets, the rest of their clothing, tack and other equine gear, and the rest of their camping supplies—were all gone. The clothes were the first thing to be replaced, while everything else could wait. Once that was done, they spent a considerable amount of time researching records from the Hall of Knowledge, usually while Tynx was working with the healers. Specifically, Ozzie, Taryn, and Smitty were looking to learn more about Terturelia, become more familiar with its geography, and get an idea of what else they might encounter. The possibilities seemed endless.

England was huge, easily the largest country in Terturelia, which meant there was a fair bit of it that was unexplored, or at least unmapped. Ozzie, Taryn, and Smitty had to piece together bits of information they found in scrolls and books and half-drawn maps. There were some well-established areas like the city of London and then there were great swaths of land that went by different names depending on the source. Never-Never Land was an island off the west coast of England, and Wonderland was tucked up to the north. There were some mountains to the east, which created a border between England and Germany. The mountains were labeled *The Carpathians*, which confused all three of them.

"The Carpathian mountain range isn't in England," Taryn said. "I don't think England has much in the way of mountains, do they?"

"I think there are some, but, no, the Carpathians are somewhere else in Europe. Are they in Germany?"

"No, they're further over," Ozzie replied. "I'm pretty sure they're in Romania or something."

"That sounds right," Taryn agreed, "Eastern Europe area."

"So why are they here?" Ozzie asked.

Taryn snapped her fingers and looked at Smitty, saying, "*Dracula*. Mr. Arthur's class."

"Yes!" Smitty agreed. "Wait, Stoker was Irish, wasn't he? Oh, but he lived in London."

"Another point for the Irish," Taryn said, making an imaginary tally mark in the air.

"What is it with you and vampires?" Ozzie cut in. Taryn shot him a look, and he added, "Smitty, did I ever tell you about Ralen?"

"Oz, I will poison your food," Taryn began.

"I can tell this is going to be good," Smitty laughed.

Ozzie wasn't a few sentences into his story before Taryn decided she needed to be anywhere else, but that didn't stop her from hearing about it for the rest of the day.

# Chapter 14

Ozzie, Taryn, and Smitty felt as close to experts as possible by the time the arrow wound on Ozzie's leg had closed up properly. It was still a little stiff, which Tynx warned might never go away completely, but it was healed. For Ozzie and Taryn, it felt a little like they had two lives, which had suddenly come together to merge and mix.

On the one hand, having Tynx and Heinz back in their lives made them feel like they were back in Leleplar. They felt independent, separated from all things of the world they knew. Getting back into a routine with them was old hat...until they looked at Smitty. Smitty was the link back to college and parents and exams and television, and, despite how much he enjoyed Arbor Glen, he was an outsider. Taryn and Ozzie made every effort to make him feel included, and Tynx was always congenial and inviting, but, underneath everything, there was a common knowledge. Smitty had not been with them the first time. Smitty was not on the same level of understanding. Smitty could never truly conceive of the horrors they had endured together. No one said anything about this, but every time someone mentioned something about the adventure in Leleplar, the knowledge was there, sitting amongst them like another person, drawing a line between them.

It was decided after Ozzie's leg was completely healed that Tynx would venture back out with the group and act as a guide. It was an easy decision to make. After all, Tynx had better survival skills that Ozzie, Taryn, and Smitty put together. Plus, they all had to admit it seemed far more than a coincidence that they had crossed paths again. Tynx helped Ozzie, Taryn, and Smitty get their supplies restocked, pulling from what he had in his cottage first and then instructing them what to buy and from whom. He also had to ask Erandiar for his blessing to leave. After all, the elves had taken him in and provided for him. Erandiar was easily amenable and wished the group his best. Ozzie, Taryn, and Smitty had accompanied Tynx to see Erandiar so that they could thank him again. He had a look on his face when they were leaving that said he knew more than he was saying, but none of them were willing to try and pry it out of him. After that, there were the logistics to work out. Which way would they take? Who would be responsible for what? How would they handle the sleeping arrangements, which was quite possibly the most difficult subject of all.

"I don't have much money, certainly not enough to rent a room every night," Tynx confessed. "I'll have to camp where I can and meet up with you each morning."

"No," Ozzie and Taryn objected together.

"It's stupid for you to camp out by yourself," Ozzie added.

"Heinz can stay with him, can't he?" Smitty asked.

Tynx shook his head and said, "There's no way he'll be that far from Taryn for so long."

"But can we really afford two rooms every night?" Smitty asked.

"We don't need two," Taryn said, genuinely baffled at the idea. "We'll rent one just as we've been doing and we'll all share it. Why would we do anything else?"

"I wouldn't presume to leech from your finances and become a burden on you," Tynx explained seriously.

"Please, dude," Ozzie replied, slapping Tynx on the back. "We're way past that."

"Um, it's already pretty cozy as it is, though," Smitty said dubiously. "You want to add to that?"

"Do you have a better idea?" Taryn asked him.

"I think Smitty's just uncomfortable because you don't split three ways, Ryn," Ozzie joked.

"I don't follow," she said, giving Ozzie a look.

"Think about it," he laughed. "You've been a bedtime-buffer between Smitty and me this whole time. Now one of us has to snuggle with another dude."

Taryn couldn't help but laugh at that, especially as Smitty looked more uncomfortable than ever. Tynx even smiled a little.

"Don't worry, Smitty," Taryn said after a moment, trying to make him feel better. "We'll all take turns sleeping on the floor each night."

Ozzie laughed harder and said, "That doesn't help! What about the nights you're on the floor?"

"Well, you can have Heinz be a buffer instead," she said, putting her hands up helplessly.

"I think it would be better if you just never sleep on the floor," Smitty suggested, trying to feel less awkward.

"I won't say no to that," she said agreeably. "But, purely in the interest of fairness, let me know if you guys decide you're okay snuggling."

Ozzie then made a joke about elf-cuddles and gave Tynx an exaggerated eyebrow waggle. Smitty never took Taryn up on her offer.

The group set out bright and early the next morning, already feeling somewhat worse for wear. Tynx had celebrated his farewells with his friends—elven and otherwise—the night before, and Ozzie, Taryn, and Smitty had all learned that elves didn't do anything by halves. They were exhausted but optimistic as the morning sunlight slipped down through the trees into the valley. Progress without the horses was slower than Ozzie, Taryn, and Smitty were used to, but they felt good about their guide and guardian.

After all the research Ozzie, Taryn, and Smitty had done, and with Tynx's learned knowledge of the country of England, the group was able to discuss at length where they were headed and what they might encounter. There were bound to be inns around and within the major settlements, so that probably meant comfortable nights...provided Heinz didn't frighten the clientele too much. In between was less certain, so they planned to camp more often than not just in case. Almost immediately, the improvement in Tynx's skills showed. He helped Heinz hunt in the evenings now and easily identified food that was good to eat. The first time he pointed out some wild mushrooms they could gather, however, Taryn vehemently objected.

"Very well, no mushrooms," Tynx conceded, "but I promise I wouldn't let that happen to you again."

Taryn had sworn off mushrooms of all kinds after a mix-up in Leleplar had almost killed her. Camp was set up quickly and efficiently, and Tynx was judicious when he assigned responsibilities to his charges.

Where Tynx could not help was in speculating what other stories they might come across. It became a regular thing, a highly useful game almost, for Ozzie, Taryn, and Smitty to suggest various books or characters they might yet encounter. Taryn and Smitty, being English majors, were better read than Ozzie, but most of their knowledge was based in classical literature. Ozzie enjoyed reading when he could as well, but he mostly read more modern works of fiction, and nearly all of them were of the sci-fi or fantasy genre. They all felt rather good about their circumstances, what with all of their collective literary knowledge plus skillful protectors. Things eventually got back to as close to normal as they could. Even the sleeping arrangement awkwardness seemed to ebb, though that took a bit more time and depended on what type of rooms were available at each stop, if any.

It was several days before the group had made it out of the deep woods and even longer before they emerged into an area that was simply called The Moors. It was cold and eerie, and fog crept along the ground late into the morning and started again in early evening. It put everyone on edge, and there wasn't any lodging to be found, so they were forced to camp in the dank grass. The howling began the first night, and Ozzie, Taryn, and Smitty all looked at each other at once.

"Werewolf," Smitty said.

"We don't know that!" Taryn snapped, clearly more afraid than angry.

Thankfully, nothing bothered them in the end that night, save for the strange, glowing figure that appeared over the ridge of a hill, which Heinz warded off with a salvo of fierce threatening barks. Nevertheless, Tynx assigned watches every night until they were out of The Moors. The stress of the experience and lack of sleep, however, made for very crabby travelers. Ozzie snapped at Taryn, who snapped back, and they both quickly agreed to keep their mouths shut for a good while. Smitty started complaining about Tynx's task assignments, and Ozzie joined in to defend Tynx.

"Tynx knows better than us," Ozzie said.

"We did just fine before without him," Smitty retorted.

"You'd rather I leave?" Tynx asked calmly.

"Are you crazy?" Taryn demanded, joining the fray.

"No! I just don't want to always have to do what he says," Smitty said.

"How would you have it go then?" Tynx asked.

"I don't know," Smitty said petulantly.

"Look, let's go for a walk," Ozzie suggested. "We've all probably had too much together-time lately."

"So why are we going together?" Smitty asked.

"Because something bad always happens when one person goes off by themselves," Ozzie said.

"Do you think they'll be okay?" Taryn asked, looking in the direction Ozzie and Smitty had gone.

Ozzie and Smitty had just left, leaving her, Tynx, and Heinz alone at camp.

"I should think so," Tynx replied.

He knew Ozzie wouldn't do anything foolish and was fairly certain he could keep Smitty from doing the same.

Taryn felt Tynx's hand wrap around hers, and she looked up to see him looking back down at her. He was smiling, which made Taryn smile too, and Tynx pulled her close. Wrapping his arms around her, he held her tightly.

Since they had been reunited, Taryn and Tynx hadn't had a great deal of time to themselves. They had taken walks now and then in Arbor Glen, but they had never been long—neither of them had wanted to make Ozzie or Smitty feel left out—and there was the rest of the city all around them. These walks had been happy but hesitant. Taryn and Tynx were still catching up, getting reacquainted, and there was of course that universe-sized roadblock of knowledge between them. What could happen between them when, eventually, Ozzie, Taryn, and Smitty were all meant to go back home? That, along with Tynx's incredible chivalry, had kept things nearly platonic between them…nearly.

"I still can't quite believe you're here," Tynx said. "I feel like I'm dreaming and about to wake up to disappointment again."

"Again?" Taryn asked, though she didn't stop hugging him. "Did you dream about me?"

"All the time."

With that, Tynx kissed Taryn on the top of her head, and Taryn's heart quickened. Tynx had never kissed her before. This was very exciting! But wait…what was she supposed to do now?!

"I'm sorry," Tynx said, releasing his grip on her. "I didn't mean to be forward, I just—"

"No, you're fine!" Taryn stuttered awkwardly. "I—how did you—of course! Your super-sense thing." She could feel her face getting hot. This was so embarrassing! How was she able to face off against monsters but couldn't help babbling like an idiot in front of Tynx? "Can you maybe turn it off? Just for a minute?"

Tynx looked baffled and then pleased as understanding dawned on him.

"Taryn Kelly, do I make you nervous?" he teased.

"What? No! I mean…seriously, can you turn it off or can't you?"

"Why would you ever be embarrassed in front of me?"

"Gah! Why do you have to call it out like that?!" She covered her face with her hands, wishing to be anywhere but here at the moment, trying to calm herself.

She felt Tynx grasp her wrists gently and pull her hands away from her face. There he was, not inches from her face, smiling affectionately. Taryn still felt mortified. Tynx could sense every emotion she felt. He had to know how happy that little kiss had made her, but that was surely being overshadowed now by great waves of humiliation rolling off of her.

"Don't hide," he said simply and drew her back into his arms.

Tynx kissed the top of her head once more as he held her, but nothing more. Taryn still felt stupid about her reaction, but Tynx was making it better. What was more, he had given himself a do-over on the kiss, which gave them both an opportunity to experience the happiness it brought…properly this time.

"What's going on, man?" Ozzie asked seriously, sitting down on a rock.

The two had walked in silence for about five minutes until Ozzie decided they had gone far enough. There was nothing around them but more rocks and grass. Mist was crawling across the ground like languid, creepy eavesdroppers. Smitty said nothing, but scowled angrily at the ground.

"Come on," Ozzie urged, "this isn't helping anything."

"I just want to go home," Smitty said finally.

"I know, dude. We all do. We're working on it, remember?" Smitty was looking away now, and Ozzie was getting frustrated. He took a deep breath and then asked calmly, "Did you hear what I said?"

"I hear something," Smitty said distractedly. "It's coming from over there."

He pointed further out into The Moors, and Ozzie's brain switched gears. He listened hard and, sure enough, he heard something, too. It sounded like voices, but they cracked as they spoke, and sounded odd. Were they singing? No, it was more like chanting. The two crept towards the sound, crouching low and hiding behind rocks as they went. It wasn't long before they found the source of the sound.

Three women were gathered around a small fire tossing what looked like hair into it. Or maybe it could have been moss or grass or something. It was difficult to tell from this distance, but the smell coming from the fire was pretty good confirmation. A grey cat was there as well, sitting patiently and watching the fire. The women all looked strange; it was unclear whether they were old or young. From one angle, as they revolved around the fire, one would look old and haggard and hideous. Then, as they made the turn, the features would shift and look young and fresh and gentle. Their hair was either blond or white or silver, but the drab cloaks they wore never changed. Neither Ozzie nor Smitty could make out what the women were chanting, but they couldn't be sure if it was because their voices seemed to keep on changing, or if it was the wind, or if they were speaking a different language.

They had only been there a few minutes before Ozzie motioned to Smitty that they should leave. He didn't know who these women were or what they were up to, but he didn't want to risk finding out. Smitty shook his head at first, indicating that they should stay just a few more minutes. Ozzie scowled and shook his head firmly. Too risky. Smitty didn't look happy, but, after a huff and a great rolling of eyes, agreed. They turned back to leave when one of the women called out shrilly above the other two, pointing a gnarled, filthy finger straight at Ozzie, her face vacillating between youth and hag.

"The sapling cannot bear the weight of water. Grasp it not! Lest it break and you be drowned! Turn to the flame; guard it. Embrace sovereignty!"

Both boys had begun to back away by now, frightened by the scene before them. The other two women joined the first in pitch, but they couldn't be understood. Ozzie and Smitty turned and ran, thinking they might be turned into toads or killed or cursed at any moment. They ran all the way back to the camp, where they found Taryn leaning against Tynx watching the sunset.

"What's wrong?" Tynx asked at once.

"Are you guys okay?" Taryn asked, breaking away from Tynx.

Both Ozzie and Smitty were panting and holding their sides painfully. They were pale with wide eyes and shaking.

"I...I don't know," Ozzie managed to gasp.

"There are people back there," Smitty said. "They're doing something weird. They started screaming at us."

"Were you pursued?" Tynx asked immediately.

Ozzie and Smitty, after exchanging a few notes, decided they didn't think they had been. They then recounted everything they could remember about the incident, which shook them up even further.

Putting a hand on Tynx's arm, Taryn asked, "Do we go looking for them?"

"Best not," Tynx said. "We don't know if they could actually cause us harm. If they can, I'd like to hope they either can't or won't try to find us. We'll set another watch for tonight."

"But what about what they said to Ozzie?" Taryn pressed. "What does it mean? Shouldn't we try and find out?"

"At best, they were mad gibberings," Tynx replied.

"And at worst?" Ozzie asked.

"Dude, they were probably just crazy," Smitty said, clearly trying to convince himself as much as Ozzie.

Ozzie said nothing, but was still clearly upset. He knew Tynx was making the right decision to stay put; that kept everyone as safe as possible, but what if that woman had done something to him? What if she had put some kind of a hex on him? He mentally checked himself for any bad feelings, looked at his skin for marks or warts or something, and recited to himself the names of those people in his life most dear to him.

*Smitty walked through a sunny field of tall grass, letting his hand idly brush by the blades. Why was he here? Why didn't he really care?*

*"Hello, Loren," came a voice. It was soft and lovely.*

*Smitty turned and looked to see a woman standing about fifty feet away. She had long black hair and a warm smile. Her eyes were green a bit like Taryn's but brighter.*

*"Hello," Smitty replied curiously. "Um, where are we?"*

*And why was he so calm about all this?*

*"I needed a place where we could talk in private...away from your friends."*

*"So am I dreaming?"*

*The woman smiled wider and nodded.*

*"Oh!" That made sense. No wonder he wasn't weirded out by their surroundings or this strange yet beautiful woman. "If you don't mind me asking then, ma'am, who are you? Galadriel? Mab...erm, sorry, Queen Mab?"*

*The woman's smile nearly faltered. She knew of the Galadriel Smitty had mentioned and, unfortunately, knew Mab personally. Besides that, projecting herself into Smitty's dream was tiring. She was running out of time.*

*"That is not important now. I have come to warn you. You cannot trust your companions."*

*"What?" Smitty asked, worried now. "What are you saying?"*

*The boy was getting upset, which made the web of the dream unsteady. She had to stabilize his feelings again.*

*"Allow me to clarify, my dear," the woman said soothingly. "The enfield, he is a danger. Your companions mean you no harm, but they trust the beast's judgment too much. You know that creature does not trust you."*

*"Taryn won't let Heinz do anything to me," Smitty argued defensively.*

*Too defensively. The seed had been planted. The woman approached Smitty carefully and reached out to place a hand on his shoulder. It was now that Smitty realized she was tall, about his height actually, and she was looking at him with a mixture of care and sympathy.*

*"Just be careful, my dear," she said softly. "Be cautious. If you need me, I will be there. I'll be watching; I will find you if you look for me."*

*With that, the dream began to fade. Smitty tried to call after the woman as she receded from him, but it was all over before he had the chance. He felt himself falling back into dreamless sleep, but he wouldn't forget about the dream even after he awoke the next day.*

"Hey! You're not green or hairy," Smitty said tiredly the next morning, rubbing the sleep out of his eyes and trying to switch gears back to his friend's plight instead of his dream.

Ozzie tried to laugh, but it came out as a weak chuckle. It had been a rough night. Ozzie had volunteered to take the first watch, thinking if an attack were coming, it would follow close on the heels of his encounter. The howling was heard again, but it was much further off, which was good, but also bad. Bad because it put one more idea in Ozzie's head as to what might become of him. After his shift was over, he had tried to lie down and sleep, but sleep wouldn't come. He was too afraid of what he might find when he woke up. He ended up sitting with Taryn for her watch, which was the last of the night, and confided his fears in her.

"From what you said, it didn't sound like a curse or anything," she said, trying to be optimistic. "It sounded...like...well, cryptic."

"Yup, I got cryptic marked off the list already. Thanks for that," Ozzie joked, trying to lighten the mood for them both.

Taryn smiled at him and bumped him with her shoulder. Even at the worst of times, he looked out for others.

"Like Tynx said, maybe it's nothing."

Ozzie nodded and spent the rest of the night and the waking hours holding onto Taryn's hand like an anchor. She distracted him for a bit, even made him laugh, by telling him about her absurd post-kiss freak out in front of Tynx. By the time Smitty had made his comment that morning, the worry was no longer fresh, but had found a niche within Ozzie's mind like an unpleasant tenant with no intention of leaving anytime soon.

Everyone was so thrilled to be out of The Moors a few days later, they actually allowed themselves an extra day of rest from traveling. Thankfully, the people that lived around that area were tough and not easily frightened by Heinz, despite his size. The group spent most of their time there sleeping. The constant tension coupled with the lack of sleep—they had shared night watch duties every night—plus the energy it took to travel fast enough to get out of The Moors as soon as possible had exhausted everyone. There probably would have been more arguing had everyone not been ready to pass out at any moment. Being able to rest properly, however, gave them energy to refocus on their conflicts. Smitty was still clearly unhappy and he got into it with Taryn when she accused him of sulking. Ozzie and Tynx had to step in to separate them.

"I'm so sick and tired of him pouting like a baby!" she cried. "He's acting like such a victim."

"Well, we don't all have a personal guard dog and knight on a white horse, do we?" Smitty snapped back. Heinz began to growl at Smitty, to which he said, "Rein your beast in already!"

Taryn opened her mouth, ready to let fly a barrage of insults, but Ozzie interrupted her.

"Taryn, can it! Think back to your first time here. How well did you take it? Smitty, I don't know how to help you, man. It is what it is, but at least we're all in this *together*."

"I know how you feel, Smitty," Tynx added calmly. "It's—"

"You do not!" Smitty snarled. "Leave this to the humans."

Tynx's lips stretched into a thin, angry line as he forced himself to keep his mouth shut. Though he knew Smitty had been told of his ability to sense the feelings of those around him, he also knew this fact must have been forgotten. Tynx sensed fear, anger, jealousy, and loneliness in Smitty. He had sensed it since they had first met, and it had only gotten worse. That made Tynx concerned for what Smitty might do.

"Look, let's all calm down," Ozzie said, forcing himself to be calm as he said this. What Smitty said to Tynx made Ozzie angry, but, like Tynx, he knew it would only make things worse if he retaliated. "I know what a tough spot you're in. What can we do to make it better?"

"I don't know!"

"You keep saying that; it doesn't help us. You have to meet me halfway here. We're friends, remember?" Smitty huffed petulantly, and Ozzie added, "This is your chance to say your piece."

Smitty shrugged coldly. Ozzie took a deep breath, doing his best to keep his patience.

"How about this: Let's start fresh. Can we all just start over? New adventure, clean slates, all of that."

"What, we just let go of everything? Just forget about it?" Taryn asked incredulously.

"Yes," Ozzie replied simply. "Burn all our grievances against each other."

"Just like that?" she asked.

"We did, and the stuff between us went a heck of a lot deeper," Ozzie replied.

Taryn's brow furrowed unhappily. She knew he was right, but she didn't like it. Taryn held grudges. She didn't just drop unresolved issues like they didn't matter. They mattered! True, Ozzie and her issues had been patched up quickly, but they were facing death, and she didn't want to die with discord between them, especially since they had been best friends all their lives. She didn't have that history with Smitty, nor were they staring death in the face…at least not at this current moment. Smitty wasn't being particularly fair or, in her personal opinion, brave. She didn't respect that, and this wasn't a situation wherein they had the luxury to be scaredy cats. True, she had been…well…okay, she had been fairly horrible upon first arriving in Leleplar, but she couldn't have been as bad as Smitty. And she had learned and knew now that her behavior could have had much worse consequences. Despite all of this, she couldn't think of a really good argument to make against Ozzie's idea, mostly because, as frustrated as she was with Smitty, a little part of her understood and sympathized, even if the rest of her wanted to disregard that.

"Where'd this idea come from?" she asked for lack of anything better to say.

Ozzie shrugged and said, "Marriage counseling, my mom and dad's when they went through a rough patch. What do you all say? Can we begin again? I'll start. Hi! My name is Ozzie, and I kind of dig this even if I don't know a lot of these characters and stories. I don't have many discernable skills, but I think my winning smile makes up for that."

He grinned widely like a lunatic.

Taryn and Tynx couldn't help but smile at that. Smitty looked more receptive than he had a moment ago, but he was keeping his face hard.

"Hello, my name is Tynixenal. You all may call me Tynx," he said, joining in. "I'm a half-elf and, while I do have healing skills, my goal is to keep you all so safe I won't have to employ any of them."

Taryn looked at Smitty, who looked back at her. She dearly wanted to hold onto her grudge, to lash out at Smitty—her anger from before hadn't ebbed much—but she looked to Tynx and Ozzie, who looked back at her plaintively. She so hated being wrong…

"My name is Taryn," she blurted quickly, putting the force of her anger behind her words in the hopes of expelling some of it through her silly, fake introduction. "This is Heinz, my enfield, who chose me because I'm full-blooded Irish—and proud of it, thank you very much—and I have a bad temper, which has a tendency to get me into trouble. I'm working on this."

Smitty sighed and said, "My name is Smitty. Don't call me Loren because I hate that, and I'm new to this whole other world thing."

"Great to meet everyone! We should have food to celebrate our reintroductions," Ozzie said cheerfully.

They each ate a quarter of a pear as their peace-reestablishing ceremony. Ozzie, quite dramatically, asked life, the universe, and everything for a blessing on their fruit before anyone was allowed to take a bite. Taryn didn't know about anyone else, but she was still having trouble just dropping everything, but it was so difficult to stay angry when Ozzie was continuing to be so entertaining about the whole thing.

*Erik watched the two men from the shadows, sizing them up and wondering if this was really worth his time. Clopin had said they would be easy to buy. He had said this as he stood surrounded by his men. Erik was not unknown in the criminal underworld of Paris, but they avoided each other, and that seemed to suit everyone just fine. Everyone knew if he had the desire Erik could be King of the Truands instead of Clopin, but he had no such ambitions. Still, Clopin didn't know that and the infamous Phantom, who was apparently not nearly as dead as the papers said, was here before him now. He seemed pleased when Erik asked for information about whom he could hire in England. Perhaps that meant the Phantom was leaving the city.*

*The road here had been long and full of setbacks and questions. Now, as Erik watched the two men argue about some game they were playing, he could feel his patience growing very thin.*

*"You two bicker like old women," he snapped, sweeping out from his hiding place.*

*The new voice was sudden and unexpected. The two men spun to face the owner, hands on swords, but recoiled automatically when they saw Erik.*

*"What grave did you roll out of?" one of the men jeered.*

*Erik reached out and grabbed the man who had spoken by the throat, lifting him up and cutting off his air in one swift motion.*

*"You must be the one they call Conrade. I heard you were a bit of a cretin." Looking to the other, he added smoothly, "Borachio, I presume?"*

*Conrade gasped and fought, but his attacker was extraordinarily strong. Borachio stood and unsheathed his sword. Erik effortlessly caught Borachio's wrist with his free hand and squeezed until he dropped the sword.*

*He then dropped Conrade, straightened his waistcoat, and said calmly, "Come now, gentlemen. There's no need for any of this. I've come to offer you employment."*

*"We have employment, sir," Borachio scoffed.*

*"Whatever you are being paid, I will double it."*

*Borachio and Conrade, who was gingerly rubbing his neck, exchanged a glance. They nodded together and turned back to the stranger.*

# Chapter 15

The next major stop was London. They arrived, but not before quite a bit more travel time, a few nights camping out, and a chance encounter with a funny, mismatched group of people on a quest of their own. All of them, save for a one, had been very kind and courteous, and Tynx was keen to compare notes of the land, news, and other information with them, but he could not offer much to help them in their search. He did, however, share some of his healing supplies and what knowledge he could.

Ozzie was bothered because he thought the group seemed familiar, but he couldn't recall why. Taryn seemed to remember something from their childhood that might explain why, but not much more than that. Something in the gaps in Ozzie's memory made him afraid for the group. He believed he needed to warn them of something, but couldn't remember what exactly. It bothered him quite a lot, but Smitty reminded him, even if he could remember, he couldn't risk altering their storyline. Taryn disagreed, mainly because they already had altered the storyline just by their meeting, but couldn't deny that Smitty might have a valid point as well.

One very fortunate bit of information did come forth when Tynx mentioned the encounter with the strange women in The Moors. The group's leader was excited to hear of this and revealed that these were very likely the same three they were looking to find. Ozzie was at first frightened to learn the three women were enchantresses, but Taryn quickly reminded him that nothing had happened to him so far and therefore probably never would. The two parties went their separate ways after only an afternoon and the following night together, and Ozzie asked them to please take care on their journey.

It wasn't long after that Tynx, Ozzie, Taryn, Smitty, and Heinz finally reached the city of London. It was magnificent! As had been predicted, the time period was at least one hundred years in the past, if not more. It was hard to tell, as the Terturelian calendar system went by centuries, years, and then days...or something like that. The first newspaper they found, which was a surprising discovery in itself, was dated *13th Century, Year 93, Day 8-22*. Not even Tynx knew what to make of that, as the elves had a completely different lunar calendar system. Even so, the technology in England had come far enough for there to be daily newspapers, which said to Ozzie, Taryn, and Smitty that it was somewhat recent, historically speaking.

The city spread out like a great, sleeping creature, breathing in and out, shuffling this part or that limb in its turn. It was clearly the longest-established place the group had been so far, save perhaps for Arbor Glen. Massive stone buildings rose up from the cobblestone streets like monoliths. Mustachioed men armed with canes and dressed in black coats walked about what must have been the business sector of the city, while ladies in long dresses and bustles walked the parks, some pushing prams and others with small companion dogs. The sky was overcast, a solid sheet of steely grey, but it fortunately was not raining.

Taryn and Smitty immediately wanted to explore, to discover what landmarks existed here as they did back home and what was different. Ozzie was for that plan as well, but Tynx, who disliked and distrusted human cities, especially those of this size, insisted that they get settled and do some reconnaissance first. He already had a plan as to where they would stay, too.

Knowing they would be stopping here, Tynx had asked for advice from his fellow elves before they left Arbor Glen. The more experienced scouts had recommended The Falcon and Bairn. It was a popular stopover for travelers of all kinds including sailors, as it was close to the docks. That also meant it was a little rough around the edges, but it would also be cheaper than some of the nicer inns closer to the city center. Because there were so many different types of people coming through, The Falcon and Bairn was also tolerant of unique needs...like housing a massive enfield.

Tynx was adamant on this point, so the group headed there first. At the front desk, which also served as the bar, Tynx dropped a few names that seemed to mean something to the taciturn innkeeper, James, paid for their room up front—standard practice here apparently—and was given a key. The establishment was really quite large, larger than most of the places the group had stayed before, and so the room they were given was of good size as well. The best part was that there were actually three beds, so Smitty and Tynx each got their own, while Ozzie and Taryn shared. It was late afternoon and still mostly light outside despite the clouds, so Tynx agreed that they could have a walkabout in the immediate area and get to know their surroundings.

"London isn't next to the ocean, is it?" Ozzie asked as they walked.

"Nope," Taryn replied. "It's inland."

The area around Falcon and Bairn was busy with shops of all kinds, people coming and going, and lots of pubs. The populace was very nearly entirely human, but the group spotted one or two people who were clearly of a different heritage. What type of heritage wasn't exactly clear, however. Ozzie wanted to follow these few individuals and make friends, but no one else thought that was a good idea. That being the case, he settled for making note of all the different places to eat around them. They ended up grabbing dinner from a pie shop and headed back to The Falcon and Bairn for an early night.

"I'm telling ye, Sir Danvers Carew was clubbed to death right there in the street. 'Parrently, it was some small, mean bloke by the name of Hyde. Stick broke right in half."

"Where'd you hear that rot?"

"From the maid who seen it happen. She said he was like a wild animal when he did it."

Ozzie, Taryn, Smitty, and Tynx listened carefully to the man who recounted the story of the murder to his friend. They were one of only a few groups there in the great common room of The Falcon and Bairn, and the man was so excitable he was forgetting to watch his volume.

"No one goes out by themselves," Tynx whispered seriously.

That was easily agreed upon. It was their day for sightseeing, but the shine had been taken off of the event by the heinous murder that all of London was buzzing about. Nevertheless, they headed out and were astonished by what they saw.

Many of the historical monuments—Nelson's column and the lions of Trafalgar Square, all of the museums, Big Ben (but not the Houses of Parliament)—were missing. Buckingham Palace was there, but it was smaller and not quite as grand as Ozzie expected and Taryn and Smitty knew it to be. Granted, it was still very impressive, but actually less so than the Tower of London. The Tower looked just as it was supposed to and was in full use as a prison. They decided against trying to get closer when they learned of this and saw a group of men being led inside in chains. The group was pleasantly surprised to come across a few places they hadn't expected, like 221B Baker Street. The layout of the city was very different as well, which they had expected given that Terturelia's London was a seaside city and earth's was not. The Thames was a harbor that eventually turned into a river, and Tower Bridge did span it, but closer to the outer edge of the city. The bridge, interestingly, supported a number of small merchants that had set up shops and booths along either side of it. The current reigning monarch, the group learned, was an elderly but adventurous king by the name of Henry Wyvernbain, or Henry the Eleventh.

"Do the elves recognize his authority?" Smitty asked.

"Oh no," Tynx explain. "He only reigns over Middlesex."

Both Smitty and Ozzie started sniggering at that, and there was a great rolling of eyes from Taryn.

Ozzie, Taryn, and Smitty couldn't feel like proper tourists simply because there were no others here. No tours going through Westminster Abbey, no guides on top of buses telling their passengers to look left and right, no shops or street vendors hawking Union Jack souvenirs, none of that. The people that walked the streets were just everyday denizens going about their business. It was so refreshing! Ozzie, Taryn, and Smitty were free to immerse themselves in the culture of this new England without the hassle of ogling crowds. Tynx was happy to be along for the ride, having already been all over Terturelia.

Tynx's experience as a half-elf in Terturelia hadn't been anything like what it had been in his native country of Leleplar. Back home, both humans and elves alike had shunned him for his mixed heritage. He was seen as an outsider by both races, unable to completely fit in anywhere. Here, however, he was regarded mostly with curiosity. The people of Terturelia were familiar with strange and magical things, and elves, though only slightly less reclusive than their cousins across the water, were common knowledge. There were even some, hardened travelers mostly, that weren't even fazed by the idea of a half-elf. Tynx had quickly found he liked being unimpressive. Even with this understanding, though, he still couldn't shake his dislike of cities.

As his charges walked and looked and whispered to one another, he kept a watchful eye on them and their surroundings. He often looked to Heinz for cues, but the day went peacefully. It had been long and full of walking, however, and everyone was ready for a good meal that evening. They eagerly ordered dinner in the common room of The Falcon and Bairn and then settled before the fireplace to recount the adventures of the day. At one point, Ozzie offered to get them all something to drink and headed up to the bar. It seemed like it was going to be a very nice ending to a very good day. That is, until Heinz noticed trouble approaching.

A large group of men came rowdily in through the door, at least a dozen of them, happily congratulating each other with boisterous cries and much back slapping. They were seamen like many of the other patrons but rougher looking. Heinz stood and stared at the men warily. Taryn and Smitty noticed Heinz's protective behavior as a warning, and Taryn looked to Tynx for some kind of confirmation. Tynx was watching the men carefully, though he did so more subtly than Heinz. Tynx didn't turn to them, but rather watched from the corners of his eyes. He then looked to the other patrons and seemed to be trying to decide something. He made no other move than that, however.

The newcomers quickly filled the room. They were clearly drunk on their happiness over whatever success they were celebrating—alcohol was quickly being added to the mix—and soon made it impossible to converse without shouting.

"I don't like this," Taryn said, leaning over to speak into Smitty's ear. "It's obnoxious."

Of course, by "it's obnoxious" she meant, "It makes me nervous".

Smitty nodded, but said nothing back. She couldn't be sure if he shared her feelings or not. Smitty had heard what Taryn said, but his brain was busy with other things. Amidst the muddle of building noise, he thought he had heard the word pirate, but he couldn't be sure. He was busy trying to listen for the word again or for anything else that would give them more information about the group. From the looks of them, he wouldn't be surprised if they were pirates.

Taryn then saw Ozzie coming back and gave him a meaningful look. He was carrying their drinks and was distracted by whatever message she was trying to get across. He didn't see the peg leg that had been stretched out into his path and tripped over it in a spectacular way, tossing the drinks far and wide as he threw his arms out to catch himself. He was successful...kind of. He didn't land on his face anyway. The atmosphere of the room changed entirely in that moment: the air stood still, silence fell thick and heavy, and it seemed to grow warm and close. Ozzie looked up and saw several of the pirates standing over him, drenched in cider.

"I am so sorry," Ozzie managed before one of them picked him up by his shirt and threw him onto one of the nearby tables.

It was with that the silence exploded. Tynx, Taryn, and Smitty sprang into action with Heinz close behind. Several other patrons started forward, though whether to intervene, join in, or simply get a better view was unknown.

Ozzie didn't even have a chance to try and roll away before another one of the pirates picked him again and landed a punch square in his nose.

"Now hang on a second," Smitty cut in, jumping between the two. "It was an accident. There's no—"

The pirate then delivered the next punch, which had been intended for Ozzie's face, into Smitty's. Smitty went reeling back into Taryn, who was trying to help Ozzie up, creating a haphazard pile of arms and legs and bodies. The pirate lunged forward again, but stopped and began howling in pain mid-step as Heinz sank his teeth into the man's backside and pulled. It created enough of a distraction to allow Smitty, Taryn, and an unsteady Ozzie to get to their feet, but more of the pirates—most had been content to simply watch until their side stopped winning—were moving forward to join in now. They were surrounded. Heinz, who had released his victim for the time being, was carefully circling back around towards his mistress, while the pirate was swearing and holding his bleeding buttocks. The pirates advanced slowly, knowing there was no escape for the little group, probably imagining the most effective way to pummel their faces. Suddenly there was an insane shout, and Tynx came flying down from the rafters on top of a massive chandelier. Tynx and his ride landed right on top of the pirates who stood behind Ozzie, Smitty, and Taryn.

"Run!" he cried.

They didn't need to be told twice and took off, bounding over the bodies of the pirates underneath the chandelier and out the door. Tynx followed directly behind.

The pirates wasted no time in giving chase, shouting and swearing angrily. The sound of their boots pounding off of the streets was like a herd of enraged rhinos.

Ozzie, Taryn, Smitty, Tynx, and Heinz ran madly down alleyways and across streets without any sense of direction whatsoever. Smitty was in front, while Taryn and Ozzie were neck and neck behind him. Tynx and Heinz trailed behind, pulling down nets and crates and whatever else they could to slow down their pursuers. Suddenly, the lane they were barreling down opened up into a wide open space, beyond which were wharfs; jetties; ships of nearly every shape, size and time period; and the ocean.

"There!" came Tynx's voice from behind them! "It's shoving off!"

Since they couldn't see him or where he might be pointing, Ozzie, Taryn, and Smitty could only assume Tynx meant the great wooden ship that was beginning to pull away from the pier. It was still moving slowly enough for the group to make it, as it had only been partially unmoored. There was more crashing behind them as Tynx continued to try to trip up the pirates, but the furious shouts were still too close to guarantee any kind of successful escape. Ozzie, Taryn, and Smitty all put on an extra burst of speed and ran pell-mell for the departing ship. Just as they were coming close, though, the world turned on its head.

Heinz rushed forward and tackled Smitty. Taryn and Ozzie leapt for the ship, just managing to clear the gap before the ship gave a hard lurch forward, pulling it free from the last few ropes.

"Ahoy there, Captain Codfish!" rang out from the crow's nest of the ship.

Taryn and Ozzie looked up to see a young boy there, calling down to the pirates. They then turned to see Tynx picking Smitty up off the ground as he looked back at them desperately. Smitty looked furious and was yelling, while Heinz was looking mournfully at Taryn.

The pirates, meanwhile, were now distracted by the theft of their ship by a gang of little boys and a pixie. They ran back and forth, cursing and shouting. Some valiantly thought they could still reclaim the ship and jumped for the deck. They fell short and into the water, as the ship was sailing away faster now, propelled by some form of pixie magic. Taryn and Ozzie watched speechlessly as Tynx, ignoring Smitty's protests, pulled him away from the chaos. Within moments, they were lost in the crowd.

"Come on, we can still swim back," Ozzie said quickly.

As soon as the words left his mouth, however, two boys half their height flew in front of them, brandishing small swords.

"Not so fast!" one said.

"You're our prisoners now," said the other.

"Against the mast," said the first.

"Until Captain Pan decides what to do with you," the second finished.

Taryn and Ozzie exchanged looks and shrugged. Raising their hands in surrender, they walked over to the mainmast and sat down with their backs against it. They knew they were prisoners, but it was very difficult to be frightened when their captors were only three feet tall and could probably be bribed with candy. Nevertheless, they had swords, and the time for swimming back quickly passed.

"What's your problem, man?!" Smitty demanded, as Tynx pushed him into a deserted alleyway of crates. They stunk of forgotten fish cargo.

"My problem is that you are acting like a fool!" Tynx hissed. "Now lower your voice before you get us both killed."

"No! Why should I listen to you? You let Taryn and Ozzie get away while your freaking dog tried to kill me! I'm done with all of this!"

With that, Smitty began to storm off, but Tynx grabbed him and shoved him against the wall. He shook Smitty roughly by the collar once to get his attention and then spoke angrily.

"Shut it! Do you know why Heinz attacked you? Because you're a danger to Taryn. I don't know how, but you are, and neither of us trusts you. I would let you go your own idiotic way, but you are Ozzie and Taryn's friend, and for that reason—and that reason alone, mind you—I won't let you toddle off to get yourself killed. You are going to stay with me, you're going to do what I say, and we are going to find and rescue Taryn and Ozzie. Do I make myself clear?"

Smitty said nothing and only scowled furiously at Tynx.

Tynx shoved him hard against the wall again and snarled, "I said, do I make myself clear, Smitty?!"

"Sure," Smitty sneered angrily, "you've made yourself clear." Tynx let go of him, and he added, "So what's your genius plan to find them? It's not like we can just use a GPS to track them down."

"I don't need that," Tynx said, ignoring the fact that he had no idea what a GPS was. "Heinz will lead us straight to them."

Heinz, who had been tagging along with Tynx since Taryn had sailed away, suddenly chittered enthusiastically and wagged his tail.

"Hold still. This is going to hurt," Taryn said.

She was trying to sound confident even though she wasn't. The hit Ozzie's nose had taken at the pub earlier was looking bad. There was blood all down his face and shirt, though he had been too busy running to notice at the time. His nose and the corners of his eyes had turned purple with bruising. Worst of all, his nose was flatter than it had been, and Taryn was pretty sure it was broken. The current plan was for her to pinch it back into shape. When Ozzie asked if she had ever done this before, she had simply said it looked easy on TV.

Now, Taryn had one hand on the back of Ozzie's head and the other poised to do the deed. She let out a breath and went for it. She squeezed cartilage and flesh back into what she hoped was its proper place, and Ozzie screamed in pain, but he resisted the urge to jerk away. His nose started to bleed again, and Taryn pulled away to see if her work was successful. Unfortunately, it was difficult to tell. Ozzie was still groaning and growling in pain, gripping his leg tightly to stave off the worst of it.

"Oy! You there!" came a voice. "Who are you?"

Taryn and Ozzie looked and saw the boy—Peter Pan, they both knew—levitating before them. He had an impish face and looked ready for trouble in whatever form it would come.

"Stowaways," Ozzie replied before Taryn could.

He hissed through his teeth at how much that made his face throb.

Following Ozzie's lead uncertainly, Taryn added, "We were trying to get away from the pirates."

Peter looked dubious. Taryn and Ozzie both knew the story well enough to know that he probably didn't trust anything two adults had to say, but it probably seemed interesting that these two appeared to be enemies with his.

Finally he spoke again, making a big show of taking command of the situation. "Very well. You'll come with us."

"Are we your prisoners?" Taryn asked, raising a skeptical eyebrow.

She was having a very hard time taking Peter Pan and the lost boys seriously. They were just children playing a game, after all, and she wasn't really in the mood for games. They needed to get back and find Tynx, Smitty, and Heinz.

"Yes!" Peter declared excitedly. "You are prisoners of the fearsome Captain Pan!"

"No, we're not," Taryn stated in a very motherly tone of voice, fed up with this silliness.

"What if we were part of your gang instead?!" Ozzie interjected suddenly. "Ow!" More carefully now he added, "I can be your...your bodyguard, and Taryn here knows loads of stories!"

Taryn stared at Ozzie agape. She was able to stop herself just short of demanding what on earth Ozzie was doing. He was treating their situation like a game.

"You know stories?" Peter asked.

"Yes, of course," Taryn said distractedly, still looking at Ozzie.

"Tell us one now!" Peter demanded. "You, guard, stand watch."

The other lost boys began to gather from various ends of the ship, and Taryn looked at them all in surprise.

"What about the ship?" she asked.

"It knows where to go," one of the boys replied.

"Oh, you should tell them about the time with the bandits!" Ozzie suggested before heading for the bow of the ship.

Taryn was flabbergasted for a moment and looked around at her audience. All of the lost boys were sprawled out before her, half-tangled in the shrouds, lying on the deck, leaning against the mizzenmast, and one was even scooting next to her.

"Okay then, I think it's important for you to know the characters of my story first," Taryn began.

She was immediately interrupted by a tiny furious noise, like bells tinkling in a heavy wind. Taryn looked to see Tinker Bell flying back and forth and yelling in her own little pixie language.

"Cool your jets, Tink!" Taryn snapped. "I'm just here to tell stories. That's all, so don't try anything. Got it?"

Tinker Bell said something that seemed calmer, but Taryn couldn't be sure if the pixie was threatening or agreeing with her. Either way, she flew over to Peter and settled on his shoulder.

"As I was saying…the characters," Taryn said, turning back to the lost boys. She pointed at Ozzie and said, "Ozzie was there, and so was I. My name is Taryn, and our friend Tynx was there, too. Tynx is half-elf, and Heinz is an enfield."

"What's an enfield?" the little boy next to Taryn asked.

And so the stories began. They were interrupted often with questions, which Taryn was actually glad for, because it kept the lost boys occupied. She wasn't even halfway through her second—the tale of how she met Heinz—when Ozzie called *Land ho!* from his spot near the forecastle. The boys all looked to him and then started shouting excitedly as they raced towards the bow.

"We're home!" they cried. "Land ho! Land ho!"

Then, without warning, they took off and began flying around and around the ship.

"Is that…Never Land?" Taryn asked, not believing her eyes, sidling up to Ozzie.

In the distance was an island. It was impossible to tell how large it was from this distance, but there was a mountain surrounded by tropical forest on all sides, which was pretty telling.

"How do you know about Never Land?" Peter asked, narrowing his eyes at them.

"How do you think," Ozzie said petulantly. "She's always asking for more stories. We heard about it from a traveler in a pub somewhere. You're pretty famous, you know."

Peter then smirked, and Taryn was overcome with an urge to hug him. How could one little boy look so skeptical one moment and then cuter than anything she had ever seen the next. He just looked so happy! Kyla, as well as Kael before he had died, could do that, but not to the extent Peter could.

"Yahoo! Never Land!" Peter cried suddenly, as he shot higher into the air. He then took off towards the island, followed by the lost boys.

"Hang on!" Ozzie called. "What about us?"

But Peter wasn't listening. He was calling to his gang, giving them some new order. Ozzie saw Tinker Bell racing after him, and he called to her.

"Hey, beautiful!"

Tinker Bell stopped short and flew back, tinkling something neither Ozzie nor Taryn could understand.

"I'm sorry, darling, but I can't understand a word you're saying," Ozzie said, smiling at her. "I just wanted to know if a sweet thing like you could help us. We want to fly."

Tinker Bell said something and seemed to indicate Taryn.

"Ryn? You don't need to worry about her. She's harmless." They both had to fight to keep from laughing at that. Ozzie went onto to whisper conspiratorially, "Between you and me, I don't think Peter's going to want to keep her around that long. She's a bit of a nag really."

Taryn, who could hear every word he said, looked nonplussed.

"What do you say? Help us out?" Ozzie said, winking at Tinker Bell.

Tinker Bell made a happy sounding noise and began to zip around their heads, effusing fairie dust as she did so. It could barely be seen, save for when the sunlight caught the specks at just the right angle, at which point it flashed for moment and then disappeared again.

"You and fairies," Taryn said, shaking her head but smiling. "Happy thoughts then?"

"Happy thoughts," Ozzie agreed. "Like when we became friends again…after we were back home."

"When we met back up with Tynx."

"When I got accepted into college."

"When you threw me a surprise party for my eighteenth birthday!"

"When we stayed up all night that time eating nothing but chips, queso, and cookies and watching movies!"

Taryn laughed, and they began to lift into the air, gravity losing its grip on them.

"Oh! What now? How do we steer?" Taryn asked.

They looked back to ask Tinker Bell for help, but she was long gone, having flown off on her own again.

Ozzie shrugged and said, "Hang onto me, just in case."

Taryn grabbed his outstretched hand, and they rose up further.

"Okay, let's think about what we want to do," Ozzie said.

At that, they did so and flew in opposite directions. Their grip on one another broke instantly, and they were quickly on the starboard and port sides of the ship.

"Ryn! What are you doing?" Ozzie called, getting his thoughts together and drifting back towards her now.

"I don't know! I thought maybe we should go back, you know, so that Smitty and Tynx don't think we're dead." She too had managed to get control of herself again.

"You know Tynx," Ozzie said, taking her hand again. "He's probably already on his way here. We should stay put. Heinz will find you."

"You might have a point," Taryn said, "but Heinz will find us if we go back, too."

"Do you really want to risk running out of fairie power?"

Taryn looked back over the ocean and thought about how long they had sailed. They were miles and miles from England now. No, it wasn't something she wanted to risk.

"Alright then, where to now?" she said finally.

"Let's find the lost boys again. We'll probably have a better chance with them than without."

Taryn couldn't deny that logic and nodded. Then, very carefully and awkwardly, they began to learn to fly. Ozzie had been right; they just had to will themselves where they wanted to go. It took a bit of practice, though, as they could easily send themselves zooming if they were careless with their thoughts. It was a bit like riding a bicycle or driving, though, in that, after a while, the movements became more familiar. Still, they were careful. After all, there was nothing to protect them from impact except the clothes on their backs.

Even with these difficulties, flying was the most incredible thing Taryn and Ozzie had ever experienced. They could look down on forests and beaches from above, float upside down, hover above a tide pool and watch the creatures on the very bottom through the clear blue water, and swoop through flocks of birds. The only drawback was that it got colder the higher they got, so they mostly stayed just above the trees. When they got hungry, they just grabbed some fruit growing up in the treetops and began to look for the lost boys in earnest.

"There," Tynx hissed, pointing at a small sailboat.

He, Smitty, and Heinz were crouched behind some cargo boxes in almost complete darkness. The only light came from gas lamps that lined the street at the other end of the wharf and the occasional lantern hanging from a ship. Their target was one of those with a lantern, which could be good or bad depending on one's perspective. Originally, the plan was to hire a boat and at least one mercenary before sailing to wherever Heinz directed them. They were laughed off by every captain, sailor, and sword-for-hire they spoke to. No one wanted to go to "that mad island", especially not when the crew of the Jolly Roger was involved. Smitty informed Tynx that the ship that had taken Ozzie and Taryn belonged to the pirates who had chased them—and who they were still trying to avoid—and the thieves were Peter Pan and his lost boys. Tynx had been skeptical until Smitty told him more of the story. That was when they decided they would set out without help—well, voluntary help—and find their friends alone.

They checked to see if anyone was coming, saw that the coast was clear, and then scuttled across the wharf to the sailboat. Their footsteps sounded so loud! They were sure the patrol that had passed by a little while ago could hear them. Nevertheless, they reached the boat and slipped down into it. Heinz was immediately uncomfortable on such an unstable surface, and began to whine as he tried to make the floor stop moving by digging at it, which of course only made it worse. Tynx told him to stop and lie down, which he did, but he wasn't happy about it. Tynx had obviously learned a lot about sailing during his voyage to Terturelia. Almost immediately, he was untying ropes and raising the sails. After stashing their packs, which had been carefully and quickly retrieved from the room that evening, Smitty sat there dumbly watching him, trying to think of something he could do to help. As much as he didn't like Tynx or Heinz, he disliked this anxious waiting even more.

"So what would Ozzie and Taryn think if they knew you were stealing a boat?" he asked, trying to distract himself.

Tynx actually chuckled at that and said, "Don't you know? I was actually trying to rob them when we first met."

"That's right. It didn't go well, did it?"

"No. Taryn knocked me on my rear and gave me a head wound."

"Well, this should be a piece of cake then."

At that, there was the all too familiar *schink* of a blade being drawn. Smitty swore as he felt a sharp tip press against the back of his head. Through the darkness, he could see Tynx standing stock still, scowling at whoever was standing behind Smitty.

"It's a bit late for a turn about the harbor, isn't it," a smooth voice said.

"Very late, indeed," another voice agreed.

"And in the vessel we've had our eye on, no less." The first voice grew serious as he continued, "I recognize you lads. You were with those little urchins that took my ship."

"Um, slight correction," Smitty said carefully. "We weren't really *with* them. A couple of our friends ended up hostages on the ship the urchins stole...yours, that is."

"You were running like a couple of yellow-bellied dogs," the second voice countered.

"To be fair," Tynx said with a smirk, "the odds weren't exactly in our favor. Run to fight another day and all that."

"I'm not impressed," the first voice said.

Smitty felt the blade tip press harder, and he made an incoherent noise.

"Sorry, I couldn't quite make that out," the first voice said as he watched a small bead of blood begin to seep out from Smitty's skin.

"Wannacomwitus?!" Smitty splurted.

"Beg pardon?" both voices said together, obviously taken aback.

"Think about it," Smitty continued quickly. "We're both going to the same place, looking for the same people. You like this boat, we like this boat. It just makes sense."

Tynx was fixing Smitty with a look, but he couldn't quite make out what it meant.

"We could just kill you," the first voice purred.

Smitty swallowed hard and looked to Tynx for help. Surely he was about to come up with something brilliant and elfy. Tynx didn't move, but just stared off at the men behind Smitty. Heinz also didn't move, but lay tensely on the floor of the boat.

"Don't kill us," Smitty finally pleaded. "Please. You don't want to do that."

"Why not?" the second voice asked. It almost sounded like an innocent question.

"Because..." Smitty stammered. "Because...we can...help each other...maybe." It sounded more like a question than a suggestion.

"Oy! Who goes there?" came a voice through the thick silence.

All heads turned to see the patrol, a handful of armed men, coming back around. They had heard the voices, which had initially tipped them off that something was wrong, and now saw the little group standing off against each other. The assailants suddenly leapt into the boat, causing it to rock violently.

"Your idea seems to have some merit after all, lad," the owner of the first voice said. "Shove off, Mister Smee!"

Smitty snapped his head around and saw a man with dark, curled hair and a hook for a hand standing next to him now. Smee and Tynx were rushing to get the last of the moorings untied. Tynx pushed so hard away from the dock, he overstretched and fell forward into the water.

"Crap! Tynx!" Smitty cried.

A moment later, the half-elf resurfaced hanging onto the mooring rope. He disappeared underwater again just before the bolts came flying down at him. The patrol was firing crossbows at him since he was the closest target. By now, the sail was up and had caught a bit of wind, so the boat was making slow progress away into the harbor. They weren't far enough yet, however, as the next bolts came for the rest of them. Smitty, Smee, and Hook hit the deck, barely avoiding being shot. Smitty found himself face to face with Heinz, who was thankfully too distressed to be very threatening at the moment. Smee's hand was still on the rudder keeping them fairly straight as crossbow bolts continued to whiz by. Smitty couldn't believe he was going to die this way. If he wasn't shot, pirates were going to kill him. It was just ridiculous! The sailboat then jerked forward and began to speed away. Smitty looked up and saw the sails full of wind, but how was that possible? The air was fairly calm. That was when he heard it, the choked grunting from behind the boat. Tynx! Smitty crawled to the stern and carefully poked his head up. They were well beyond the reach of crossbows now, as the dock shrank behind them more quickly than should be possible. He stood unsteadily and looked into the water behind them. There was Tynx with the rope wrapped around one arm to keep him above water while the other was up and making a throwing motion around and around repeatedly.

"You're alive!" Smitty exclaimed.

"Spot on! Now pull me up!" Tynx yelled before inhaling a mouthful of water and choking.

Smitty reached over and grabbed the rope, pulling as hard as he could. The water pressure was working against them, though, pulling Tynx back.

"Smee! Help me!" Smitty called.

Smee was there a moment later, and they both were soon huffing and puffing as they made slow progress in getting Tynx up and out of the water. Tynx had stopped whatever it was he was doing with his other arm, which made the boat slow down, and he was able to pull himself over the edge as soon as he was halfway up.

Sitting next to Tynx on the deck, Smitty said between breaths, "Can you imagine...what Taryn and Ozzie...would do to me...if you had died?"

174

"Well, lucky you don't have to find out," Tynx gasped before choking up more water.

"That was quite the rescue you just pulled off," Hook said suddenly.

Smitty and Tynx looked up to see him sitting languidly on the side of the boat, while Smee had retaken his place at the rudder.

"Don't make it have been for nothing," Tynx said sternly.

"I wouldn't dream of it now that I know you're good for something," Hook replied. "I suppose that means we should be properly introduced, now that we're not going to kill you and all. Captain James T. Hook here and my first mate, Mister Smee."

"Pleasure," Tynx replied. Pointing at each of them, he stated, "Smitty, Heinz, and Tynx. I'll be happy to help sail."

"Much obliged," Hook replied with a nod.

With that, Tynx went back to work, and Smitty settled down next to Heinz. It was uncomfortable and silent aboard the boat, but they weren't dead. This didn't seem quite as exciting as it initially had, though, as soon as Heinz started to get seasick. And thus began a very unhappy voyage.

Taryn and Ozzie found the lost boys' camp easily enough since they vaguely knew what to look for, but the noise was really what led them there first. They were running around, yelling after one another, and fighting and rolling on the ground. Taryn went into big sister mode before she even realized what was happening.

"Hey! Knock it off!" she shouted, followed by a sharp, two-fingered whistle.

Most of the lost boys stopped where they were, while others took this opportunity to steal from their fellow boys. The ones that stopped immediately started calling for Peter, who emerged a moment later from one of the secret tree trunk entrances.

"It's a wonder the pirates haven't found you already," Taryn called to him over the noise of the boys.

"We would have killed them if they had," Peter said arrogantly.

"I'm sure," Taryn said rolling her eyes.

"We're back!" Ozzie interjected excitedly.

"Who are you again?" Peter asked.

"Ozzie, personal bodyguard.    Taryn, storyteller," Ozzie reminded him.

"Oh, yes!" Peter replied, remembering. "Why are you back?"

"Because we made a deal," Ozzie replied simply.

A wide, satisfied smile broke out on Peter's face.  It was another one of those purely gleeful impish looks, and he whooped to his lost boys, "Gather round, lads!"

The lost boys did as they were told and were quickly assembled before Taryn and Ozzie.

"Um, hi!" Ozzie said, as six pairs of eyes stared at him. Meanwhile, Peter was looking both Ozzie and Taryn up and down. "What are your names?"

"Well, that's more like it," said one of the boys in a snooty sort of way.  "There's a right way and a wrong way to do this, you know.  Slightly, at your service."

"Nice to meet you, Slightly," Taryn said sweetly.  She looked to the sweet-faced boy that had sat next to her on the ship and asked, "And you?"

"Tootles," he said smiling.

"Oh, Tootles," Taryn said fondly.

"Curly," he said almost apologetically.

"Nibs!" he said happily.

"Twins," the two who had initially held them up on the ship said together.

"Are you going to finish your story from before?" Tootles asked.

"I'd love to," Taryn said, "but what do you say?"

"Oh, please, if you would be so kind," Slightly began.

"Now, of course!" Peter chimed in.

Taryn glowered at Peter, but said nothing.  Turning back to the lost boys, she asked where they'd like to hear it, and they led her and Ozzie into their underground hideout.  Within the cozy hideout, Ozzie and Taryn quickly found space for themselves and settled in.

That night, after an especially long day—or maybe it had been several.  It was hard to tell—the two laid on a pile of animal skins on the floor and whispered to one another so as not to be overheard.

"Do you really think Tynx and Smitty will find us?" Taryn asked.

"Psshh!" Ozzie replied.  "Of course!"

Taryn smiled and placed a hand on Ozzie's.

"I'm so glad you're here. What would I do without you?"

"Jail time. You totally would have killed someone by now."

"Oz!"

Ozzie laughed and said, "Just kidding...sort of. Love you really!"

Taryn smirked at him and cuddled closer.

"Just don't do anything crazy without warning me first, okay?" she said.

"I'll do my best," Ozzie said, wrapping an arm around her. "Good night, Ryn."

"Good night, Oz."

"Are you two going to kiss?"

The voice came from one of the lost boys, but Ozzie and Taryn couldn't make out which one at the moment.

"Nope," Ozzie replied. "Sleep tight, buddy."

Neither Tynx nor Smitty could tell how long they had been sailing. The sun didn't so much rise and set as disappear, leaving dim twilight, and then reappear with proper daylight again. Thankfully, they had water and a little food from their supplies, but no one had much of an appetite with Heinz retching every so often and then groaning pitifully when there was nothing left in his stomach.

"The island might not be looking for us," they heard Hook say to Smee at one point, but neither knew what that meant.

Smitty and Tynx had eventually been able to strike up a conversation or two with the pirates to try and get a feel for how much danger they were in. Captain Hook spoke congenially enough, but Tynx recognized it as a façade. Hook's voice was oily smooth, and he smiled widely, too widely, when he looked at them. The last person Tynx had heard speak like that was Vurnal in Leleplar, and it set every particle in Tynx's being on high alert.

"So why didn't you and your crew simply commandeer another boat and come back together?" Tynx had asked.

"After what Pan did, the men needed a night off to carouse and lift their spirits," Hook replied.

What Hook didn't tell them was that coming to the mainland had been a mistake from the get-go. They had been pursuing Peter

Pan and his gang, who had craftily led them out beyond the borders of Never Land and then "let slip" that they were headed for London. Peter and the lost boys had snuck below deck under the cover of night, and the Jolly Roger and her crew had followed the occasional lost boy sighting all the way there, despite the occasional request to turn back. None of the crew wanted to go to the mainland—too strange, too far, too many other people. In Never Land, the pirates were free to be lawless, but Hook was determined. Each time they caught sight of a lost boy, they got so close! Only to see their quarry slip through their grasp each time. The crew of the Jolly Roger had no clue they were being pulled along like a bass on a line. That is, not until the ship had been stolen. Then everything made sense, and the pirates were furious with their obsessive captain.

Captain Hook had threatened and swore at the men. They weren't mutinying, probably because there was no ship to be had if they did, but they refused to help Captain Hook steal another vessel. What if they failed? What would happen to them? Only Smee, ever-faithful Smee, agreed to follow. Hook finally gave up and, with great bravado, promised them all that he would be back with the Jolly Roger and they'd all be very sorry when he was. Like his crew, the authorities here concerned him. He couldn't simply kill a crewman as an example here like he could in Never Land. No, coming upon Smitty and Tynx had actually been a stroke of luck.

Hook's reply sounded fishy to Tynx, which only increased his distrust of the captain. Finally, however, they came within sight of the island and made for a lagoon of blue water, surrounded by rocky walls covered in greenery. A few thin waterfalls sauntered down the cliff faces, spilling into the lagoon and creating mini-rainbows. It was beautiful, as was the singing. Wait, singing?

Smitty was on guard immediately. After what happened at the underground lake in Paris, he didn't want to be caught unawares again. He looked to Tynx and then to Hook and Smee as well. Tynx was scanning the island and surrounding water, clearly looking for the source of the music. Hook and Smee, however, did not look concerned. That might be a good sign since they probably knew everything that was dangerous in Never Land, but it also might mean nothing. The singing got louder as they approached the lagoon, where Smitty could only guess they would disembark, but he didn't feel his mind slipping away or anything, so maybe it really was harmless. Finally, as they sailed in through the mouth of the lagoon, both Smitty and Tynx were able to identify the source of the music: mermaids.

There were at least a dozen of them scattered across the lagoon sunning themselves on rocks, braiding each other's hair, lazily swimming to and fro, and all singing together. Their voices were beautiful, harmonizing with one another, a symphony of voices, and they did it effortlessly. The mermaids themselves were just as beautiful as their voices, with long, elegantly finned tails that changed from gold to teal to violet and bronze to emerald to fuchsia in the sun. Their eyes were wide, glassy, very large, and dark.

When the boat came within sight of the mermaids, several of them waved, and Smitty waved back.

"What do you think you're doing?" Tynx asked.

"Saying hello," Smitty replied innocently.

"Don't encourage them," Hook said darkly, "unless you like the idea of being made a pet."

"He may," Smee chuckled.

Hook laughed at that, while Tynx rolled his eyes. Smitty just shrugged and looked back to the lagoon. They were all just being paranoid. The mermaids seemed perfectly nice. They weren't nearly as scary as he thought they might be, certainly nothing like the Phantom, and not at all like the Greek myths and other stories he had read about them. No, he wasn't worried anymore. Smitty then snuck a look at Hook and Smee again. Well, he wasn't worried about the mermaids anymore anyway.

They docked the boat near the bank and had to wade a little to get to shore, all except for Heinz who leapt from the boat and took off as soon as his feet touched dry ground.

"Heinz!" Tynx and Smitty called after him.

They began to run after him, but the pirates were faster and had their swords drawn before Tynx and Smitty could take two steps.

"Not so fast," Hook growled. "As a crew, we stay together."

"He is our only way of finding our friends!" Tynx cried, pointing to the direction in which Heinz had run.

"And why should I care?"

"Because they're probably still with Peter Pan," Smitty said.

Hook thought only a moment before he lowered his sword, Smee following suit.

"Very well." Turning back to Tynx, he asked, "You. Can you track your dog?"

Tynx nodded and then took this opportunity to slog the rest of the way out of the lagoon. Heinz's tracks were easy to follow; his claws left deep gashes in the earth while his paws made perfect impressions in the soft ground. Their progress was fast, which was both good and very, very bad because Tynx had no idea what they were going to do when they found Taryn and Ozzie.

In the time that Ozzie and Taryn had been apart from Tynx and Smitty—however long that was…it was still hard to tell how time passed in Never Land—they had come to look more like the lost boys. They wore animal skins like the boys did now, but only for warmth over their own clothes. Taryn had plaited her hair down the sides, making her look much younger, while Ozzie…Ozzie had simply let it go wild. They ate when they were hungry and slept when they were tired. Taryn told stories whenever the boys were not off on adventures and was left to her own devices when they were. Ozzie, however, was always with Peter Pan and his gang, but he didn't seem to mind. In fact, Ozzie seemed to be really enjoying himself as they went out to hunt pirates—they never seemed to catch any, probably because all of them were still on the mainland—or attend the Indian's festivals—yes, he had met Tiger Lily—or whatever idea, no matter how ridiculous, came to Peter. At first, Taryn had objected and been concerned for Ozzie's safety, especially since Ozzie was usually sent into potentially dangerous situations first. Her fears were quickly assuaged, though, when Ozzie confided to her that nearly all of their excursions were pretend.

"They're little kids," Ozzie whispered. "They're usually playing make-believe."

Despite this, Taryn still asked him to be careful, which he was. Better than that, he knew how to get along with the boys in a way that Taryn didn't. Taryn was an older sister first and foremost, but the lost boys had no interest in being told what to do, especially by a grown-up, so most of what Taryn said, besides her stories, went ignored or ridiculed. Ozzie, however, was a master of reverse psychology and had an uncanny talent for understanding the boys' way of thinking. Taryn once said that this was because Ozzie was still a wild, little boy at heart, but she meant it affectionately. He could usually convince the boys to do something else if things got too dangerous, but he was careful about how often he did it. Peter was clever and usually skeptical of Ozzie, so he was always watching for any signs of treachery. It was a careful balance, especially among so many unruly children, but Ozzie seemed to manage it pretty well for the most part.

"I saw a monster!"

Taryn turned from her perch in a tree and looked down to see Tootles running around the camp, red-faced and out of breath. Taryn had been watching a group of fairies go about their work, but they had scattered at the announcement, so she flew down and took Tootles into her arms.

"What do you mean you saw a monster?" she asked.

"It was huge!" he said.

At that moment, the rest of the lost boys began to emerge from the woods and the underground hideout.

"A monster?!" Nibs cried. "Oh, boy! A monster!"

"A monster? A real monster?!" Curly asked uncertainly.

"Looks like we're going on a monster hunt!" Peter declared, flying up above them all. "Gather the weapons!"

The lost boys were running every which way now, grabbing their swords and bows and arrows from their hiding places. Taryn scanned the area for Ozzie and spotted him as he came around a tree.

"You think it's actually anything?" she asked quietly.

Ozzie smiled and shrugged. "No way to know. You staying here?"

"Yeah. Be careful."

"I always am."

Taryn smiled back at him. It was true; he always was careful, but she still always worried. The boys were haphazardly assembled in no formation whatsoever within minutes and headed out with shouts and hoots loud enough to alert the entire forest to their intentions. Taryn watched them go and continued to listen after they were gone. She could usually tell how far away they were and always kept an ear out for trouble. Everything sounded pretty normal, and Taryn soon began to wonder if maybe her fairie friends would come back.

"Taryn!" came Ozzie's voice from somewhere in the forest.

It had been several hours since the lost boys had headed out. Dusk had fallen, and the sound of the hunting party was phasing in and out as they circled back around closer to the camp and then away again. As soon as Taryn heard Ozzie, she knew something was wrong. She thought she heard him shouting something else, but couldn't make it out over the sound of the underbrush being crushed beneath her feet. Taryn half-flew through the trees. All of the time alone had given her plenty of opportunity to take walks through the forest, which served her well as she tried to figure out just where Ozzie might be.

"I saw it! It went this way!" Ozzie called frantically.

The lost boys were running around madly, yelling to each other, weapons drawn. He had to get a handle on the situation. The hunting party had been tromping through the forest just as they had been for the last few hours with no sign of any monster. Not surprising. Then it happened. A red-gold streak of fur ran by them so close Ozzie could feel the wind as it passed by. The lost boys screamed and ran after it, quickly scattering. Ozzie, however, didn't move. It was Heinz! Heinz was the monster, and he was helping hunt him. That meant Tynx and Smitty were here somewhere now too, didn't it? Probably, but Heinz could have come by himself. You couldn't put anything past an enfield bent on finding its charge. The lost boys were only children, but they might actually kill Heinz given the opportunity. They might not even mean to, but it was a very real danger, especially if Peter had anything to do with it. Or Heinz could hurt them. Enfields were far smarter than average canines, but he would defend himself if it came to it, children or no. Then there was the fact that every lost boy was armed. What was to stop them from injuring one another in the fray? This could in no way get any worse. Ozzie had to get them off the trail. He gave one quick shout for Taryn and then began the misdirection. Ozzie could only count two, maybe three, lost boys at the moment, but he tried to get them to follow him anyway. He shouted his commands in the hopes that the others would hear him and follow.

Taryn could hear the hysteria long before she found anyone. Ozzie was yelling, most of the boys were either screaming or shouting, and Peter was giving commands that contradicted each other at every turn. Taryn, throwing all caution to the wind and only adding to the cacophony, was shouting for Ozzie. Then there was the wolf's howl. At least it sounded like a wolf, but there was something odd and kind of chirpy about the call. Great! Just what she needed! A wild animal. She jumped and tripped when she saw it. The creature, the monster they had been hunting, was Heinz!

Heinz was on Taryn in a moment, licking her face and chirping excitedly. That was when the first of the lost boys showed up, the twins, and they began to shout for Peter. The others arrived within moments, all ready to strike with their weapons.

"We've got it now!" Peter cried, leaping into the air.

"Now wait just a minute!" Taryn snapped so sharply it made the boys jump. "This is *not* a monster! He is my enfield!"

"He's ours!" Peter argued.

"He's mine!" Taryn yelled. "And if you so much as lay a hand on him, so help me, I will hang you up by your ears! Do you understand me, Peter Pan?!"

There was solid silence for a moment, wherein Ozzie appeared with Slightly and looked around the tense scene.

"Hey! New pet!" he exclaimed.

"Traitors!" Peter cried.

"New pet?" some of the lost boys said to one another. "New pet!"

The ranks, small as they were, were divided. Some of the lost boys didn't know what to do, as their leader was crying revenge for the betrayal, but the idea of a new pet as grand as Heinz was hard to pass up. Plus, Ozzie had become something of a friend to them, and Taryn was terrifying just then. Most of them backed away for lack of a better option. They were, after all, still little boys despite being part of Peter's gang.

To add to the chaos, Heinz suddenly stepped forward and started barking. Taryn knew that bark: he sensed danger approaching.

Switching gears, she looked to Peter and his gang and said sternly, "Something's coming."

Ozzie was immediately on the same page as Taryn. They needed to identify this new threat. Peter Pan and the lost boys were way ahead of him, though. Every one of them flew upward to get a better view of the forest beyond, and Ozzie followed close behind.

Peter turned to the others and commanded their attention with a determined wave of his arm.

"It's the codfish!" he whispered seriously. His eyes suddenly went wide, and his face lit up. "Let's go kill some pirates!" he hollered, rallying his mini-army.

"No, don't!" Taryn protested.

It was too late. The lost boys were already off, having instantly forgotten about the monster dispute.

"Oz!" Taryn cried in exasperation.

"Come on!" Ozzie said. "If Heinz is here, Tynx and Smitty might be with them."

"But what about the boys?"

"You know, Ryn, they were doing just fine way before we got here," Ozzie teased. "They'll be okay."

Taryn huffed at him because she couldn't argue with that and took off after him, but she stopped short when she heard Heinz whimper. Looking down, she saw her faithful enfield padding back and forth on the ground, whining unhappily and staring up at Taryn.

"Oh, baby dog, I'm so sorry," she said quickly.

Poor Heinz. He had come all this way to find her, following his deepest instincts, and now she had found a new way to be separated from him: flying. She didn't really have time to comfort him properly just now, so she flew back down and opted to run through the trees with Heinz by her side while Ozzie flew above and ahead.

Peter Pan and the lost boys were many things, but subtle was not one of them. Hook and Smee knew Peter was capable of such a feat on his own, but when the entire pack of them was on the hunt, their prey always had early notice. The shrill battle cries ripped through the night sounds of the forest like claws through linen. Immediately, Hook began sizing up the situation.

"You lads, I assume you know how to fight?" he asked, looking to Smitty and Tynx.

"Of course," Tynx replied, with absolutely no intention of doing so.

He began to form a large mote in his hand for good measure, just to be convincing. If he was lucky, which he was counting on, Hook and Smee wouldn't have the slightest inkling that the mote was completely harmless. Whoever was coming, they were under no circumstances getting involved. Rather, Tynx planned on using the incoming conflict as a distraction to escape. Tynx remembered Smitty telling him about a band of children led by one in particular named Peter, but he still couldn't quite believe this was Captain Hook's enemy. The voices they heard were undoubtedly very young, though.

"Good. To arms!" Hook ordered.

The little group circled up back-to-back and waited tensely. Smitty had his hunting knife drawn, Tynx his scimitar in his free hand, and Smee and Hook their cutlasses. Then, just as the cacophony reached fever pitch, the lost boys and Peter exploded through the canopy. Tynx immediately released the mote, causing a flash of light to burst all around them. He then ran, grabbing and dragging Smitty behind him. They both ducked and dodged miniature swords as they went, hoping the pirates were too busy to give chase. Fortunately, the exploding mote had created the very distraction they needed. As soon as the mote had dissipated back to its elemental compounds, the lost boys regrouped and focused their efforts on their long-time nemesis.

"Get back here!" Hook screamed after them.

Already, Peter Pan and his gang were beginning to overwhelm Hook and Smee, but they both fought tooth and nail. If only the lost boys weren't so quick! Tynx looked back only long enough to make sure they weren't being pursued. He couldn't believe it, but Smitty had been right. This unruly pack of little children was battling against the pirates as bravely as any army.

"Ah!"

Tynx easily regained his footing after smacking into something...someone...and looked ahead again. It was a pair of wildlings along with Heinz, one of which had been knocked onto her rear when she had run into Tynx. No, not wildlings, Taryn and

Ozzie! Smitty clearly didn't recognize them either, as he was brandishing his hunting knife towards them, making Heinz snarl angrily.

"Hey!" Ozzie said excitedly. "We found you!"

"Ozzie?" Smitty said, recognizing the voice first.

Reaching for Taryn to help her up, Tynx added, "What happened to you two?"

"What do you mean by that?" Taryn asked, thinking she should be offended without being sure why.

"Later. Let's get out of here," Tynx said.

They all ran on back the way Smitty and Tynx, and Heinz before them, had come. When they all finally emerged back out onto the beach, Taryn and Ozzie were so excited they turned loops in the air.

"So...this is new," Smitty said as he watched them.

"Oh, yeah," Taryn giggled. "Little trick we picked up while hanging out with the lost boys."

"It's probably going to wear off soon, though," Ozzie added. "With no more faerie friends, no more pixie dust."

"Pixie dust doesn't make you fly," Tynx argued. "It makes you invisible. Remember?"

Hanging upside down in front of him, Taryn touched his nose affectionately and teased in a singsong voice, "Here it does!"

"You two had some adventures while you've been here," Tynx replied, smiling back.

"Yes, and that's great, but shouldn't we be going?" Smitty asked, cutting in.

Heinz whined pitifully, and Taryn came back down to kneel beside him.

"What's wrong, baby?" Taryn asked.

"He doesn't like sailing," Tynx told her unhappily.

Despite Heinz's feelings on the matter, the group was soon back at the lagoon and making ready to head back to the mainland. They needed to restock their supplies first, however, since no one actually knew how long it would take to get back. Ozzie, who had gotten to know Never-Never Land pretty well, led the effort, while Tynx assigned duties. Taryn and Smitty were left with the boat to make sure no one—pirate or lost boy—came by and stole it. They were also in charge of arranging everything so that the trip back would be as comfortable as possible for everyone, given Heinz's proclivity for seasickness. Thankfully, with Ozzie's help, Tynx was able to find some ginger plants there on the island, which would hopefully help. Fruit was harvested and packed, but Heinz refused to leave Taryn's side to hunt. He was clearly convinced she would disappear again if he did so and tenaciously followed her every step. The sun was beginning to set while they were making preparations, which wasn't so bad given that all the pirates—save for Hook and Smee, who might still be fighting the lost boys—were still on the mainland. Ozzie had developed a good relationship with the Indians and had told Taryn what to do if any came along, so they were not a concern. All in all, everyone felt pretty good about the extra time they would need to take before leaving.

"So what did you and Tynx do to find us?" Taryn was asking as she tended the little fire she had built. "I know you didn't *buy* this boat."

She laughed at that, but Smitty didn't respond. That didn't matter so much. It was pretty relaxing there on the beach, what with the crackle of the fire, the sound of the lapping waves, and the tittering of pixies somewhere just beyond the tree line.

"I want to spend some more time in London when we get back," she continued. "I know it's probably not smart to stick around, but it's so cool! Cooler than the one back home, don't you think?"

Smitty didn't respond again, and Taryn turned around to look back at him. He was gone. She stood up from the sand and frantically looked all around. There! In the water! Smitty was standing in the lagoon up to his waist.

"Smitty!" Taryn called worriedly.

What in the world was he doing?! She hurried out to him, splashing loudly as she went. Before she was halfway there, she saw them: The large, dark, gleaming eyes catching the light from the fire. The eyes belonged to something swimming in the water near Smitty, half hiding behind a rock. It looked human, but definitely was not. The mermaids! Ozzie had told her about them and mentioned that the lost boys were friendly but careful with them. But why? She couldn't remember. Were they sirens? What was the difference?

"Hey!" Taryn cried, not sure of what else to do. "Leave him alone!"

In response, she heard giggling. Not just from the one floating near to Smitty, but from all over the lagoon. The giggling made Taryn scared and angry all at once, and she doubled her pace, or at least as much as she could through the water. The mermaid behind the rock smiled widely at Taryn before looking back to Smitty. She opened her mouth, but no sound came out. Smitty smiled at that and walked forward. Whatever he was hearing, Taryn was clearly immune to its power.

"Smitty, don't!" Taryn screamed. "They'll kill you!"

The giggling resounded again even louder this time. Taryn finally reached Smitty and grabbed his arm, pulling him back violently. She didn't bother responding to the mermaids, but instead focused on Smitty. He didn't fight...at first. The mermaid there opened her mouth again, singing her silent song, and Smitty lurched forward towards her. Desperately, Taryn looked around for something, anything, she could use. There was nothing but water, so she did the only thing she could. Taryn tried to stop the mermaid. She swam towards the creature, doing her best to splash it on the way, maybe break whatever hold it had on Smitty. Was it stupid to take on a lethal sea creature in its own domain? Incredibly. But what else could she do? Let it take Smitty? The mermaid didn't seem much affected by the pitiful splashing—why would she be?—but she looked annoyed, possibly even angry, as Taryn came closer. The water was deeper here, and Taryn found she was submerged nearly to her shoulders when she stood again, several feet from the mermaid.

"Come on now," she yelled. "Let him go!"

With one swift move of her tail, the mermaid lunged towards Taryn, but was stopped mid-attack as something tackled her from above, something huge and furious. Taryn retreated straight back into Smitty, who had woken from his trance just then. She jumped and screamed, thinking another mermaid had swum up behind her. Relief filled her when she saw it was only Smitty looking bewildered but himself again. She looked back and saw Heinz swimming towards her and the body of the mermaid, now dead, floating in the water. Her throat had been torn open, and the dark stain in the water around her could only be her blood. Taryn and

Smitty looked around, expecting to see the rest of the mermaids coming for them, crying revenge for their fallen sister. There was nothing but silence. The other mermaids had disappeared, which was more terrifying than the first option had been.

"Go," Taryn whispered fearfully. "Go. Go! *GO!*"

Smitty didn't actually need to be told so many times. He was already on his way after the first, as was Taryn. They half ran, half swam back to shore, full-on panic driving them the entire way. Mercifully, the mermaids didn't give chase, and Taryn was content to think they had escaped to the safety of their coral caves, terrified by the ferocious land creature.

Taryn and Smitty stood close to the fire, while Heinz sidled up to Taryn looking very proud of himself. Taryn was trying to avoid looking at the faint traces of blood around his muzzle.

"What happened?" Smitty finally asked after he had caught his breath.

"The mermaids…" Taryn began. "They were trying to lure you."

"Lure me? Lure me where?"

"To your death, most likely."

"To my…what? The mermaids? No, they're perfectly nice."

"Oh, get a clue, Smitty!" Taryn cried. "They're mermaids! That's what they do. I should tie you to the mast for good measure."

"And so your stupid dog killed one?!" Smitty yelled back, even louder.

"He just saved both our lives, so stop calling him stupid!" Taryn shouted, loudest of all.

Smitty didn't know what to say to that, so he said nothing. Taryn put a hand on Heinz's head, scratching him behind the ears. She looked down at her faithful enfield and found herself profoundly grateful that she was his charge. She often forgot how dangerous a creature he was. Dangerous to those that would do her harm, that is. Heinz had simply done what came naturally, but, in doing so, he had snuffed out the mermaid's life as quickly as he did a rabbit's. And he had no concept of the magnitude of what he did. All he knew was protecting Taryn. She looked to Smitty and saw him looking at Heinz too, but his expression was markedly different from her own. Smitty was afraid and angry and distrustful. Heinz was tolerant of Smitty at Taryn's behest. Everyone knew it, especially after he had prevented Smitty from escaping on the Jolly Roger with Ozzie and her. If it weren't for her, what would Heinz have done about Smitty by now? Taryn didn't like thinking about that. It was pointless; Heinz wouldn't do anything to Smitty because Smitty wouldn't do anything to Taryn. It was just that simple.

Things were quiet for a little while after that, but the mermaids returned when night had set in properly. Thankfully, they were no longer interested in bewitching Smitty, but the alternative wasn't much better. The mermaids gathered en masse, hundreds of them, all over the lagoon, sitting on the rocks and floating in the water, and wailed eerily, calling to the moon above. This was not the same song they had sung during the day in the sunlight. No, that was light and joyful. This was something else entirely. It was just as beautiful, but frightening and mournful. Ozzie and Tynx returned soon after this had begun, having heard the wails all the way inland, only to find Taryn, Smitty, and Heinz soaked, the former two looking sullen and silent. After hearing the story of what had happened earlier that evening, it was decided they would wait until daylight to sail.

The night had been long and tense. The mermaids had cried long into the wee hours of the morning, only stopping when the sky began to lighten. Ozzie, Taryn, Smitty, Tynx, and Heinz all climbed into the boat once the sun was shining and the mermaids could be seen frolicking and playing once again as if nothing had happened the night before. There was no sign of the mermaid that Heinz had killed, and they were all glad for that. Smitty sat at the opposite end of the boat from the little bed that had been laid out for Heinz, though no one could be sure if that was coincidental or not. Taryn made sure he chewed his gingerroot, which seemed to help enormously, and everyone on board was much happier for it.

*Hook ran, cursing Peter, the lost boys, and those two useless scabs that had run with their tails between their legs. He had barely escaped, pushing Smee into the circle of boys that was closing in on them, sacrificing the faithful bosun to whatever they had planned. He had to think, to formulate a strategy, but first he had to get somewhere safe in order to do so. The lost boys would undoubtedly pursue him, but Hook knew of a few good hiding places there on the island. He headed for the closest one, a cave further into the jungle, and kept his ears and eyes out for any of those vexing children. He was surprised that none seemed to have picked up his trail, but who was he to complain? Once hidden within the shadows of the cave, just within sight of the mouth, he sat down on a boulder to catch his breath.*

*"Hardly a fitting refuge for the fearsome Jas Hook."*

*Hook leapt to his feet again and swung his hook around, pulling his cutlass from his belt. Something flitted in Hook's peripheral vision, but was gone when he turned. Soft laughter chimed behind him. He spun again to find nothing.*

*"What trickery is this?!" Hook demanded, superstition leeching into every thought. Was it possible this cave was cursed? Were there ghosts about? Or demons?*

*"Tricks are for children, like that creature that abandoned you," replied the voice from before.*

*Then, as if collecting and assembling herself from the shadows, a woman appeared. She was not like any woman Hook had ever seen, however. She wasn't even human, if he guessed correctly. Her green eyes glowed unnaturally there in the dark, and her long black hair moved like the waves on the ocean, its curls undulating with every move. There was a wildness about her, and yet something familiar.*

*"Pleased to make your acquaintance, lady fae," Hook said carefully.*

*The woman raised her eyebrows appreciatively, impressed with Hook's cleverness already.*

*"And yours, Captain James Hook," she replied. "You'll be glad to know I took the liberty of throwing those urchins off your trail."*

*"And for that, I thank you," Hook said, bowing. He was really turning on the charm now. "This doesn't seem like a fitting refuge for one of your kind either. Surely, you aren't here by choice. Have your heartless kin banished you here?"*

*The woman laughed and said, "Oh, how they wish they could. No, I'm here to make you an offer, one that involves those miserable cowards who left you for dead."*

*"I'm listening."*

The voyage back to London was much like the one to Never-Never Land: surreal and disconcerting. Once again, time, not days, passed oddly. Only when they began to draw closer to the mainland did the sun begin to set and the moon to rise properly. The group did not sail back into the harbor, but rather allowed themselves to run aground on a deserted bit of beach just outside the city proper. They were glad to find that it didn't seem to take very long, even if they couldn't be sure how long it actually was. The new plan was to spend one night on the outskirts of the city before continuing on to Wonderland. Taryn seemed to be the only one still even a little interested in seeing more of this London, but she quickly changed her mind when Ozzie pointed out that the Jolly Roger's crew was probably still there and still very sore about their ship being taken. Tynx spent most of the evening taking stock of their supplies and deciding what they needed to buy before heading out again. According to what Ozzie, Taryn, and Smitty had learned while studying Terturelia in Arbor Glen, human civilization pretty much dropped off as one approached Wonderland, so they needed to be prepared for anything.

"I mean *anything*," Taryn told him. "Talking plants and animals, flying toast, sentient playing cards, mad queens…you name it, they've probably got it."

Tynx smiled and said, "I think your imagination is getting the better of you again."

Since they had met back up with Taryn and Ozzie—barring the sobering event between Heinz and the mermaid—Tynx had noticed that both of them had gained a new kind of lightheartedness about them. They laughed more easily, expressed excitement more often, and seemed to imagine bigger. The changes were subtle enough that Smitty might not have noticed them, but Tynx certainly had when he used what Taryn and Ozzie called his sixth sense. He was certain this was a result of being with Peter and the lost boys, but he also suspected some kind of magic from the island had had something to do with it as well.

"No, dude," Ozzie chimed in, "she's right. The place is pretty wacky."

"And don't eat anything that says *eat me* and don't drink anything that says *drink me*," Smitty added.

"Right. Talking flowers, airborne breakfast, and don't ingest anything with suspicious labels," Tynx said. "I think I can manage."

The list was made, the path was planned out, and everyone was able to turn in for the first good night's sleep in a long while. Out of consideration for all they had gone through, Tynx and Smitty were offered the bed...with Taryn as the bedtime buffer, of course.

The job was so easy it was laughable. Conrade and Borachio's new employer only cared about the girl; the rest of them were expendable. First, however, there was the little matter of getting the innkeeper to look the other way. Luckily, they were bankrolled well, for their employer had heavy pockets. It took a bit of coaxing, but greed coupled with fear won out in the end, as it usually did. Up the stairs they crept, being as quiet as humanly possible. The last thing they wanted to do was wake the beast. They needed to catch it sleeping in order to kill it. The corridor was short but turned once, and the girl was in the room on the end, so they padded carefully and slowly on the wooden floors. When they reached the door, Conrade put his ear to the wood and listened. The only sound was muffled snoring. Good, this should be quick.

Heinz shifted his head from one paw to the other. He was watching the one that mewled closely. He didn't like that one sleeping so close to his beloved mistress and he couldn't rest when he wasn't certain of her safety. It just wasn't in him to do so. Why couldn't her favorite one be there instead of here on the floor next to him...snoring...like a troll in spring? After the eternity he had spent on that horrible rocking floor, he was exhausted. Wait! What was that? Heinz felt every muscle tighten. His ears perked up and listened hard. He looked towards the door and saw something. Shadows. He could see them moving through the crack between the floor and the door. Heinz sniffed the air. They didn't smell familiar, but he sensed their intentions. Mistress! Heinz leapt up and ran for the door, bounding for it just as it had begun to open. He overshot his jump—why were these human dens so small?!— and slammed against the door. It flew beneath Heinz's massive weight and slammed violently onto the arm that had been reaching through. There was some kind of weapon attached to that arm, which jerked and sent a piece of it flying towards the bed.

Conrade screamed and tried in vain to pull his arm back. He had heard the sound of his own bones breaking when the door had smashed against him. The crossbow went off, and that thrice-cursed fiend was making the most awful racket, barking, growling, and clicking. Borachio tried to pull Conrade back, which sent jolts of searing pain through his arm.

Ozzie, Taryn, Smitty, and Tynx were all yanked from sleep when a hellacious din of shouting, swearing, and snarling exploded in the room. A split second later, a crossbow bolt buried itself into the wall not inches from Tynx's head. Tynx shot out of bed, grabbing his scimitar, and took no more than one second to size up the situation. No matter why the man in the door with the crossbow was here, Heinz had it handled. Whoever he was, though, he was in trouble. The door might actually sever that arm if Heinz kept pushing on it as he was.

"Taryn!" Tynx yelled over the clamor. "Get Heinz!"

Taryn, whose brain didn't work as fast as Tynx's, was desperately trying to make heads or tails of what was happening. On hearing the command, she leapt out of bed and grabbed Heinz by his ruff. Ozzie was suddenly there too, pulling the enraged enfield back.

"Heinz, back off!" Taryn shouted.

That did it, but only just. Heinz got off the door and took a few steps back, but he didn't stop his furious tirade.

Tynx swung the door wide open and held his sword to the injured man's throat. There was a second one there as well, but the other patrons of the inn had already begun to emerge to see what all the commotion was about, blocking any chance to escape.

"You there!" Tynx commanded to a pair of onlookers. "Secure this one!" Looking to Borachio, Tynx said, "Resist and your friend will die. I will make sure of it."

Tynx didn't know if the second man actually cared about the welfare of the other, but he wasn't about to let either of them go without a fight.

Borachio glared at Tynx and then looked back to size up the two inn guests. It wasn't just them anymore, however; another had joined with them. They looked serious about their task, and he knew Conrade's death would be on his head if he ran. Reluctantly, he allowed himself to be taken prisoner.

With the second taken care of, Tynx turned his attention to the man whose arm was now a bloody, mangled mess.

"Smitty, I'm going to need fire, a hot poker and perhaps a shovel, clean water, bandages, and my kit."

"You're not actually going to help him," Smitty protested.

"Yes, Smitty, I am! Now are you going to help or are you going to quibble?"

"No way!" Smitty insisted, shaking his head.

"I'm going," Ozzie broke in and began to assemble the items as fast as possible.

Taryn remained with Heinz, watching everyone.

Tynx was a machine as he went about his craft. He gave succinct instructions to Ozzie, who was dutiful and attentive, and concentrated hard on saving as much of the arm as possible. Besides the damage the impact of the door had done, Heinz had maimed the end of Conrade's arm that had been trapped inside the room. Preventing any more blood loss had been the first priority, which was tricky at best. The flesh had split under pressure and been torn away by teeth and claws until it hung in strips. Before anything else was done, Tynx had to cauterize most of the wound just to keep the man alive for the moment. After that, even with all of his healing skills, magic, and herbalism, it was clear the shredded and now burned limb was a loss. Thus began the gruesome task of amputation. Conrade was given some strong liquor and a thick belt to bite. Ozzie assisted, the local constable arrived with a handful of men, all of whom watched the operation fearfully, and Tynx saved the life of the man who had tried to kill them.

By daybreak, things were finally wrapping up. Borachio had been taken away, but not before Taryn and Smitty got a chance to question him. Borachio was silent and sullen, however, and would say nothing except his name.

Conrade, similarly, told Tynx before he was taken away, "I am a man of my word, sir, and I have taken an oath to give you no more than that."

"I don't suppose your life is worth telling us to whom you made that oath, Conrade?" Tynx asked firmly.

"I am a man of my word."

"Very well. Gentlemen."

Tynx nodded to the constable and his men and watched them leave. He then looked to the innkeeper, who stank so strongly of guilt Tynx could sense it from across the room without even trying. He glared, but said nothing. Turning on his heel, he headed back up the stairs and was thankful when he saw everything packed up and ready to go.

*Imbeciles! How could they have failed so miserably? Clearly, this was a job he would have to do himself.*

# Chapter 16

*Smitty opened his eyes and realized he was back in the dream field. He turned, looking for the woman from before and saw her there. She was standing just as she had been before, and Smitty hurried towards her.*

*"You're here again," he remarked, curious about this second visit.*

*"I am, and I am so glad you're safe. I've been watching you, as I promised I would."*

*"Oh, um…thanks," Smitty said, smiling bashfully.*

*The woman smiled, but then her face turned serious.*

*"I am concerned for your safety, Loren. The creature is growing more bold."*

*"I—he," Smitty stammered. He finally confessed, "I don't know what to do."*

*It felt so good to get that off his chest! Taryn would never understand; Heinz protected her. Why should she be concerned? Tynx was too enamored with Taryn to see any side but hers, of course. Ozzie was the only one who might understand, but how could Smitty get him alone to talk about it without arousing suspicion in the other two? He couldn't, so the dream woman was the only one in whom he could confide.*

*"I understand," the woman said, "but why haven't you come to me if you felt this way? I told you, if you search for me, I will find you."*

*"I almost did," Smitty confessed, "but Tynx wouldn't let me."*

*"Ah, yes, after the beast attacked you."*

*"Yeah, after that."*

*"He's killed a mermaid, he maimed a man, and he could have killed you there on the wharf. What do you plan to do?"*

"I don't know. No one will listen to me."

"You are master of your own life, Loren," the woman said soberly. "You have a choice. I cannot help you until you do, however."

Smitty nodded, saying nothing. He couldn't imagine leaving Ozzie and Taryn. How would they all get home if he did?

"Can you help us get home?" he asked suddenly, coming to a realization. "Are you my guardian angel or something?"

The woman smiled again and said, "If it helps you to think of me as such, you may do so. And, yes, I have the power to help you."

"Really!? That's great!" Smitty gushed.

Relief was spreading through him. They had a way home!

"Beware, Loren Smith!" the woman said sternly. "Think of how your companions will react if you tell them of me."

"But...but they'll be so excited. It's so simple!"

"I guarantee they will not. They will be disappointed. They will turn on you!"

The woman's suddenly harsh tone coupled with her accusations was like dumping ice water on Smitty's excitement. More than that, it was making him indignant. He might not have been getting on great with them lately, but they were still his friends.

"Why would they do that?" he demanded.

"Think. Your friend, he loves this world. You can see the joy on his face as he walks its paths. And her, she rejected you for the half-elf, did she not? They want to be together."

"I—no!" Smitty objected. "They have families back home, friends, lives! They wouldn't leave them all behind."

The woman said nothing, but fixed Smitty with an expression of pity. The dream field suddenly began to fade. The woman receded, and Smitty called out to her, pleading with her to come back, but she was gone.

Travel to Wonderland was swift, as there wasn't much traffic going that way, and the group wasn't taking any chances. As they discussed the events of the previous night, it was quickly deduced that Conrade and Borachio had to be connected to the pirates somehow, if they weren't pirates themselves. The hope was that, after Conrade had been maimed so badly, no one else would dare come after them. That coupled with the fact that no sane person seemed keen on traveling into Wonderland. From what the group understood, it was a bit of an island unto itself. Scarcely any trade was done with the country, as there weren't really any exports to speak of. There were some rumors of poaching, which were then followed by rumors of what happened to those poachers. It would have been terrifying if it weren't so insane.

Besides the uncertainty of what they were headed into and the fear that lingered from their last night in London, there was still tension in the group. The elephant in the room was Smitty. Everyone knew that Heinz didn't trust him and that he didn't trust Heinz. Smitty knew that Tynx didn't trust him either, but Taryn did not. Tynx had time to confide in Ozzie as they were gathering supplies in Never Land. Ozzie objected to Tynx's fears, insisting that Smitty was just scared and having a hard time dealing with the situation.

"Taryn had a hard time dealing with the situation," Tynx had argued, "but she was loyal. Despite what she felt about you at that time and even me in the beginning—she didn't trust me as far as she could throw me, if you remember—she was true to both of us. Smitty...I don't know what he wouldn't do to help himself given the opportunity."

"Tynx, I've lived with the guy for two years. I know him."

"You've never lived with him in a situation that truly tested his mettle."

The argument had died there. Ozzie had said they would just have to agree to disagree on that point and that he had faith in Smitty.

Taryn, who hated for things to remain unresolved, was frustrated with the whole situation.

Smitty, on the other hand, was bothered by his latest visit from the dream woman. How could she say Taryn and Ozzie would just abandon their families? She obviously didn't know them at all. Smitty had seen both Ozzie and Taryn with their parents, and they all had good relationships. Then there was Kyla, Taryn's little sister. It was obvious to anyone with eyes that she was precious to Taryn, possibly more so since the death of their brother Kael. No, that was crazy. Smitty needed to get his thoughts straight, to make things right. This tension wasn't helping anything, but he couldn't shake the feeling the dream-woman's words had given him. She had been right about everything else. She had *known* about them. Maybe…just maybe…he needed to find her. Thankfully, or perhaps not, there wasn't really time to discuss these things. Once they entered into Wonderland, everything changed.

The first thing they noticed was the color. The color of everything was brighter, more lurid, and everything seemed to be outlined in sharp contrast. After that, there were the creatures. Ozzie and Tynx found them hilarious, starting with the butterflies. They were literally zippy, little pats of airborne butter.

"Puns," Taryn groaned. "Great."

"Puns are the highest form of humor, my dear," Tynx teased.

Taryn giggled when he smiled at her, and Smitty rolled his eyes. That was something else that was making him unhappy: Taryn and Tynx were getting closer. Since Never-Never Land, Taryn had been showing affection for Tynx more freely, which had been one of the barriers between them. Granted, their relationship was still incredibly tame by modern standards—they barely held hands—but the teasing, the looks, the giggling and flirting…it was sickening. Smitty said nothing, however.

Some of the other pun-creatures they saw included irises—variously colored eyeball-like creatures on stems that looked this way and that and even blinked—dragonflies—tiny dragons that flew on gossamer wings, which Ozzie immediately wanted for pets—and mockingbirds—horrible birds that insulted Taryn's freckles and Ozzie's hair and anything else they could. Thankfully, a warning bark from Heinz quieted these birds instantly.

"So how do we find these creatures of yours?" Tynx asked. "A cat and a caterpillar."

"Alice just ran into the Cheshire Cat, didn't she?" Taryn asked Smitty.

"Yeah," he replied simply. He then looked up and let out a startled shout. "On your head, Ozzie!"

Ozzie suddenly doubled over to fling off whatever was on him and started batting at his own head frantically. The thing, a floating pair of eyes that glowed even in the bright daylight, lazily disappeared and reappeared above Taryn's shoulder.

Heinz was looking at the thing curiously, uncertain whether or not to bother with it. The thing, whatever it was, confused him because he could see it, but he couldn't sense it properly. Tynx had his hand on his scimitar, but hadn't drawn it, also baffled by the odd eyes-creature.

"Know Alice, do you?" the creature asked curiously.

"In a way," Taryn said, doing her best to look at the thing she could not feel resting on her shoulder. "Who are you?"

"That depends on who you're looking for," the creature purred.

"Cheshire Cat?" Smitty asked. "You must have heard us talking about you."

With that, a smile appeared to join the eyes. It was an unnatural smile, far too wide for any face, and very toothy. The body began to appear as well. The Cat was slender and grey and very fluffy.

"I heard you speaking of Alice," the Cat said evasively.

"And?" Taryn asked.

"How do you know her?"

Ozzie opened his mouth, but Taryn stopped him.

"A question for a question," she said. "We don't answer one of yours until you answer one of ours."

The Cat looked intrigued and purred unsettlingly, "Very well. Ask your question."

Taryn then looked to Ozzie and Smitty, unsure of how to proceed.

"Is there a way to escape this realm to go to another one?" Smitty asked quickly. "I don't mean from Terturelia to Leleplar. I mean from Terturelia to a different...dimension, I guess."

The Cat narrowed his eyes at the group, landing on Heinz last. He hissed at the enfield, which set Heinz off barking madly.

"Heinz, settle down!" Taryn commanded.

Heinz obeyed, but still let slip a growl or two at the odd feline.

"Well?" Tynx asked. "Give him an answer, or you won't get yours."

The Cat smiled too widely and replied craftily, "Only one of the greater powers of this world would have the ability to do what you ask."

"Really?" Taryn urged. "Because Alice just fell down a rabbit hole."

"I wouldn't know about her means of getting here or getting back," the Cat replied easily. "My turn. Where is Alice?"

"No idea," Ozzie replied quickly. "Not sure she was ever real."

Taryn and Smitty remained silent. They knew Alice Liddell had been a real person, but she was dead and gone now. The Cat narrowed his eyes at Ozzie, and he opened his mouth to speak again.

"Our turn," Taryn interrupted. "Do you or the Caterpillar know who or what power in this world could send us back to a different realm? If so, which one or whom?"

"Two questions," the Cat purred. "Three, technically."

"No, the first was one question," Taryn insisted.

"Very well. No."

"No what?" Smitty asked.

"It's my turn now. Are you from the same world as Alice? And how did you get here in the first place?"

Ozzie, Taryn, and Smitty looked at each other, unsure how to answer. They all shrugged.

"No idea on either."

The Cat narrowed his eyes distastefully.

"Dull."

The Cat then disappeared.

"Wait! No!" Ozzie, Taryn, and Smitty said together.

But it was too late. The Cheshire Cat was gone. They all looked at each other desperately.

Camp was somber and unsettled that night. Taryn was pacing, Heinz following her like a monstrous shadow, while Smitty and Ozzie sat together in front of the fire, neither of them saying anything. Tynx stood a little way away watching all of them as he inspected his equipment.

Tynx could sense all of their disappointment, their despair, their fear, and their loneliness. They were aliens here, separated by an impassable gulf from their loved ones. Tynx felt for them, but had no words. Secretly, Tynx was more than a little pleased. Smitty he didn't much care for, but Taryn and Ozzie were the only two people that had completely overlooked his mixed heritage and accepted him for who he was. Granted, that was mostly because they were ignorant of what it was to have mixed parentage in his world, but their ignorance had changed him. It was warm and uplifting and gave him strength. And then they were gone. Much of that strength they had given him stayed because they had given him confidence, and he had learned there were advantages to being mixed race, but it was cold again without them. That's why he had gone to such lengths to find them in this country's America. Finding Arbor Glen had been fortunate, because Tynx had been growing desperate by then. That was most of the reason he traveled there with Roelrhir and Nariel in the first place; he had nowhere else to turn. Tynx had felt sick after Taryn told him their America wasn't here in Terturelia. What would have happened to him? How long would he have searched only to find nothing, never realizing they were still in another dimension? He didn't want them to go again. He didn't want to lose the friends who had looked at him unlike anyone else ever had, careless of his lineage. He didn't want them to go.

This didn't even touch how he felt about Taryn. Tynx watched her pace, wanting to take her in his arms and tell her it was all going to be fine. Why? Because he would keep her safe forever. Back in Arbor Glen, his elf friends had encouraged him to find someone that would make him happy, someone to settle down with, but no one was like Taryn. He smiled as he thought back to the times he had observed the she-elves in Arbor Glen. They were strong, yes, and lovely, but none of them had the same fire in them that Taryn did. Tynx couldn't help but be glad they had run into a dead end, and he felt terrible for his selfishness.

"What do you think he meant when he said no?" Ozzie asked softly.

"Who?" Smitty asked despondently.

"The Cheshire Cat."

"He meant we're screwed."

"What if he was just being evasive?"

"Even if he was, dude, what can we do about it? Nothing. We're stuck here!"

"No! We can't be," Ozzie insisted. "Something brought us here, so something has to be able to send us back."

"We don't know that whatever brought us here is benevolent! What if it's evil and just wants us to suffer?"

"Evil is not in control!" Ozzie said, angry now. "You can't let yourself believe that. We're going to get home."

Smitty sighed and covered his face with his hands. A part of him deep down, buried beneath his misery, was pleased with Ozzie's reaction. It reinforced what he had told the dream-woman in the field. They wanted to get home as much as he did.

Taryn watched and listened to Ozzie and Smitty's exchange in silence. Ozzie, ever positive, was doing his best to support his friend. She felt a hand on her shoulder and turned to see Tynx standing there. He had crept over, noiseless without even trying, while the boys were having their talk.

"What can I do?" he asked softly.

Taryn shook her head, not trusting herself to talk. Seeing Tynx unsteadied her already frayed resolve to remain tough. Since the Cat had disappeared, Taryn had been fighting to hang onto anger. Anger drove her when Ozzie couldn't hold her together, and he was busy. She didn't want to break down; that felt too much like defeat. She knew why Tynx was standing here now. He wanted to be the one to hold her together or, if it came to it, hold her up when she couldn't.

Tynx had done that before. One night, back in Leleplar, when Taryn had been reminded too strongly of her brother Kael and what had happened to him and of her anger and guilt towards Ozzie over it, Tynx had been what she needed that night.

Tynx reached out to take her hand, but she flinched away before she realized what she was doing. Taryn's face grew hot, and she looked down to avoid Tynx's eyes.

"Why are you running from me?" she heard Tynx whisper.

He reached for her again, and she shook him off as she turned and walked away into the trees. Tynx followed, sensing Taryn's embarrassment, her frustration, and—what surprised him most—her fear. What on earth did Taryn have to fear from him?

"What are you afraid of?" he hissed, not wanting to draw attention to them.

"Tynx, stop. Okay? I don't want to talk about it," Taryn replied tersely.

"What did I do?"

"For goodness sake, nothing!"

"Then why are you spurning me?"

"I'm not trying to! I just...you can't...ugh!"

"Taryn, I can't make sense of you right now. Everything you're feeling, it—"

"Stop it!" Taryn snapped. "Stop reading me or whatever it is you're doing! You don't get to be inside my head whenever you feel like it."

"Taryn, I care about you. I want to be here for you."

"That's exactly the problem!" Taryn exploded. "You can't be here for me because I can't afford to depend on you, not if we're trying to get home! Not that it seems likely at the moment."

At that, the first tears broke through the wall Taryn had built. She turned away from Tynx as she did her best to stop crying before she really got going. She could feel his eyes on her back. She waited stubbornly for several minutes, willing him to leave and knowing he could sense it...or something like it. When he didn't take the hint, she spoke again, trying to keep her emotions in check.

"Tynx, please leave me alone. I told you I don't want to talk about it."

"Then don't talk." He hesitated a moment before continuing slowly, "Taryn...I know you all want to go home. I have no doubt you will when the time is right, but this...this is all the time I have with you. While I have you, please, let me have you."

Taryn sighed. She was being selfish. She wasn't the only one in this...whatever it was. Tynx too had and would hurt again. She turned back towards him and hugged him tightly. Breathing in the woodsy scent of him, Taryn immediately felt better. She didn't cry, but she also wasn't angry anymore. She relaxed into Tynx as he held her and said nothing.

The sunrise the next morning was horrible. It shed light on the ugly fact that the group was lost. They had no idea what to do next; they didn't even have a direction to go. Before, they hadn't had a direction to go either, but they'd had a plan. The plan had been to aimlessly wander until they found the Cheshire Cat or Caterpillar. Well, now they didn't even have that, as poor a plan as it had been. They had been left with nothing.

"What if we try to find the Caterpillar?" Ozzie asked.

"I don't know that we'd be able to," Taryn replied with a sigh. "Alice was tiny when she ran into him. We run the risk of either stepping on him or missing him if we looked while we were big, and I don't think we should risk shrinking ourselves to find him."

"Plus, the Cat said he couldn't help us," Smitty added.

"We don't know for sure that's what he actually meant!" Ozzie insisted.

Taryn put a hand on Ozzie's and said gently, "Oz, I think it's safe to say he meant that wasn't going to work."

Heinz growled uneasily.

"If nothing else, there are places we can go for more information," Tynx suggested.

"Good thinking!" Ozzie said, jumping on the idea. "Give me the map again."

They had looked over the map the previous evening, but hadn't been able to agree on anything. It was too far to head back to Arbor Glen, and no one was keen to travel back through London. They could go the long way around, but that seemed to just invite danger. They had lost the light before much more discussion could take place.

Heinz barked once, twice, three times before Taryn shushed him.

"Now, let's think. We need magic. Obviously," Ozzie began determinedly. "Friendlies…"

"Magic isn't always the answer," Taryn said.

Tynx nodded appreciatively.

"Merlin," Smitty chimed in, catching Ozzie's drift. "Good fairies."

"Yes, dude, that is what I'm talking about."

"I don't follow," Tynx confessed.

"Potential allies," Smitty explained. "Magical ones."

Heinz was barking again and had begun circling the group in agitation. He nudged Taryn hard, growling.

"Heinz, what?" she snapped.

"Get up," Tynx ordered suddenly. "Now!"

"Tynx, wha—" Ozzie began.

"All of you! On your feet right now!"

Ozzie, Taryn, and Smitty obeyed but saw and heard nothing. Heinz was facing the trees and snarling now as he stood protectively in front of Taryn.

"Tynx," she whispered carefully, "what is it."

"I can't tell, but we should leave," he replied, concentrating on the forest beyond.

"Now? What about camp?" Smitty asked.

"No time. We need to go. Now. Carefully."

Tensely, the group retreated from camp, Ozzie clutching the map possessively. As they walked, they began to hear leaves rustling riotously, undergrowth surrendering beneath the crushing weight of something huge. There was a sickly, incongruous, gurgling noise too. Tynx stepped in front of his friends, hoping that perhaps whatever was coming might be benevolent. They were out of options, after all, so he didn't want to lose a potential opportunity for his friends, and there was no telling what surprises this mad land held.

The creature that emerged from the trees was horrendous to look upon. Its eyes glowed bright orange and its slender hands were mostly long razor sharp claws. Huge teeth dripped saliva while the thing burbled hungrily as it came.

The group stared fearfully at the thing, unable to believe the monstrosity they beheld.

"Run!" Ozzie cried suddenly, and they all took off.

The creature screeched angrily and followed as quickly as it could. It had an awkward gait, but the size of its legs made up for this.

"Taryn, Smitty, what is it?!" Tynx demanded as they ran.

"I don't know!" Taryn replied, focusing only on running faster.

"We're in Wonderland!" Ozzie called. "Surely, that thing must have been mentioned somewhere."

"There weren't really many baddies besides the Queen of Hearts!" Taryn said.

"Jabberwocky!" Smitty cried suddenly.

"Faster!" Smitty, Taryn, and Ozzie all yelled together.

As if in response, the Jabberwocky roared angrily. They could hear it crashing through the brush behind them, but it was impossible to tell if it was gaining or not. Suddenly, there was another figure, smaller than the Jabberwocky but massive still, joining the chase. This one was faster than the three humans, and it scooped up Taryn as it lumbered by.

"Taryn!" Ozzie yelled, seeing her disappear up into the trees, followed closely by Heinz.

"Where did she go?!" Tynx demanded, stopping short. He hadn't seen her taken, but he could sense her getting further away...or at least the sense of her fear was.

"Keep running!" Smitty yelled, the sounds of the Jabberwocky not far behind.

"They went into the trees!" Ozzie said.

"What was it?!"

"No idea!"

"Climb the trees!" Tynx commanded.

The half-elf was suddenly leaping up to one of the lower branches, spinning up and around it, and effortlessly alighting to another.

"Wait for the humans!" Ozzie called, scrambling after him.

Tynx quickly helped Smitty and Ozzie up just as the Jabberwocky came into view again.

"Quickly! Go!" Tynx told them, pulling his bow from his back.

He took a shot, but it bounced off the monster's scaly hide. Meanwhile, Ozzie and Smitty were trying to navigate the branches with almost no success. Smitty had already tried to leap to another branch, but had nearly slipped and fallen in his haste. Ozzie was trying to look anywhere but down, repeating Taryn's name to himself over and over again.

"Tynx, we'll never catch her this way. We're not squirrels!" Smitty said.

"Then climb down. I'll lead it away. Try to find Heinz's tracks."

"How will you—" Ozzie began.

Then Tynx took another shot, aiming for the creature's eyeball. The arrow met its mark, though not as directly as Tynx would have liked. The arrow hit the Jabberwocky's eye, but it only grazed it, slicing it open. Tynx had been aiming for a dead-on strike that would travel straight through to the brain. Nevertheless, the creature screeched in pain and rubbed at its injured eye uselessly.

"Here!" Tynx taunted. "Come and get me! There's more where that came from!"

With that, he took off through the trees back the way they had come, making sure to make lots of noise as he went. The Jabberwocky gave an angry, gurgling growl and turned to chase after Tynx, giving Ozzie and Smitty their escape. The two boys climbed down from the tree as fast as possible, stumbling at the dismount.

"Heinz's tracks," Ozzie said aloud, looking around. "Where'd he go?"

"Here!" Smitty called, chasing after the deep gouges of Heinz's talons.

The two followed the tracks, thankful they could no longer hear the Jabberwocky but also fearful of what they were pursuing.

Taryn screamed and fought and bit and scratched and whatever else she could to try and escape her captor. The arms that held her, however, were massive and she got nowhere…not that that stopped her.

"You are hurting me," came a voice suddenly. "Please, stop."

"No!" she screeched. "Let me go!"

"Why? Do you fancy the idea of being eaten?"

"I—no! I—where are you taking me?!"

"To safety."

"What about my friends?!"

"I will also rescue them if I can."

"Ah—oh…thank you," Taryn finally said, unsure of what else to say.

This was not quite the situation she thought it was. That being the case, she took stock of her…rescuer. He was a giant, that was clear. He had to be at least twelve feet tall, but she couldn't see much of him due to the cloak he wore. They were running and then climbing and then running some more. Finally, they reached their destination, a rundown dwelling—house, cottage, shack…none of these really seemed to apply to the haphazard place—that half stood on its own and was half supported by the trees around which it was built. The giant lifted Taryn to a little platform built into the tree branches and set her there gently.

"Stay," he said simply.

He then turned to find Heinz standing before him expectantly and wagging his tail.

"He likes you," Taryn called down.

The giant nodded to the enfield and then took off again. Heinz watched him go and then looked back up to Taryn.

"I think I have to stay here," Taryn called down. "Go help the boys." Heinz hesitated, and Taryn told him, "I promise I'm safe."

Heinz then did as he was told and took off.

Tynx stepped lightly from branch to branch like a dancer, looking back now and again to make sure he knew where the beast was. It had begun to falter. Tynx had probably blinded it in that eye, even if it was temporary, but the Jabberwocky was furious at him. Anger was driving it, which was never good. Tynx had taken a few more shots, but he hadn't been able to really wound it again. At least Ozzie and Smitty should be safe. Taryn...he prayed she was as well. She was tough, but there were things here much tougher. He looked back again and saw the creature had slowed. He had been making less noise now than before, hoping to confuse or lose the Jabberwocky. He needed to go back for the others, so he aimed his arrow for the forest on the other side of the Jabberwocky, pulled way back on the bowstring, and let the arrow fly. Success! The arrow hit a tree trunk with a satisfying *thunk*! The Jabberwocky heard the noise but had not seen it with his bad eye. It roared angrily and picked up its pursuit in the wrong direction. As soon as he saw it was safe, Tynx took off through the trees back towards where he hoped he would find Ozzie, Smitty, and Taryn.

Smitty and Ozzie continued to run despite the stitches in their sides. Only when the hulking figure came crashing through the trees did they stop...and scream. It was huge! It blocked out the sunlight behind it and was undoubtedly what had taken Taryn.

Ozzie yelled—angrily this time, not fearfully as he just had—and lunged at the creature.

"What did you do with her?! Give her back!" he ordered.

The giant, however, simply dipped down and caught Ozzie around the waist, lifting him up into the air and plucking his knife from his hand. Smitty, seeing he was no match for this behemoth, turned to run, but he too was caught and then carried like a football under the creature's arm. Both boys fought in vain as they were carried away.

Heinz caught up with the giant fairly easily and barked happily when he saw the giant's living cargo. Mistress will be so happy! Her favorite is coming back! Heinz also laughed to himself because the one that mewled seemed rather upset about being carried. Well, Mistress' favorite didn't seem too happy either, but it was what it was.

"Heinz! Sic him! Get him! Bite his legs off!" Mistress' favorite yelled frantically.

Heinz laughed to himself, lolling his tongue out before rushing ahead, back to see his mistress.

Tynx heard the cries of his companions long before he could see them. They were in danger, and he rushed through the trees to intercept. When he saw the gargantuan creature, however, he remained hidden, uncertain whether or not he could take on such a monster. The thing was covered in a cloak, disguising its true nature. If it was a troll or something of that ilk, arrows would do no good against its thick hide. Therefore, Tynx followed silently. Ozzie and Smitty seemed unharmed for now, which gave Tynx time. They finally arrived at what Tynx could only assume was the giant's lair.

Wood and mud blended together around tree trunks and boughs, creating a lumpy shanty of sorts. The roof was some mixture of reeds and thatching and more mud. What could only loosely be described as towers rose up into the trees, battlement-like platforms topping them higher than Tynx could see at the moment. Taryn had to be here as well, but the sense was faint. Where was she?! Was she injured?! That was it; he had to attack. The creature had just lifted Ozzie onto one of the high platforms and was reaching his now free hand for Smitty when Tynx leapt out from the trees and onto the creature's back.

The giant cried out in alarm and spun, flinging Tynx off him. Tynx flew and barely caught himself, landing on his feet before spinning to face the creature again. The giant had released Smitty onto the ground in order to face the crazed half-elf. Tynx leapt again, but stopped when he heard Taryn's voice call out.

"No! Tynx! Don't!" she cried.

He looked up to see her attempting to scramble down the side of a crooked turret. In her haste, however, she lost her grip on the uneven surfaces and went tumbling down through the air.

Tynx instinctively dropped his sword and reached out to catch her. He was too far away, though; he wasn't going to make it. The giant was suddenly there and caught her like a baby bird, gently but securely. Tynx stood staring in shock as the giant carefully placed Taryn on the ground before him.

"He saved me," Taryn said, trying to catch her breath.

"I saw," Tynx said.

"No, I mean earlier, when we were running from the Jabberwocky."

Tynx turned to the giant, who was staring down at him from his hood, and bowed his head as he knelt.

"You have my deepest apologies, sir," Tynx said gravely. "Had I known you were protecting my friends, I never would have raised a blade to you. I owe you a great debt."

"Can someone please save me?" Ozzie called down from his own perch.

"He doesn't like heights," Taryn said to the giant.

"You have my apologies as well, then," the giant replied.

He reached up and helped Ozzie down. Smitty, who had been hiding around the side of the shanty for most of this, uncertain of what to do, reemerged now and joined his friends.

"What can we do to repay this kindness?" Tynx asked.

"Nothing but stay a while and enjoy a meal with me. It has been a long time since I have had company."

"Very well," Tynx replied gladly.

The inside of the house was tidier than the outside by far, though shelves and other items were a bit lopsided due to the uneven walls and floor. There was also an odd, semi-circular fireplace in the floor, which served as a cooking station as well. They sat on the floor, as there was nearly no furniture to speak of, save for a large sleeping pallet, which was rolled up and leaning against a corner at the moment. The giant doffed his cloak, at which all four of the group tried not to recoil. The man was a mess of stitching and different flesh tones. Even his eyes were two different colors. He was completely bald as well, though whether or not that was a side effect of being reanimated was unclear.

"Are you…" Smitty asked. He exchanged a look with Taryn, who subtly shook her head, and he finished, "Are you okay?"

"Besides a few scrapes, I am fine," the creature replied with a smile.

"That's probably my fault," Taryn confessed sheepishly, hoping to take the attention off of the giant's horrible appearance. Placing a hand on the giant's, she added, "I'm really sorry."

"Nothing I cannot handle, my dear," the giant replied with a smile. He then turned his attention to the iron pot sitting over the fire and asked, "Now then, what are the likes of you young ones doing in Wonderland?"

At this, Ozzie, Taryn, Smitty, and Tynx all exchanged helpless glances. They couldn't tell their host the truth, not that there was much to tell now. The silence went on for too long, making it clear the group wasn't about to share.

"I understand," the creature said calmly. "We all have our secrets."

"Changing the subject entirely…or maybe not," Ozzie said, trying to hide his relief, "what can we call you? Giant-savior-man doesn't really roll off the tongue, you know?"

Their host laughed at that and replied, "You may call me Adam."

"Very nice to meet you, Adam," Tynx said, still wanting to make up for his attack, and the rest of the group agreed.

After this, the only conversation that occurred was about either Adam's lunch or the need to go back and salvage what they could of their camp. Adam volunteered to go back and help them with the camp, but the group politely declined. They needed to talk more about what to do next. It seemed rude, however, for all of them to run out so soon after Adam had been so kind, so Taryn and Ozzie stayed behind while Tynx and Smitty headed back to the campsite. If there was any damage, Tynx would have to decide what to do, and Taryn and Ozzie felt it would be better for them to stay with Adam since Smitty hadn't been exactly congenial lately.

# Chapter 17

The walk back to the campsite took a lot longer than Smitty remembered, though they had been running and then carried earlier that day. It was quiet and uncomfortable, and Smitty was still trying to think of ways to make nice.

"It's awfully nice of you to take such good care of us," he said awkwardly as they walked.

"Taryn and Ozzie are good friends," Tynx said tersely. "Besides, it's the right thing to do."

"You still don't trust me, eh?"

Tynx sighed and stopped. Turning to Smitty he asked, "Do you truly want to have this conversation? You might not like what I have to say."

Smitty shifted uncomfortably. Tynx was fixing him a hard look that made him feel somewhat vulnerable. He might be using that superpower or whatever it was Ozzie and Taryn said he had. Feelings-reading or something like that. Smitty was suddenly angry at the idea of Tynx intruding into his brain like that.

"Don't do your mind games on me!" he snapped.

"Beg your pardon?" Tynx asked evenly.

"That...that thing you do. The elfy sense-thing. That's an invasion of privacy!"

"Smitty, I can't turn it off. It'd be like asking you to stop seeing," Tynx explained calmly. "I can understand your objections, however. Therefore, would you feel better if I told you how I am feeling?"

"Wait...are we talking about our feelings?" Smitty asked, suddenly feeling as if he'd stumbled into a very uncomfortable trap and wasn't sure how he'd gotten there.

"I don't know. Are we?"

Smitty hesitated before shaking his head and saying, "Nope. Seems a little too…mmm, touchy-feely."

Tynx smiled suddenly and chuckled. "I can see why you and Ozzie get on." Turning, he started forward again and said, "I'm sure you're very pleasant under normal circumstances. Admittedly, however, yours are far from normal circumstances."

"You can say that again," Smitty said. Switching gears, he added, "And was that a shot or some kind of a pass?"

"I'm simply sharing my thoughts," Tynx replied nonchalantly.

Smitty didn't know what to say to that, so he said nothing in response. Instead, he turned the attention onto Tynx.

"So what do you imagine is going to happen between you and Taryn? I'm asking as her friend, of course."

Tynx knew that wasn't completely true. He had been able to sense Smitty's affection for Taryn, which had then soured to jealousy and was now something between bitter annoyance and apathy. Maybe that meant he was getting better about it? Nevertheless, he felt the need to be candid in the interest of peace.

"Heard that little exchange last night, did you?" Tynx joked.

"I'm pretty sure the whole of Tulgey Wood heard that little exchange," Smitty countered amicably.

Tynx laughed and then sighed heavily before admitting, "I have no idea what will happen between Taryn and I. Our…path together seems doomed to failure. You will all eventually go back home, I will stay here, and that will be that. I won't pretend knowing this makes the idea of her being gone again any easier."

The thick emotion in Tynx's voice as he said this was shocking to Smitty. Both because he suddenly saw just how deeply Tynx cared for Taryn and because he couldn't believe Tynx could be so willing to reveal so much to him. Something else from what Tynx had said stood out to Smitty even more than that, though.

"You really do believe we're going to get back. I mean, Ozzie says so, but he's always like that. Optimistic to the end. I'm just surprised you think so."

"Why wouldn't I?"

"Because you're realistic. Every time you make a decision, you look like it might be your last."

Tynx smiled and said warmly, "Ozzie just has a brighter spirit than I; it's his nature. He's not wrong, though. You all will get home, and I will be your guide until then."

Smitty was surprised then to find himself feeling better than he had in a long while.

"How do you think the camp fared?" Ozzie asked, pulling another weed from the ground.

Adam had some gardening to do—no one was surprised to learn he had a large vegetable garden plus a small herd of goats behind the house, seeing as how he had to sustain himself—so Taryn and Ozzie had volunteered to join him outside. Ozzie was idly pulling weeds here and there. It wasn't serious work, as Adam tended his garden very well, so there weren't many weeds to begin with. Meanwhile, Taryn was stretched out across Heinz as he lay in the sun. His tongue lolled out of his mouth as she raked her fingers up and down his back and shoulders.

"Debatable," Taryn replied. "I mean, the Jabberwocky came straight after us, so anything that was in its way might have gotten trashed. No telling."

"You think Smitty and your boy-toy are getting on okay?"

"Whoa, timeout!" Taryn said, making a T with her hands. "Since when is Tynx my boy-toy?"

Ozzie grinned widely at her, glad that he had incited a reaction from her. She was the best to tease. Taryn made a derisive sound in her throat and rolled her eyes, seeing exactly what Ozzie had done. She refused to dignify his taunts with any other response and sat up to scratch Heinz's belly. Heinz happily rolled onto his back and opened his mouth wide in a silent, bared teeth, slack-jawed smile of ecstasy. Ozzie came over and crouched down in front of Taryn.

"Seriously, do you think they're okay? Smitty hasn't been happy for a long time."

Shaking her head in exasperation, Taryn replied, "I have no idea. Probably. Tynx won't let Smitty do anything stupid."

"He's scared, you know," Ozzie prodded.

"I know he is, Oz. How well I know. It's just...eventually you have to suck it up and do what needs doing, whether it's walking across a fictional country to who knows where or to your own death with magic rocks. All that sulking isn't helping."

Ozzie smiled, remembering the morning Taryn had woken him up in Leleplar and told him they were leaving, specifically without Tynx. Not that it mattered much because Tynx followed them anyway, but she had stepped outside of her fear then and made the hard decision. He reached out and hugged her, knowing those memories were hard for her. Taryn had legitimately thought they were going to die back then and yet here they were, alive and well...watching Frankenstein's monster harvest cabbage.

Taryn hugged Ozzie back, feeling the waves of understanding rolling off of him. She was so thankful for that. Heinz, however, was not happy about this situation, as his belly was no longer being scratched. He pawed insistently at Taryn's arm, always careful not to slash her with his talons. Ozzie broke away from Taryn and joined her in loving on the massive enfield.

"Even so," Ozzie said, referring back to their conversation, "let's be sure to see if we can't cheer him up when they get back."

"Okay," Taryn agreed begrudgingly.

There were a few minutes of contented silence before Ozzie spoke again.

"So how does the story go?"

"Which story?"

"The Jabberwocky story."

"It's a poem, not really a story, by Lewis Carroll," Taryn explained. "I used to know it really well..." Her voice trailed off as she tried to remember. "'Twas brillig and the silthy tove, did gyre and gimble in the wabe. All mimsy were the borogroves, and the momeraths outgrabe. Beware the Jabberwock, my son, the jaws that bite, the claws that catch. Beware the Jub-Jub Bird and shun the frumious Bandersnatch. Something something vorpal blade...sword? Uffish thought...snicker snack...Callooh! Callay! Oh, frabjous day! And he went galumphing back."

Taryn waved her hand around through the parts she didn't really remember and shrugged at the end. Ozzie had fixed her with a confused look.

"Is that even English?" he asked.

"Eh," she said, wagging her hand back and forth uncertainly.

"Did you say you saw a momerath?" Both Ozzie and Taryn jumped, surprised by Adam's sudden intrusion, and he added, "My apologies. I did not mean to startle you. It's just that they have been eating the tops off of all of my vegetables."

Without the context of his statement, Adam would have looked frightening as he wielded his hoe like a weapon. As it was, Taryn and Ozzie couldn't help but smile.

"No, sorry, we didn't see any," Taryn said.

"Oh, but, hey, can you tell us if we need to worry about Jub-Jub Birds or Bandicoots—"

"Bandersnatches," Taryn corrected."

"—what she said?" Ozzie finished.

Adam laughed and replied, "The Jub-Jub Bird cares nothing for people unless they go near her nest." He motioned to Heinz and added, "As for the Bandersnatch, keep that one close and you'll have nothing to worry about."

Heinz chittered happily, knowing they were talking about him.

The camp wasn't exactly trashed, but there was considerable damage. The tent was completely destroyed; not even the fabric was salvageable. Two of the pallets were okay, as were most of the packs. Animals had gotten to their food reserves, however, and pretty much decimated them. It was disappointing to be sure, but Tynx reminded Smitty that Heinz could hunt for them, so that was something. Smitty was doing his best not to be scared, but it was difficult. Not only did they have no idea what to do now, but there was nowhere nearby to replenish their supplies. They were out of food! How long could they last now? A growing panic was gathering in his chest, and he began to think back to the dream woman.

Twilight had settled over everything when Smitty and Tynx arrived back at Adam's hut. Heinz was hungry and very disappointed at being told he wasn't allowed to eat any of Adam's goats, so he had gone off to hunt. Ozzie and Taryn were harvesting crabapples from a tree for dinner, which was a harder task that it had initially seemed. The crabapples had sharp pincers just like a real crab and snapped at anyone who came close. Adam warned that they could lose a finger if they weren't careful, so the best strategy was to knock the mature crabapples off the tree with a stick and then bash them to death before they could crawl away. Taryn was frankly disturbed by this, and Ozzie couldn't stop laughing about it.

"Get it? Crabapple! That's great!"

"Yeah, Oz, I get i—Oh! Get it! Get it! Get it! It's getting away!" she shrieked.

Taryn had just knocked a crabapple down, and Ozzie took out in one shot. Taryn cringed at the sound of its chitinous skin breaking, while Ozzie picked it up and added it to the large wooden bowl Adam had given to them for the task.

"Everything okay?" Tynx called, running around the side of the house.

Taryn's cries had alarmed him, but that was already wearing off now that he saw her safe and sound.

"Yes, it's fine," she groaned, embarrassed that he had seen her act so stupidly.

Tynx laughed at sensing her embarrassment, and relief that she was okay washed over him. He put an arm around her and kissed the top of her head before looking to the tree to try and figure out what they were doing. Meanwhile, Ozzie was giving Taryn a what-just-happened look. Tynx had never really been openly affectionate towards Taryn, not in the way that Ozzie was used to couples acting anyway. True, they had snuggled together while sleeping on many occasions, but Ozzie usually did the same when he was sleeping next to Taryn. More than once when there were three of them in a bed and Smitty was on the floor, Ozzie had awoken to find Tynx's arm draped over him because he had stretched it out over Taryn. That was just kind of something they did; it came with the territory. Just now, though, that was new. Tynx had kissed Taryn on the head so casually like it was something they did all the time. Taryn looked back at Ozzie uncertainly, but she was smiling too.

"Are these…crabapples?" Tynx asked curiously.

"Yeah, dude, get it?" Ozzie said, suddenly distracted by the punny produce.

Tynx laughed and looked back to Smitty, whom he could sense had come around the back of the house as well. There was something going on with him. He had been really anxious since coming back from gathering up the campsite, and Tynx couldn't understand why.

"Smitty?" he asked curiously.

Taryn and Ozzie turned to look at their friend as well and could see the conflict in his expression even without a sixth sense.

"What's going on, man?" Ozzie asked.

"Guys…I think I might know a way to help us," Smitty started uncertainly.

"Yeah?" Ozzie pressed excitedly.

"Yeah, I…" Smitty started. He wasn't quite sure how to explain things to his friends without sounding crazy, but they were out of food and options. "There's this woman. She's been coming to me in my dreams. She says she can help us get home."

"In your dreams?" Taryn asked quizzically, like she didn't quite grasp the concept.

"I know how that sounds, but she's real. She can help us get home. She said we just have to go look for her."

"Does she have a name?" Ozzie asked.

Smitty sighed with relief. At least Ozzie was taking him seriously.

"I don't know it," Smitty said more steadily than before, "but we can find her even without that."

"I don't know," Tynx said thoughtfully.

Smitty shot him a glare, immediately angry with him for shooting down his idea. Tynx thought he was so smart, but he certainly wasn't coming up with any solutions.

"It seems odd that she would appear only to you," Tynx said. "Why wouldn't she show herself to any of the rest of us? Or appear in person?"

Was Tynx suggesting Smitty was making it up? Smitty couldn't tell, which only made him angrier.

"She's real!" Smitty insisted. "I can't tell you how, but I know. And she can help us."

"I'm with Tynx," Taryn said. "It's sketchy that she only came to you."

"Of course you're with him," Smitty spat. "Your precious elf can do no wrong."

"Whoa, calm down," Taryn snapped. "I'm just trying to be sensible here. I wouldn't trust a stranger on the street who volunteered to give me a lift home, much less a magical entity in a strange land I know nothing about."

"Taryn's right, Smitty," Ozzie reasoned. "We don't know anything about this person."

Smitty gaped in disbelief at all three of them, unable to believe his ears.

"You're all crazy!" he finally cried. "We have a chance to go home, and you two are sitting there telling me that we shouldn't take it?!"

"Not without knowing more about this person," Ozzie said. "How do you know she's not trying to lure us into some kind of trap?"

"If someone who can walk through dreams wanted to catch us in a trap, I think she would have by now."

"We don't know that," Taryn countered. "We don't know anything about this person. I mean...sorry, but is it possible she's really just a dream?"

"Is that it? You need proof?" Smitty snarled. "Fine, I'll show you."

He then reached out and grabbed Taryn by the wrist. He began to drag her towards the trees, calling for the dream woman. Taryn was about to show Smitty just what happened to people who tried to move her against her will, but Tynx beat her to it. Tynx leapt forward and grabbed Smitty's arm. He contorted it the wrong way, making Smitty to grunt painfully and let go of Taryn.

"Keep your hands off her," Tynx growled, his expression deadly serious.

Smitty scowled at Tynx and rubbed his arm but said nothing as the half-elf stood in front of Taryn protectively.

"I know you're frightened, Smitty, and I'm sorry for that. I understand how badly you want to get home, but now is not the time to give into fear. We need to be intelligent and cautious."

"I'm not frightened! I'm just smart enough to know when to seize an opportunity. Your insane way of thinking is going to get us all killed or, at best, keep us here forever! And I get that. You love Taryn, but she doesn't belong here any more than the rest of us," Smitty snapped. Turning to Taryn, he ordered, "Little Fire Warrior of the Irish Hills, come!"

Taryn looked at Smitty in confusion at first, but her expression darkened to stormy rage as realization dawned on her.

"You're trying to…to *command* me with my true name?" Taryn snarled. She advanced on him as her voice raised in volume to a furious yell. "Seriously?! And just what were you thinking? That we'd run off to your friend who might be a member of the dark side? That she'd actually help us? Are you completely mental? She might stab us in the back, and maybe then we'll be *lucky enough* to be left in a ditch!"

"She'll send us home!" Smitty yelled back. "We'll finally be out of this deathtrap!"

"Guys! Both of you calm down!" Ozzie shouted over them. "Taryn's right, even if she is being a little dramatic." Taryn shot him a withering glare, and he replied evenly, "You are. Take it down a few notches."

"Then what are we supposed to do?" Smitty demanded. "I don't want to die here."

"You fight!" Taryn cried. "We all fight to make sure that doesn't happen! And we don't go running blindly into the arms of mysterious beings. We use our brains to figure out who she might be. Sorry if that seems too hard to you."

"Taryn," Tynx said gently.

She spun around to face him, still fired up, but he just looked at her levelly. Taryn took a deep breath and let it out slowly.

"Okay, that was kind of harsh," she admitted through gritted teeth. "We're not saying it's a no-go for sure. We just need more intel. Can you…I don't know, try to speak to her in your sleep tonight."

Smitty was shaking his head stubbornly before she even finished.

"No. We're out of food. We need to do this *now*."

"Dude, it's okay. Heinz can hunt fo—" Ozzie began.

Smitty cut him off furiously, "No way! I am not trusting my survival to Frankenstein's psychotic demon dog! We're probably all lucky it hasn't killed us in our sleep!"

"Smitty, Heinz is—" Tynx began.

Smitty swore at Tynx and threw up his hands. "I'm out, guys. Good luck with everything. I'm gonna go ahead and save myself."

He then turned on his heel and sprinted into the forest.

"Smitty, wait!" Ozzie cried, starting after him.

"No, wait here. I'll get him," Tynx said.

Ozzie stopped and watched as Tynx took off after his friend. If anyone could catch up with him in the growing darkness, it would be Tynx. He sighed heavily. Well, so much for cheering up Smitty. Turning to Taryn, he started to speak, but stopped when he saw her looking fearfully back at the house. He turned as well to see Adam there looking livid and dangerous.

Tynx ran, following Smitty's footprints in the grass. They were hard to see with so little light in the trees, but he was managing. What he couldn't understand was why he hadn't caught up with him yet. Smitty was fast, yes, faster than Ozzie and Taryn, but he wasn't this fast. Tynx was running at a steady pace that he knew was faster than what most humans could do. He didn't have time to think on that for long because he then heard Taryn and Ozzie screaming.

Smitty hadn't gone far when he saw movement in the trees. He stopped short, uncertain whether or not he should be scared. It could be a predator or Heinz or something harmless. It could also be the woman. Hesitantly, he walked forward, watching and listening for growls or something equally bad. The figure approached, and Smitty could see it looked human. Could it be? Was it? Yes! It was the dream woman that stepped out from the darkness now!

"You really came!" Smitty gushed.

"Of course I did," The woman cooed.

"Smitty!" a voice came echoing through the woods just then.

"Hey! That's Tynx! You have to show him you're real," Smitty said.

The woman shook her head, making her long hair float as if it were caught in a breeze.

"No. I do not reward naysayers. We are hidden. He won't find you now to try and drag you back there."

"But...but my friends," Smitty stuttered.

"They will find their own way," the woman said reassuringly.

"You're sure? How can you know that?" Smitty asked.

"It will all work out," she said, smiling warmly.

Smitty still felt his stomach twist with guilt at the idea of leaving Taryn and Ozzie. Ozzie especially, but the woman had said they'd be okay. The woman was holding out her hand to him, so he reached for her and, as soon as he took her hand, they blinked out of sight.

"A-Adam," Taryn stammered, her mind racing.

Smitty had mentioned Frankenstein. Adam must have heard it. What must he be thinking now? He looked ready to rip their arms off. He marched towards them, his huge feet pounding on the ground. Ozzie and Taryn grasped one another by the arm protectively, as if that would somehow do something against the enraged giant.

"Hang on," Ozzie said plaintively. "It's not—"

Adam scooped both of them up while Ozzie was midsentence and hoisted them above his head.

"How did you find me?!" he bellowed.

"Find you?" Ozzie cried, not making the connection. "What do you mean find you?"

"Lies!" Adam cried, and prepared to spike Ozzie like a football.

"Adam, don't!" Taryn shrieked. "Please!"

"Tell me what you know!" Adam commanded.

"Put us down, please!" Taryn begged. "Put us down, and we'll tell you everything!"

Adam growled unhappily and said, "You will tell me now, or I will crush him!"

To demonstrate, Adam squeezed Ozzie just enough to make a point. Ozzie groaned in pain, feeling everything in him compress.

"Stop! Stop!" Taryn screamed. "I'm sorry Doctor Frankenstein rejected you! It wasn't right! You were his responsibility, and he left you alone in the world. I don't know where you are in your story besides that because things are obviously different here, but you don't have to be afraid. We're no threat to you, so *please*! Stop hurting him!"

Adam then placed them on the ground, and Taryn rushed over to Ozzie to check on him. He was doubled over on the ground, gasping for breath, and Tynx suddenly emerged through the tree line. Adam growled at him, but Taryn spoke up before he could do anything.

"He doesn't know anything!"

Adam looked back down at Taryn, anger still contorting his stitched-together features into a hideous war mask. He reached for her again, pulling her from Ozzie's side, and lifted her to his face.

"Explain," he snarled.

"I-it's crazy, and you won't believe me."

"Explain," he said again.

"Okay! Okay!" Taryn said frantically, not wanting to get squeezed to death. "We're not from here. Where we're from, you're a character in a book, but like I said, everything here is different, so I don't know any more than what I already said!"

"It's true," Ozzie said cautiously, his voice shaking. "Frankenstein brought you to life with lightning, didn't he? Electricity."

Adam looked to Ozzie and back to Taryn and then to Tynx.

"I swear, it's the truth," Taryn insisted.

After a moment, Adam let out a massive sigh and sat down, Taryn still in hand. He released her and then put his head in his hands.

"Forgive me," he said, the words muffled behind his huge hands. "I thought he had sent you to find me...to kill me."

"No...no," Taryn said shakily. "We're...we're just lost."

Adam continued as if he hadn't heard her, "He's sent others after me...before I came here. He wants me destroyed." He finally lifted his face from his hands and looked to Ozzie. "The doctor would never share the secret to my birth. He's too afraid someone else will try to create another."

"I know," Ozzie said, even though he didn't.

"Forgive me," Adam said again. "I do not wish to be the monster he claims I am."

"You're not," Tynx said adamantly. "Our actions define us, not our makeup."

Taryn smiled at him when he said that, knowing he never would have been able to when they had first met.

"Your friend," Adam said, looking around, "where did he go?"

Tynx sighed and shook his head. "I don't know. It's too dark to track him now. Hopefully, he'll come to his senses and returned soon."

Adam apologized several times more and helped gather a few more crabapples for dinner. He dispatched them with unsettling ease. He also pulled some butterflies from a trap to go with dinner. He made crabapple soup, a strangely sweet and savory dish, and toasted the butterflies before serving it all with some warm goat's milk. Odd as it was, it was good, but Ozzie, Taryn, and Tynx couldn't appreciate it. They were all too worried about Smitty. Taryn was also still fairly angry with him over his use of her true name. She argued the point that he had basically tried to strip her of her free will, but both Ozzie and Tynx argued that he couldn't use it against her and it was stupid of him to try, so she should just let it go. Only because she knew they needed to find Smitty, get back on track, and that it wouldn't help anything to keep harping on it did she drop the subject. After this little discussion, it was quickly decided that Tynx would take Heinz out tomorrow if Smitty didn't come back that night. Surely, the enfield would be able to track him down. In the meantime, Tynx checked Ozzie and Taryn for injuries, though Ozzie was of the most concern.

"Two cracked ribs and a lot of contusions," Tynx finally pronounced. "You have to take it easy so the ribs heal."

"Got it," Ozzie sighed.

Taryn too was covered in bruises, which Heinz licked comfortingly when he returned from hunting. Thankfully, that was the extent of her injuries. Adam apologized again, and they told him not to worry about it.

"You must stay here," Adam insisted. "It is the least I can do."

"Thank you. That's very kind," Tynx replied.

"Maybe that will give us some time to figure out what to do now," Taryn suggested bleakly.

"You had mentioned you were lost," Adam said. "What do you mean?"

"Not all who wander are lost," Ozzie cut in, but no one seemed to notice. He still smiled at his own joke.

"We..." Taryn began uncertainly. "Like I said, we aren't from this world. We came here from France hoping the Cheshire

227

Cat or the Caterpillar could tell us how to get back. We ran into the Cat, but he couldn't, or maybe wouldn't, help us. Now we don't know where to go."

Adam shook his head and said, "That is a shame you came all this way. The Cat is a fool, and the Caterpillar…unreliable at best."

Taryn sank at these words. They had come all this way for nothing.

"We don't know what else to do," Ozzie confessed. "We thought about finding a wizard or something. Have you heard of Merlin? Maybe we could go to Camelot and find him."

"I do not know of this Merlin, but that does not mean he is not there or that he wouldn't help you. Whether or not he can do what you need is the bigger question. The fairies, though—"

"Yes, we've had some experience with them," Tynx cut in, grimacing.

"They have incredible power," Adam finished. "I believe you must take the risk."

"What risk?" Ozzie asked curiously.

"The fae can send you home," Adam said seriously. "I can tell you how to find their Court. One of their members saved me during a dark time in my life. You should know, however, they may exact a price from you."

Ozzie and Taryn exchanged a hesitant look, and she put a protective hand on his. Back in Leleplar, Tynx had warned that the fae folk might want to keep Ozzie after he had flirted with them. That wasn't a price they were willing to pay, but what if the fairies *could* help them? What if they got there and became prisoners anyway? Weren't there legends about fairies keeping people for hundreds of years just for fun? Was it worth the risk?

"What other options do we have?" Ozzie asked Taryn.

"I don't know," she replied softly. "We could try Camelot first, but it might be a wasted trip. I mean, the sooner we get home the better, right? The more we travel, the more we risk running into all kinds of trouble."

"I know what you mean," Ozzie said.

Taryn hesitated for a moment and then said more boldly, "I think we should do it, go to the Fairie Court. This might be our only shot."

Ozzie nodded.

Taryn then squeezed Ozzie's hand in hers and said firmly, "Hear me when I say this, Ozzie Thomason. I am *not* losing you to a fairie. Turn off your charm, your cute, your funny, and anything else they might find appealing. Got it?"

Ozzie's face broke into a huge smile, and he hugged Taryn.

"I love you too, Ryn." There was a pause before he added quickly, "There's nothing you can do to stop this charm."

"Stop!" Taryn laughed. "That's exactly what I'm talking about!"

Ozzie laughed with her, and Tynx smiled sadly as he watched them. They had hope again. They even had multiple options. If the fae refused to help—and assuming they escaped the Fairie Court safely—they could always try this Merlin chap. This was for the best, but Tynx couldn't help but feel sadness fill his heart. What if they found their way home this time? His friends would be gone again, for good this time, he was sure. Either way, whether or not this new plan was successful, he made a decision in that moment: if a price was demanded, he would pay it.

# Chapter 18

That night, as Ozzie, Taryn, and Tynx lay down to sleep, Taryn and Ozzie struggled to get comfortable. Everything was tender, so there wasn't any way they could lay that wasn't painful. They had other, more pressing concerns, however. Mainly, where had Smitty gone? It was dangerous out in the Tulgey Wood by himself. Why hadn't he come back? What if they didn't find him tomorrow?

Tynx, sensing Taryn's anxiety, gathered her gently into his arms as they all three lay there together, Heinz acting as a gargantuan pillow.

"Don't fret," he said soothingly. "It's going to be fine."

He then kissed the top of her head again, and Taryn exchanged another happy but quizzical glance with Ozzie. She certainly wasn't complaining. After his admission last night, she felt better about letting down her guard around him. After all, this was the only time he got with her, and she was enjoying the attention far more than she realized she would.

"Just don't kick me out of the bed, you two," Ozzie teased.

Of course, by "bed" he meant "Adam's oversized pallet"— Adam had insisted they use it, especially now that they were healing from injuries caused by him. Tynx smiled at Ozzie and kissed Taryn's head again, playfully this time. Taryn was grinning widely as she snuggled against Tynx.

*Things were not going well. Erik had been following the group for what seemed like an eternity. The beast was still there protecting Taryn, which made it impossible to get close. The monster posed a dire threat as well, and Erik knew he would never be able to reason with the hideous creature. Erik had begun to grow weary of this venture, questioning whether or not this was really the path he was meant to follow. When he saw Tynx kiss Taryn so tenderly as she and Ozzie gathered crabapples, though, his fury burned within him. Erik was tempted to rush out from his hiding place just then and snap the half-elf's neck, but that would have given everything away. Instead, he had watched and then followed when Smitty ran off. Erik watched from under cover as Smitty disappeared from sight right before his eyes. There was more happening here than Erik knew, something he wanted no part of. He would have to retreat for now. Very well. He had some things to prepare anyway.*

The next morning, Ozzie awoke to see Tynx gone, but Taryn still slept just next to him. Heinz was gone as well, which probably meant they had already left to search for Smitty. Ozzie was keen to be up and about, even if he couldn't do anything to help. His body complained at him loudly as he sat up, but Ozzie winced through the pain as he scooted closer to Taryn. He touched her nose gently and whispered her name. He knew how she could be in the mornings, so he was careful. Taryn stirred slightly, but nothing more, so he tried again. She finally opened her eyes, but her face turned into an annoyed scowl almost immediately.

"Good morning, gorgeous," Ozzie teased.

Taryn made a sound at him like an angry cat.

"Happy to see me?" he asked, grinning too widely.

Ozzie stared at her, keeping his smile fixed in place. It went on for too long and just became weird, and Taryn couldn't help but eventually laugh at Ozzie's maniac impression.

"Come on!" Ozzie said now that she was awake.

"Be careful!" she scolded, seeing him get up with some difficulty. "You'll hurt yourself!"

Taryn followed begrudgingly, but they found no one outside. Not even Adam was anywhere to be seen. Maybe he had gone out to help search for Smitty? Taryn and Ozzie exchanged worried looks, but neither said a word.

Tynx and Adam jogged after Heinz, but it wasn't long until they came to a dead end. Heinz was tracking Smitty's scent despite his unhappiness over doing so. The pointy-eared one had a way of speaking to him the humans couldn't. When Tynx had told Heinz what he wanted him to do, Heinz had growled and lowered his head obstinately.

"Heinz, this is what your mistress wants, and you know it!" Tynx had snapped at him, looking Heinz straight in the eyes.

This was a challenge, especially as Tynx refused to break eye contact with Heinz. He was doing something else too as he stood there. He was projecting his will towards Heinz, or rather his will on Taryn's behalf. Heinz snorted angrily, but his heart was being tugged in the opposite direction. The pointy-eared one was right; Mistress wanted to find the one that mewled. Therefore, Heinz began to sniff the ground to find the stink of the one that mewled. When he found it, he took off, not bothering to wait for the giant and the pointy-eared one.

Tynx ran after Heinz with his heart in his throat. He had worried all night about Smitty, about where he might be or what might be happening to him. Tynx was angry, too. He was angry with Smitty for his stupidity and cowardice and selfishness. He had to remind himself not to throttle Smitty when they found him…if they found him. There was a terrible fear in the back of Tynx's mind that something had happened to him during the night, the one time he was separated from the rest of the group. He prayed desperately that they would find him safe and sound.

The trail ran on only for a short while before it stopped. Heinz went back to check, sure that he had missed something. He followed it carefully. Suddenly, it was gone again. Just…gone. Heinz looked up, thinking the one that mewled must be hiding up in the trees. That was the only way his scent could have disappeared. No, he couldn't have made that jump. Only the pointy-eared one could make a leap like that. There was another scent here, though, but it was strange and confusing. It almost smelled like the wind before a storm, but it was…thinner. Heinz circled the spot in agitation, unsure what to make of it.

Tynx and Adam had caught up and were watching the enfield work. Not knowing what else to do about the strange smell, Heinz finally decided there was only one thing to do. He lifted a leg and peed on the spot, proclaiming his dominance. Tynx sighed and leaned back against a tree. He ran his hands through his hair, trying to think of something, anything, to do.

"You cannot blame yourself," Adam said, watching Tynx with concern.

"He was my responsibility," Tynx replied angrily. "I promised to keep them safe, to keep them *all* safe."

"You cannot control them," Adam said sensibly.

Tynx didn't respond. Instead he ran his hands through his hair again. Suddenly, he drew his sword from its scabbard and lashed out at a nearby branch, letting out a furious yell as he did. The branch fell cleanly from the bough to which it had been attached and landed on the ground with an indignant rustle and an angry thud. Then Tynx dropped his sword and fell to his knees.

"I can't go back and face them," he whispered more to himself than anyone else. "I can't tell them Smitty is gone. I can't tell them I failed, not when they put so much faith in me."

Adam said nothing for a long moment.

"People make their own choices for good or ill," Adam said finally. His voice was grave as he spoke. "You made a vow to them. You will most certainly have failed if you don't follow through for the two that remain."

Now it was Tynx's turn to take a moment before answering. When he did, his voice was still despairing, but it was stronger than it had been.

"I know. Just…just give me a moment. I need to think about what I'll say to them."

"I don't know, Oz," Taryn was saying uncertainly. "They look pretty serious."

"No! They're full of lies! Here, don't look at them. That way they can't cast their spell on you."

Holding Taryn by the shoulders, Ozzie turned her around, at which point the bleating started. The two were standing in front of the goat pen. Taryn had been lured over by the sound of goat horns banging on empty food troughs. She was concerned they were hungry and needed breakfast, but Ozzie wasn't buying it. Now that the humans weren't looking at them, the goats had begun to complain…loudly.

"Adam knows his business," Ozzie said loudly to be heard over the noise. "If he needed to feed them before he left, he would have done."

"But…but they look so sad."

"Just wait till Heinz gets back. Then you can pour your maternal-ness over him. Come on."

Ozzie led her away from the goat pen. He had been trying to distract her all morning. They were both worried for Smitty, but now without Tynx or Heinz, Taryn was especially concerned. What if whatever had taken Smitty—he surely must have been taken since he never came back—had taken Tynx and Heinz and Adam now, too? What if she and Ozzie were all alone? She had then reasoned that anything would be hard pressed to take on all three and survive. Plus, Smitty was probably just being stubborn, the stupid jerk, but she couldn't shake off her worries completely. Ozzie could tell Taryn was struggling internally even if he didn't know the exact details.

"So if you could choose to meet any character here, who would it be?" Ozzie asked.

"Any character?" Taryn asked curiously.

"Sure."

Taryn looked flabbergasted. "I honestly don't know. Kind of changes the game now that we potentially could, doesn't it? What's that saying? Don't meet your heroes."

"You think you'd be disappointed?" Ozzie asked curiously.

"Maybe," Taryn replied shrugging.

Ozzie nodded and looked back out to the trees. Taryn had noticed him doing this all morning. He was also really concerned, but he had been hiding it for her sake, putting his fears aside to make sure she was okay. Taryn reached out and hugged Ozzie—gently so as not to hurt him—and leaned her head on him. He really was the best friend anyone could have. She already knew this, but it still floored her sometimes when she saw it come out like this.

"Thanks, friend," she said happily.

Ozzie smiled and returned the embrace.

"Of course, friend," he said.

"He'll be okay," Taryn said, hoping to console him as well as convince herself. "If there's one thing Smitty's good at, it's self-preservation. I don't mean that as an insult. It's just a fact."

"Yeah," Ozzie agreed.

He had to admit, Smitty was pretty good about knowing what to do to save himself. That had been pretty apparent this entire trip, even if that meant they sometimes disagreed. Ozzie kissed Taryn's forehead, thankful for her in that moment.

Tynx and Adam walked back into Adam's clearing slowly, Tynx taking up the rear. He was still trying to decide on the best thing to say. Heinz had trotted ahead happily, glad this whole business was over with and excited to be getting back to his mistress. When Ozzie and Taryn saw Heinz come round the corner of the house, they rushed around to meet Adam and Tynx and Smitty. Heinz was making that somewhat difficult, as he was insisting on getting some hello cuddles before he would let Taryn go off. He was still bumping his head against Taryn's hand when Tynx came within sight. Both Taryn and Ozzie's hearts sank when they saw no sign of Smitty.

"Tynx," Ozzie said fearfully.

Tynx shook his head. "I'm so sorry," he said softly. "There's no sign of him. I'm so, so sorry."

"He's gone?" Taryn asked in disbelief. "How can he be gone? Where could he possibly go?"

"I don't know," Tynx said, his voice full of shame. He took Taryn's hands in his and said, "I'm *so* sorry."

"Why do you keep saying it like that?" Ozzie demanded suddenly. "You said there was no sign of him. What did you see?"

"The trail ran cold," Tynx explained, Ozzie's tone sending darts into him. "It just stopped. I'm so sorry. I know I said...I know I said I'd keep you all safe."

"Is Smitty dead?!" Ozzie asked angrily.

"I don't have any reason to think so. I just don't know where he's gone."

"Good! Then pull yourself together, man."

"Ozzie, calm down," Taryn interjected. "You're being a little harsh."

"I just don't understand why he sounds like it's all over," Ozzie replied. "It's not like we're just going to abandon Smitty to whatever. We're not done looking. We'll go back out. We'll find something."

"Ozzie, there is nothing to find," Tynx said. "I promise I will do anything I can to help find Smitty, but he did not get away on foot or by any natural means I know. I'm so sorry."

"Why are you still saying you're sorry?!" Ozzie cried in exasperation.

"Because I said I would protect you all!" Tynx shouted back. "I vowed to keep you all safe, and Smitty is *somewhere* out there now, and I have no idea where to look or how to find him! I failed you and I'm sorry for it!"

"Dude! You can't blame yourself for Smitty running off! You tried to go after him, but he got away. We don't blame you for that. Just stop sounding so defeated."

Tynx looked at Ozzie in confusion. He was frustrated with Tynx, which made sense, but what he was saying about why didn't. He was frustrated over Tynx's reaction to the failure? But why?

"Tynx, just spidey-sense me so we can move on," Ozzie said.

"I am," Tynx replied, his face unchanging. "I don't understand."

Taryn didn't understand either. Tynx and Ozzie were arguing, which was new, so she wasn't sure what to do. She decided to stay out of it for the moment.

"Did I just stump your super-sense?" Ozzie asked, a smile playing at the corner of his mouth.

"Yes, in fact, you did." Tynx replied. "Why is my remorse so vexing to you?"

"Because you can't give up on us, man!" Ozzie replied emphatically. "Not now, not when we need you more than ever!"

"You still trust me? Even after I failed to keep Smitty here?"

"You can't control him," Ozzie replied. "The important thing is that we find him."

Tynx was a little bit floored. Ozzie wasn't angry with him for Smitty's disappearance. Neither was Taryn. Ozzie, ever resilient, just wanted to start planning on how to find Smitty and get him back. How could they not blame him for this? Tynx snuck a glance at Adam, who simply smiled and nodded.

"So where do we start?" Taryn asked, carefully venturing back into the conversation.

Smitty wandered from a stone hallway out to a copse of trees and back to a stone hallway again before coming out to a garden. The...palace?...was a strange and beautiful rambling sort of place that was some combination of castle and nature. There was some kind of design or logic here, as Smitty had found a few pathways so far, mostly from his...room?...and back.

He and the woman had arrived the night before, materializing out of nothing, appearing in a round room with stone walls, a floor of soft grass, and no roof whatsoever. The moon was fat and full and hung low in the sky, shining brightly down on them, while fireflies glided to and fro, shining for a moment before going out again. Smitty was so entranced by the beauty of the place for a moment, he forgot what had just happened. He turned and saw the woman, though, looking so pale as if made from ivory and quickly came back to himself.

"You did it! I think...is this home?"

"This is my home," replied the woman wearily. "I know you have many questions, but we should wait to talk until morning."

She then turned to leave.

"So...what should I do?" Smitty asked, suddenly feeling very lost.

"Rest. You can sleep here," the woman said simply.

Smitty agreed quietly, though his hostess hadn't stopped to answer his question, so she was gone now. Well, she had looked pretty tired. Truly alone now, he looked around the room and was somewhat disappointed at the scarcity of the space. There was a tree there, just large enough for Smitty to fit his arms around, and nothing else. The grass was very thick, though, and provided a surprising amount of cushion. Smitty sat down on the ground and rested his back against the tree. He found himself oddly tired, though, and fell asleep within minutes.

As Smitty walked around the palace now, he was still working kinks out of his neck and back. He had awoken to sunshine and birdsong and decided to go exploring on his own.

He was thinking now about the argument from yesterday. Guilt twisted his insides when he thought about Ozzie and Taryn. He had abandoned them, but the woman had said she didn't reward naysayers. She wouldn't help them. Then again, she had also said they would be fine and that they'd find their own way, so that was okay, right? Hadn't they made a choice? They had wanted to find out more about the woman, question her probably. If it was Taryn or Tynx, interrogate was probably a better word. Smitty couldn't believe he used to have a thing for Taryn. She was harsh and judgmental and insensitive to him while Tynx and Ozzie could do no wrong. Well, Ozzie was a good guy, so no offense meant there. He'd stuck by Smitty this whole time. Yeah, Smitty felt guilty about leaving him, but not Taryn or Tynx. Those two were made for each other. Ozzie would be okay, though; that kid always landed on his feet.

Smitty eventually came into a little glade and found a roughly hewn table laden with food. Setting out the food was the woman, his rescuer.

"Hey! Good morning!" he beamed.

The woman turned and smiled at him evenly.

"Good morning, Loren."

"Please, call me Smitty," he said congenially, cringing internally at the use of his given name. "And thank you."

"For what?" the woman asked, motioning towards the table.

"For picking me up. You saved me, you know."

"I know, my dear. I know. Please, eat. Restore yourself."

Smitty looked down and couldn't decide what to eat first. There were apples and pomegranates, seared meat, and some kind of hot gruel…or maybe it was a stew. He grabbed an apple and some of the meat and tucked in.

"If you don't mind me asking," he ventured carefully, "what should I call you? I don't know your name or anything."

"Deianira," the woman replied simply.

"That's a pretty name," Smitty replied. He trailed off there because he realized he had nothing else to share and only one thing to ask: when can you send me home? "Is that a…family name?" he finally floundered.

Deianira laughed gently and replied, "Many of us bear names you are probably not familiar with."

"Us?"

"You may have realized, young Smitty, that I am not human."

Smitty hadn't realized that, but now that he thought about it, it made sense. Sure, she could have been human and just had magic or something, but what did that mean she was? His face must have given him away because Deianira answered his question without him having to have asked it.

"I am fae," she replied.

Now Smitty was really curious. "Fae? As in fairie? Like, tiny with wings and stuff?"

Deianira laughed again and said, "True, some of my kind are very small and have wings, but we come in many forms. I have sisters that take the forms of trees and protect forests and glades and others that look like humans and ensure that crops grow. Some of my brothers make volcanoes spit fire and lead mortals to drink and revelry. Different abilities, different domains, you will never meet two alike."

"Ah," was all Smitty could think to say for the moment. That did explain her slightly…aloof nature. "So what's your…domain?"

"I am a spirit of the world. I wander here and there…"

She trailed off as if the rest was implied, but it wasn't. Not for Smitty anyway; he still had no idea what she did.

"I guess that's how you're able to blink between places?" he asked.

"Indeed, though that is a very difficult thing indeed, even more so with another."

"Have you recovered?"

"Not yet. It will take time."

"And then I can go home?"

He hadn't meant for it to come out like that. He was so eager to get back, though, it had just come out. He was terrified of ticking her off and losing his chance forever. She seemed pretty even-keeled, but he really didn't want to push his luck. Smitty immediately tried to backtrack, but Deianira raised a hand to silence him.

"I know how you feel, young Smitty, but you must understand the energy it will require. I may look young, but I have lived for eons. You must be patient while I prepare. In the meantime, we have a task."

Smitty might have made a joke about how good she looked for her age, but instead he knitted his brows together in confusion and asked, "A task?" She'd never mentioned a task.

"The enfield who travels with your friends, he is a danger. You know this. It is our task to end the creature."

"Whoa! You mean kill him? Deianira, I hate that thing, but Taryn and Ozzie and Tynx...they'd never forgive me. We can't kill Heinz."

"They will understand in time, as I'm sure you do now, it is the right thing to do. The creature is a danger. He has killed already and will kill again. It might be one of your friends next. We must destroy him for the safety of all."

Smitty's mouth went dry. What Deianira said made sense. Heinz would never hurt Taryn, but what about Ozzie? What if they argued and Heinz decided Ozzie was a threat? Would he end up like that mermaid in Never-Never Land? He looked at Deianira fearfully, quailing inside at the idea of going up against Heinz, but she looked so calmly and confidently at him that he knew she must have a plan.

*Hook sneered at the banal conversation between Deianira and Smitty. He'd wanted to kill the boy in his sleep, but Deianira had forbidden it.*

*"The half-elf is the one you want," Deianira hissed at him. "This one is only a simple pawn, but he's my pawn now, so I expect you to keep your hand and hook off him. Do I make myself clear, Mister Hook?"*

*"Aye," Hook growled.*

*Deianira may have been worn out from her journey, but she was still fae and unpredictable. She could turn on him at any time, so he did as he was told and remained out of sight.*

It had been several days since Smitty's disappearance, and everyone had been busy. Adam volunteered to replenish what supplies he could, but Heinz would have to hunt for them to supplement their meals until they reached another town, which would apparently be a while. The group would have to make their way out of Wonderland and towards an area Adam called Gloriana's Green. He didn't know if that was actually its name, but it was what his fairie rescuer had called it when she had rescued him. He didn't know her name, but he had taken to calling her Gloriana for lack of a better option. Both regions had vast stretches of wilderness and almost no mapped settlements to speak of. Adam told the group they might run across traders on their way or perhaps even some villages, but not to count on anything. Tynx told Ozzie and Taryn to take it easy so their injuries would heal, Ozzie especially, but they were both too anxious. Everyone except Heinz would often glance at the tree line in the hopes that Smitty would miraculously return, but he never did.

To help prepare for their journey and to keep their minds off of their AWOL comrade, Taryn and Ozzie agreed to any task that was asked of them. Hard labor and anything strenuous was left to Tynx and Adam, but Taryn and Ozzie worked together to sew a new tent and repair their packs, made lists and inventoried their slowly growing pile of supplies, and anything else they could do to either hurry things along or replenish what Adam was so generously sharing. Adam, however, seemed to need no help at all.

Having traveled and lived alone for so long, Adam's survival skills were even better than Tynx's. He provided goatskins— "From good goats whose time had come."—for the tent as well as the pattern, and he showed them the best way to lay out the skins so there was the least amount of waste.

"Oz, this should be right up your alley," Taryn teased. Turning to Tynx and Adam, he said, "Straight A's in Home Ec. class, this one."

"What is that?" Adam asked curiously.

"It's a class we were required to take in Middle School. We learned to sew and cook and other domestic type things like that."

"You have to take a class for that?" Tynx asked in confusion.

"Yup," Ozzie replied. "And it's a great way to impress the ladies."

Taryn laughed so hard at that she snorted. "Oh, you guys should have seen him! When we were learning to make pancakes, he decided he was going to make this enormous monster pancake, as big as the pan. Then, he turns to this girl next to him—"

"Lexi Smith," Ozzie added.

"—and he says to her, 'Hey, wanna see me flip this? No hands'." Taryn made her voice very low and dramatic when she impersonated Ozzie, but she was practically crowing the next sentence. "Then, he goes to flip the pancake in the pan, but it wasn't cooked yet because he forgot to turn the burner on, and he flung batter all over himself and Lexi!"

"Had she not gone to wash the batter from her hair, she would have been impressed by the mega-pancake once it was finally done," Ozzie replied confidently.

Taryn smirked at him and nodded sarcastically.

So the tent was easy enough, and Tynx made the poles for it. Adam foraged for food, taking Heinz out with him to sniff out as much as possible. Within a few days, they were ready to set off again. The goodbyes were difficult, as Ozzie, Taryn, and Tynx had become quite attached to Adam over the last few days, and the former two knew they would never see him again.

"Stay strong, okay?" Taryn said, hugging Adam around his gigantic neck.

"I'll come back if I can," Tynx promised.

Ozzie gave Adam a high five, wherein Ozzie's hand barely covered the giant's palm. Adam watched them go, and it wasn't long before they disappeared into the Tulgey Wood.


"So what should we expect to find in fairie land?" Tynx asked. "I mean, from your perspective as readers?"

Adam had given the three advice on travel and Gloriana's Green from his own experience, and he had asked Taryn and Ozzie to refrain from sharing anything with him about what they knew.

"We should not know so much about our own lives and the world in which we live," Adam had said sagely. "Whatever is meant to happen will happen."

Now that the group had left Adam, they were free to discuss possibilities.

"So many things," Taryn said heavily. "There's no telling. I mean, for us, the word fairie is kind of broad. It could mean a wood sprite living in a tree or a spirit of the air or even a dwarf."

"Truly?" Tynx asked, looking dubious. "I've met a few dwarves that would take offense to that. What's the tale like?"

"Tales, plural," Ozzie said. "Fairytales is a common term for all kinds of magical stories."

"Yup," Taryn confirmed.

Taryn and Ozzie then began to share the various fairie-related stories they had grown up with. The name Gloriana's Green wasn't familiar to either of them, which only led to more speculation as to what the name meant. Tynx was floored by the popularity of fairies, mostly because of how annoying he found them.

Smitty clung closely to the tree, gripping the smooth bark like a dangling man holding onto a cliff's ledge. The plan was simple, so simple that Deianira deemed it necessary to only go over a few times. Smitty, however, had been over it in his head hundreds. He repeated it again and again, a mantra that helped to ease his panic.

"You will be fine, Smitty," Deianira had assured him. "I will be there. I will shield you and make sure nothing happens to you."

It was hard to tell how long Smitty had been with Deianira, passing the days in her retreat like he was on vacation. Her home was either endless or changed by the hour. Smitty could spend an entire day exploring and then find all new places the next day. Food was readily available, and Deianira would appear if he sought her out. She wasn't much for company, but then again she wasn't human. What would they talk about anyway? "Read any good books lately? Oh, right, you're a possibly-immortal creature. You probably don't need to read books." He had thought of a few questions to ask her:

"So do you visit with other fae? Or do they visit you?"

"No," was all she said in response, as if it was simply not a done thing.

"How long have you lived?"

"It's difficult to keep track. I do not view the world as you do, each day passing with the sun's cycle. I see time in the life of a tree, the journey of a mortal, the song of a bird."

Smitty could understand that a bit better now. The sky went from light to dark and light again in her glade or wherever it was, and night came and went, but there didn't seem to be any set cycle. They could be entirely outside of time for all he knew. Even so, he was curious, but Deianira eventually grew weary of his questions. She told him she must rest and prepare for their next step, and Smitty unhappily withdrew from her presence.

Then, suddenly and without warning, Deianira had come to Smitty and told him it was time. They must destroy the creature that threatened his friends' lives. It was time to kill Heinz.

Smitty hated the idea of what he was about to do. He knew it was going to break Taryn's heart, probably Tynx's and Ozzie's, too.

They loved Heinz despite how dangerous he was. Smitty may have been at odds with Taryn and Tynx, but he didn't want to cause them pain. Still, it was necessary.

He heard them before he saw them, Ozzie's voice ringing out excitedly about something he had just seen. They were near the border of the Tulgey Wood, so there was no telling what type of punny animal or strange thing they had seen now. Smitty readied himself, knowing he'd have to be fast. If he wasn't, he'd surely be dead. A moment later came Taryn's voice, and then a flash of red hair just around a turn in the almost nonexistent path, and Smitty struck.

"Now!" he called, his voice more frantic than he had meant for it to be.

Ozzie, Taryn, and Tynx all looked around in excitement when they heard Smitty's voice. A half-second later, however, a bright light exploded all around them, blinding them to everything.

Smitty was able to see through the light. It was apparently some trick of Deianira's, and she had granted him immunity to it. This was good, as Smitty kept his eyes on Heinz every second as he leapt out from his hiding place. Everything seemed to play in slow motion as Smitty moved. He saw the expression on Ozzie, Taryn, and Tynx's faces change from happy to alarmed. Heinz was looking for him, probably to tear his throat out, but he couldn't see so he began trying to sniff Smitty out instead…Smitty made sure to stay as far from Heinz as possible.

He grabbed Taryn around the midsection, pinning her arms to her sides, and everything began to speed up again. He pressed his knife to her throat before she could begin to fight and, driven by anxiety, he spoke more loudly than he meant to in her ear.

"Don't move!"

Startled by the yell in her ear, Taryn jumped, causing Smitty's blade to slice into her neck. It wasn't deep, but it started bleeding immediately. The light had just begun to dissipate, but Heinz was already snarling ferociously at Smitty, sensing danger for his mistress. When Ozzie and Tynx could finally see again, the scene looked bad. Smitty was holding Taryn at knifepoint while blood ran down her neck and soaked into her top. Heinz was nearly mad with fury, and Smitty was looking angry and terrified all at once.

To top it all off, Captain James T. Hook was suddenly there now, looking positively gleeful.

"Rather fitting, don't you think?" Hook purred, brandishing his hook and sword at Tynx. "Caught by the very same trick you pulled on me."

"Smitty, what are you doing?!" Ozzie demanded furiously, trying to keep his eyes on both Hook and Smitty.

"Stay back!" Smitty shouted, his voice panicky and still too loud.

What was this? Why was Hook here? This didn't make any sense!

*I will create a distraction while you pull Taryn away from the others. Then, we can kill the beast.*

That was what Deianira had said. Surely, Hook wasn't her planned distraction. Despite his alarm at seeing Hook, he held his ground, knowing Heinz would kill him for sure now that he was threatening Taryn.

"Smitty," Taryn said carefully, "whatever is going on, we can talk about it. Okay? I know how I can be, but I am sorry for anything I did to hurt your feelings. Okay? I'm very, very sorry."

Taryn was really and truly frightened. Smitty sounded like a maniac, and she couldn't be sure of his mental stability in that moment. Had he suddenly gone crazy? Where had he been since he'd gone missing? Anything was possible in this land. She was trying to judge whether or not she could get away by stamping on his foot or something, but that knife was awfully close to her throat. How much further would it have to slice before it did real damage?

"You have your instructions, lad," Hook sneered. "Go and be glad I don't gut you like a fish with this one."

Smitty swallowed hard. This was getting worse. Hook was here to kill Tynx! Maybe…maybe he would be okay, though. Tynx seemed pretty capable. He suddenly spotted Heinz coming close and doubled down, gripping Taryn more tightly and pressing the knife dangerously into her flesh. Right! The plan. He had to get Taryn away.

"Back off, you psychotic mutt! We're getting out of here!"

Heinz barked angrily at Smitty, but for the sake of his mistress did as he was told. He followed at a safe distance, however, while Smitty began to pull Taryn backwards with him.

"Smitty, don't!" Ozzie called fearfully.

Hook was still there, languidly watching the scene disintegrate into chaos, obviously waiting for to Smitty to leave. Ozzie couldn't abandon Tynx. There was a good chance Hook was a better swordsman than even the half-elf, but his heart was being dragged away with Taryn as he saw Smitty leave.

"Ozzie, go with him," Tynx said firmly. "He's here for me, so I'll take care of him. Protect Taryn."

"I'll be back," Ozzie promised.

Then he was off, running in the direction Smitty had disappeared with Taryn.

As soon as Ozzie was gone, Hook got down to business. He had been instructed to let the others go, much as he was loath to see Smitty get off scot-free. Nevertheless, he'd take the obviously not-quite-human Tynx. Tynx parried his first strike and then his second and his third after that, which surprised Hook. What Tynx lacked in technique and skills he made up for in strength and speed. Hook guessed this was caused by his heritage, whatever that was. Hook didn't let that deter him, however, and struck out with his hook. He gouged deep into Tynx's arm and then moved to disarm him. Tynx suddenly leapt up and back further and higher than any human could, tearing away from Hook's hook, slashing down as he went. His blade cut through curly, black hair and flesh, slicing deep down Hook's face and chest. Blood flowed into his eyes, and Hook swore as he was half blinded. He jumped back to avoid the next attack, but it didn't matter. Tynx was already running away, following his friend's tracks. Hook screamed after him, but Tynx ignored him, hoping he'd limp off to nurse his injuries. There wasn't time to worry about the pirate for now.

"Think about what you're doing," Ozzie said gently. "Taryn is your friend, remember? You don't want to hurt her."

Smitty had led Ozzie to a thicket of reedy bushes with red berries. They should be pretty well hidden here until Deianira came for them. Where was she anyway?! Taryn was thankfully being fairly docile. That had been one of Smitty's main concerns. Taryn was, after all, a pretty tough and fighty girl.

"I'm going home, Ozzie!" Smitty insisted for the third or fourth time.

That point didn't really seem to be coming across the way Smitty intended.

"I know. We all are," Ozzie said. He was holding his hands up and coming closer very slowly. "This, though...this isn't helping. We can get home without hurting each other."

"I have to wait here," Smitty said firmly.

"Okay. We'll wait here. Can we wait without weapons drawn?"

"It's to keep that *thing* away," Smitty snarled, jerking his head towards Heinz.

Heinz was still standing faithfully by, ready to strike as soon as the opportunity presented itself.

"Heinz won't hurt you," Taryn said. "I won't let him. Heinz, you absolutely cannot under any circumstances hurt Smitty. Do you hear me? Stay!" She paused and added, "Please, Smitty, you're hurting me. See, I've told him no. He listens to me. He knows what I want."

A vision of Heinz ignoring Taryn and leaping for his throat flashed through Smitty's mind.

"No! Tie him up!" Smitty commanded.

"If that's what you want," Ozzie said.

He then pulled a length of rope from his pack and approached Heinz. The enfield wasn't having any of it. He snapped at Ozzie's reaching hands and held his ground.

"See! He'll even attack *you* given the chance!" Smitty cried.

Before another word could be said, Tynx came running into the thicket. Taryn felt Smitty's grip loosen ever so slightly as they both saw the gash on his arm and the blood that was pouring from underneath his hand where he was trying to apply pressure.

"Ow, Smitty, you're really hurting me," she said in her most helpless voice.

Smitty reacted automatically, his mind focused on the possibility that Tynx might actually die because of him. He loosened his grip, and Taryn took her opportunity. Ripping an arm from Smitty's grasp, she pushed the knife away from her throat, spun, and punched Smitty in the face. Smitty's hands flew to his face, but he was still holding his hunting knife, and so he rammed the hilt into his eye and cut his forehead with the blade. He then dropped the knife and cradled his face in his hands.

As soon as she was done with Smitty, Taryn turned to Heinz and grabbed his ruff in both hands.

"Heinz, stay!" she commanded. "I said you are *not* to hurt him!"

Heinz had been split seconds from leaping for Smitty, but stopped short at Taryn's command. He barked unhappily at her.

"You heard me!" she snapped.

As soon as Taryn was free, both Tynx and Ozzie moved in on Smitty. Ozzie picked up the knife where Smitty had dropped it after smashing it into his face. Meanwhile, Tynx was keeping himself between Taryn and Heinz and Smitty. He wasn't certain in that moment whether or not Heinz would attack Smitty. Despite Taryn's command, Smitty had threatened and injured her, and Heinz was making his intentions very clear. He was pawing the ground angrily, growling deep in his throat, all while Taryn stared him down and kept a hold on him. The enfield was clearly fighting against his own instincts only at the behest of his mistress. Her will was the only thing between his teeth and Smitty's throat.

Tynx tried to herd Smitty away from Heinz and Taryn. "Let's head over here, Smitty. We need to have a look at that cut."

Smitty was still gingerly holding his face, refusing to look at anyone. How had it all gone so wrong?! Where was Deianira? She should have been here by now! He could hear Heinz to his right, practically begging Taryn to let him loose. He wanted nothing more than to sink into the ground and disappear. He allowed himself to be ushered away.

"Tynx, your arm needs attention first," he heard Ozzie say.

"Heinz, stay *put*! I mean it!" Taryn was adding. "Whose injury is wor—Tynx! Look out!"

Smitty's head snapped up to see a bloody Captain Hook charging through the brush, cutlass drawn and thrust out before him, heading straight for Tynx. Tynx reacted too late to defend himself, and Ozzie was a step behind. Taryn, however, was already half running, half leaping towards them. She pushed Tynx, shoving him out of harm's way while taking his place. Then a massive bulk of fur and claws and snarling overtook the scene. Hook went down under Heinz's massive weight. Heinz made a terrible fox-like shriek but he did not retreat. That is, not until Hook was safely pinned and Heinz had a chance to look back and ensure his mistress was safe.

"HEINZ!" Taryn screamed.

Sticking out of Heinz's chest was Hook's cutlass. It was buried to the hilt in his flesh and fur, and Heinz looked back to Hook. The strange and angry human wasn't dead, but he would be soon. Heinz's claws had slashed the side of his throat down to his chest, criss-crossing Tynx's scimitar slash from earlier, and hot blood was gushing from the wound. Heinz would have done more, but the human's weapon had pierced him. Nevertheless, Mistress was safe, and Heinz was glad for that.

Taryn rushed forward and tried to pull Heinz off Hook. The pirate was wounded and didn't seem to be a threat any longer, but that was the most energy she allowed her brain to expend on that problem. She had to help her beloved enfield. Heinz took a step to the side, yelped, and stumbled agonizingly to the ground. Mercifully, he fell onto his side where the pain was less.

Smitty still wasn't sure what to do with himself after he had failed so miserably, but now he was filled with a strange mixture of relief and regret. Heinz looked done for, which meant he was safe, but Taryn…she was his friend, or at least had been at one time. She was panicked now and pale with terror. She shook as she knelt down next to Heinz, her eyes wide. Smitty felt a hand on his shoulder and looked up to see Deianira.

"Finally!" Smitty gushed. It would all be okay now.

"Smitty!" Ozzie cried, seeing a strange and not-quite-human woman suddenly standing behind his friend.

The woman and Smitty then evaporated into vapor, disappearing without another word. Tynx and Ozzie stared at one another in silent shock for a moment, but were quickly pulled back by Taryn's voice.

"Tynx!" she cried frantically. "Tynx, please! Help him!"

Tynx's mind had already begun to process the situation, however, and he had already come to a conclusion.

"There's nothing I can do," he said simply.

"No!" Taryn shrieked. "You have to do something! Use your magic! *Please!*"

Tynx shook his head and, almost whispering, explained, "Anything I do will only prolong his pain. Taryn, he's...he's already dying."

Heinz lifted his head and looked back at Hook as he heard a strange gurgling noise emanating from the human. Oh, it was just his breath leaving him, so Heinz looked back at his mistress, smiling a toothy canine smile. Good! The job was done, and the one that mewled was gone as well. Even better!

Taryn looked back into Heinz's golden eyes and did her best to smile at him through her tears. Her smile disappeared, however, when she turned back to Tynx.

"No, I can't accept that," she said adamantly. "You have magic, Tynx. Do something. Now. Save him, Tynx. Please, save him for me."

Tynx's heart broke at Taryn's words. She believed in him. She believed he could do anything, and this one crucial request...he couldn't do it. Tynx sank down onto his knees next to Taryn, tears filling his eyes as he spoke.

"I can't. Taryn, I'm so sorry. I can't save him."

Taryn's face crumpled as she heard his words. Walls came crashing down around her as truth rang through her ears. Tynx wouldn't lie to her. He would try anything he could before giving up. There really was nothing to be done. With tears erupting from her eyes, she reached for the cutlass.

"This is going to hurt, okay, baby?" she said, her voice shaking and cracking.

"No, let me," Tynx offered. "I'll make it as painless as possible."

Taryn nodded, and Ozzie came to sit by her, wrapping his arms around her tightly. Carefully and very gently, Tynx slid the blade out from Heinz's chest as smoothly as possible. Heinz whined as flesh and blood and bone came loose and fell to places they weren't meant to. Taryn then scooted forward and lifted Heinz's enormous head into her lap, stroking his fur lovingly and pulling at his ear the way he liked. Blood was flowing freely from the wound now; it was only a matter of time.

Ozzie and Tynx sat with Taryn, holding her while she held Heinz, all three of them shedding tears for the faithful enfield. Taryn spoke to Heinz like a mother to a child, assuring him it would be okay and she'd see him later. Ozzie expressed what a great and noble friend he was and how courageous he had been. Tynx told him he had brought honor to his line and been a true warrior of his kind. When Heinz was just slipping away, Taryn began to sob great racking sobs that shook her whole body. She bent over Heinz and begged him not to leave her. Heinz kissed her teary face, licking away the saltiness and wishing for her to be happy before his strength finally left him.

They sat there long after Heinz had slipped away. Tynx eventually made camp while Taryn keened into the twilight, still held in Ozzie's arms. Hardly anything more was said that evening, and Taryn fell asleep weeping.


"What are we going to do about Smitty?" Ozzie asked somberly.

It was sometime in the middle of the night. Taryn was sleeping restlessly, and Tynx was taking proper care of his arm. He had hastily staunched the bleeding earlier by pressing a bit of bandage to the wound, which had partially dried now, so the gauzy fabric had to be carefully extricated. Ozzie had already attended to the cut on Taryn's throat while she fell asleep. The girl had not protested to his ministrations and lay crying while he worked.

"I don't know," Tynx confessed. His face was hard, and he didn't look at Ozzie as he spoke.

Ozzie couldn't be sure, but he suspected there was a part of Tynx that didn't want to go find Smitty. After all, he had been responsible for Heinz's death. More than that, he was a traitor. Tynx was dealing with his own pain as well as the sense of the grief both Ozzie and Taryn were feeling. None of that was exactly incentivizing the half-elf to go off and risk his life for Smitty, a would-be stranger save for the fact that he was Ozzie's friend. Ozzie steeled himself, knowing he was able to make a very unpopular decision.

"We have to go after him. We need to find allies—powerful ones—and find out who that woman was."

"And how are we to do that, Ozzie?!" Tynx snapped, finally looking at him. His eyes were cold and glinting with anger. "What reason would anyone have to help us, much less that little snake? I say let him rot wherever he is."

"Tynx," Ozzie argued, "he's my friend."

"You should choose your friends better!" Tynx exploded. "Did I not tell you, warn you, of his duplicitous nature?! In case you've forgotten, not only did he all but cut Heinz's throat himself, he set me up to die as well!"

"He doesn't belong here," came a voice from the other side of the campfire. Ozzie and Tynx looked over to see Taryn sitting up.

"Taryn…" Tynx sighed as he tied off his new dressing, "I'm sorry I woke you. Go back to sleep."

Clearly ignoring him, Taryn continued, "Smitty can't stay here. He has a family."

"So he should simply go back home?" Tynx asked, getting angry again. "You think he shouldn't have to pay for what he's done?"

"Of course not!" Taryn snarled. "He'll pay dearly before we go home. Away from any authority that can save him, he'll answer to us."

"I don't think that's a good idea," Ozzie said carefully.

"Agreed. There's nothing you can do that will fit the crime."

"Want to run that by me again, Tynixenal Delalewyn?!" Taryn demanded. "He killed my baby Heinz! You don't think I can make Smitty regret that?"

"Enough!" Ozzie broke in. He spoke with a tone neither Tynx nor Taryn had ever heard from him, and it gave them both pause. As he spoke, Ozzie addressed the murderous glare in Taryn's eyes and the cold glint of revenge in Tynx's. "Now look! Taryn's right; Smitty doesn't belong here. He has a family back home. It's not our place to decide that they should lose him forever. Tynx is right too, though. Yes, Smitty's a coward and a dirt bag. We all know that, but who made us judge and jury? Huh? No one! He'll pay for his own actions in time and *not* at our hands.

"Tomorrow morning, we'll bury Heinz and Hook—yes, Hook as well!—and then we're going to go look for Gloriana's Green."

"Are you insane?!" Taryn asked.

"Regarding which part?" Ozzie asked seriously.

"All of it!"

"That's what's happening. I'm sorry if you don't like it, Taryn."

Taryn screamed and swore in frustration. She then marched towards Ozzie, intending to push him, slap him, something to provoke him, wanting to fight, but Tynx caught her first. He wrapped his arms around her, holding her arms there, keeping her restrained with his superior strength as she pulled away. Tynx wanted to keep her from striking Ozzie, from making a bad situation worse, but he didn't know what he was doing beyond that. He suddenly rested his head on her shoulder in defeat. Taryn continued to protest, fighting weakly against Tynx, insisting that Ozzie's idea was idiotic, but her rant quickly disintegrated into tears, and she sank down towards the ground, Tynx holding her up. Tynx squeezed her tightly, beginning to cry again and sat down with her. Ozzie came and sat opposite them. He reached out and took one of Taryn's hands in his own. She didn't pull away. He didn't expect her to; she wasn't really angry with him, after all.

The night was long and passed fitfully. Tynx couldn't sleep, nor could Ozzie, and Taryn didn't want to, but her two friends encouraged her to. They lay together on their pallets, Ozzie on one side of Taryn and Tynx on the other, the comfort of one another helping slightly against their heartache. As soon as the sun finally made its appearance the next morning, they began the arduous task of digging graves for Captain Hook and Heinz. Taryn buried herself in the task, trying to empty her mind and heart of everything and anything and focusing only on moving dirt from one place to another. Tynx gathered what rocks he could to top the graves, and Heinz's was marked with a stick with which they had often played fetch. Not much was said. It had either already been said or didn't need to be. The task took more than a day, and sleep had been sparse, so it wasn't until a few days after the horrendous event that Ozzie, Taryn, and Tynx could move forward.

"What happened?!" Smitty demanded.

They were back at Deianira's retreat now, the deed done, and Smitty could feel his head still buzzing with adrenaline and anxiety.

"After sending you ahead, it was more difficult for me to transport myself than I expected," Deianira said wearily.

"Okay, I get that, but what about Hook?!" Smitty replied. "Where did he come from? Did you send him?"

Heaven and earth, this human was irritating. While teleportation did always take it out of her, Deianira was beginning to think dealing with Smitty and keeping up this charade was even more tiresome than that.

"He was a terrible man," she said soothingly. "It was regrettable that he should lose his life, but it was the path he chose."

"I don't understand," Smitty said, deflating under the confession.

"Hook chose his path," she repeated calmly, willing Smitty to simply accept that and shut it. "What matters now is that the task is complete, and we must now focus on getting you back to where you belong."

Smitty brightened at that, all dark thoughts disappearing at the prospect of home.

"Really? What do we do first?"

"Get some rest, young one. I will begin work tomorrow," Deianira said, petting Smitty's hair like a child.

Smitty was feeling pretty wiped out after everything that had happened that day. Yeah, he'd get a good night's rest and start fresh tomorrow. His friends were safe and, even though he didn't know how they were going to get home, he was feeling optimistic for them and himself.

As Smitty lay on the soft grass to fall asleep that evening, however, something was tugging at his mind. It was the numerous gaps in information, the unanswered questions that spun around inside his head. It kept him up all that night and refused to allow him the reprieve of sleep.


"Taryn, what do you think the fairies will ask of us?" Tynx asked.

The two were sharing a quiet moment while Ozzie had stepped away. Since Heinz's death, Tynx had been trying to make sure he didn't let Taryn out of his sight much. He shared the pain of losing Heinz with her—and Ozzie as well, of course, but in a different way—but he was worried about her as well. One didn't need his sixth sense to know how broken she was over the loss of her enfield, but he felt the emptiness in her. She was so filled with grief, Tynx felt as if he could almost touch it when he touched her skin. It was like a layer of rime just beneath the surface of her, cold with the potential to harden and thicken. He was concerned she might drift away from them if he didn't hold onto her, despite her attempts to suppress her pain and appear strong. He had told Ozzie about what he sensed, but Ozzie had already been on it.

Tynx may have his super-sense, but Ozzie had history with Taryn. He knew her so well that every movement, every look, every inflection, spoke to Ozzie like a story. The way she took a breath before speaking told him that she was steeling herself to not cry. The way she pursed her lips showed how hard she was working to remain tough in front of them. More than once, Ozzie had simply reached out and held her when he saw these things, but he was trying to be better about that. Taryn usually started crying when he did this, and she had already expressed more than once how tired she was of crying.

Questions were an easy way for Tynx to remain engaged with Taryn. There were plenty to be asked, both inane and not. This one in particular was on the serious side, and Taryn looked uncertain how to answer it.

"I've been afraid to think about it," she began. "I don't think they'll kill any of us, but they refuse to help unless we answer an impossible riddle. Or they might just...um..."

"Hold us prisoner?" Tynx suggested.

Taryn nodded emphatically and replied, "Yes! What if they want us as pets or court jesters or something? Fairies seem kind of...unpredictable, you know?"

"Yes, I know."

"I have to believe it will all work out, though," Taryn said, her voice soft now. "Like Ozzie, I just can't believe that we'll never see our families again. I can't let myself believe that. Otherwise...otherwise..."

She let her voice trail off at that, worried she might break down again. Tynx nodded and left it at that. Leaning over, he whispered into Taryn's ear.

"I love you, Taryn Kelly."

Taryn jumped and looked at Tynx in shock. She gaped at him, opening and closing her mouth several times, unable to find the words to say. This was not the first time Tynx had expressed that he loved her. He had told her one other time, back in Leleplar after they had defeated Vurnal. Tynx had said he wanted to tell her in case anything else happened, which was good because that had actually been the night she and Ozzie had been sent back to their world. She hadn't reacted like this then. No, she had taken it calmly and in stride, mostly because she already knew it. The way he'd said it that night, though, had been with a tone that was more like an FYI. Tynx's tone now, though, had a completely different feeling behind it. It was fervent and necessary, like it pained him to keep it in. Taryn looked at him, and she was shocked to find that her heart ached at hearing those words. Was this grief talking, or was this something different and separate? In that moment, she wanted nothing more than for Tynx to take her in his arms and tell her that it was all going to be okay. She wanted him to do the very thing, to be the person, she had been fighting against for so long.

"You look like a fish," Ozzie said gently.

Taryn looked to see Ozzie walking back. He was smiling at her, obviously hoping his tease would make her smile. She stuttered and ultimately failed to find words with which to respond.

"I'll make us some dinner," Ozzie volunteered, ignoring whatever had just happened.

He realized too late that he had intruded on something serious but couldn't tell what. He didn't want to make either Taryn or Tynx feel self-conscious about whatever it was, so he made himself as scarce as possible.

Taryn looked back to Tynx, but her defenses were back up. The moment had passed, but Tynx had sensed what she had felt in those moments before Ozzie had interrupted. Taryn's heart had reached out to him, but it was pulled away again now, hiding behind sensibility and protections against being hurt. His heart had leapt at that and, had Ozzie not shown back up, Tynx would have taken Taryn into his arms and been everything she needed in that moment. Seeing the uncertainty on Tynx's face now—and was that a bit a disappointment as well?—she instinctively reached out for Heinz as a distraction, stretching out her hands to run through his fur. Heinz had never been more than an arm's length away if he could help it. Of course he wasn't there now, and a slash of anguish ripped through Taryn as her fingers closed on nothing. Taryn tried unsuccessfully to choke back a sob, and Tynx really did reach out to her this time. Taking her into his arms, she hunched over and cried, drawing into herself, not wanting to share her pain with Tynx.

Tynx sat with the bundle of Taryn in his arms, stroking her back comfortingly, his own heart twisting in pain as he felt hers blocking his out.

# Chapter 19

The first sign that they were nearing Gloriana's Green—or at least some part of fairie land, as Tynx kept calling it—was that the colors of the landscape around them faded to more normal tones. The land was still rich and beautiful, but in a more quiet and long-established way. Wonderland always held the feeling that the scenery might just get up and rearrange itself on a whim. Gloriana's Green felt more orderly and had a majesty to it that Ozzie, Taryn, and Tynx had never beheld before.

As beautiful as the rocky cliffs and waterfalls and plains and woods were, however, what they really hoped to find were some traders or a village or something. While Adam's supplies were still somewhat plentiful, the trio could see themselves running into some major trouble now that Heinz was gone and they were in a sparsely populated area. Tynx tried his hand at hunting, but felt apprehensive about it now that Taryn and Ozzie had told him some of the animals here might be fairies or fairie-victims in disguise. What if he accidentally shot an innocent person or a potential ally? He quickly decided that fishing was a better option…hopefully.

The group stuck as close as possible to the river. The fishing was good, though tricky to time. They had to either get up before dawn or stop earlier in the afternoon to do so, and one person had to be dedicated to it, as they had no fishing nets or traps, nor did they know how to make them. This one person usually ended up being Ozzie because neither he nor Tynx wanted to leave Taryn by herself, and Ozzie kind of wanted to give Taryn and Tynx some alone time. Although, he wasn't very good about getting up before dawn and so more often than not ended up going in the afternoon.

Everyone kept their eyes open for both wild animals and sentient plants. They soon realized, however, that they might have seen something that could help them—a deer, that weeping willow, a hawk—and not realized it. How many different forms could the fae folk take? The way Taryn and Ozzie explained it, it sounded as if the very water flowing next to them could be a nature spirit of some kind. After that, the three started saying hello to every creature and tree they saw. This turned out to be hilarious and provided some much-needed laughter, as the three quickly realized they all looked like lunatics shouting hello to every bird and bush and funny looking stone that crossed their path.

"So...do I just put my hand here?" Taryn asked uncertainly, placing her hand in Tynx's.

"Of course. Where else would you put it?" he asked with a playful smile.

"On your shoulder, and yours would go on my waist," Taryn replied as if should be obvious, a small smile playing at her lips.

Tynx shrugged and said, "Well, I suppose if you want to do it like that, but it seems like an odd way to dance."

This was Tynx's latest venture to keep Taryn's mind off of her grief—teaching her elvish dancing. Currently, the two stood about a foot apart with both hands raised and clasped with each other's.

"It works if you're going round and round in circles," Taryn told him. "I think that's how a lot of people dance. Not in my family, though."

She actually smiled at that because she and Tynx had once danced together the way her family did back in Leleplar. It was in a little village by the name of Creekbend at the end of their founding festival, so Tynx already knew exactly what she was talking about, which made him smile even wider.

"This, I promise you, will be much more fun that going around in circles," he teased.

Tynx could sense that Taryn was healing, but it was a slow process. He knew she would never fully be over Heinz, but her sorrow was shrinking day by day.

"Now, push away from me, turn and jump and clap," Tynx instructed, going through the motions slowly.

Taryn did none of them but instead watched Tynx happily. She knew what Tynx was doing, and Ozzie, too. She was endlessly thankful for them. Ozzie hadn't abandoned her by leaving them to fish in the afternoons, not at all. In fact, they usually came back together in the evening while Tynx went to bed early so that he could take the late watch. Ozzie was a natural when it came to handling Taryn, and she was always open to him, so there wasn't any kind of barrier between them like there was between Taryn and Tynx. She felt a bit silly about the way Ozzie and Tynx were babying her, but she also suspected she would be having a much harder time if they weren't. She made sure to tell them how much she appreciated them and even did her best to open up to Tynx more—something far, far easier said than done—and told herself that she would be strong and wouldn't become complacent in their care.

"Now you try," Tynx told her, coming back to her.

They took their places again, and this time, as Tynx gave the instructions, Taryn followed.

"And now, hands on hips, we trot sideways back to each other."

"This must be exhausting!" Taryn joked, trotting back. "Then again...elves."

They continued to go through the steps, clasping hands, spinning together, pushing away again, and starting again in a different direction. It really was tiring but also a lot of fun.

"It's incredible to watch from above," Tynx told her, "everyone dancing around each other in unison."

"Don't people knock into each other?"

Tynx raised an eyebrow at her and echoed her sentiments from earlier: "Elves."

"Fair point," Taryn conceded.

She was suddenly inspired by how happy Tynx made her and, before he could sense her feelings, she stretched up onto her tiptoes and kissed his cheek. It was light and chaste, but it was the first time she had initiated any contact like it. Tynx smiled at her, but knew better than to push his luck. They went back to the lessons after that, and eventually Taryn wasn't completely abysmal.

Ozzie had found a kind of solace in fishing. He and his dad had been countless times. His dad loved it so much he owned a boat, the boat that crashed. Ozzie didn't go fishing back home. The places to go there were all familiar, all places he and his dad had been together. It was still too painful to try, but here...it was fairie land, it was in a way one of the fantastical places of his childhood. When Ozzie fished here, it was as if he was experiencing Terturelian fishing for his dad. Ozzie mused on what his father would have thought of the places they stopped, whether there were good spots under fallen logs or rocks for the fish to hide. Was the bank of the river muddy and mosquito infested, or was it pretty dry up to the water's edge? How was the current? Too fast and it eliminated certain species of fish from living there, too slow and the water might grow stagnant. Ozzie knew his dad would have liked most of the spots he had found there in Gloriana's Green, and he believed his dad would be proud of how Ozzie now used the knowledge he had gained from all of those fishing trips.

Tynx could always sense the feeling of peace and calm emanating from Ozzie when he returned from his fishing endeavors. He had since learned it was because of Ozzie's father and the history there. Tynx would occasionally ask Ozzie about his father—Taryn already knew the answers to the questions but sometimes didn't feel it was her place to say—and Ozzie spoke fondly of him.

Ozzie was sitting cross-legged next to a steep embankment and smiling about a dumb joke his dad used to tell.

"What do you call a fish with no eyes?" he asked to no one in particular. "Fsshhhh!"

Ozzie laughed out loud at the punch line and then laughed even harder when he thought about how Taryn would react. He decided he was going to tell her when he got back. He stopped laughing, but he was the only one. Someone else...no, two were still going, and Ozzie's heart quickened. The laughter was coming from the other side of a huge stack of boulders just down the riverbank. Very carefully, Ozzie set down his homemade rod and crept over to the boulders. The laughter was fading now, and he skirted carefully around the edge of the mound and down the steep slope of the bank. There was no shore to speak of here, as the land just stopped a few feet down before dropping off into the river. That's when he saw them: two enormous bears standing in the river. Ozzie hadn't been able to see them past the rocks from his vantage point, nor could they see him, but they saw each other now.

"Human!" one of the bears cried in alarm.

"Bears!" Ozzie shouted, trying to scramble back up the embankment.

The grass was long and slick, and Ozzie lost his footing, sending him sliding down into the river. The bears screamed and ran further into the river as Ozzie went backside first into the water. The current was strong enough to tumble him once, but Ozzie got his bearings after a moment and gasped as his head surfaced. The water wasn't too deep here, only about waist high, but the current got progressively stronger further from the bank. Ozzie steadied himself, knowing he could be in real danger if he strayed too far. Then it dawned on him. Those were talking bears!

"Hey!" Ozzie called, spotting them further downstream. "Wait! I want to talk to you!"

He wasn't really thinking. A small part of his brain told him that just because the bears could talk didn't mean they wouldn't eat him, too. The rest insisted that the bears must be humans imprisoned in bear bodies. He did his best to run after the bears, but even with the current pushing him along, it was difficult to run and not get his feet swept out from under him.

"Oz!" he suddenly heard Taryn shout.

It was faint, and he looked to see her on the bank downriver a ways, the bears in between them.

"Oz! Bears!" she suddenly screeched in fear.

Tynx was there too, and Oz saw he was armed with his bow, but he wasn't taking aim yet.

"Don't hurt them!" Ozzie shouted at the top of his lungs to make sure he was heard. "*Talking* bears! Furry friendies!"

The bears were standing up on their hind legs now, looking back and forth between Taryn and Tynx on the shore and Ozzie, clearly unsure what they should do.

"We won't hurt you!" Ozzie shouted to the bears. "I'm sorry we scared you. We just need to talk to you."

The bears looked at one another and were clearly discussing what they should do, but it was impossible to hear them from this distance. They kept glancing back and forth and motioning at Taryn and Tynx.

"Tynx, put down your bow," Ozzie called. He gestured exaggeratedly to drive home his point.

Tynx looked like that was the last thing he wanted to do, but Taryn placed a gentle hand on his and helped lower the weapon. Tynx finally dropped the bow and showed his empty hands. After that, the bears motioned for Ozzie to come close. Ozzie slogged through the water and when he got close enough did an awkward half bow that he wasn't even sure was appropriate.

"Hey, sorry about that," he said. "Really, I didn't mean to freak you out. Those are my friends; they're okay."

"You're a human," one of the bears said. "You're not supposed to be here."

"Of course they are! How else would they have gotten here?" the other bear crabbed at him.

"They could have used tricks," retorted the first.

"You can't trick your way into Sídhe."

"Nope, nothing like that," Ozzie interrupted. "But, hey! I'm really glad we found you guys…bears."

The bears eyed the trio nervously.

"We've been trying to find someone to talk to this whole time," Ozzie said, realizing just then how little sense he was making. "Look, we got off on the wrong foot. My name's Ozzie. The half-elf over there is Tynx, and Taryn's the redhead. We're all friends. What are your names?"

"Bramblebee," said the first bear, who was slightly darker than the other, pointing at himself.

"I'm Tumbleburr," the other said. He had sandy flecks in his fur.

"Great to meet you! Look, can we maybe go talk up on the bank? I'm getting cold…disadvantage of not having fur."

A few minutes later, all five of them were on the bank. Taryn and Tynx had to help pull Ozzie up onto the bank, and Bramblebee gave him a helpful boost as well. Both bears had given themselves a good shake, which ended up half soaking Taryn and Tynx.

"Are you two brothers?" Taryn asked.

"Half," Tumbleburr replied.

"What are you doing here?" Bramblebee asked, the same edge of worry coming into his voice as before.

"We're trying to find the Fairie Court," Ozzie said.

Both Tumbleburr and Bramblebee gasped and stared at the three.

"We know, we know," Taryn said before either of the bears could say anything. "We could also use a trading post or somewhere to get fresh supplies."

The bears exchanged glances and then whispered back and forth to one another behind their massive paws. Finally, after almost a full minute, they turned back to the humans and spoke.

"Where's your camp?" Bramblebee asked.

"Just over that rise," Tynx replied, "near the stream."

"Go back to your camp and wait there," Bramblebee explained. "We have to go speak with someone. We might be back."

"Might?" Taryn asked. "Why might?"

"We *might* be back," Tumbleburr said, clearly trying to sound authoritative.

With that, the bears turned and started lumbering away.

"I don't understand!" Ozzie called after them. "I thought we were cool!"

The bears ignored him and soon disappeared into the landscape.

"Now what?" Taryn asked, throwing her hands up.

"I guess we wait at camp," Ozzie replied with a shrug.

Dinner was quiet and tense that night. Ozzie hadn't caught anything, which didn't help anyone's mood, and all three of them kept glancing out to the horizon for any sign of Bramblebee and Tumbleburr. An owl hooted nearby as the three sat anxiously around the fire.

"Perhaps we should see if someone can act as a liaison between the fairies and us," Tynx suggested, trying to be helpful. "If no one will take us there, we can see if someone is willing to go on our behalf."

"What do you think is the deal with Tumbleburr and Bramblebee?" Ozzie wondered aloud. "Are they cursed?"

"They didn't seem cursed," Taryn replied. "The only thing they seemed worried about was the threat we might pose."

"Then why can they talk?"

"Well, why wouldn't there be talking animals in fairie land?"

Ozzie sighed and let his head fall back, gazing unhappily at the sky. He knew Taryn had a point, though it didn't make it any easier. If anything, it was more complicated now. He hadn't considered normal—as normal as talking animals could be— denizens of Gloriana's Green as a possibility. Why did he think it would be all ethereal sprites and incoherent pixies? Maybe this was better, though. Maybe this meant more potential allies. The owl was circling overhead now, and Ozzie called out a despondent "Hullo" to it out of habit.

"Good evening," the owl responded cordially. "You must be Ozzie. I heard of your little...encounter."

At this, the owl laughed, a whistling, repetitive hooting sound.

"Hey!" Ozzie cried excitedly. "We thought you guys had abandoned us."

"We may yet. I don't know for certain."

"Oh, please don't!" Taryn pleaded. "We're sort of lost and need to replenish our supplies. We can't even hunt because we don't want to risk accidentally killing one of your people."

"Not to be rude, but you three look a bit more than sort of lost," the owl countered.

"Is it that obvious?" Taryn asked.

"In your faces, yes."

Taryn sighed and slumped. She was sure the owl was right.

"You can come down if you want," Ozzie offered. "We have food we can share."

Taryn nearly started at the offer. They had limited supplies, and her primal survival side was the first to react. The rest of her brain soon caught up, however, and calmed the other part of her.

"That's very kind, but I am content to stay up here," the owl replied. "Until I know better what you are about, that is."

"Honestly, they...we're trying to find our way," Tynx added, tripping over his words.

"Aha! You're hiding something," the owl said before letting out an ear piercing screech.

"I'm helping them!" Tynx snapped. He did not add that he was as lost as they were, not knowing what he would do when this was all over.

"Please," Taryn said, her voice cracking. "We're not trying to trick you. It's just...it's such a long story."

At that, Taryn allowed a few tears to eke out of her eyes. Tynx wrapped his arm around her, but kept his eyes on the owl.

"It's so complicated," Ozzie agreed. "How can we prove you can trust us? We'll do anything."

The owl said nothing, but circled a few more times before descending and alighting on a tent pole.

"Lucky for you, you've already had someone vouch for you. Duskhollow, at your service." The owl bowed as he introduced himself, stretching out his wings and fluttering them in a funny sort of way.

"Thank goodness!" Ozzie gushed. "I thought after we scared Tumbleburr and Bramblebee so bad, they—"

"It was not Tumbleburr and Bramblebee," Duskhollow said sharply.

"Wait, if not them, then who?" Taryn asked. "No one else knows we're out here."

"As you say—Tara, was it?"

"Taryn."

"Pardon me. Yes, well, as you say, Miss Taryn, the people of the mounds are already aware of your predicament."

"People of the what?" Ozzie asked.

"Aos sí," Taryn answered immediately, shooting Ozzie a look. Turning to Duskhollow, she said, "We are honored."

"If you don't mind me asking," Tynx ventured, "how long have you been here?"

"Long enough," Duskhollow replied.

"The fae folk came to you then?" Ozzie asked. "They talked to you about us?"

"They did, even before the bear brothers did."

"And what did they say?" Ozzie pressed.

"That I will hear of you and I must assist. Thus, here I am."

"So all of that stuff about possibly abandoning us..." Taryn asked, doing her best not to narrow her eyes at the owl.

"A test. I trust our leaders implicitly. Even still, I wish to know who I am inviting into my home. Well, not mine precisely. Not unless you can fly, of course."

"Sorry, no," Ozzie replied. "Though that would be cool, wouldn't it?"

Duskhollow raised his feathery eyebrow-equivalents at Ozzie in that moment. He said nothing, however, and motioned with his wing to the camp.

"Come now. Gather your things."

"We're leaving now?" Taryn asked in surprise.

"Fickle, aren't you?" Duskhollow quipped. "Quickly, please."

All three got to their feet and immediately, though somewhat awkwardly, fell into their usual morning cleanup routine.

"So where are we going?" Ozzie asked as he packed up his sleep roll.

"The Fairie Court, of course," replied Duskhollow simply, as if that explained everything.

That was enough for Ozzie, but Taryn's head still buzzed with dozens of questions. She didn't like the idea of being called out for being fickle again, though, so she said nothing. Less than an hour later, the three were doing their best to trot behind Duskhollow as he flew ahead. He was a graceful silhouette against the starry sky, but he flew rather fast and was difficult to keep up with. It was deep night now as well, and Tynx's little mote of light was the brightest thing around for miles. The dark made time pass strangely, and they nearly lost sight of Duskhollow once they climbed down into a woody dale.

"Here, little humans," Duskhollow called to them. "Follow the sound of my voice."

He then started hooting every minute or so. Tynx could see fairly well in the dark, but he had to take Taryn's hand with his free one as they picked their way through the trees. Taryn, in turn, held onto Ozzie's hand.

It was impossible to tell how much time had passed when the orange glow of fire appeared in the distance, but it suddenly didn't matter because they were nearly there! Their tired eyes found new energy as they headed for that beautiful warmth. When they entered the clearing where the fire burned, they found it was a dying bonfire of sorts, and Tumbleburr and Bramblebee were there waiting for them.

"Evening, gents!" Ozzie said, both excited and tired at the same time.

"Oh! Hello," Bramblebee said nervously. "Duskhollow found you then. Right where we told him?"

"Of course he did," Tumbleburr said, rolling his eyes. "They're here now, aren't they?"

"They could have moved," Bramblebee retorted, shaking his head at his half-brother.

"Thank you, lads," Duskhollow said gently, and both bears quieted down at that. "Ozzie, Tynx, and Taryn, welcome to the Fairie Court. I realize you may not be able to see much of it at the moment, but you are welcome nonetheless. I'm afraid we have not worked out living arrangements for you, what with the short notice and all, but I expect you can camp out one more night."

"That's fine," Ozzie replied. "We can make do."

"Very good," Duskhollow said. Then, with another fluttery bow, he added, "Well, I am late in getting my dinner, so I leave you to it."

Duskhollow instantly and silently disappeared into the darkness once more. Tynx, Taryn, and Ozzie were all happy to lay out their pallets and fall asleep by the bonfire remnants. They thanked Tumbleburr and Bramblebee again and were asleep within minutes.

With the sunrise came new hope and new faces. Taryn opened her eyes that morning to see a fox nosing around their packs.

"Hey, handsome," she whispered, thrilled at being so close to a real fox.

"Hey yourself, beautiful," the fox replied, giving her a crooked smile.

"Oh gosh! I'm so sorry! So rude!" she exclaimed.

"Anytime, sweetheart," the fox said, winking at her before turning and trotting away.

Taryn watched him go, aghast at the fact that she had just inadvertently come onto a talking fox in the Fairie Court. She then turned and saw Ozzie standing there, obviously trying not to laugh.

"Not a word!" she said firmly.

Ozzie's smile spread slowly at that before he let out a huge guffaw.

"Seriously, say nothing," Taryn said, starting to laugh as well.

"What did I miss?" Tynx asked, walking around the perimeter of what had been the bonfire.

"You've got some competition," Ozzie managed to reply. "With a fox!"

At that, Ozzie lost it again, and Taryn covered her face with her hand.

"I'll fight a fox for you," Tynx teased, ruffling her hair affectionately. "You think I can take him? Very sly, those foxes."

"Vampires, half-elves, foxes..." Ozzie said. "At least you don't discriminate, Ryn."

"I'm warning you, mate," Taryn said to Ozzie, a feisty glint in her eye. "One more sideways comment and you're going to be sorry."

"Equal opportunity flirt," Ozzie goaded.

He laughed again at his own joke...until Taryn took him down onto his backside. She wrestled with Ozzie, trying to pin him down, relying on nimble quickness. It was her only advantage against his superior strength.

"Ahem, friends," Tynx said over the ruckus. He was ignored. He then said more loudly. "Guys. *Guys.* You're being rude to our host!"

Taryn and Ozzie stopped tumbling around long enough to look up and see that a leopard had sidled up to Tynx. A very large, severe looking leopard. Immediately, they stood back up and awkwardly brushed themselves off as best they could. There were some awkward apologies until the leopard shook her head.

"Cubs. It doesn't matter how they come, they never change," she said with a low, purring voice.

Both Taryn and Ozzie opened their mouths to object to being called cubs, but immediately realized they had no argument.

"Ozzie, Taryn, this is Windstalker."

"Pleased to meet you," Taryn and Ozzie said together.

"Welcome to the heart of Sídhe," Windstalker said. "Your friend has been telling me about your journey."

"Has he?" Ozzie asked, looking meaningfully at Tynx.

"What was his to tell, that is," Windstalker amended. "The people of the mounds have spoken for you, so you are welcome in this place. Come. I think we have identified a suitable dwelling for you."

Windstalker then turned and began padding away slowly.

"You totally started it," Ozzie whispered to Taryn.

"Me?!" Taryn hissed. "You wouldn't stop baiting me. You brought it on yourself."

Ozzie stuck his tongue out at Taryn, who returned the sentiment. They picked up their packs and trotted to catch up with Tynx and Windstalker. They walked through the trees for a few minutes, past what might be any number of animal homes. There was a hollow log on the ground, under which nestled a family of hedgehogs. There was also a very large nest high up in a tree. A pair of squirrels chased each other, chattering in perfectly understandable English.

"There is a brook nearby," Windstalker said as they walked. "Remain quiet, if you can, and then follow the sound you hear."

Eventually, they came to a clearing where a little garden sat next to a mound of grassy earth.

"Here we are. We call this place the burrow. The owner, Miss Sally Brighteyes, has graciously opened her home to you three. She's stepped out for the moment, but she will be back soon."

"Thank you very much," Taryn said, "but did you speak to your...monarchs? Did they say anything else about us? Will they see us?"

"That honor was Duskhollow's," Windstalker replied. She saw the desperation in Taryn's eyes and bumped her head against Taryn's hand encouragingly. "Do not fear, little human. You are not alone."

Windstalker had been planning on leaving them there at the entrance, but offered to stay with the three until Sally Brighteyes came back.

They gathered in the sitting room of the burrow, which was apparently mostly underground. The mound above ground was mainly only there so that others didn't tread on top of the house. The front door opened to a short stairwell leading down, and the walls were all very hard packed earth. Taryn and Ozzie shared a confused look when Windstalker told the three that Brighteyes was a bit persnickety about cleanliness and so they should remove their shoes at the entrance. They might have made a comment about the fact that they were surrounded by dirt, but knew that would probably be rude. Windstalker also explained that many members of the community would gather that evening around the bonfire for fellowship.

"It's important for us to come together," Windstalker said. "We are a small community and so must look out for one another. We need to be aware of things happening in one another's lives."

All three of them smiled at that, remembering back to the little village of Creekbend in Leleplar. Everybody knew everyone else's business there; they had heard numerous conversations about it. It was looking more and more like Gloriana's Green...the Fairie Court...whatever the proper name was might be similar, only populated by talking animals. Sally Brighteyes, who insisted that Brighteyes was fine and turned out to be a plump and kindly wombat, returned home soon after her guests had arrived and immediately began apologizing for not being there to greet them. She wittered on about someone named Ebony as she made tea and explained that she was further removed from the other homes in the Court, what with needing space for a proper burrow and all.

"And so, if you'll forgive me, darlings, I had to toddle all the way to Ebony's tree to borrow supplies for breakfast. Watch yourselves now, it's hot."

Taryn's eyebrows shot up at tasting the tea, and she said, "This is fabulously strong!"

"Tunneler's tea, my dear. That's what I call it. You need it to be strong first thing in the morning, don't you?"

Ozzie was doing his best not to make a face, and Taryn was doing her best not to laugh at him. She had always thought he made his tea far too weak. Tea flavored water was what she called it. Brighteyes served the three breakfast—toast and root vegetables— and they settled into their new living space.

# Chapter 20

Smitty wandered around the strange palace, trying to distract his mind from the creeping boredom. Deianira was busy, as she had been for a while now, working on some project…presumably the teleporter or whatever it was that was going to send him home. As fascinating as the constantly-changing scenery around him was, there really wasn't anything to do. He was always discovering new rooms and outside areas as he wandered, but he eventually needed something more than just nature and old architecture to hold his interest. What he wouldn't give for a good old book, which he found rather ironic considering the situation. Smitty opened a set of doors he wasn't sure he had seen before and stopped short. The room gave him the distinct feeling he shouldn't be there. There were only three walls, one with a large gilded mirror on it, and a raised bed that was, quite literally, a tangled bed of begonias. Beyond where the fourth wall should have been was a large garden, a cluster of apple trees serving as a divider. Despite the heavy feeling that he should turn back, Smitty crept in, hoping for some kind of diversion in here. He headed over to the mirror and smiled.

"Mirror, mirror, on the wall…" he began, whispering childishly.

Despite his joke, the mirror's surface swirled, and then a voice emanated from within.

"What do you wish of me?"

Smitty jumped back, looked around, looked back, looked around again, and finally back to the mirror.

"You talk!" he hissed, knowing for certain now that he should not be here talking to the obviously magic mirror.

"What do you wish of me?" it repeated.

"Show me…" he began.

He first thought to say his family, but decided that might be too painful, especially if he had really been missing from home for weeks and weeks. That might make him even more anxious and desperate to be home.

"Show me my friend Ozzie," he said instead.

He didn't want to see Taryn or Tynx for a variety of reasons, but he wanted to make sure Ozzie was okay. He was also curious where they were in their journey. Were they worried about him at all? Where were they heading now? They hadn't had a plan when he left, and Smitty had no clue where they had been when they set the trap for Heinz.

The mirror's surface swirled again and showed Sally Brighteyes' sitting room. Smitty was shocked to see Ozzie, Taryn, and Tynx sitting around a low table drinking tea with a leopard and...what was that thing? Some kind of fat gopher? He rubbed his eyes, suddenly thinking he had to be hallucinating. Nope, they were still there with their animal friends. Even stranger, he could see their mouths moving, but could hear no sound. Abruptly, the image broke and reflected a massive lioness, who suddenly roared so loudly the stones of the walls shook and looked as if they might come loose. Smitty cried out as fear and regret and shame struck him down to his very core. He ducked down to the ground, holding his hands over his head and breathing hard. The roaring stopped after but a moment, but the sickening feelings remained. Smitty tried to calm himself by talking to himself, convincing himself it was some kind of security device on the mirror, but it didn't help much. Was this what a panic attack felt like? He couldn't be sure. He just knew he felt more awful than he ever had in his life. He dared a peek back up to the mirror and saw all the images were gone.

"Ozzie?" he barely whispered.

He hesitated for a minute, knowing he should leave but unable to resist this new window to the wider world.

"Show me Ozzie again," he finally said.

The surface of the mirror swirled once more and Smitty saw Ozzie again. He was somewhere else now, his features distorted and wavy.

"Ozzie," Smitty said in confusion.

Smitty had had a sense that time worked oddly here. He was certain of it as he saw Ozzie outside now, treetops and sunshine behind him.

Ozzie jumped, clearly startled, but appeared to recover almost instantly. Smitty had to guess because he could see Ozzie's mouth moving but could hear no sound. Smitty was pretty sure he could see Ozzie say his name, but he couldn't make out anything else.

"Ozzie! Ozzie! I can't hear you!" Smitty said. "Talk slower. I'll try to read your lips."

Ozzie could apparently hear Smitty just fine, as he immediately slowed down, using his face to exaggerate every word.

"Where am I?" Smitty repeated back. Ozzie nodded, and Smitty replied, "I'm in Deianira's castle. She's...she's, um...a good spirit? Or something?"

"Where is that?" Ozzie mouthed.

Smitty shrugged and said, "I don't know. We sort of teleported here."

Ozzie looked frustrated for a moment, keeping his eyes on Smitty. He then mouthed, "Are you okay?"

"Yeah, I'm fine!" Smitty replied. "Deianira's been—"

Smitty was abruptly cut off as someone grabbed him by the shoulder and yanked him away from the mirror. He was dragged completely out of the room by the time he realized it was Deianira doing the dragging.

"What do you think you're doing?!" she snarled, throwing Smitty away from her and slamming the door behind her.

"I—I found—I didn't mean to—" Smitty stuttered, too taken aback to think properly.

"Silence!" Deianira commanded. "Save me your pathetic excuses. Keep out of my private rooms, lest I confine you to yours permanently."

"Yes, ma'am," Smitty mumbled, his mind reeling with shock.

Deianira stared daggers at Smitty for a long minute, and Smitty was worried she was about to make good on her threat. Finally, however, she turned, swept back into the room, and slammed the door behind her. Smitty heard the lock *shink* into place, and he was left alone, confused and hurt and frightened in the corridor.

*Stupid boy! Deianira thought to herself as she stomped back inside her rooms. She looked around. Where was the lion? She could see nothing, and Smitty had been talking to the mirror, so the lion must have disappeared almost as soon as he had appeared. Deep down, Deianira was terrified. When she had heard the roar, she had collapsed to the ground, shaking and petrified. The sound had cut her down to her very essence, and it was several minutes before she had been able to collect herself enough to investigate. It looked clear for now, but she was going to be on her guard now...and perhaps keep Smitty contained.*

"Smitty!" Ozzie yelled into the water. "Smitty! Talk to me, man! Smitty! Come back!"

Ozzie then angrily slammed his fists into the bank of the brook, ignoring the pain that reverberated up through his wrists. He stood up and pulled on his hair, trying to think, trying to calm down. That woman he had seen pull Smitty away, it was the same one that had appeared after Heinz had been stabbed. Was that Deianira? The person...spirit...thing that Smitty had mentioned? He had to tell the others. Ozzie ran back to the burrow at full speed and burst into the kitchen.

"What the—Oz?!" Taryn stuttered, nearly dropping the plates she had been stacking for cleaning. "What's wrong with you?"

"Goodness!" Brighteyes exclaimed. "You look as if you've seen a ghost."

"I saw Smitty! I talked to him, sort of. He's...well, I don't know where he is, but he's alive. At least, I hope he still is."

Taryn's face turned dark and stormy at the mention of Smitty's name, but she managed to keep her tongue in check only for Ozzie's sake.

"I'll go get Tynx," was all she said through gritted teeth.

Minutes later, Ozzie was recounting the experience he'd had to Tynx and Taryn. He had been getting water for the washing up when Smitty's face appeared in the water. For some reason, Smitty couldn't hear Ozzie, but Ozzie could hear Smitty. At this, Tynx explained that it sounded as if Smitty had found some way of scrying for Ozzie. Ozzie shared the little information he'd been able to gather and described what he could of the room he had seen

Smitty in and the woman, supposedly Deianira, who had yanked him away from the mirror. After that, the image had disappeared.

"A spirit?" Tynx asked when he was done. "What kind of a spirit?"

"I don't know," Ozzie said. "Smitty said she was a good spirit, but I think he drank the Kool-Aid a long time ago. I don't think he realizes that she's evil."

None of them actually knew if this Deianira was truly evil, but what else could she be? She had absconded with Smitty and convinced him of something, though none of them knew what exactly. Everything that had happened regarding her had been so confusing. They thought back and seemed to remember Smitty claiming that she could send them home. He wasn't home, though. He was...somewhere else. At the very least, she seemed deceitful.

They talked on and on about where Smitty could be, who and what Deianira was, and how they could find out. It was a conversation heavy with anger and grief and frustration. Tynx was still struggling with the idea of going to save the person that had conspired, unwittingly or not, to have him killed. Grief over Heinz's death rose in all of them, but Taryn most evidently. Nevertheless, they had agreed that Smitty needed to return home with them, and so they trudged through the conversation and accompanying emotions, but hours of talk got them no further than where they had started. Eventually, they gave up and decided to go for a walk and help Brighteyes around the house and whatever else they could do at the moment. The three joined the rest of the Gloriana's Green community that night around the Fairie Court bonfire, which was a welcome distraction, and got to know their new neighbors a bit better. Tumbleburr and Bramblebee were there, as were Windstalker and Duskhollow. They met Brighteyes' friend, Ebony, and her three fledglings. The fox that Taryn had spoken to that morning arrived, introduced himself as Brushfire, and then disappeared among the activity. They met several others including a funny and playful otter named Finnymore Jest, a couple of warblers who simply referred to themselves as the Lightsingers, and Windstalker's mate, Shadowpaw. The denizens of Gloriana's Green shared food and chatted with one another about this and that. It was fairly mundane conversation—How are your nest renovations coming along? I tried a new fishing spot today. The onion shoots are coming in nicely!—but Ozzie, Taryn, and Tynx all found it comforting. It was nice to be able to forget about the conversation from earlier that day and lean into the everyday lives of these folks. It was simple and comforting and gave the three a much-needed reminder that things were still normal in other parts of the world…normal being a relative term in this case.

That night, as Ozzie lay awake on his pallet in Brighteyes' front room, he thought back to his conversation with Smitty. The get-together that night had been a wonderful and refreshing distraction, but now that it was over everything came back to him. He replayed every word in his head, tried to focus in on every detail. As much as he enjoyed being here at the Fairie Court and as thankful as he was for where they had ended up, he had watched his friend get dragged away by that…whatever she was. It had struck a spike of icy fear into his heart. Had Deianira hurt Smitty? His life might be in very real danger now and they had no clue when, or even if they would get an audience with the fairies themselves. There had to be something he could do. They couldn't just wait around forever. It was possible even if they got to talk to the fae folk, they would refuse to help. Where were they anyway? If they had told their…subjects?...to look after the trio, why hadn't they shown up yet? They knew what was happening! The fairies knew they needed help? What was the holdup? Ozzie found himself suddenly very uncomfortable with this situation. Without even realizing it, he began to think of alternative solutions.

The scariest and first thought was: *what if the fairies had already taken them captive without them knowing it?* Ozzie concentrated hard, rewinding through events in his head. There were the bear brothers. They had said no one could get into Sídhe without being allowed in. If that was true, was that a good thing? Everything had felt okay so far. Everyone had been really nice. But what if it was a trick? No, that seemed unlikely. If the fairies were as powerful as Adam had said, they wouldn't need trickery to trap feeble humans. That, and Tynx would have spotted something. Plus, Adam vouched for the fae folk. No, Ozzie had to think they hadn't been deceived. The fairies were probably just caught up in their own business. The problems of two humans had to be small potatoes to magical beings. He was getting nowhere. Ozzie almost wished he could go back and find those women from The Moors.

Maybe if he hadn't turned tail so quickly, he could have asked them for directions. From the sounds of them, they might have been able to help…if they had chosen to and didn't turn them all into frogs or something.

Something clicked in Ozzie's brain at this. The women or hags or sorceresses or whatever they were, they had said things to Ozzie, pointed straight at him. What had they said? It had been cryptic and frightening, but maybe it hadn't been a curse at all. Maybe it was what he needed to hear. He closed his eyes and concentrated. Something about water and drowning. He remembered that because it had scared the crap out of him. What had that been about? A branch breaking and drowning. Yes, that was the gist of the first part. And something about fire as well. He remembered he had to guard fire from…from what? Was it from the water? From going out or something like that? But what did any of it mean? It did no good if he couldn't figure any of it out!

"I don't mean to complain, mate, but could you turn it down?" Tynx suddenly whispered from the other side of Taryn. "All of your feels, as you call them, are making my hair stand on end."

"Sorry, dude," Ozzie said with a sigh. "I'm trying to figure something out."

"Can I help?"

In order to keep from disturbing Taryn, Ozzie and Tynx decided to take their conversation out to the garden. Ozzie gave Tynx a very abridged version of what he had been thinking.

So abridged, in fact, all he said was, "I'm trying to figure out what those weird sisters meant back in The Moors."

Ozzie told Tynx what he could remember, and Tynx helped him to fill in a few of the blanks. Tynx remembered what had been said only slightly better than Ozzie, but it was a good start. Tynx reminded him that there was a part at the end about embracing power or something to that effect…something to do with his true name possibly. Tynx remembered making some connection in his mind to Sovereign Gift Brother when he had heard the story the first time, but he couldn't remember the words exactly now. They couldn't agree on what the fire part had been or what that meant, save for one possibility.

"If there is a connection to your name, then what are the chances there's a connection to Little Fire Warrior of the Irish Hills?"

Ozzie swallowed hard. That logic followed. Guard the fire. Protect Taryn. Protect her from what? They talked on and spun more theories, but nothing solid came of it. No plan, no revelation, nothing that would help them save Smitty. Finally, an idea struck Ozzie, but it turned his expression into one of grim determination.

"A wise man once said the quickest way to find out someone's plans is to get captured," he said flatly.

"Ozzie, that could be suicide."

"I know. But there's no other way, not that I can see anyway. We have to help Smitty."

Tynx sighed. Inside, he was quietly reminded why he respected Ozzie so very much. "I don't like it. I don't like it at all, but I think you're right."

"Taryn can't come," Ozzie said, more serious than ever.

"Ozzie, you know how she'll feel about that."

"I know," Ozzie said resolutely. "Look, I don't know what those women meant when they said what they said to me, but I can't let anything happen to Taryn. It will be better for her to stay here where it's safe…relatively. That way, if we don't make it, at least she will."

The next morning did not go as well as hoped. It was a good thing they waited for Brighteyes to go out before telling Taryn their plan.

"You know what, Ozzie Thomason?" Taryn said angrily. "You're out of your bloody mind."

"If I may—" Tynx began.

"No you may *not*, Tynixenal Delalewyn!" Taryn snapped. "You're both mad if you think I'm just going to sit here like the helpless damsel while you run off to who knows where."

"Anyone who has ever met you knows very well you're anything but a helpless damsel, Taryn," Ozzie replied sternly. "That's actually completely beside the point, though. You're staying here. Of the options available, none of which are great, it's better. When the fairies show up, someone needs to be here to talk to them."

"No," Taryn argued, "I'm coming."

"Taryn, it's not safe. You're staying here so you can be safe."

"Ozzie, if it weren't for that harpy, I would be safe because Heinz would still be alive! It's because of her that he isn't here to protect me! Because he's *dead*! All because of her! So, as I said before, I. AM. COMING!"

Her voice had risen to a roar as she spoke. Ozzie stood firm against the force of her determination. In contrast to hers, Ozzie's voice was softer now when he replied.

"I know, Taryn. I know that, and I am so, *so* sorry about that, but consider this me filling in for him. Just like Heinz was, I'm committed to protecting you."

"As am I," Tynx added, sidling up to Ozzie.

"You can't stop me from coming," Taryn snarled defiantly.

"We can," Tynx said, stepping forward. "Please, don't make us."

"I'd like to see you try."

She crossed her arms over her chest and narrowed her eyes at her two friends, waiting for their next move. It looked like a stalemate, and Taryn was fine with that...until Tynx took another step forward. He moved quickly and adroitly, grasping Taryn gently yet very firmly by the wrist. She reacted before she knew what she was doing. Pulling her free arm back, she swung at Tynx and connected with the side of his mouth. His lip exploded, splitting open and bleeding immediately. Tynx let go of her wrist and stumbled back. He hadn't expected her to fight back, not when it was them, much less fight so well.

"Put your hands on me again and see what happens!" she growled furiously.

Inside, Taryn was shocked and hurt and angry. How dare they try to force her to stay! What kind of friends did that?! Well, she wasn't going to stand for it.

Tynx moved quickly again, on his guard now. Taryn tried to punch him again, but Tynx caught her hand this time and held tight. He wished he could say it was easy, but she was fierce and made it very difficult to restrain her without hurting her. In fact, he had to take even more of a beating in order to do so. When Tynx caught Taryn's hand, she changed tactics and kicked for whatever she could reach. He had to move quickly to avoid being struck, but managed to make her foot graze the meaty side of his leg. In the next movement, he swooped under her and scooped her over his shoulder, at which point she started beating against his back mercilessly. Ozzie stepped in at that point to hold her hands. He needed Tynx in one piece to rescue Smitty.

"Ozzie, you black-hearted hypocrite!" Taryn screeched at him. "You don't care about anything but your own selfish ambitions!"

She swore at him, and Ozzie's heart broke inside as her words pierced him like swords. He didn't blame her. He'd be lucky if she ever forgave him for this, but wouldn't be surprised if she didn't. This…this was way beyond anything their friendship had endured, and that was saying something. If he was honest, if this wasn't a kind of abuse, it was very much akin to it. Ozzie had known the price of protecting Taryn might cost him their hard-earned friendship, but he loved Taryn too much to risk her. He was strong and silent for now; he had to be. He would have to take time to be sad later.

With Taryn fighting and screeching the whole way, Ozzie and Tynx tied her to a chair for Brighteyes to find later. Brighteyes would untie her and…and, well, Taryn would tell her whatever she wanted. Once Taryn was securely restrained, Ozzie and Tynx apologized again and bid her goodbye.

"I love you, Taryn," Ozzie said softly.

"Piss off, traitor!" she replied venomously.

This was not the way they wanted what was potentially their final farewell to go, but Taryn fought to the bitter end, and they left.

"Deianira!" Ozzie called to the sky and trees and whatever else would listen. "Deianira! We want to join you! Look, we left the doubting one and everything."

This part of the plan was not very well thought out, and it was the most thought out bit, which admittedly didn't bode well for their venture. Ozzie and Tynx had traveled quickly out of the Fairie Court and then began calling for Deianira. Smitty had something about just having to go look for the woman from his dreams—that was supposedly Deianira—so that's what they were doing. They didn't have any more than that to go on, though, so they had come up with this.

"Man, I really hope this works because, otherwise, it's going to be really embarrassing going back to face Taryn," Ozzie said, more to lighten his own mood than anything else.

His insides were twisting with guilt at what they had done, and Ozzie wasn't ashamed to admit that he wanted nothing more than to cry then and there at probably losing his best friend. There was a bitter part of his mind that was actually thinking, *Smitty had better be frickin' grateful for this*, but he tried to push that thought back down. That's not what this was about; it was about doing the right thing.

*Deianira heard the call on the wind as she worked on the formulations for her project. She didn't recognize the voice, but it addressed her by the name she had given Smitty. That was curious indeed. Deianira went straight for her magic mirror and found the owner of the voice: Smitty's friend, and the half-elf was there as well. They were calling for her, she continued to hear from the wind, and they had left the girl behind? That was very interesting. A quick check in the mirror confirmed this and, from the looks of things, she had not stayed behind willingly. Well, she should answer then.*

Tynx sensed the strange and magical presence first. It was easier now that he recognized it for what it was. He stopped short, grabbing Ozzie to stop him, too. The air before them shimmered for just a moment before she appeared. Glossy, black hair billowed gently in the breeze as she looked on the two with bright, inhuman eyes.

"You called?" she said, every word honeyed and dripping.

"Hey!" Ozzie blurted. This had worked a lot faster than he had expected, and they hadn't really talked about what they were going to say. "I mean, yeah, we did. Hi! Thanks for coming. Um, how do I say this? We want in on the deal you made with Smitty."

Deianira's eyebrows shot up at that, and she smiled unsettlingly. "Both of you?" she asked. "You're not even from their world, elfling. And what of your friend?"

"She's with the fae folk. She will find her own way," Tynx said firmly. "As for me, I am tired of this land. This realm offers me nothing. Allow me to come with Smitty and Ozzie as well. This is the only way I will be able to enter their world."

Deianira looked at the two for a long moment, studying them, considering all the possibilities. This could very well be a trick, but they had left the girl, Taryn, behind. She had watched the group long enough to know how close these two were to her. They wouldn't have abandoned her unless they were truly desperate. That was for the better, actually. That Taryn had looked to be more trouble than Deianira wanted to take on. Should any of them try to fight her, she would be all but powerless to fight back. Then again, having Ozzie in addition to Smitty would speed her plans along significantly. The half-elf Tynx was useless—his elven heritage would disrupt her magic more than his human side would help it— but that was easily solved. He would just be left to languish in her palace for eternity. This could actually be very advantageous, but she would have to be doubly careful to keep their trust. She was suddenly very pleased she had decided against imprisoning Smitty.

"Very well," she said finally. "I will take you in like a mother hen to chicks. You must do everything I say, however. We are at a vital step in the process."

"Oh, great! Thank you so much!" Ozzie gushed. "My name's Ozzie, and this is Tynx! Thanks!"

"Hands, please," Deianira said, holding out her hands.

Doing their best not to hesitate, Ozzie and Tynx reached out and each took one of Deianira's outstretched hands. As soon as they did, all three of them winked into nothing.

What could have been moments or days later, Ozzie, Tynx, and Deianira reappeared in Deianira's castle.

"Whoa," Ozzie said, looking around him. "That was crazy. Do you always travel like that?"

"No, dear, thankfully not," Deianira said, slightly out of breath like she had just been running. "It is difficult on my own, exhausting with others. Oh, how I wish for my younger days."

"Don't worry about that," Ozzie said. "You look great."

Deianira smiled at him. She was almost sad about what she had in store for Ozzie because he seemed so genuinely kind. Only *almost* sad, though, because the payoff was going to be completely and utterly worth it.

"Thank you. Now, if you will excuse me, I must rest. Please feel free to make use of anything within the palace. Find Smitty; he can show you around. My private chambers are off limits, however, which I believe he will also tell you."

"Thanks again, Deianira! You're the best!" Ozzie called after her.

As soon as she was gone, he motioned to Tynx that they would go the opposite direction to look for Smitty. Tynx nodded and followed silently. Tynx was dealing with his own emotions about the day, not least of which was his anger with Smitty. He had to remember to keep up the ruse, which might be very difficult once he actually met up with Smitty again. That being the case, he was more than happy to let Ozzie take the lead on this, and his happy-go-lucky act seemed to be working perfectly.

"Ozzie!" Smitty said, both shocked and overjoyed at seeing his friend. "And Tynx," he then said, sounding less so.

They had run into each other in a dining room, Ozzie's nose following the smell of food.

"Smitty! We found you! You're okay!" Ozzie gushed. "Thank goodness!"

"Yeah, completely," Smitty said dismissively, keeping an eye on Tynx. "What are you guys doing here?"

Ozzie then looked around and, not sure if Deianira had spies, he decided to play it safe.

"We're here to join back up with you," Ozzie said, looking at Smitty meaningfully.

"And Tynx?" Smitty asked, still keeping an eye on the half-elf.

Tynx was glowering at Smitty, eyes burning with anger and possibly hatred. It was hard to tell, but it definitely wasn't friendly.

"He's here to join the party," Ozzie explained with that same meaningful look. "He's a bit miffed about that thing with Hook, but we are getting over that, aren't we?"

"We are getting over it," was all Tynx said in response, and it sounded for all the world like a euphemism for an ugly swear.

"Um…great? So do you guys want to eat?" was all Smitty could think to say to that.

There was obviously something else going on here, but he didn't have the slightest idea what. Like Ozzie and Tynx, though, he wasn't sure what was safe to share, so he kept his own thoughts to himself for the time being.

Taryn sipped at her tea and kept looking to the wall absently. She wasn't sure if she was happy or upset there was no window there to look out of. Brighteyes had indeed found Taryn several hours after Ozzie and Tynx had left. The wombat was appalled when Taryn told her what had happened. By this time, Taryn was a mess of tears and raw wrists and ankles from trying to escape from her bonds. Brighteyes had immediately untied Taryn, made some tea, and was bustling around the girl, doing everything she could to comfort her. Brighteyes covered her with a small quilt—all of Brighteyes' blankets and furniture and dishes were small—and had just put down some toast. Taryn absently nibbled at the toast just as she sipped at her tea and kept glancing out the window that wasn't there. If the quilt fell down from around Taryn's shoulders, Brighteyes would fix it without Taryn noticing. Brighteyes didn't say much because she didn't know what to say, but she stayed by Taryn's side nonetheless.

Taryn felt more alone now than she ever had in her life. Her friends, who apparently weren't really her friends, were gone. Heinz was gone. Even Smitty, who she would very happily beat the snot out of right now, was gone. Taryn was alone in this strange land, left to wait. For what? For Ozzie and Tynx to maybe come back? And what if they didn't? What was she supposed to do then? How long was she supposed to wait for them? Could she really go home by herself if it came to it? She felt utterly desolate, but was thankful for the small comfort Brighteyes' presence provided. It was no more than a tiny prick of light in a black sky, but it was there, and Taryn did her best to open herself up to that light, but her heart was too broken to open more than a hairline crack.

Deianira looked over her setup with satisfaction. Having both Smitty and Ozzie here now would provide her with twice as much power, so she could save that much more for herself. She wasn't sure what she would encounter in this new world, so she needed to be prepared. Doing things like cursing people and transforming them into beasts took a lot of energy, and she just wasn't sure she was up for things of that magnitude anymore. Thankfully, guile took no effort whatsoever, and it had served her well throughout the ages. From what she could tell, it would take her even further in their world. Yes, things were ready.

# Chapter 21

Smitty was doing his best to act as normally as possible as he walked through the corridors of the palace with Ozzie and Tynx, pointing out rooms he had seen before and commenting on ones he hadn't. Ozzie was unnaturally cheerful and childlike, looking around at everything as they walked and acting no different the he would at an amusement park. Well, Ozzie was always optimistic, always the first one to make a joke and get others smiling too, but this took it to a whole other level. Smitty wasn't stupid; he knew Ozzie had to be upset with him for leaving and Heinz and Hook and everything. So what was going on? Tynx was surly and silent, which wasn't surprising at all, but it was unnerving. And what on earth was all that about Tynx joining the party? Smitty had tried to ask, but it was difficult when he was trying to act like everything was fine and not terrifyingly amiss. And where the heck was Taryn?! When Smitty asked about her, all he got was a curt reply from Tynx about leaving her behind. Smitty had a feeling Tynx's fat lip was a goodbye present from Taryn.

The day looked like it was beginning to draw to a close, though it sort of felt like three days had passed since Ozzie and Tynx had arrived. They had both immediately noticed and commented on the way time seemed fluid and inconsistent here.

When Smitty couldn't explain it, Ozzie had simply shrugged and said, "Oh well. The Doctor did teach us that time wasn't in a line anyway."

He had smiled at his own joke and looked around at his friends for their smiles as well. Smitty had smiled too, but more because he hadn't realized till that moment how much he missed having other people around. Tynx had not smiled for multiple reasons.

This was a strange situation for the half-elf. Granted, for most of his life he had been a pariah. He was faster and stronger and more skilled than humans, but they wanted nothing to do with him and looked down on him. Among other elves, he was the village idiot. When it came to Ozzie and Taryn, though, he was the one in charge, the one who knew best how to keep from getting killed, the one who usually had a pretty big hand in getting them out of sticky situations. That is, until he had agreed to Ozzie's mad plan. Now he was clueless and floating along after Ozzie and doing his best not to say anything to Smitty for fear of giving the game away in his anger. There was a part of him that dearly wanted to give into the fury simmering inside him, to wring that little betrayer's neck. Taryn's temper served her very well half the time, so why not? Then again, the other half of the time it got her into serious trouble. At that thought, Tynx decided to continue to say nothing and follow Ozzie's lead.

The three came to a set of double doors, and Smitty took a step back.

"I don't think we should—" he started, but Ozzie had the doors open and was inside before he could finish.

Ozzie looked around the room and immediately recognized it as the one he had seen Smitty in. Was that just yesterday? It felt like a week ago. Smitty hung back looking like a nervous mouse on the lookout for a cat.

"Guys, we really shouldn't be in here," Smitty said. "It's…it's off limits."

Both Ozzie and Tynx heard the fear in his voice and knew that there was something significant about this room, but Ozzie ignored him. The way this place changed all the time, they might never find this room again, and he knew this room had to have useful things in it. If he was right, and he suspected he was, these were the private chambers Deianira had mentioned, the ones that were forbidden. Ozzie spotted the mirror on the wall first, and his brain quickly deduced that it had to be how Smitty had spoken with him…scryed for him, as Tynx had put it. In that moment, his heart dearly wanted to use it to check on Taryn, but he pushed the feeling down. They didn't have time right now. He saw the bed of begonias and, while that was super weird, it didn't help. There were no armoires, wardrobes, cupboards, or anything else that could hold magical items or weapons or anything else in here. Why? Didn't Deianira need *things*?

Tynx stood between Smitty and Ozzie, just barely in the room, keeping an eye on both of them. Smitty was really frightened, so Tynx was on high alert. He didn't know why Ozzie was so keen to investigate this room, but he trusted him and said nothing.

"Gentlemen," came Deianira's purring voice from behind the apple trees.

They all looked and saw Deianira gliding into the room from the garden looking pleased as punch. Smitty was craning his neck so that he didn't actually have to set foot in the room.

"I'm sorry, Deianira," he immediately began. "I told them we weren't allowed in here, but they didn't listen. I did tell them."

It was all Tynx could do not to reach back and introduce Smitty's face to his knee.

Deianira held up a hand to quiet Smitty and then said sweetly, "It is fine, my pet. You may have noticed the door was *unlocked*. I left it just so for you today. Today is *the day*."

She then looked to three expectantly. Oh, she did like a bit of drama. Smitty's eyes grew wide, while Ozzie and Tynx had looks of…confusion? Skepticism? She was slightly disappointed her announcement hadn't caused more of a reaction.

"Allow me to show you," Deianira said, beckoning them to follow her.

Smitty was shaking, but Ozzie couldn't tell if it was with fear or excitement. Tynx could sense both in him. Smitty was obviously afraid of Deianira, which was different from his feelings about her back in Wonderland. Something had happened to make him afraid of her, but he clearly still believed she was going to send them back to their world. Both Ozzie and Tynx followed more slowly than Smitty. They were on their guard now, certain that she was up to no good.

They all walked past the apple trees and out into the garden, which was teeming with life. Besides the apple trees, there were pomegranate trees and low shrubs with blue berries so dark they were almost black. There were also neatly arranged beds of all kinds of flowers: rhododendron, hydrangea, oleander, snapdragons, monkshood, nightshade, and several varieties of clematis. Bees, butterflies and birds flitted back and forth and paid the visitors no mind.

"This is really pretty," Ozzie commented. "Are you a fairie?"

Deianira chuckled at that and replied, "Of a sort. As Smitty may have told you, I am a spirit. Fairies, spirits, nymphs, we're all very much of the same kin."

They then arrived at what was obviously their final destination. A very magical looking staff topped with a fist-sized white opal had been driven into the ground, and three lines had been carved into the soil leading away from the staff. All three of the lines ended in circles also carved into the ground. What was even odder, each trench appeared to be lined with a black and silver glitter or shiny grit, save for one. One of the trenches was filled with a white, crystalline substance.

"Cool! Is that your wand?!" Ozzie exclaimed, pointing at the staff.

"If by 'wand' you mean a conduit for amplifying my power, then the answer is yes," Deianira replied. "It will allow me to focus the energy needed to send you all back to your world."

"What's the white line for?" Ozzie asked, his eyes wide and inquisitive.

Deianira could feel her patience wearing thin with all of these inane questions, but she reminded herself she was nearly done with these irritating mortals. She smiled extra sweetly and responded like a mother indulging a child…because that's what she felt a bit like at the moment.

"That is for Master Tynx. You see, I will need you and Smitty to concentrate very hard on your home to direct my magical energies. Tynx, not being from your world, cannot add his thoughts to the ritual. He will still be included, as he has his own teleportation ring, but his thoughts will not be able to disrupt anything."

Tynx was on high alert now. He may have always been fairly rubbish at magic, but he had learned plenty of magical theory back when he was an apprentice to Cormin. This entire layout screamed of something nasty. The biggest red flag was his special teleportation ring. That was salt in the energy channel. Salt would block all magical energy from reaching him. Whatever Deianira was planning to do, Tynx was being walled off from it completely.

He didn't know what he could do, but he had to do it fast. Deianira was already beckoning Ozzie and Smitty to their spots.

"What do you need us to do?" Smitty asked, his voice tight. He was still fighting with himself over what to feel, but he was beginning to be more eager than afraid.

"Remain in your places no matter what happens," Deianira instructed. "Things may become somewhat frightening for a time, but you must remember we are crossing dimensions. It is not an easy thing, so remain steadfast. When I tell you, you and Ozzie must think of a place, the same place, together. That will direct us to the location we are to arrive."

"Us?" Tynx asked, trying to sound innocent. He wasn't nearly as good as Ozzie at this.

"You three. My apologies," Deianira said, widening her smile.

"Oh! Where do you wanna go?" Ozzie asked Smitty. "We could stop off somewhere cool. We have our wallets, so we can just get a bus back or something. What do you think? Grand Canyon?"

"No, Ozzie, let's just go back home. We'll go back to campus."

"Bo-ring!" Ozzie complained, giving Smitty's idea the thumbs down. "Come on, man. This is one chance to literally teleport anywhere in the world."

"Dude, don't be an idiot," Smitty retorted. "We have to choose a spot we've both been."

The two continued to argue like this for a minute or two, Ozzie growing more and more petulant and ridiculous with each reply. Tynx could see what he was doing: he was playing for time. But how could Tynx use that to his advantage? Or perhaps he didn't need to. Maybe this stall wasn't for him. Tynx could feel the anger rising in Deianira. She'd done a fantastic job of hiding her feelings all this time, but everyone had a breaking point, and Ozzie was an expert at winding someone up.

"ENOUGH!" Deianira finally exploded. "Silence, you infantile cur! Smitty will choose."

Ozzie opened his mouth to object, but no sound came out. His eyes widened with shock as he realized Deianira had taken his voice. He was afraid in that moment for what else she could do and remained still.

Tynx glared at Deianira and moved to defend his friend, but she stopped him before he could.

"Stay put, half-elf!" she spat, extending a cruelly curled hand towards him.

Tynx was instantly rooted to his spot. He could move from the waist up, but his legs were frozen and stuck to the ground.

"Okay! Okay! We get it! We'll behave! Um…I think…er…" Smitty stammered, dread filling him up just as it had when Deianira had thrown him out of her room. He thought fast and hated the only idea that came to him, but it was all he had. "I think we should go to the Mel Brooks theatre where we saw praying mantis. It should be safe enough with both of us concentrating."

Ozzie's expression was unreadable for a moment. Smitty was willing him to understand what he meant. Meanwhile, Tynx was simultaneously trying to make sense of Smitty's words and both their feelings and think of something to do. Finally, Ozzie nodded once and smirked in a mad sort of way. Smitty's idea was idiotic, but they had made do with worse.

"*Aiiiiiiieeeeeeee!*" Smitty cried insanely, turning on Deianira.

Both he and Ozzie rushed her, Ozzie's mouth a silent mimic of Smitty's strange battle cry. Deianira disappeared from sight just as Smitty and Ozzie were jumping to tackle her. Both boys landed hard on the ground, and Deianira reappeared several hundred feet away.

"You insolent wretches! I have poisoned monarchs, started wars, and you dare challenge me. I will turn you into fleas! Slugs! Or better yet, my favorite: *frogs!*"

Deianira raised both hands, and Ozzie and Smitty scrambled in separate directions, as if they could dodge Deianira's enchantment. As she swept her hands back down, one toward each boy, she doubled over and sank heavily to the ground, gasping at the feel of her core being stretched painfully beyond its limits. The power was not there, and she managed to stop the spell just before it drew on her life force to finish.

"No!" she wheezed fearfully at realizing what had happened. Transformation was too much.

Ozzie and Smitty both stopped and looked back at Deianira. Within moments, they changed directions and were barreling down on her. On his way past, Smitty grabbed the staff from its place, ripping it from the ground, and held it like a baseball bat. Tynx tried shooting what fireballs he could conjure at Deianira, but she was too far away. They extinguished before they could reach the terrified woman.

"Please! Don't hurt me!" she pleaded desperately as Ozzie and Smitty came close. "I'll give you whatever you want."

"Fix Ozzie and Tynx!" Smitty commanded, wielding the staff just out of Deianira's reach.

"I—" she stammered.

"Now!" Smitty shouted.

Deianira looked even more frightened now, but eyed her staff, which was potentially about to become the weapon of her undoing. Weakly, she waved her hand and Tynx fell forward just before catching himself.

"Tynx!" Ozzie called. "Hey! I have my voice back!"

"Tell us what you were planning," Smitty demanded. "The truth!"

Tynx joined Smitty and Ozzie and held a fireball in his hand for both emphasis and security.

"I was going to send you home," she began as innocently as possible.

"Lies!" Tynx snapped. "Silver's an excellent conductor, true, but black starleaf crystal would kill them, draining their life force. If you really wanted to help them, you'd have used the gold variety."

"Like a magical Wikipedia, this one," Ozzie smirked.

Deianira's eyes grew wide with fear. She had underestimated the half-elf. She had underestimated them all.

"Please, do not kill me," was all she said.

"Can we use her?" Ozzie asked the other two.

"I don't trust her," Smitty said darkly. "She might try to kill us again."

"Nor do I," Tynx replied, "but I can assist with that." He reached for the staff, which Smitty was clearly unwilling to hand over. "I won't brain you with it or anything," Tynx assured him.

After a moment, Smitty conceded and passed the staff to Tynx, making sure to keep it away from Deianira.

"Rowan base," Tynx said to Deianira. "Clever. Gents, with this in our hands and what defensive magic I can muster, we should be at least somewhat protected from anything this fiend tries to pull." Tynx was careful not to mention how poor his command of anything beyond novice magic was.

"Can you still send us back home?" Smitty asked.

"No, it's far beyond my capabilities now," Deianira said, still obviously trying to garner some sympathy.

"Can you send us somewhere else in Terturelia?" Smitty then asked.

"Can she send us back to where she picked us up?" Ozzie suggested.

"Good question," Tynx replied. "Well? And, please, try not to lie."

Deianira looked helplessly to each young man, afraid to answer.

"It might kill me," she finally whispered.

"Makes you wish you hadn't gone and cursed us earlier, doesn't it?" Ozzie said mirthlessly.

"If you don't, we will kill you," Tynx said.

"Please, don't ask this of me," Deianira begged. She was no longer hiding anything, no longer pretending. She was terrified.

"You didn't have any problem killing us," Ozzie said flatly.

Deianira turned to Smitty, grasping his trouser legs, and pleaded, "Smitty, please don't let them hurt me. You know me better than they do. You know I don't deserve death."

Smitty knit his eyebrows in confusion. "What do you mean? You lied to me! You drove a wedge between my friends and me! Taryn's never going to talk to me again! Who knows how much damage you've caused?"

"I...I'm sorry! Forgive me. *Please!*" Deianira shrieked, pulling at the others now.

"That's enough, witch!" Tynx said, shaking her off. He offered the staff to Ozzie and Smitty and said, "Grab a hold at the base and don't let go. Good. Take my hand with your others." Tynx, now holding onto Smitty and Ozzie's, offered their joined hands to Deianira as a faint blue glow began to surround them. He had summoned up a basic but reliable defense spell. "Now, you, send us back."

Deianira trembled and placed her fingertips across all three hands. In the next moment, they disappeared.

Brighteyes had gone round to Ebony's again to deliver some herbs. She had asked Taryn to come, suggesting it would be good for her, but Taryn had politely refused. It had only been a few days since Ozzie and Tynx had tied her up and left her behind, and she wasn't at her best. Taryn didn't like strangers seeing her in this state, but she promised she would come out to the bonfire that night. Taryn had avoided that particular event these last few evenings as well. In order to further appease Brighteyes, Taryn had also offered to get outside and work the garden a bit. Brighteyes liked that idea, mentioning that the northwest quadrant had been fallow for a season and needed a wakeup call. The quadrants of Brighteyes' garden were not large, but it would provide at least a few hours hard work. That should help Taryn take her mind off things. It didn't.

Brighteyes, being a wombat, didn't need garden tools, so Taryn had found a sturdy stick about the length of a broomstick handle and twice as thick instead. She had pared one end down to a sharply tapered paddle in order to pierce and move the soil. It wasn't nearly as efficient as a hoe or a shovel, but it made a good start. Taryn stabbed at the ground with her makeshift auger before levering it up, breaking the ground apart. Her anger was driven behind every thrust. How dare Ozzie and Tynx leave her! Being alone had allowed Taryn to rehash everything in her mind, and all the anger from that horrible time a few days ago came bubbling back to the surface. Hot, furious tears eked from her eyes as she thought about them out there in danger. There was no way to know where they were just then or if they were okay. Taryn had vacillated between anger and sorrow these last few days. There were times like this when she would slap both of them if they magically appeared before her, but then there were times when she prayed and bargained. If they just came back safe, she wouldn't say anything, she wouldn't be upset. She would just hug them and let everything go if they would just come back to her. Taryn started thinking about other things, too. She thought about Heinz, sweet faithful Heinz who had protected her so valiantly, about Smitty and his pathetic cowardice. The tears began to come faster, too fast to see, and Taryn's efforts turned from plowing to thrashing. Finally, after beating the earth around her so violently it had actually undone some of her work, she folded onto her knees and began to sob, hanging onto the stick for support.

*Taryn*...she heard faintly. She ignored it, but a moment later it came again. *Taryn*...lilted musically, floating gently on the breeze to her ears.

Taryn lifted her head and looked for the source of the sound through bleary eyes. She heard it again and felt comforted. Getting up, she began to walk forward, feeling pulled in that direction. It was only when she was close to the tree line, when she had blinked away the worst of the tears, that she saw it. A figure, cloaked and half concealed behind a tree, had become visible. Taryn's brain went into defense mode. She stopped short and stared at the figure, scowling.

"Show your face," she said simply.

The figure did so without hesitation, and Taryn gasped and took a step back.

"Erik!" she said, her voice shaking.

Erik, the Phantom of the Opera, was dressed for traveling but still looked impeccable. All except for the mask, of course; that hadn't changed.

"Lovely to see you again, Miss Taryn," he cooed. "Your gentlemen friends are out, I see. That is good, because I very much wanted to have some time alone with you."

"Erik," Taryn stammered, "how...what are you doing here?"

"To be frank, my dear, I have come to discuss your betrayal."

With that, he began to approach her carefully, almost gallantly. Every movement was fluid, every gesture lovely. Taryn, on the other hand, backed away fearfully, trying to put as much distance between her and the Phantom as possible. She couldn't flat out run. No, he would catch her, and then she'd be done for. Erik was insanely strong. She had to try and figure something else out. She realized her sharp-ended stick was still in her hand, but could she really do what had sprung to mind?

"Erik, please, think about this..." Taryn began.

"I have had plenty of time to think about this," Erik replied smoothly.

Taryn could feel her mind grow fuzzy when he spoke. She didn't know if he was doing it on purpose, but the power of his voice was working on her, which was very, very bad. If he was going to try to kill her, she needed to be sharp enough to fight back.

"You were so very clever with your words: everyone does what you tell them to. You were right. My dear Christine, I sent her away with that prat. For the sake of her love, I sent her away. And you *knew* it! Why? Why didn't you tell me?! After all I did for you!"

He slammed his fist on the trunk of a tree with that last question, making Taryn jump and yelp fearfully.

"I'm sorry, Erik!" Taryn cried. "I was so scared and didn't know what would happen if I told you. You might have killed Raoul! You were going to kill *us*!"

"Yes, I very well might have killed him in the end, but now we will never know. We will never know what might have happened between Christine and her Angel of Music. Not unless you can tell me what happens next."

Taryn pursed her lips together, fighting hard against the fear that was quickly growing in her and the tears that were threatening to return. She didn't blame Erik for how he felt. She had known of the heartbreak that was coming to him and did nothing to stop it. Possessive and obsessive though he was, Christine was the dearest thing in the world to him. What was worse was that Taryn couldn't do anything to help now that the damage had been done.

"What. Happens?" Erik demanded, his voice more musical than ever now.

"Nothing," Taryn whispered, not daring to meet his eyes.

"Nothing?" Erik pressed.

"That's where the book ends. Christine and Raoul leave together, and that's it. Nothing else. I'm so sorry."

The Phantom's eyes were burning. There was a heavy, uncertain moment wherein he didn't move, and Taryn risked a few more slow steps backward, hoping against hope that he would turn away in despair. He did no such thing. Instead, in a fit of anger, he leapt forward and grabbed Taryn. She screamed and pulled away, but his grip was too strong.

"Help!" Taryn shrieked, praying that someone might hear her.

"Since there is no ending, I will create my own!"

"No! Erik! Stop!" Taryn said, fighting against him.

With that, she swung the branch around and struck the side of his head with it. She had wanted to stab him with it, but her angle was wrong. He let go of her for a moment, and she used that to make a break for it, still hanging onto her only weapon. She ran pell-mell around to the front of the burrow. Erik raced after her, gaining quickly. Taryn could hear Erik close behind, too close. She turned suddenly, bracing the flat end of the stick against the ground and angling the pointed end towards the Opera Ghost. Erik, chasing Taryn at such a speed, was unable to stop himself from running onto her spear. She felt victorious for a moment as she watched the end sink with sickening ease into Erik's side. Erik clutched the weapon in his hands and took a step back. Taryn let go of it as he did so, waiting for him to collapse. Impossibly, he pulled the stick from his flesh and then snapped it in half as easily as he would a twig. He began to advance again, and Taryn, knowing the level of superhuman strength she was dealing with, realized she had only one defense left. She kicked fast and hard between Erik's legs, sending him to his knees, and then she was off again, shouting at the top of her lungs for help.

There was a horse tethered to a tree beyond, and Taryn debated with herself for a moment. She would lose time if she took the horse, but would make it up quickly, and Erik couldn't catch her once she was off on horseback. The risk was greater if she tried to get away on foot, despite the time she'd initially save not fussing with untying and mounting a horse. She headed for the horse, a great black steed, and attacked the knot that secured him to the tree. Thankfully, it was no more than a loose slipknot, and Taryn had it undone in a matter of seconds. She hooked her foot into the stirrup and leapt up onto the horse's back faster than she knew was possible. It was only another few moments before she had him turned and heading away to safety. The horse was picking up speed when Erik ran into their path and stared furiously at Taryn. He didn't move even as the horse barreled towards him, and Taryn realized they were playing a game of chicken. She steeled herself for the impact. She was going to get away. If that meant running the Phantom of the Opera down, so be it. The horse ran on, and

Taryn hunched down in the saddle, making herself as small as possible just in case he tried grabbing her. Unlikely, but she was ready just in case. She was not ready for what Erik actually did.

Just before the horse reached him and trampled him into the ground, Erik threw up his arms and shrieked horribly like a thousand tortured violins, spooking the horse and making him rear up and whinny fearfully. Taryn was thrown from the saddle and landed hard on the ground. She cried out as a horrible pain racked her shoulder. She was dazed, but struggled to get up and run again. She made the mistake of trying to push herself up with the arm she had landed on and cried out again when another wave of agony ripped through her. Then she heard the snarling, the roars and furious yowling, and sounds of animalistic pain. Taryn managed to crane her head around and saw Shadowpaw and Windstalker. Erik was just ripping Shadowpaw from his back and tossing him aside like a cub, while Windstalker grabbed his leg with teeth and claws. Erik grabbed her by one ear and bashed her head repeatedly with his fist.

"NO!" Taryn shrieked. "Leave them alone!"

She tried to get up again using her other arm while the opposite drummed pain all down her side. There! She was on her feet. Erik was still fighting Shadowpaw and Windstalker, doing more damage to the leopards than should be humanly possible. He was ruthless, ripping at ears, breaking limbs, kicking organs, anything he could to stop the attack. Taryn hadn't made it one step before Erik was suddenly there, dragging her towards the horse by the back of her shirt. Taryn tried to pull away, but he squeezed her injured shoulder, and her knees nearly buckled from the pain. He half dragged, half carried her back to the horse, who was pacing back and forth nervously. Erik spoke soothingly to the creature, which immediately calmed it, and lifted Taryn back onto the saddle. It was excruciating. Every time her arm moved, it sent waves of agony through her. When she was finally back up on the horse, she could barely focus. Devising another escape attempt was impossible, and Erik moved quicker than ever now despite his injuries. Taryn was able to just barely catch out of the corner of her eye Shadowpaw leaping towards Erik again, but Erik swiftly kicked the leopard in the jaw, sending him sprawling to the ground. Windstalker was lying motionless just beyond. Taryn began to shed tears for the noble leopards while Erik quickly bound his wounds just enough to stem the bleeding. Then, climbing up onto the horse, he sat behind Taryn and gently lifted her injured arm. He held it tightly against her body as he held her securely around the waist. Not that it mattered now. The best Taryn could hope to do at this point was fall off and crawl away. Erik steered the horse towards the trees and took off. The jostling of the ride was brutal on Taryn's shoulder, but she suspected it would have been worse had he not been holding it secure.

Ozzie, Tynx, and Smitty materialized in the middle of a gullied and woody wilderness, but what wilderness and where was anyone's guess.

"Did we make it?" Ozzie asked, looking around.

There were only grass, trees, and birdsong to answer his question.

"Where are we?" Smitty asked.

Tynx looked around slowly and said, "It's certainly not Wonderland, but it also doesn't feel overly familiar."

"Are we back in Gloriana's Green?" Ozzie asked. He then shouted, "Hello! Fairies!"

"Subtle," Tynx joked.

"What happened once you guys made it here? How did y'all survive without food?" Smitty asked.

While in Deianira's palace, they hadn't talked much about what Ozzie and Tynx had done since Smitty had disappeared. All he knew was that they had made it to the Fairie Court and somehow left Taryn behind.

"Oh, you mean after you murdered one of the most noble creatures to ever walk the earth?" Tynx replied waspishly. "After you colluded with that blackguard to have me killed? Not much. Just risked our lives to save your miserable one. We all but assaulted Taryn to keep her from coming with us."

"Dude! So not the time!" Ozzie snapped. "Seriously, all I care about right now is getting back to the burrow. Please, save it for later."

Tynx glared at Smitty for a long moment. He wanted so badly to lay into the little scoundrel, but his better judgment won out in the end. He too was more than keen to get back.

"Come on!" Ozzie said as soon as he saw he had won Tynx over.

Ozzie didn't bother to wait for Smitty to agree. Somewhere inside, he too was furious with Smitty for everything, but Ozzie didn't have a temper like Taryn or even like Tynx, especially when there were far more important things to attend to.

They began to jog, Ozzie taking the lead. It was quiet and might have been awkward as well, but they were all too busy with their own thoughts. Both Tynx and Ozzie were trying to think of the best way to apologize to Taryn. A little sorry was not going to do the job this time. Meanwhile, Smitty was wondering what he had missed, but he wasn't about to risk asking again.

"How do we know we're going the right way?" Tynx asked.

He had been looking for any signs that they were close to the Fairie Court, but he simply was not familiar enough with the area to be able to tell.

"We don't, but we can't just stand around," Ozzie replied. "You make a good point, though."

With that, Ozzie started shouting as he jogged. He shouted hello and called the names of the animals from the Court and anything else he could think of. They ran on for a bit when suddenly there was a flash of gold over the edge of a ridge. Ozzie felt sure it was one of the fae folk and turned sharply towards the ridge.

"Where are you going?" Smitty asked, turning to follow Ozzie.

Ozzie didn't answer. He couldn't explain it, but he just *knew* this was the right way. He led the little group up the ridge and spotted a thickly wooded forest beyond. Standing at the tree line was a huge lioness. Tynx stopped in his tracks, dumbstruck at the size of it. It was enormous, bigger even than Heinz had been! He was afraid when he saw her, but not for his life. He was afraid because he knew this was a being of incredible power, but he was at the same time full of awe and wonder and joy. Ozzie was already running at full speed for the lioness, who disappeared into the trees just then. Tynx started off again, while Smitty, who was taking up the rear, came trudging over the crest of the ridge just as the Ozzie was entering the trees. When he saw the others so far ahead of him, he picked up his speed to catch up.

Ozzie had lost sight of the lioness, but he ran on anyway. A familiar voice began to resound from above, faintly at first, but quickly grew louder.

"Mortals!" it crowed.

They looked up to see Ebony flying above them.

"Hey! We found you!" Ozzie exclaimed excitedly. "How close are we to the burrow?"

"Come quickly," Ebony cawed.

Before they could ask any more, she flew ahead.

"I really hope she's not still mad," Ozzie said to Tynx as they ran.

Tynx said nothing. Something was wrong; he could sense it in Ebony. He ran ahead faster than either human could ever hope to and ignored the calls that followed behind him.

The scene that met the three in the burrow's clearing was grim. There was blood on the ground, and a strong wooden tool or weapon of some sort lay broken in half on the ground.

"Taryn?" Ozzie called when he saw these things, worry filling his voice. "Taryn!"

Ozzie ran inside, ignoring whatever Ebony was saying. He burst into Brighteyes' front room to find Windstalker and Shadowpaw laid out and looking as if they'd been hit by a bus. Brighteyes was trying to usher Ozzie out, but he wasn't hearing her. He ran back outside, shouting frantically.

"Tynx! Tynx! Taryn's gone! Something's…"

He stopped short as he saw Tynx examining the ground. He was tracking Taryn and Erik's movements. Tynx could see the marks where their scuffle had taken place. Taryn, whose feet left smaller imprints, had turned here and taken off again. Her assailant had gone down, but he had pursued. Taryn had gone one way—for a horse apparently—while the other had gone another. Something happened, someone had gone down. There was more blood on the ground. Was it Taryn's? Leopard prints were here as well and deep gashes in the earth. Whatever had happened here had been bad. Two sets of prints led away, back to the horse. Ebony was trying to fill him in as he worked, but he was only catching about half of it.

"Brushfire is following," Ozzie heard Ebony say.

"Following who?" he demanded. "What happened? Where is Taryn?!"

"A man in a mask took her," Ebony explained quickly.

"A mask?" Ozzie said, feeling as if he had been punched in the chest.

He turned to find Smitty. Smitty was hanging back and surveying the scene with wide eyes. His face was white. Was Taryn dead?

"Smitty!" Ozzie called over to him, snapping Smitty's attention back to him. "What happens in the end of that story?"

"What story?" Smitty replied, still reeling from the nightmare they had stumbled into.

"The Phantom or whatever it's called. What happens? You saw it. Think!"

"I—I," Smitty stammered. "I don't really remember. I think the girl, Christine, and the guy live happily ever after."

"What guy? Erik?"

"No, the other one. The normal one."

Ozzie swore. That didn't tell him anything.

"What are you talking about?" Tynx asked. "Who's this masked man?"

"It has to be Erik, the Phantom," Ozzie replied. "We met him when we first got here. Remember the guy we told you about who almost killed us but then helped us? It's him, but why would he take Taryn? What did she say to him? She convinced him not to kill us by telling him how his story ended. Ebony, when was he here?"

"Midmorning," she replied.

Ozzie and Tynx looked to the sky. It was late afternoon now. That meant they had a few hours head start on horseback. The decision was already made; they were going after Taryn and the infamous Opera Ghost. Smitty made one objection, and Ozzie said something very unkind to him, something that would have made his mother admonish, *language!* Tynx followed up by telling Smitty to either help or get out of the way and stay put until they returned. Smitty sat dumbly on the ground then, staring blankly at his feet. They were ready within minutes, and Brighteyes gave them what little food she could from her stores. Both Tynx and Ozzie spared but a moment to speak softly and encouragingly to the two unconscious leopards in Brighteyes' front room. They thanked the wombat deeply for her hospitality and apologized for the trouble they had brought.

"You should go," Brighteyes said seriously.

Had they not been in such a rush, Ozzie and Tynx would have felt guilty about Brighteyes' comment. Surely, she blamed them for Taryn being taken. They had left her here alone, after all. As it was, they simply nodded in response and set off at a run.

# Chapter 22

Erik and Taryn rode until the sun had begun to dip down behind the hills and a blanket of twilight had begun to spread. He steered the horse into a little copse of trees and carefully helped Taryn dismount. The pain in her shoulder had become constant, making it seem as if it had always been there, but she didn't know if that made it better or worse.

"Stay," Erik told her firmly.

Taryn obeyed tiredly, leaning back against one of the tree trunks while Erik went about securing the horse and whatever else he needed to do. Taryn didn't care at the moment. She was too tired and in too much pain. She needed to figure out a way to get away, but her arm was a major impediment. She liked to think she had begun to learn to stand the pain after enduring it most of the day, but a slight test-twitch told her that sharp agony was awaiting her if she got too brazen about moving it.

Erik was eventually back at her side. She could tell by the smell of him. That scent of death had made her feel dizzy and ill during the ride, but the wind rushing by them had helped considerably. Now that they were stationary, it hung next to him and wafted over to her when he was near. Her eyes were closed, trying to concentrate, but she felt him take a hold of her arm. She resisted the urge to shudder at the cold clamminess of his touch. When he jammed her arm back into its socket, however, she screamed and pulled away, which made the pain worse, if that was possible. He took her arm into his hands again, and Taryn could feel his intentions in the strength of his grasp to keep a hold of her this time. She braced herself against the bolts of pain shooting through her as Erik tucked her arm into a sling and tied it tight.

Taryn finally recognized what was happening, and she spoke through gritted teeth.

"Why are you doing this? I thought you wanted revenge."

"I do not think revenge is the right word," Erik replied smoothly. "Restitution is perhaps better. I provided you and your friends with quite a bit of help. This is my repayment."

"That still doesn't explain why you're fixing my arm," she said, trying not to snap at him. The pain of her arm mixed with the fear of the situation was putting her fight response into overdrive, but she knew this was a fight she would lose.

"What purpose would it serve to allow it to heal improperly?" Erik asked.

Taryn was losing the battle against her frustration. "So you're not above kidnapping or murder, but you're highly logical in this situation?"

"I do nothing without a purpose."

Taryn growled through her teeth at that, mostly because she knew this to be true somewhere in her mind.

"You are a very intriguing young lady, Taryn. You are very brave…and impetuous."

"Not like the other women you're familiar with, huh?" she said dryly.

Erik chuckled at that and replied, "No, not at all. The women I am familiar with are far more demure than you."

"I won't replace Christine Daaé for you," Taryn said boldly.

She knew she was being stupid. She really should be choosing her words with more care, but she was so pained and tired and frustrated and scared and angry. That, and she suspected the game between her and Erik had changed now that she was his chosen prisoner instead of Christine. She was fairly certain he wouldn't kill her, but that still left plenty of unpleasant options.

"No one will ever replace my Christine," Erik said, and the note of sadness in his voice shot through all of Taryn's pain and anger and hit her heart like an arrow.

She thought of Tynx and what it had been like when she had woken up in her own bed, away from Leleplar and him. She knew then that she would never see him again. How much worse was Erik's pain over Christine? A different dimension over which Erik had no control didn't separate them, Christine's choice of Raoul over him did. Taryn sighed unhappily, not knowing what to say to that, especially now that her feelings for Tynx were warring against each other.

Erik then spent some time re-dressing his wounds, taking great care to check his side where Taryn had impaled him. He stitched it up in the end; continuing to stuff the wound with more bandages was only going to cause problems.

"Come," Erik said finally. "You know all about me, yet I know nothing about you. Tell me while I make us supper."

Taryn didn't know what to share. What was safe to share? She decided to tell him about her family back home. They were there and out of Erik's reach. Plus, maybe Erik would feel badly for her and let her go if he heard about everything he was tearing her away from. She told him about her parents and Kyla. She shared about Kael and his death, but left Ozzie's part out of it. She made sure to emphasize how hard losing one child had been on the family. She looked to Erik for any kind of reaction, but he was facing away.

"What exactly is your plan for us?" she then asked suddenly. "I hope you don't expect much from me. Not being from this world and all, I'm fairly useless because I don't really know how to do anything. Back home, machines do most of our work for us."

Erik chuckled at that, a warm, leisurely sound, and replied, "Let us wait and see what fate has in store. I should think, however, that this animosity will not last."

Taryn stared agape at Erik for a moment, unable to wrap her mind around what he had said. Did he really think she would just get over kidnapping her and keeping her captive?

"I thought we already discussed this," she said sternly, suddenly wanting to reinforce some boundaries. "I am not going to replace Christine for you."

"Nor do I expect you to. Despite all your redeeming traits, my dear—barring your treachery, of course—you will never be as sweet, as gentle, or as innocent as my Christine. She is a lamb, while you are a lion. You are not someone I would have chosen to know, but the choice is apparently out of my hands."

"Fate's consolation prize?" Taryn said acidly.

What Erik had said made Taryn angry. Not the part about Christine's traits. No, that was all fine. It was the part about fate.

Taryn didn't believe in fate; she believed in the consequences of people's decisions. Erik had made the decision to spare Raoul's life and send Christine away with him. Taryn had made the decision to hide the truth from Erik. Erik had decided to come after her for answers and then to kidnap her. It made her furious that he was blaming that on fate.

"That's your explanation?" she demanded. "*Fate* took away the love of your life? Christine loved Raoul, and you killed people! That's why she didn't want to be with you. She was afraid of you! It's not that hard to under—"

Erik backhanded Taryn midsentence. He said nothing, but she could feel the heat of his eyes on her even as she looked away. She took a deep breath and looked back to him. She wasn't about to cower or let him break her. She knew she had crossed the line, but she still didn't buy this fate story he was selling. Erik was clearly furious, but this wasn't like back at the burrow. This was a cold, controlled fury, and she wasn't sure what he would do next. Thankfully, he only turned away and finished with supper.

A few minutes later, he served them both bowls of the vegetable soup he had made. Taryn had to balance her bowl on her knees and then in her lap to try and accommodate her injured arm. Neither was working well, so she finally just ended up dropping her spoon next to her and drinking straight from the bowl. Erik stared at her while she did this, which bothered Taryn—*What?!* she thought—but she said nothing. Her face was still throbbing a little from where he had hit her, and she didn't want to push him again, not unless it would be worth it.

Erik watched Taryn with interest. She was a very curious creature. She had forgone good manners for practicality, a highly unattractive trait in his mind. There was none of the sophistication in her that he was used to. How must they raise their women in her world? It must be chaos. Nevertheless, she was here now; his mission was complete.

Erik had retraced his steps back into Wonderland, back to the monster's cottage, and then followed the trail to Gloriana's Green. He found the graves Ozzie, Taryn, and Tynx had dug, but could not guess at what had happened. He also could not take the time to investigate. He was already far behind them, and the trail was very nearly gone now. Thankfully, he was on horseback and catching up quickly. When he had finally reached that odd underground den—which had been very difficult considering the number of magical animals living in the area—Erik couldn't believe his luck. There she was, his quarry, all alone and so vulnerable. The emotionally compromised were always more susceptible to his call. Taryn had been stronger than he expected, however, making his job that much more difficult...not to mention painful. All in all, though, he was now satisfied with his decision to bring her back with him. Already, even before he had begun to scratch at her foundation, he could see her walls cracked and beginning to crumble. Best of all, she was oblivious to the power it gave him.

Brushfire peered through the darkness at the two sleeping forms, keeping a close eye on the disfigured one. The fox had just caught up with them and surveyed the scene with a shrewd, calculating gaze. What he saw was not promising. Taryn was injured and Erik had caused it. Brushfire was not powerful enough to defend her, but he also could not help her escape. Erik kept one hand on her arm even as he slept. Taryn, however, was not sleeping. Her eyes were open, watching Erik carefully for any sign of wakefulness. Brushfire silently crept around her other side. Taryn saw the bright, glowing eyes approaching, but she said nothing. Between Erik and this potential new foe, she would risk the golden-eyed creature first before waking Erik.

"Hello, beautiful," Brushfire whispered so softly that it was more hiss than words.

Taryn smiled and breathed back, "Hello, handsome."

Brushfire drew closer, right up to Taryn's ear, and said, "You won't be able to slip away tonight. He's only half sleeping."

Taryn barely nodded, suppressing a sigh. If anyone knew what a sleeping predator looked like, it would be another predator.

"Brushfire, please, find my friends. Tynx and Ozzie and even Smitty. I need help."

The fox nodded once and then silently slipped away. Taryn tried to be brave as she watched him go, leaving her alone. He was *going* to find them and tell them what had happened. He had to...

Tynx and Ozzie ran all through the night, a mote of light gliding above their heads. Ozzie could only trust the path down which Tynx led them. He knew Tynx could see at least halfway through the dark, and the hoof prints were dug deep into the ground. Ozzie, meanwhile, could only see a few feet ahead. Taryn and Erik had galloped for a little while, but Ozzie suspected the horse hadn't been able to keep up that pace with two riders because it had slowed, or so Tynx had said. Ozzie just wondered how far they had made it and if they were still going.

Taryn peeked around the corner, looking for Erik. She was currently on a mission for food, having waited most of the day, listening for any sign that Erik was occupied elsewhere. No dice, and her stomach was grumbling angrily now. She listened hard, but couldn't hear anything. No footsteps, no creaking and, most of all, no music. This was bad. It meant Taryn had no idea where Erik was. When he was composing, she was free to wander and search for an escape. He didn't compose as much as she expected. Apparently, Taryn didn't inspire him the way Christine had. While she would have preferred for Erik to be working on his music 24/7, she was relieved in a way as well. She was worried this was going to turn into some kind of *Beauty and the Beast* situation. No, thank you! She had already done that and had less than no desire to go through it again, least of all with the Phantom of the Opera. Erik very clearly only had a heart for Christine, but that didn't stop him from trying to manipulate Taryn.

Erik had tried very hard to enthrall Taryn with his voice. It was pretty hard to miss, what with the way he sang as she tried to fall asleep each night, his voice seeping through the walls of her room. It floated in and wrapped around her head, insidiously sliding into her ears and wafting through her dreams. She felt her eyelids grow heavy when his voice slipped under the door and through the keyhole. Try as she might, nothing—not pillows or walking around or banging on the door—blocked out the terrible pull of that hypnotizing music. What was worse, she always felt better when she woke up the next morning, which in turn sickened her. She woke up wondering where the sweet music had gone before she shook herself to bring her back to her senses. It was a battle for her mind, she was sure, and it never ended. Her only respite occurred when Erik turned his attention to other things. Those other things weren't always music as far as she could tell, but he disappeared before she could ever follow him to find out what they were.

Taryn had been Erik's prisoner for she didn't know how long now. He had taken her through woods and down near invisible tracks until they had finally arrived at a manor hidden deep in the woods. It had taken eight days on horseback, and Taryn didn't have any clue as to where she was now. They could be back in France for all she knew. She looked for clues around the house— architecture, maps, anything—but there was nothing helpful. She'd had nothing but the clothes on her back when Erik had attacked, so she was left with only her wits. None of the items in the mansion were any help, as they were mostly decorative in nature...*the gaudy git*, she had thought acidly. The windows were all blacked out, hiding the sun and moon from her and erasing all concept of time. It had been long enough for her shoulder to heal, though it was stiff and hurt when she pushed it too far. Nevertheless, she put herself through the best physical therapy she could think of. If she was going to escape, she'd need to be as fit as possible.

The inside of the house, while immaculate and remarkably beautiful, was always dim, lit only by candles, sconces, and fireplaces. Taryn supposed Erik would have preferred another underground lair, but only he and Batman seemed to have those. Erik would never go back to the Opera House—too many painful memories, she knew—and Batman...well, she could really use a Batman right now.

Taryn decided to chance a trip down to the kitchen. Erik didn't like her to go there for food. He preferred she eat with him, but Taryn made every effort to avoid him. Today, she was not successful. She slipped around the corner and padded down the hall as stealthily as she could. She hadn't made it far when she heard the voice.

"Taryn, my dear. Won't you come and join me?"

Taryn put her hands over her ears and ran on, filling her head with her own, rebellious cries.

*No! Not this time! No! No! No!*

"Taryn..." came the voice again, musical and otherworldly.

Taryn's breath caught in her throat. The beauty of that voice snared her muscles, pulled her senses and her attention back. She stopped and caught herself on the wall, fighting against the pull of the voice. She trudged a few steps forward, mentally switching gears.

*Think of Ozzie. Think of Tynx. They're out there. They're coming for you. They're...*

And Taryn had to shake her head. What else were they? They had left her. They weren't here, but that voice was. Taryn suddenly gasped when a cold hand grasped hers. A musty corpse smell invaded her nostrils, and Taryn closed her eyes. Erik must have been waiting for her. She was bound to fall into his trap sooner or later.

"Come, my dear," he crooned. "Let us sit and enjoy a meal together. I have more questions for you."

"No," Taryn growled, trying to pull away.

Erik's grip on her was too strong. She couldn't get away, but she couldn't stand to run through more of her memories with Erik.

Since they had arrived at the manor, Erik had taken to asking Taryn further questions about her life and adventures in Terturelia. She hadn't seen the harm in it that first night, but then, as he asked more, she realized what was happening. He was invading her mind. She had begun to feel it happening, his words weaving like vines inside her head. He made comments as she spoke, cutting words that undermined her faith in herself and others. She found herself beginning to question things she had known for years, but she resisted as best she could. Perhaps Erik was looking for more material for his music. He had taken advantage of the sadness in Christine Daaé's soul after all. Whatever the reason, he used that damnable voice of his to draw it out of her slowly like threads from a tapestry, one by one. She would spend days on one story, and Taryn wondered if the process was as exhausting for Erik as it was for her. She had already told him of their harrowing encounter with the Beast and relived the experience of first meeting Erik from her perspective. He now knew of Ozzie's troubles back home and how they had met Tynx.

She yanked at her arm again, but it didn't budge from Erik's grasp. He reached out and brushed her hair gently with a hand, that horrible smell of decay invading her nostrils.

"Come. Now."

"Piss off!" Taryn snarled, and she was pleased because her clarity was coming back. That seemed to happen whenever she got her ire up.

Erik responded by forcibly dragging her back to the little room where he had been lying in wait for her. Laid out on a table there were tea, toast, cheeses, meats, crackers, nuts, compotes, and more. He pushed her towards a chair, and Taryn just managed not to trip into it. She stood defiantly next to it, staring hatefully at Erik.

"I see you wish to try my patience today," he sneered.

"I do my best," Taryn snapped.

Days like this she counted as victories. She was resisting him and planned on continuing to do so, but there would be a price to pay. She picked up a piece of toast and bit into it violently, not caring to wait for Erik.

"Take care, Miss Taryn," Erik hissed, "lest you push me too far."

She said nothing, but continued to stare daggers at him. Erik turned from her and began to hum. She stuck her fingers in her ears to block out the noise, knowing immediately what he was doing. It was just another way for him to use the power of his voice, but this was more subversive. It dulled all of her senses like a light tranquilizer, making her just a bit less fighty. Somehow, the sound still penetrated her ears, and she immediately felt the heaviness that began to come with it.

"Shut it!" she screeched, picking up a plate and hurling it at Erik.

It connected, shattered over his head, and made him stumble for a moment. Taryn immediately realized she had made a huge mistake. She had defied Erik, of course, in the time she had been his prisoner. She had been insolent, but she had never physically struck out at him since the burrow because she knew she was outmatched. She was frightened now, but she stood her ground, knowing there was nowhere to go, and waited for whatever punishment was to come. Erik turned slowly towards her again, eyes blazing furiously.

"Just how long do you think this can go on, Miss Kelly?" he growled, approaching her slowly. He leaned heavily on a chair. "You are *alone* here. No one knows where you are. You are my property and forever will be because *no one* is coming for you! Ever!" His voice rose in volume and melody as he spoke until it eventually resembled church bells, the tune of his words and will crashing through Taryn's head.

Taryn put a hand to her chest as she felt a piece of her heart cry out and die. Her knees buckled beneath her, and she sank to the floor, suddenly feeling empty and cold. Erik was still there, no longer leaning on the chair but looming over her and smiling wickedly. What had he done to her? She had to get away. Taryn feebly got back to her feet and walked uncertainly around the table, making her way for the door. Erik didn't even have to move.

"Your friends were not there when I found you," he said, his voice a deep purr. Taryn stopped in her tracks, the ache in her chest growing again. "Tell me, where had they gone? Why, pray tell, did they not hear your cries for help and come running?"

Taryn felt sick as tears welled up in her eyes. She didn't want to think about the answers to those questions and she certainly didn't want to tell Erik. Taryn had been telling herself all this time that Ozzie and Tynx *would* come back for her. They were going to save her! Then Erik, with that accursed voice, had dug up the secret fear she had been keeping even from herself, and it was now staring her in the face.

"Tell me," Erik whispered victoriously, just behind her ear now, "why were you crying that day? Alone?"

Ozzie felt like whooping into the air when the manor appeared before them, hidden in a small but deep valley thick with pine trees. He didn't, though, for fear of being discovered. After Brushfire met them on the trail and told them of what he had seen, Tynx had led an impossibly grueling march across Gloriana's Green and into Greece. They had slept only when Ozzie couldn't go on without stumbling and ate as they doggedly followed the trail. Tynx was thankful for the big horse and the deep tracks it left. There had been times they worried they had lost the trail completely at river crossings or in very wet and marshy land where the ground was so pocked and divoted everything and nothing looked like tracks. Tynx had summoned up every bit of magic he could to help them in their endeavor, which exhausted him as well. Ozzie was convinced this had saved their bacon more than once. Not only did the divining spells help to identify the tracks they needed when they lost the trail, but the spells Tynx cast to make them silent and camouflaged had gotten them through some very unwelcoming looking places.

Greece was full of strange and frightening creatures. Some were friendly or indifferent towards the two young men that passed through their domain. Others, however, looked like they were just itching for a victim to prey upon. Erik seemed to have taken them a pretty safe route, but it was not perfect by any means. Tynx asked Ozzie what they could expect in this country, but Ozzie could only name a few creatures he thought he remembered from Greek mythology. He had never read any of the plays or stories, and most of his knowledge came from the fantasy fiction he read, so he wasn't completely certain even if centaurs and Pegasus were Greek. The land seemed to be on their side, however, as more than once Tynx spotted a dryad or some other spirit tagging along at a distance. He was always wary when he saw these creatures, for he had always known them to follow no rules but their own. Nevertheless, they always stayed a safe distance away and remained even through the night, like a strange sentry guarding the two as they snatched their short rests.

Now that they were finally here, they could barely believe it. Ozzie wanted to approach the manor immediately, find a way in, and ambush Erik. Tynx wouldn't allow it, though. As worried as he was about Taryn, he knew they needed to get an idea of what they were up against first. So they waited…and waited…and waited. They waited all that afternoon and into the night, Ozzie growing increasingly frustrated with Tynx. There was nothing to see! They should just risk it! Who knew what Taryn was enduring in there right now? Ozzie forced himself not to think about that; it made him even more anxious and frantic. He took a deep breath. Tynx was just as concerned for Taryn. He knew what he was doing. Tynx was frustrated as well, but for an entirely different reason. Why hadn't they seen anyone? Weren't there guards or something? Didn't they feel the need to check the perimeter? Surely this Erik wasn't so foolish as to…wait…what was that?

A lone figure on horseback was approaching. The horse was laden with something, but it was impossible to tell what at this distance. The figure had arrived from the direction almost opposite where Tynx and Ozzie were hidden and it was hard to keep track of him since the trees grew right up to the manor. The figure dismounted near the house and walked to the side of it. Tynx and Ozzie could no longer see the figure, and Tynx motioned silently for Ozzie to follow. Noiselessly, Tynx crept down the hill faster than Ozzie could understand. Ozzie was doing his best to be quiet, but the slope was so steep he kept having to grab onto tree trunks to avoid slipping and falling down to the bottom. Tynx did not wait for Ozzie and skirted around the side of the house, watching carefully for any movement. He dreaded the idea of making it this far, to have waited this long, only to get caught by a guard. There was no one there, and Tynx carefully crept along the edge of the manor, sticking to the shadows and wondering to where the figure could have disappeared. He heard Ozzie coming up behind him and held out a hand to stop him. Tynx had just seen something that caught his eye. There was a cellar door set into the ground and partially covered by branches. This door had been used to go in very, very recently. Tynx made a decision: they were going in.

The cellar doors, unsurprisingly, led to a root cellar. After that, a set of stairs took Ozzie and Tynx up to a locked door. Thankfully, Tynx had learned to pick locks back when he was "living off the involuntary charity of others" in Leleplar, and his skills had improved. The door led into a massive kitchen, which looked old even by Tynx's standards. Despite its apparent age, however, it was well kept and orderly. It was also not empty. Someone was moving around in the pantry, the doors of which were standing wide open.

Tynx led the way as they snuck towards the open doors and peered in. Inside was a smallish man, shorter than Ozzie even, dressed in strange travel garb. It was completely foreign to Tynx, but it looked like something Ozzie had seen in a few films...is that what a toga really looked like? He didn't look to be armed, but it was hard to tell with all those folds in his robes. Tynx rushed the man, grabbing him easily and putting a hand over his mouth before he could call for help. Ozzie pointed the tip of his knife towards the man's throat.

"Make no sound," Tynx hissed quietly. "Do as we say, and you will be allowed to live. Nod if you understand."

The man nodded once.

"Very well," Tynx said. "I am about to let you go. Take care, for I am in a killing mood."

Ozzie knew some of what Tynx said was for show. Ideally, they could intimidate the man to get information quickly. Some of it was serious, though, too. Ozzie suddenly found a new reason to be grateful Tynx was a friend. If he wanted to, he could make an exceptional bandit.

Tynx removed his hand, and the man dared to look behind him at his inhumanly strong captor. Was this one kin to the Ghost? The cold look in Tynx's eyes made him quiver.

"There's a girl here," Ozzie whispered. "Red hair and very loud. Have you seen her?"

The man, remembering the threat about making a sound, nodded.

"Where is she?" Ozzie pressed.

The man shrugged and held up his hands.

"Speak quietly and tell us all you know," Tynx said.

"She...she sometimes comes down here," the man whispered, trembling. "I hide, for the Ghost does not want me to be seen. She sneaks through, looking for food and...and trying to get through the door, which I keep locked."

"You didn't try to help her?" Tynx demanded, his voice hissing angrily like a snake. "Even though you knew she was looking for a way out, you just...just...sat here?!"

"The Ghost! He will kill me! He will kill my family!" the man blubbered too loudly for Ozzie's liking.

"Shhhh!" Ozzie said. "Okay, we get that. Moving on, is she okay? The girl?"

"Last I saw, yes. She was well enough."

"What does well enough mean?" Tynx demanded.

"Her arm was injured when she first came, but it is better. Her eyes, however, they are haunted."

"When did you last see her?" Ozzie asked.

"I have not seen her for days. I am only a lowly cook, though. I do not go beyond this kitchen."

"Besides the Ghost and the girl, is there anyone else here?" Tynx asked.

"No. No one."

"Good!"

He and Ozzie then looked at each other, trying to decide what to do with the man.

"Go. Now. Never return," Tynx began.

"But...but the Ghost!" the man quailed.

"The Ghost is going to die. Tonight," Tynx said, his voice low and determined. "Fear not. He will never darken your door again."

A look of relief—and was that joy?—passed over the man's face. He thanked the two, and Ozzie got his key from him before he left. Then, with the man gone, they were free to start their search in the nearly empty manor.

Tynx took up the lead again as they searched. He was trying to sense Taryn's emotions, but it was difficult if not impossible in that vast place. The stronger the emotion the better Tynx could sense it, but if Taryn was sleeping somewhere he likely wouldn't be able to sense her at all until he was in the room with her. He kept watch, so to speak, for Erik as well. Granted, he couldn't identify people based on their emotions, but he had learned the intensity of Taryn's feelings, and anything foreign was likely Erik.

They started at the bottom floor, skimming down hallways and peeking into rooms. It was dark in the manor as candles, burned down to their wick, had gone out or were guttering fruitlessly in an attempt to shine on just a little bit longer. There was nothing to be found on the ground floor and, as a heavy foreboding pressed down on them in the dark, Tynx and Ozzie were thankful to find a stairway up to the next level. Tynx looked around often. He felt something, but could not identify what.

There were intruders in the house. Erik had spotted them as they poked their heads into the library. Erik, who was roaming the interior of the walls, as he did every evening, peered out through a grate in the wall. He recognized them both, but only knew Ozzie. The elf, however, was the same he had seen kiss Taryn in Wonderland. Oh, this was a grand treat. Erik had to be careful, though. There was more to the elf than met the eye. He had some extraordinary power, though Erik had never been able to figure out what. He would follow and wait to see what these lads were planning.

Ozzie and Tynx eventually found some bedrooms, and Tynx whispered that he could sense something, but it was very faint. They proceeded with care. It could be Taryn sleeping, or it could be Erik. Ozzie peeked into one room and, yet again, saw nothing. Tynx was checking the room across the hall. Ozzie was about to close the door when his eyes hit the far corner. It was faint but unmistakable, the bright orange glow of Taryn's hair reflecting the dim candlelight. Taryn was crouched in the corner behind the bed, as if hiding. Ozzie wasted no time. He hurried over to her and stopped short, staring in shock at the disheveled mess of his friend. Taryn was staring down, eyes empty and blank, while her hair hung forward limply. Her fingernails were bitten down to the quick, and her skin was so pale, much paler than it usually was. Even her freckles had faded. She looked broken and lost; the fire had gone out in her. She lifted her head to look at Ozzie, but made no other movement.

"Taryn," Ozzie whispered fearfully.

What had Erik done to her? Was she blind now? Couldn't she see him standing right there? Ozzie knelt down and put his hands on her face.

"Taryn, it's me, Ozzie. Are you okay?"

"Ozzie," Taryn replied dully. "Why are you here?"

"To get you, of course!"

"Why?" She was confused more than anything.

"Taryn, what has he done to you?" Ozzie demanded. "What has he told you? You remember who I am, right? It's me, Oz, your brother from another mother. Remember?"

"Yes, you were my friend a long time ago. You went off, though. You left…went about your own life."

"I'm sorry!" Ozzie moaned. "This is all my fault. We were only trying to protect you!" Tears shone in Ozzie's eyes as he searched Taryn's face for any sign of recognition. Cupping Taryn's face in his hands, he rested his forehead against hers and said, "I'm sorry, Taryn. I'm so sorry."

There was a noise, and Ozzie spun around to see Tynx in the doorway. He looked sick.

"She's…she's so full of despair," he stammered.

"I know," Ozzie replied, shame filling his voice. "We never should have left her. She must have been a sitting duck for Erik."

At the mention of Erik's name, Taryn gasped and looked around fearfully as she began to shake.

"Taryn, it's okay," Ozzie said, gathering her into his arms. "I've got you. He won't hurt you anymore."

"Follow me," Tynx said quickly.

"Do you see, Ryn?" Ozzie whispered. "Tynx is going to get us out of here. You remember Tynx, right?"

She didn't respond. She kept on looking back and forth between the two, as if something was bothering her, but didn't quite know what. Ozzie gently pulled her to her feet and slowly led her out of the room. Tynx went ahead.

"We're here now," Ozzie whispered as they went. "We've got you."

In response to that, Taryn stopped and then reached out to touch Ozzie. She pulled back and then touched him again as if testing to make sure he was actually there.

"You want to hit me?" Ozzie teased, hoping for some kind of normal reaction. He actually wanted her to hit him; that would be the most normal reaction possible.

She said nothing but just looked at him quizzically. Ozzie's heart sank even more, but he kept his smile on for her and pulled her forward by the hand. They came out into the hallway, but Tynx was nowhere to be seen.

"Tynx!" Ozzie hissed down the dark hallway. "Where'd you go, man?"

Ozzie swallowed hard. Something wasn't right, but he had to get Taryn to safety. He led on, deciding that he would get her out and then come back for Tynx. Tynx was smart and strong; he could take care of himself for a little while. Right? True, they were both fatigued from their journey, but it was just Erik after all...ridiculously strong Erik. Ozzie suddenly thought back to the lake under the Paris Opera House, remembered how defenseless he had felt when Erik had pushed him under the water. Ozzie had fought so hard, biting and scratching and scrabbling, but it had hardly made a difference. He probably would have drowned had it not been for Taryn...Ozzie shook his head. No! He couldn't think about that now. Looking around again, he grimaced. He suddenly hated this place. Any place of Erik's seemed suffused with fear and despair. He wouldn't succumb to it. He was going to get them out! All of them.

"Come on, Taryn. Let's go," he whispered, moving her onward.

Painstakingly slowly, they made it down to the first floor. Taryn was petrified, stopping to look back and all around her every so often and then back to Ozzie with an odd look. There was something there, something that looked like it was waking up. It was disbelief and uncertainty and fear and just a tiny spot of hope all wrapped up into one. Ozzie didn't know how badly Erik had messed with her head, but he focused on that little bit of brightness that had appeared in Taryn's eyes.

"Hey, guess what?" he said, trying to smile at her. "I love you!"

Taryn suddenly looked at him strangely, and Ozzie had to choke back tears at that, barely keeping his smile in place. That was not the reaction he had been hoping for. They had just made it a little way down the hall of the first floor when a voice resounded ahead of them.

"Taryn, my dear, you should have told me you were expecting a guest. I would have provided refreshments."

Ozzie spun around to see Erik emerging from the shadows. Taryn squeaked and huddled down behind Ozzie. Erik was but ten feet away. How had he snuck up on them so fast?!

"You had better back off, pal!" Ozzie snarled furiously.

"Oh, I see you have some interest in my dear Taryn. I've seen this story before, and it won't end well for you."

"Taryn's my best friend. Do you hear me? Mine to protect."

"Oz, don't," Taryn heard herself saying. Through the haze of fear and desolation, something was coming back to her, something important. Ozzie was right. Something had been waking in her since the moment he had appeared before her. She said it again, louder this time.

"Well, your dedication is admirable, but you have wasted your time. If you leave now, I give you my word no harm will come to you."

"Not without Taryn."

Erik began to walk forward slowly, gracefully.

"I remember meeting you, lad. You seemed sincere then, just as you seem sincere now. That is a rare thing. I respect that, so I will give you one last chance. Leave now without Taryn, and your life will be spared."

"Don't...hurt him," Taryn stuttered.

She couldn't look Erik in the face; she couldn't look into those horrible eyes. She felt terror down to her soul when she heard his voice, but here was Ozzie who she somehow knew from before. He had gone away, both physically and emotionally. He had left her alone and broken, and she no longer knew the him that was here, the Ozzie that had come to rescue her. She was coming to know him again, though, somehow. It had been like waking from a dream, except the other way around. When she saw him, she had begun to remember. She remembered that she knew him, but there was something else. He was...important somehow. He meant something. Just now he had said she was his best friend. He had said he loved her, but that couldn't be true. Had they been close? It was so hard to see through the fog, through the pain and emptiness, but there was a new fear in her, something that was battling against her fear of Erik. Erik, who she had been abandoned to, who sang loneliness and fear through her soul each day, who had shown her that terrible face and reminded her that *this* was her life. Forever. He had filled her head with nightmares at night because she had defied him. This was her punishment for his pain, this misery. What stirred in her now, though, was a fear for Ozzie. She didn't know why it was there or why it was so strong, but it was here and growing, and she couldn't ignore it.

"Please," Taryn said again, avoiding that face. She took a frightened step forward, holding Ozzie's hand behind her in her own trembling hands, and pleaded again, "Don't hurt him."

Erik's face turned dark and in one smooth movement he grabbed Taryn by the arm, ripping her away from Ozzie. He grabbed her jaw and lifted her face to his, forcing her to look at him.

"Have you forgotten your place?" he hissed.

Taryn yelped in fear and struggled to look away. Ozzie roared and lunged forward, shoving Erik back, freeing Taryn from his grip. Ozzie pushed Erik back towards the wall and held him there, one arm across his shoulders and the knife pressed to his throat.

"What did I just say?!" Ozzie yelled. "Not without Taryn! Give me one reason, just one, why I shouldn't kill you here and now."

Erik began to laugh, and Ozzie felt his determination begin to slip. He pictured Taryn in her room huddled in the corner, Erik holding her by the jaw, and his clarity returned.

"Knock it off!" Ozzie growled. "That's not going to work on me, not after what you did to Taryn. I should cut out your voice box for that."

Erik continued to smile. Then, very suddenly, he shoved the boy away as easily as he would a small child.

"Oz!" Taryn cried, rushing forward to shield Ozzie from whatever Erik would try next.

No attack came, however. Erik was calm as he looked down on the two. Ozzie was crouched in front of Taryn now, holding his knife at the ready. Erik began to laugh at them. He was *enjoying* this! He beckoned with his hand at them and spoke congenially like he hadn't just been trying to kill them.

"Come with me. I have something to show you."

"No, Ozzie, don't," Taryn pleaded, tugging at his shirt. "Please, he'll kill you."

Erik was waiting for them. The last thing Ozzie wanted to do was follow, doubly so with Taryn in tow, but Erik would surely kill him if he didn't comply. Cautiously, he followed, holding Taryn's hand the entire way. Erik led them into a parlor. A fire was crackling away in the grate, covering everything in the room with a soft, orange glow. Ozzie didn't notice that, though. What he saw there made him stop short, and Taryn felt her heart break, though she didn't understand why. Tynx was sitting in a chair with a gag in his mouth, hands tied behind him, and feet bound together. Ozzie stopped dead and glared murderously at Erik.

"Okay, dude, what's your game?" Ozzie demanded.

"I caught this creature lurking around my manse," Erik explained calmly. "Naturally, I plan on questioning him. And you, Taryn, my dear."

Erik reached out his hand, waiting expectantly.

Ozzie turned back to Taryn and hissed, "No! Taryn, don't!"

She looked at him sadly and barely shook her head. She then released Ozzie's hand and obediently stood in front of Erik, and

Ozzie thought she looked suspiciously like a human shield. Tynx was raging within his bonds, pulling and struggling against them as he uselessly grunted angrily at Erik. Ozzie felt sick as he surveyed the scene.

"Firstly, I must ask that you surrender your weapon," Erik said as congenially as if he were offering Ozzie tea. Ozzie hesitated, and Erik then took Taryn's arm and twisted it behind her back, making her cry out in pain. "Now, please. On the mantel, if you don't mind. Then you can have a seat next to your friend."

"Okay," Ozzie said placatingly, "just don't hurt Taryn. There's no need for that."

Erik said nothing in response, but he grew a nasty smile at Ozzie's words. Ozzie carefully walked over to the mantelpiece and placed his knife there so Erik could see. He then walked over to Tynx and sat in the chair next to him. After that, Erik sat on a sofa opposite and pulled Taryn down next to him.

"That's better. Now, tell me about your travels. Where, for instance, is the other one?"

"He's not with us," Ozzie said honestly, hoping it would play to the small bit of humanity in Erik. "We left him behind when we found that Taryn was gone."

"And why would you do that?" Erik pressed.

"Because he's not on very good terms with Taryn at the moment." That wasn't precisely true, but it was close enough to sound like the truth.

"Why?"

"Because…" and Ozzie's voice faltered at this as he saw Taryn's face. Her eyebrows were knit with concern, fresh pain filling her eyes. She must be remembering Heinz. Had she forgotten about him completely? How was that possible? Her face made it seem like she had. "Because Smitty was responsible for the death of Taryn's enfield, Heinz."

Taryn tried and failed to choke back a sob, but finally managed to swallow back her sorrow when Erik wrapped his hand around her arm.

"Ah! I had wondered what happened to the beast. That explains it," Erik said happily. "Taryn has told me some of your tale, though our conversation eventually turned to other subjects. Didn't they, Taryn? Traitors all around you."

Erik was practically cooing at her by the time he addressed her. Taryn shuddered and turned away, trying to ignore the words that were attempting to claw their way into her ears.

"How long have you been following us?" Ozzie asked, shocked to hear that Erik knew of Heinz.

"It wasn't long after you left me that my life fell to pieces," Erik said darkly. "I began to track you then. When this one," and he gestured at Tynx here, "led you out into The Moors, I was frankly astonished he didn't sense me. Some guardian you turned out to be." Tynx's face fell at this, and Erik said to Ozzie, "Take off his gag. I'd like to hear what he has to say for himself."

Ozzie obeyed but didn't dare do any more than he was told. He knew Erik had them all at his mercy, and he wasn't about to endanger his friends. Once the gag was removed, Tynx said nothing, and Erik leaned forward to study him.

"You're not fully an elf, are you?" Erik asked curiously.

"No," Tynx said, looking at Taryn.

"Well, that might account for it. Tell me, how do you fit into all of this? You weren't with these two when they first came to see me, but you know them somehow, don't you?" Tynx said nothing, and Erik said more forcefully, a note like an angry cello entering his voice, "Tell me."

Tynx looked at Erik now, but his face was quizzical, "What are you?"

Erik laughed at that, clearly amused. "I am human, if that is what you're asking. Why I was born with this voice, this *face*, God only knows."

"Why take Taryn?" Tynx asked. "What is she to you?"

"Answer my question, boy." Erik purred.

Tynx seemed unfazed by the power of the Phantom's voice and looked boldly into the face of his captor.

"I met Taryn and Ozzie previously. This isn't their first visit to our world. We met back up through coincidence."

"And?"

"And what?"

"You love her. Do not deny it; I have seen it with my own eyes. I see it now in yours."

"So what?" Ozzie cut in, worried for Tynx in that moment. "I love her, too."

"Not the way he loves her," Erik said, waving away Ozzie's words the same way he would a fly. "Tell me."

Tynx glowered at Erik. Instead of doing as he was told, he turned to face Taryn again and said, "I love you, Taryn, but you already knew that. You've known that ever since you saw the light in my eyes for you. I have loved you across dimensions. I will never stop loving you and I will do all in my power to protect you until my dying breath."

Erik began to laugh again, this time throwing his head back in great, mocking guffaws. His laughter resounded off the walls like deep bass notes, reverberating back on itself and out again.

"Until your dying breath, you say?" Erik laughed. "Well, fear not, lad, for that will be sooner than you think." Turning to Taryn, he glared at her malevolently, his tone changing and becoming coarse and threatening. "You see, Taryn, this is what happens in your life now. You thought you had friends again? You never had friends! Don't you remember? They abandoned you, bound you up, and left you to die!"

"No!" Ozzie cried, gripping the arms of his chair furiously. "We left her to protect her! We thought she would be safe!"

"And look what good it did her!" Erik screamed at him, his voice cutting through flesh and bone and spirit. "Look at her now! This is the fruit of your labor!"

Ozzie felt his spirit crushing beneath the weight of the Opera Ghost's words. It was their fault. But wait. This...*this* is what Erik had done to Taryn. He had torn her down, made her think she was alone, stripped her of love down to her very core. No more!

"I made a mistake!" Ozzie yelled back. "I did what I thought was best, but I was wrong. It was a mistake; that's what people *do*! They make mistakes! And, Taryn, I am so, *so* sorry! I cannot tell you how sorry I am, but it doesn't mean I don't love you. I made a mistake in love and I can't take it back and I'm sorry!"

"ENOUGH!" Erik roared, rising from his seat.

Instead of quailing, as Erik had intended to make Ozzie do, he turned back to face Erik and stared daggers at him. He stood and took a step forward, and Erik stepped to meet him.

"You don't really think you can best me, do you, boy?" Erik spat.

"I can try. Anything to free Taryn from a monster like you!"

Erik growled and lifted Ozzie up by his collar as if he were nothing. He threw him across the room and sent him crashing into a priceless looking occasional table.

"Ozzie!" Taryn screamed.

The light in Taryn flared as she saw Ozzie fly across the room. It had begun to burn brighter with each word her friends said, fanned by their confessions and fed by memories that were slowly returning to her. She looked back to see Erik reaching for Tynx's throat. He wrapped his hand around Tynx's neck and began to squeeze. Tynx gasped as his airway was pinched closed. Taryn stepped towards them, but Erik snarled at her, causing her to jump and recoil. She watched tearfully as Tynx's face turned red. Tynx continued to fight, but turned his eyes onto Taryn and met hers. There was so much in those eyes, so much regret and sorrow and pain, but there was also so much love. She looked away and saw Ozzie's body lying still and silent at the other end of the room. There was heat now with the light inside her, a match blazing into life and driving away the black isolation.

"No," Taryn hissed, turning back to Erik. "You can't." Growing louder, she said, "You can't do this."

"Take care to watch your tone, Miss Taryn," Erik growled.

Erik's voice sent a cold wind through Taryn. She actually shuddered as she felt it, but she had already begun to move. Taryn grabbed the closest things at hand, a fire poker and Ozzie's knife, and leapt at Erik.

"I won't let you take them from me again!" she shrieked wildly.

Erik had been watching her, so he saw her coming, but he could not deflect her without releasing Tynx. Erik reached out with his hands to both catch and strike Taryn, but she was leading with the poker. It connected with Erik's outstretched arm first, gouging his bicep deeply. Despite this, he was still somewhat successful and caught Taryn by the shoulders and used her own momentum to throw her to the ground. Thankfully, her attack had thrown him off, and she didn't land with nearly as much force as Erik would have liked. Taryn landed behind Tynx and reached up, her mind racing for solutions, and pressed Ozzie's knife into Tynx's hand.

Tynx grasped the knife immediately and began to work at the ties on his hands. As he did, he heard a distant *bang!* somewhere outside the house. It did not stop all the while he worked at cutting his bonds or after.

From her place on the floor, Taryn quickly raised one foot and viciously kicked upwards between Erik's legs. It connected with something soft, and she pulled back to kick again. The second kick sent Erik staggering back, doubled over in pain. Taryn got to her feet quickly and looked for her fire poker. It had been sent flying halfway across the room. She grabbed for anything else and laid her hands on a vase. She smashed it over Erik's head, all of her hate for him driven behind it. Erik staggered back again, but the vase hadn't done much more than that. Taryn knew she needed a better weapon. She reached for the plinth the vase had been sitting on, but found she couldn't lift it. The bloody thing was solid marble! Just as she was looking for something else to lay her hands on, however, the scent of death invaded her nostrils. Erik pulled Taryn off her feet and threw her.

Taryn couldn't get her feet under her as she tumbled down to the floor, but she managed to catch herself with her hands. Unfortunately, her hands landed on the broken shards of the smashed vase, cutting into them. Erik grabbed for Taryn again, but she scooted away and scrambled towards her fire poker, desperate for another weapon. In that moment, Tynx finished freeing himself and leapt up. He stabbed Erik in the back, who roared and spun around. Tynx jumped back out of Erik's reach, and Erik turned back to grab Taryn.

He knew he would have the upper hand if he could get the little termagant at his mercy again and then he would make them all pay so dearly! He grabbed Taryn's foot and yanked her back towards him just before she could close her fingers around the poker. Taryn kicked at Erik and screamed as he twisted her leg around so hard she thought it was going to come out of its socket. Tynx leapt again and tackled Erik from behind, grasping onto the knife still sticking out of his back as they went down. Taryn was freed. The knife came loose and fell to the floor as Tynx tumbled overtop Erik. Erik grabbed it first, but Tynx had already recovered and restrained Erik's knife hand. There was a short but vicious struggle between the two, during which time Taryn was able to scuttle forward and grab the fire poker.

As Erik and Tynx fought, Tynx found himself evenly matched. Erik was trying to get free, but Tynx refused to let go. Erik needed to die! Tynx might have had an easier time if he wasn't so exhausted, but as it stood, the battle could go either way. Tynx's face had already taken a few blows, and he saw spots dancing before his eyes. He knew Erik would happily beat his head in given the opportunity. Erik's mask became dislodged as Tynx tried to stab the Opera Ghost in the eye with his thumb. The mask was ripped off just then, and Tynx finally released Erik as he jumped back in horror at the sight of that terror of a face. It was like a skull, but so much worse. The yellow eyes blazed out of black sockets, and the hole where his nose should have been was flaring angrily.

Taryn, having just grabbed her poker, saw Tynx jump back. Then she heard a noise from across the room and turned to see Ozzie moving again. She smiled for the first time in she didn't know how long.

Ozzie was trying to push himself up, but his whole side where he had had landed hurt. It started in his hip. It wouldn't support his weigh without sending shooting pains up his side and down his leg, so he decided to crawl instead. Slowly and oh so painfully, he began to pull himself close to Taryn, watching Erik as he went. He might not be able to stand, but he wasn't going to let Erik lay another hand on her. If he was lucky, maybe he would even be able to help Tynx.

"Oz!" Tynx heard Taryn say, and there was true joy in her voice.

Despite the way his heart leapt at hearing Taryn's happiness, Tynx did not take his eyes off Erik, which is why he was able to see the look of cold fury that came over that monstrous face.

In a fit of rage, Erik leapt towards the smiling Taryn with every intention of burying Ozzie's knife into her neck. Tynx threw himself into Erik's path. Taryn looked back too late to see the blade disappearing into Tynx's chest.

"TYNX!" she heard Ozzie scream.

Taryn didn't know if she screamed. She didn't know anything but the sound of her heart being ripped apart within her chest. Her knee was racked with pain as she moved, which surprised her because she didn't yet realize she was moving. Concern over the pain, however, along with her surprise, was in the background of her mind. She was lifting the fire poker and driving it with all her might towards the character of whom she had once been such a fan. Grimacing with the effort, she pushed her weapon through skin and flesh and organs until it came out the other side. At the end of it, she found herself face to face with the nightmare she had endured for what felt like her whole life now. The expression on Erik's face was one of shock and dismay.

Taryn's green eyes burned bright with hate as she locked them with Erik's yellow ones.

Erik's face contorted in pain, but Taryn could see he still had some fight in him. How much more? She had to stop him from doing any more damage. Before she could do anything else, though, there was a great bellow. The weight of Erik was suddenly lifted off her, and the poker was ripped from her hands.

Erik was able to look down just in time to see the gargantuan creature from Wonderland hauling him off his feet and lifting him into the air.

"Put me down, you brute! Fiend! Monster!" he shrieked furiously, his fear masking the shredding pain in his chest as he did so.

"I am no monster!" Adam thundered. "Murderer!"

With that, he whipped Erik's body down across his knee with a sickening crack and hurled the Opera Ghost towards the wall, sending him sailing through it in a shower of wood and plaster. When he landed, his body flailed limply across the floor, the fire poker still sticking out of him.

*Taryn*, Tynx thought painfully as he lay on the floor. He had to get to her. He tried to get up, consumed with the agony that was blossoming out from his chest and pounding in his head.

"Ozzie! Tynx! Taryn!" came a familiar voice.

Only Ozzie turned to see Smitty running in through the doorway. He stopped short when he saw the devastation that surrounded him.

Smitty looked helplessly at Tynx. Tynx was the one who told them what to do, the one who would have helped them all get out of this alive, but instead he was lying on his back as a deep red blotch radiated slowly from the knife sticking out of his chest. Smitty then looked at Ozzie.

"What do we do?" he whispered weakly.

"Taryn…" Tynx croaked painfully, forcing himself to open his eyes.

"Tynx!" She understood what he was doing and rushed to move past that part. "I'm okay, but you…Erik stabbed you. How do we fix you?"

Taryn was desperately trying to suppress the deluge of feelings building up inside of her. Memories of losing Heinz were rushing back to her all at once, and now here was Tynx in the same position. One memory stood out, devastatingly poignant, when Tynx had told her there was nothing he could do. What if there was nothing to be done now?

Tynx groaned and asked, "Where's Ozzie?"

"I'm fine," Ozzie lied, pulling himself up next to Taryn. "You look really bad, man. Tell us what we need to do."

Tynx gritted his teeth against the pain and tried to force his brain to work faster, but it was clouded by the waves of pain reverberating through him.

What followed was a flurry of action and somewhat slower commands. Tynx gave orders to Ozzie, Taryn, Smitty, and Adam, all while fighting the pain in his chest. The pain in his head from where it had hit the floor when he fell under Erik's attack had ebbed into the background, but the new challenge was looking out for signs that he was concussed, which would make saving himself that much more difficult. Smitty and Adam were sent to fetch things when needed since Taryn and Ozzie were injured. Ozzie proved to be the most steady of any of them, so it was left to him to check how far down the damage went. Immediately after the knife had been removed, with hastily washed hands, Ozzie described in as descriptive detail as he could what he felt as he slowly probed his fingers down into the wound. Tynx guessed that the blade had narrowly missed his heart, though he couldn't be sure if the heart skin—Ozzie eventually figured out this was the word Tynx used for the sack that surrounded the heart—had been nicked. After this initial exploration, there was no time to lose. Tynx had already lost a good deal of blood and it was still flowing slowly. It was clear he was having more difficulty than before, and Tynx knew it, too. He immediately decided the treatment would have to be fast and uncertain. None there had the skill for anything more than a rudimentary fix.

Within minutes, the blade of the knife that had caused so much damage was searing hot from the still-crackling fire in the fireplace. Taryn was gripping Adam's enormous hand tightly as Ozzie sat ready to cauterize the wound. She was already looking away, knowing she might say or do something detrimental if she watched.

Ozzie felt as if he might be sick right there. It was not from being grossed out—as Smitty was, although he wasn't about to admit it—but from fear. Tynx had warned Ozzie that the knife could get stuck to his flesh if it was not hot enough and then made an analogy to beef in a pan that put Ozzie off meat for months and months afterward.

What if he didn't do it right? Ozzie wondered. What if he caused even more damage?

Truthfully, Ozzie felt helpless. It was the same as that time in Leleplar when Taryn had eaten poisonous mushrooms and nearly died. Why hadn't he done something after that when they got home? Gotten first aid training? Something? What if Tynx wasn't conscious? They would have no idea what to do! Ozzie felt his heart pounding, and it seemed only to increase his nausea.

"Get a hold of yourself," Tynx told Ozzie firmly.

The waves of fear rolling off Ozzie, while understandable, were not helping Tynx any. He was dealing with enough just then and sincerely afraid he was going to die and leave his friends alone in this strange world. He was thankful that Adam was here. If worst came to worst, he could help them.

Ozzie made himself nod confidently. His friend needed him; Tynx would die if he didn't do this. He also made a decision just then: he would never be caught in this position again.

# Chapter 23

It was quiet in the parlor, the fire making more noise than anything else in the room. Adam had disposed of the body still lying outside the broken wall. No one knew or said anything about whether or not Erik had died instantly or slowly and alone. Smitty had gotten them all some food from the kitchen, which was eaten out of necessity rather than desire. Taryn insisted on helping Tynx eat, knowing he would need his strength to recover. Tynx didn't want her to help him, his shame finally coming to rest properly with him in that moment. The two spoke in hushed tones, their tears hidden in the shadows, as they made their peace.

Ozzie's hip was feeling better but still ached. By the time he was done with Tynx, he was well enough to help splint up Taryn's knee—which he had diagnosed as "jacked up"—with bits of the broken occasional table. Now he was sitting equidistant between Taryn and Smitty, who was sitting with Adam on the opposite side of the room. Ozzie was talking idly with Adam mostly, as deep down he was furious with Smitty, more so than he had been before. On top of everything else, he was now angry with Smitty for not having come with them to rescue Taryn. It had been, to Ozzie's mind, cowardly. He had only shown up when Adam, a behemoth with the strength of ten men, had come along.

Ozzie soon learned that the banging they had heard during their confrontation with Erik had been Adam bashing the front doors off their hinges. Adam told Ozzie that he had seen Erik's trail after the Phantom had retraced his steps back into Wonderland. Sensing that anyone following the three probably held ill intentions, especially after what had happened with Smitty, Adam had followed. When he found Smitty in Gloriana's Green not long after

Ozzie and Tynx had left, Smitty had hastily explained what had happened, and the two had set off together.

"But how could you follow the trail?" Ozzie asked curiously. "It was only because of Tynx's magic that we even found this place."

"The spirits of the wood and water led us," Adam replied simply. "They answer to the Fairie Lords."

Ozzie nodded, realizing now that the people of the mounds had been helping them all along.

Tynx was not allowed to sleep just in case he had a concussion, so it was lucky that there were so many strong emotions in the room to keep him up, even if they did make his head spin even worse. Taryn had offered her lap as a pillow. She figured that was the least she could do for her half-elf hero, as she was calling him. Things were difficult between them at the moment, but they were both making an effort to make it better.

"How are you feeling?" Tynx had asked gently after his operation was over.

"You know already," she replied.

"I know," Tynx confessed, "but...but I think it's important to talk about...for your sake. That is, if you're comfortable...doing so"

What Tynx really meant was if Taryn trusted him enough with her feelings. He knew he had betrayed that trust and was prepared for her to shut him out. This time, he almost hoped she would.

"You know I didn't mean to hurt you," he added before Taryn could answer, his voice suddenly thick with emotion. "Neither of us did."

Taryn's eyebrows knitted together in consternation. She was trying to know. Goodness knew she was trying so hard. The infection of doubt that had begun at the burrow and which Erik had nourished and cultivated was still there, and she couldn't just banish it. She knew what she wanted to think and repeated it over and over, but it was going to take time for that seed of doubt to be washed away.

Tynx could sense the fight in her, the effort she was putting forth, and it filled him up with both hope and sorrow. He was so pleased that she was fighting, but it broke his heart that she had to. This time, Taryn spoke before Tynx could respond.

"I love you, Tynx. I love you, but I'm damaged. I believe it will get better. It's just going to take time. Even so, even with all the hurt, I want you with me for however long it takes."

Tynx was staring at her agape. He hadn't heard anything besides that first profession. Taryn had never uttered those words before. He had, and he had felt something like love in her, but never had she opened up to him so freely. Even in their best times, there was always a bit of her held back, but not now. He felt her openness like a balm on his soul, easing the apprehension that was curled up and rooted in his stomach.

Taryn smiled at seeing his expression of shock, which quickly changed to joy, and gently kissed his head.

At Tynx's insistence, Taryn tried to sleep, but new nightmares plagued her. She dreamed that Erik came back from the dead, that Ozzie and Tynx left her again, that she was back where she had been not so many hours ago. And so, because Taryn did not sleep, neither did Ozzie. Eventually, as the atmosphere of the room grew to a stifling heaviness, Adam suggested that he and Smitty keep watch from the now-destroyed front doors.

Everyone knew the real reason for the suggestion. Now that things had settled, there was time to turn the focus onto Smitty. Ozzie said nothing because he didn't know what would be productive to say, but he kept shooting Smitty scornful glances. Taryn also said nothing, but she very dearly wanted to and only didn't for fear of upsetting Tynx. Even so, her eyes said it all and more and made Smitty feel lower than scum.

The night had been long as Smitty and Adam kept their silent vigil outside. The sun that came creeping over the top of the hill was like a long-awaited dream. With the sun, however, came a lioness, followed by a variety of animals. Both Adam and Smitty stood when they saw them crest the hill and approach through the trees.

Smitty thought he remembered some of the animals from the Fairie Court, but could not be certain. Things had happened so quickly, and the animals had not been interested in him after Ozzie and Tynx had left. The lioness seemed more familiar than all the rest, though. Why? It didn't matter. The lioness inclined her head at the boy, a gesture beckoning him to follow. Smitty followed her back into the room where Ozzie, Taryn, and Tynx were all attempting to rest without sleeping. At seeing the great lioness and her company of creatures, Taryn's eyes lit up. She remembered them; they had been kind to her. The reminder made her feel as if a window had been opened in her mind, letting a fresh breeze blow through.

"Brighteyes! Ebony!" Ozzie exclaimed. He gasped as he laid eyes on the two leopards, "Windstalker! Shadowpaw! You're okay!"

The leopards, who had somehow made a miraculous recovery, nodded but said nothing.

"Children," the lioness said, smiling.

Suddenly, each animal began to let off a soft glow. The light blanketed them and hid their forms. A moment later, the light dimmed. Left in place of the animals were stunning creatures. They had humanoid forms, but their eyes were wild and colored like rainbows. Their faces were severe and beautiful, and their skin looked as if it was made of solid light, one colored like a sunset, another with hues of moon and starlight, and yet another resembled the earliest morning rays of sunrise. They wore clothing borrowed from nature, as if the very trees and birds and land had dressed them. They were tall, too; only Adam was taller than the creatures.

No one could speak. They were all dumbfounded by the beauty and awe that radiated from the creatures. Sensing the question all the humans were too shocked to ask, the creature that had been the lioness spoke.

"We are the fae folk, Tuatha Dé Danann, the people of the mounds."

"Or, as some of you know us, aos sí," Duskhollow added, smiling at Taryn.

Taryn smiled back and nodded at him.

The former lioness then said with a smile, inclining her crowned head. "I am Gloriana, Queen of the Fairies."

The rest of the creatures then introduced themselves. Duskhollow and Sally Brighteyes were Oberon and Titania; Ebony trilled she was Mab; Brushfire bowed and introduced himself as Puck; and Tumbleburr, Bramblebee, Windstalker, and Shadowpaw turned out to be Mustardseed, Peaseblossom, Moth, and Cobweb.

This left Ozzie, Taryn, and Tynx even more flabbergasted. Ozzie was the first one to find his voice.

"But…but why didn't you tell us?" he asked, unsure if he should feel angry. Then again, these were fairies they were dealing with, so what should he expect?

"We didn't know if we could trust you," Oberon replied, his voice deep and smooth.

"We also didn't know how you would react to us," Titania added. "The glamour put you at ease."

"How could you let Taryn be taken?!" Ozzie suddenly demanded. "You're fairies! You could have stopped this!"

"Ozzie, don't," Taryn said gently. "Moth and Cobweb, they defended me."

Ozzie didn't respond to that. True, two of the smaller fairies—they, along with Mustardseed and Peaseblossom, were the shortest of all the fae folk there—had gotten the crap kicked out of them. Titania raised an eyebrow at Ozzie's accusation, but Mab was the one who spoke, her voice like an angry nightingale's.

"Are we to be your nursemaids? Do not blame us for your folly."

"Peace, sister," Gloriana said gently. "Mortals, let us focus on the here and now. First, healing for hurts."

She then extended her hand and rested it on top of Taryn's head.

"Rest your heart, little one," Gloriana soothed. "You are never alone. May the light of the fae glow within you."

Taryn didn't know what was happening, but light was trickling back into her. Most of the darkness there remained, but it was weaker, and Taryn felt as if she could breathe just a little easier now.

Gloriana then moved onto Tynx and placed her hand over his wound.

"Sacrifice is the greatest honor one can bestow on another. You have done well. Your task has now come to an end. The time has come for all us to return to our rightful places."

Tynx felt cool relief at Gloriana's touch. When she removed her hand, all that was left behind was an angry scar, his wound now healed. Tynx sat up and, though his head was still swimming, he bowed to the Fairie Queen. He then looked to her for permission, she nodded her head in assent, and he turned to Taryn. He dreaded the first minute that she would be gone and felt the horrible weight of their limited time together now pressing in on him.

"I love you, Taryn Kelly," he said.

He wanted to say so much more, but could not decide on any one thing, for what could truly express how he felt about her? Finally, he took her into his arms and held her tightly. He kissed her head as he felt her hug him back.

Taryn had no words either and could only hold Tynx. She was leaving him this time. Even though it wasn't her fault, she knew what he was feeling in that moment. She didn't want to go. She knew she had a family back home that needed her, but she didn't want to go without Tynx. She wanted time to heal with him.

"You will see one another again," came Gloriana's voice, lilting softly into their exchange.

"When?" Tynx asked, his eyes lighting up.

"When the time is right."

Tynx turned back to Taryn and did his best to smile at her.

"Can you hang on for me?" he asked. "Until I find you again?"

Taryn smiled and nodded to that.

Tynx went and hugged Ozzie as well.

"Take care of her for me," he said, a note of seriousness in his voice.

"You couldn't stop me if you tried," Ozzie replied.

Tynx's farewell to Smitty was less congenial, but it was sincere.

"I wish you the best of luck."

"You, too," Smitty said just as sincerely. "Thank you for everything you did for us, especially for me."

"Come, children," Gloriana instructed finally. "It's time. Puck, if you please."

Puck bobbed a little bow and smiled impishly at the three humans.

"No tricks," Taryn said, unable to stop herself from smiling at the former fox.

"I wouldn't dream of it, sweetheart," he replied, winking at her.

Ozzie and Taryn were both thankful that they did not have to stand. Smitty sidled up to the two awkwardly and also took a seat.

Puck then pulled a pouch from his belt and knelt down at Gloriana's feet. He began to tip a strange, gold grit from the pouch and poured a line from Gloriana's feet, around the three humans, and then closed the circle around them. Ozzie and Smitty looked nervously to Tynx as Puck did this. Tynx was watching the process carefully and nodded his approval to Ozzie and Smitty. Taryn, meanwhile, was watching Puck. She had always loved him as a character and was excited to meet him, or rather re-meet him in his true form. She smiled up at him, and he smiled back at her.

Reaching down, he placed a small object in her hand and whispered, "For you, my lady."

Taryn smiled wider and closed her hand around the gift. After Puck was done, he rejoined the Fairie Lords and bobbed his funny little bow again.

"What is this going to cost them?" Tynx asked boldly.

"The price has already been paid," Gloriana replied.

"What price?" Smitty asked sharply. This was the first he'd heard of a price.

"Deianira," Mab said gravely.

"We do not kill our own," Titania explained, "but Deianira, she was…"

Titania looked pained as she spoke, and Oberon gently took her hand as she trailed off.

"Sídhe will not be the same without her," Oberon said softly, looking at his wife with compassion and love.

"Deianira was the price," Gloriana said. "We require nothing more from you."

Ozzie, Tynx, Taryn, and Smitty couldn't help but wonder how much of what had happened had been orchestrated by the Fairie Lords before them, or at least how much they'd had a little bit of a hand in. If Smitty had never been kidnapped, would they have sent the group after Deianira outright? There was no way to know, and it seemed far too late in the game to ask.

"Are you ready?" Gloriana asked.

The three exchanged eager but apprehensive looks and then nodded.

"Good. Now, all together, think of the place you left."

Taryn, Ozzie, and Smitty thought back to the road they had been driving down so long ago. They concentrated on the car and the moment before the deer had appeared. Taryn looked over at Tynx as she thought and unsuccessfully tried to keep the tears from her eyes. Ozzie also looked to Tynx, but gave him a sad little wave to say *see you soon*. With that, they disappeared.

> *If we shadows have offended,*
> *Think but this, and all is mended—*
> *That you have but slumbered here*
> *While these visions did appear.*
> *And this weak and idle theme,*
> *No more yielding but a dream,*
> *Gentles, do not reprehend.*
> *If you pardon, we will mend...*

Ozzie awoke to the sound of sirens, and lights flashed so brightly he could see them through his closed eyelids. Squinting, he opened his eyes to see...ambulances? There was also a fire truck as well as at least one police car. What had happened? The last thing he remembered was Gloriana standing before them.

"Taryn!" he called without realizing he was doing it until the word was out of his mouth.

Paramedics were by his side in a moment, and Ozzie realized he was laid out on a stretcher.

"Sir, you need to stay still," one EMT was telling him.

"Taryn!" Ozzie called again, ignoring her. He finally turned to the woman and asked, "Where's my friend? She was just with me."

"You need to remain still," the woman repeated sternly.

"Let me ride with her," Ozzie insisted. "She needs me. I'll lie as still as you want, just let me stay with her. Please."

Ozzie wasn't sure what was happening. He was obviously back in his own world, which was great, but he hadn't forgotten about what had happened to Taryn so very recently. He didn't want to risk her thinking he had left her again. After a quick but thorough examination, Ozzie was told he could ride with Taryn sans the backboard. Taryn was already there, but she was still unconscious.

"Taryn. Hey, Taryn," Ozzie said, trying to keep the worry from his voice. She stirred, and he added quickly, "I'm right here, Taryn. I'm right here with you."

Ozzie then asked after Smitty and learned that he was still being packed up to go in the other ambulance. He was unconscious, but he did not appear injured. They then began the short ride to the hospital.

Ozzie approved of the room. The walls were painted a pale yellow, and there was a big window to let the sunlight stream in. Ozzie wasn't allowed to share a room with Taryn, but she was just down the hall from him, and he was well enough to visit her pretty much whenever he liked. It also helped that he had already charmed his nurses.

Ozzie had suffered a general sort of beating in their "car accident", his poor hip having taken the brunt of it. He would probably be released tomorrow, as would Taryn. Some of the ligaments in Taryn's knee had been torn, so her recovery would take a lot longer, but she didn't need to stay in the hospital for it. The doctors were baffled by their injuries. They had said a car accident shouldn't have caused the kind of damage Ozzie and Taryn had suffered. And how had Smitty escaped completely unscathed? The car was totaled.

Ozzie had simply shrugged and said, "You tell us. All I know is we were driving, there were deer, screaming, scariness, wake up, paramedics."

Taryn had seconded Ozzie's shrug, corroborating his story. Smitty too said the same, although he also remembered having a crazy dream in between the scariness and waking up.

Ozzie's blissfully ignorant smile nearly broke at hearing that. Smitty honestly believed it had all been a dream.

Even when questioned about it later, Smitty said, "It was totally insane, and you and Taryn were super pissed at me, and we nearly died like ten times. I'd never do those things in real life, though. So weird."

"Huh," was all Ozzie had said in response to that, even though he was screaming on the inside.

He considered trying to convince Smitty that their adventures had been real. Surely, he wouldn't believe it, but what about their injuries? That wasn't a ton to go on. Plus, there was Smitty's delusion that his "dream" actions and decisions were unrealistic. It wasn't like when Ozzie and Taryn had come back from Leleplar with the Creation Stones in hand. There was no real proof this time. In the end, he and Taryn decided to continue to let Smitty believe it had all been a dream…even if that did mean saying nothing to him about his treacheries and pretending that they were all still the same friends.

It had been a few days since Ozzie and Taryn had been released from the hospital. Taryn's knee, which had undergone surgery to fix the torn ligaments, was bound up in a cast. Ozzie had walked with her as far as they would let him before the surgery and been there when she woke up after. Besides that, he had barely left her side. The biggest exception was nighttime. Taryn's mother, Shannon, had come into Taryn's room one morning to find Ozzie sleeping on the floor. He had never left the night before. While Shannon loved Ozzie dearly, she wasn't comfortable with him sleeping in her daughter's bedroom. The two friends were now sitting out on the back porch and talking softly to one another. Taryn was going back to school the next day, so they were getting as much time together as possible…not that they hadn't been already.

"I'm glad Gloriana fixed Tynx before we left," Taryn said, though her voice was sad. "I think I would have worried otherwise. I think I would have worried about it getting infected or not healing up right or something."

"Yeah," Ozzie agreed. "That's probably true. Hey, speaking of healing, are you going to be okay going back tomorrow? Because I was thinking I could make a little fort to live in your room."

Taryn smiled at Ozzie, who was grinning at her. She knew he was being serious, though. Ozzie would actually live in her room if she asked him, campus rules or no.

"Yeah, I'll be okay. I just hope you don't mind me being needy and texting and calling you all the time."

"Do it!" Ozzie encouraged her. "Get crazy. Call or text as much as you want."

Taryn smiled wider and slipped her hand under Ozzie's. They sat like that for a while in silence, simply enjoying one another's company. Finally, Ozzie spoke again.

"So I've got to find out the requirements for being an EMT."

"Why?"

"Because I think I want to be one. Or a paramedic, or whatever they're called. Add that to the list: find out what the heck they're called."

"You want to be an EMT? Not a doctor?"

"Nope, first responder. Is that the name?"

Taryn laughed and said, "Okay, let me know what you find out. If you need a test subject, maybe I can swing a new injury—"

"No."

"—but let me know beforehand so I can arrange my calendar accordingly."

"Never."

Taryn laughed again and leaned against Ozzie. She liked his idea; she thought it might suit him well. For now, though, she was just basking in his comforting presence, hoping maybe she could store it up to keep her nightmares at bay. She was determined to break free of the harm Erik had caused her. Things were very slowly, day by day, getting better, and she was hopeful for the future. Ozzie was, too…for the first time in a very long time.

# Epilogue

Tynx sat staring at the spot where Ozzie and Taryn had disappeared moments ago. Or had it been hours? Time had stopped for him. His closest friends were gone...again. What was he to do now? Eventually, Tynx felt a gentle touch on his shoulder and turned to see Gloriana standing beside him. Tynx couldn't even find words.

"You will see one another again," she repeated.

Gloriana then glided back to her people. Adam bowed to the Fairie Lords as they passed and watched as they made their way out. Tynx also watched, wondering if he should press them for answers. Even as he thought of it, however, he knew they had said everything they had to say.

Sighing heavily, Tynx said to Adam, "Would you like company back to Wonderland?"

~*~

# Acknowledgements

There never seem to be enough or the right words for this section. So many wonderful people in my life have supported and encouraged me throughout this process. During a visit home, my dad was the one who suggested the book cover design after I created something that simply did not work. He and my mum then let me take over their foyer while I staged the new cover design setup. Thank you both for indulging me and for your patience.

So many thanks to my sweet, amazing husband Mike for always supporting me, encouraging me, and loving me (especially when I'm being demanding and persnickety). Thank you also for always being willing to listen as I talk (at length) through my problems and feelings, writing-related and otherwise.

My sounding boards (better known as The Council), Sally, Heather, Colie, Amber, and Mary, thank you all for being willing to hear me talk on and on (and on and on and on) about whatever happens to be on my mind at any given moment.

Chris, your edits were outstanding and so much appreciated (and not pedantic at all)! I don't know how long it took you to comb through this book, but I am indebted to you. And thank you to Grace for giving him up during those times.

Finally, thank you to all the rest of my family and friends who have bought and/or promoted my book, congratulated me, and encouraged me. I don't know where I would be without the support of every single one of you.

# About the Author

Dana Fraedrich is an independent author, dog lover, and self-professed geek. Even from a young age, she enjoyed writing down the stories that she imagined in her mind. Born and raised in Virginia, she earned her BFA from Roanoke College and is now carving out her own happily ever after in Nashville, TN with her husband and two dogs. Dana is always writing; more books are on the way!

If you enjoyed reading this book, please leave a review.

Find Dana online at www.wordsbydana.com
Facebook: https://www.facebook.com/wordsbydana/
@danafraedrich on Twitter, Tumblr, and Instagram
Follow Dana on Goodreads or her Amazon Author page or you can support her on Patreon and Ko-fi: /WordsByDana for both
Sign up for exclusive access to Dana's VIP Newsletter, short stories, and giveaways on her website
Thanks!

Made in the USA
Middletown, DE
07 May 2022

65443759R00192